MASKS

A VASILY KORSOKOVACH MYSTERY

VASILY KORSOKOVACH INVESTIGATES
BOOK EIGHT

CHRISTOPHER H. JANSMANN

Ephram Cotte
& Company
PUBLISHING

ISBN: 978-1-960914-20-0 (Kindle Edition)
ISBN: 978-1-960914-21-7 (Paperback Edition)
ISBN: 978-1-960914-22-4 (Hardcover Edition)

Library of Congress Control Number: 2025902566

Printed in the United States of America

For Paula:

The quiet voice of reassurance, my partner, my love.

Books by this Author

Chronological Order

Blindsided

Pariah

Outsider

Peril

Ditched

Bygones

Downhill

Duality

Focus

Bewitched

Requiem

Vengeance

Mirage

Solitude

Masks

Belie

Sean Colbeth Investigates

Blindsided

Outsider

Downhill

Duality

Contents

ONE

A HALLOWE'EN PARTY

I'd told Sean Colbeth years earlier Halloween was the one night each year when the seedy underbelly of society felt comfortable crawling out from beneath the rock where it normally hid; while I'd originally meant it in jest at the time, I had no idea how prescient the observation would turn out to be — especially when the holiday itself happened to fall on a Monday that year. Nothing good had ever happened to me on a Monday; not in my personal life, and certainly not as a law enforcement professional. Some of the thorniest cases I had ever handled since returning to Southern California had begun on that fateful weekday; I'd briefly considered shifting the start of my workweek to Tuesday only to have my fiancé quietly remind me that it would likely not make the slightest difference to whatever deity was in charge of assigning me the next mayhem on their to-do list.

Still, I'd somewhat foolishly thought I'd dodged a bullet that particular Halloween Monday when a dead body hadn't shown up in Rancho Linda prior to my clocking out for the day. Counting my lucky stars, I'd dashed into the locker room at the station to change into my costume for the second part of what would turn out to be a *very* long day. My favorite millionaire author, Dr. Rosalia Frankenhoffer, had roped me into helping her host a charitable Halloween Ball at her mansion on the outskirts of the city; in the two years I had been back in California, I'd become a fixture volunteering with a number of the same groups that her fundraiser was geared to support, including one that worked with at-risk LGTBQ+ youth out of my favorite coffee shop at the local mall. Being named the celebrity host for the costumed ball had made me slightly uncomfortable, though, for I had a longstanding policy of not cashing in on my five minutes of Olympic fame; an evening with Rosie by her luxurious pool had been all it had taken to set aside my moral objections to the plan. While I could officially blame it on a weak moment promulgated by the excessive amount of Olive Garden table wine she had plied me with, in truth, there was little I wouldn't do for my friend when she asked — especially when it meant continuing the amazing work she had been doing in the community.

Pulling open my locker in the spacious changing area, I sighed again at the costume hanging on the hook, and then sighed deeper when I caught sight of my hair in the small mirror fastened to the door. Alejandro had been the one to select what we were wearing to the ball and had planned every detail including my having spent several hours in the chair with Giovanni changing my normal bleached-blond surfer mop top into a salt-and-pepper coloring that had felt as though it had suddenly aged me into AARP eligibility. Shifting my head left, and then slowly right, I tried not to roll my eyes for the thousandth time at the strange style Alex had insisted upon; it looked like something far more appropriate to the 1960s than the post-millennial era, but then again, love will make you do anything, won't it? Sighing one last time for good measure (and annoyed that no one in the locker room was paying the least bit of attention to my minor meltdown), I quickly stripped out of my polo-and-khakis ensemble and then shrugged into the blindingly brilliant gold tunic before pulling the black trousers on. A few minutes later, I was striding back out through the squad room and toward the main entrance for the station, thankful for once that our ongoing budget woes meant the cubicle farm was deserted. It wasn't that I didn't like *Star Trek*; far from it. My only objection to appearing at Rosie's fundraiser as the latest in a long line of Starfleet captains was that my cosplaying tastes tended to run more toward the superhero end of the spectrum — and I'd picked up a humdinger of a replica Spider-man costume during a case that summer that I had been looking forward to wearing. Much like Rosie, though, there was little I could refuse Alejandro; it hadn't hurt that he'd been *particularly* thorough the night he'd convinced me to go along with his plan.

Pushing out of the glass doors from the lobby, I spied the bright yellow New Beetle parked by the curb and hurried over to the passenger side; opening the door, I tossed my backpack into the rear and then came up short when I caught sight of my fiancé behind the wheel as I dropped into my seat. "Holy *shit*," was the only thing I could think of saying.

"And good evening to you, too," Alejandro laughed as he leaned over for a kiss.

"You don't do anything in half measures, do you?"

"I'm not sure what you mean," he replied with a smile before pulling out into the rush hour traffic.

While I'd known what he'd been planning on wearing as *his* costume, actually seeing him decked out as Mister Spock was more than a bit eye-popping. Somehow, he'd managed to stuff his mountain of luxurious curls beneath a wig of short, straight jet-black hair featuring bangs cut in a severe line across his forehead. His normally expressive eyebrows had somehow been replaced by mirrored angry looking dark slashes that tapered to sharp points; below them, his dark eyes had become even more beguiling with the addition of a subtle purple eyeshadow that would have looked hideous on anyone else. It took me a moment to realize his normally toffee-toned complexion had a slight greenish tinge to it; glancing at his hands, I felt my eyebrows go up when I realized he'd applied whatever that substance was to any skin that was exposed. The overall effect was extraordinary; Alejandro had managed to look completely alien while somehow also accentuating his normal breathtaking attractiveness.

"Wow," I managed to say after a few more minutes of stunned silence. "Just, wow. How long did this take?"

Alejandro rolled his eyes. "Longer than I expected. Plucking my eyebrows was an experience I'll never repeat, I assure you."

"You... you *plucked* them?"

He nodded. "It was the only way to be authentic," he said as he shifted lanes to make the left turn toward Rosie's mansion. "I thought maybe I could get away with powdering my natural eyebrows, but the clerk at M-A-C wasn't able to find the right shade for my skin. So, plucking it was; thankfully, they also had small kits of artificial hair that matched the wig—"

I blinked. "Wait, you actually went to the cosmetic store at the mall?"

"Of course," he smiled. "Where else would I go?"

"When you said you needed makeup for a Halloween costume, I figured... I dunno, the pharmacy just around the corner from the condo? Not a mainstream massively expensive cosmetic store."

"It wasn't *all* that expensive," Alex said, though there was a slight note of defensiveness in his voice. "Besides, they already had pre-made boxed sets for each of the major characters from *Star Trek*. Spock, Data, Uhura — you'd look good as Data," he added after glancing at me. "That and they could demonstrate how to get just the right look." He smiled slightly. "The eyeshadow was a bit harder to put on than I expected; I'm glad they gave me some tips to make it easier."

"You'd never catch me wearing makeup."

Alex glared at me. "Are you saying you *didn't* have eyeliner on when you wore that pirate outfit last month to *The Alternative Way*?"

"Last month?" I replied, feeling my face heat up slightly. "I don't know—"

"The Saturday that you read to kids at the store," he reminded me.

I knew I was caught, for it was my semi-regular session at the bookstore where I came dressed in the style of the genre I happened to be reading to the under ten set. Coughing slightly, I tried — badly — to extricate myself. "I was just trying to mimic Captain Jack Sparrow," I replied weakly. "And eyeliner isn't really makeup."

"Uh huh," Alex snorted. "Then what about—"

"Okay, *okay*," I sighed. "But I only wear it when I'm cosplaying. And all of my stuff comes from Walgreens."

Alejandro slowed to turn onto the gently sloping road that wound its way up the hill toward Rosie's mansion. "All I'm saying is you could probably upgrade your game a bit with a session at M-A-C," he said. "Hell, half the clerks in there were at Comic-Con this summer themselves. They know a thing or two about the space."

Thinking guiltily of the small chest of cosmetics holding my supplies for cosplaying hiding under the sink in the master bathroom, I nodded. "Fine. But you're coming with me."

"Happily," he said. "Do you think I look okay?"

"Are you kidding?" I laughed. "You're going to be the talk of the party."

"I highly doubt that." His eyes shifted to my hair for a moment. "You look good in silver."

I pulled down the sun visor and took a look again at what had happened to my hair and saw the frown form on my face. "I look a decade older than I should."

"No, you don't," he replied. "Though it is just like you to be hung up on that aspect."

My head snapped toward him. "I'm not hung up on my age."

"*Mi amor*, you've been obsessing for months over your birthday."

"No, I haven't." I waited a beat. "Have I?"

"Yes," he sighed. "It's just a number. And it's not like you're turning 40."

I felt myself grimace. "But I'm getting inexorably *closer* to 40."

"It's just a number," he repeated as he slowed again; the twin golden lions guarding the end of the driveway for the mansion had come into view, a landmark that always made me smile. "My *abuela* had a saying: you will only grow old if you allow yourself to."

"I feel like more than a few scientists might disagree with that sentiment," I replied somewhat churlishly.

"Nothing ventured," he smiled as the New Beetle rumbled up the cobblestone driveway. "Nothing gained."

We lapsed into a bit of a silence at that point, owing mostly to Alex's sudden focus on the traffic jam that had developed on the circular driveway in front of the main entrance to the mansion. For my part, I found myself musing on why I seemed to be so uncomfortable about my upcoming birthday; glancing at the still-down mirror and the silver hair it was portraying brought with it a cavalcade of emotions I'd been studiously avoiding. Part of my discomfort came from how 40 had seemed a long way off — until it suddenly wasn't. Flipping the sun visor up with a slight amount of disgust, I folded my arms against my chest and tried to ignore the entire concept of aging completely.

As if that were even possible.

Miraculously, Alex discovered the last remaining slot on the driveway after circling the giant fountain in the center and slid his New Beetle into it; my fiancé seemed to have the magical ability to locate parking no matter the circumstances. It was a superpower that I didn't share; just that morning, I'd had to circle the lot at the pool to find a spot for my Camaro, apparent penance for dawdling in bed with Alex. Pushing open the door to the passenger side, I slid out into the early evening and then grabbed my swim backpack from the rear seat; Rosie had offered — well, more like *insisted* — Alex and I stay over after the party ended, so I had my gear with me for practice in the morning. Shifting the bag on my shoulder, I followed him across the cobblestones and to the massive front door hiding between two more of the golden lions. In keeping with the spirit of the evening, someone had placed domino masks on each, and matched the look with a long black cloak that draped down over their back. Despite the hour still being fairly early, I wasn't all that shocked at the line waiting to get into the mansion; while Rosie's philanthropic fundraisers were widely known within the community, this was one of the few to take place at her home. I wondered how many of the attendees were there purely to get a peek at the mansion and smiled to think that they were likely to be rather disappointed; after purchasing the sprawling estate several decades earlier, the author had sold off all of the furniture that had come with it and donated the funds as one of her first charitable acts. Save for a few key rooms where she lived and worked, the rest of the mansion was essentially empty and had been for years.

The woman herself was at the door greeting guests and caught our approach as we came up the steps toward her. "There you are!" she cried out with a broad smile. "I was starting to think you were standing me up."

I smiled before I leaned down to kiss her on the cheek. "Would we ever do that to you?"

"You did in July," she observed.

"It was *one* time," I reminded her, rolling my eyes. "And I *was* in intensive care."

"Well, I suppose you couldn't help it then," she laughed, eyes twinkling. "Look at the two of you! What great costumes."

"It's all Alex's idea," I said. "He came up with everything."

"Excellent job," she said as she accepted a kiss from Alejandro. "I think you missed your calling; you should be in one of the costume departments at a big studio. Or makeup."

"That's kind of you to say," Alex replied. Despite the greenish tinge to his face, I could see a slight flame of embarrassment across his cheeks. "But it's not really my thing."

Tapping a finger on one of his pointed ears, Rosie shook her head. "I'm not so sure. I know a few people at the big studios—"

"Of course you do," I sighed, rolling my eyes again.

"—and can probably get you an interview," she continued.

"I'm happy right where I am," Alex smiled again. "But thank you."

Rosie eyed him. "If you ever change your mind, let me know."

"I won't," he replied after a quick glance at me. Rosie looked like she wanted to press the point, but Alejandro quickly changed the subject. "Speaking of Old Hollywood, I absolutely love your outfit. Hepburn from *The African Queen*, is it?"

"That it is," Rosie confirmed. She took a moment to twist a bit, showing off what appeared to be a 1940s-era dress that complimented her form before tapping at the massive brim of the hat atop her bun; the bright red ribbon tying it beneath her chin was a vibrant slash of color against the otherwise off-white ensemble. "I adore that movie and had the costume shop down at the Rancho Linda Mall order me a reasonable replica."

"I've always seen you more as Lauren Bacall," I said, a slight note of teasing in my voice. "This is seriously going to mess with me."

"Good," she laughed again, filling the air with, well, that Bacall-like laugh I had grown to love over the years. "You'd better get inside," she continued as she shooed us into the grand foyer of the mansion. "The charity auction starts at the top of the hour, so you don't have much time to grab something to eat before you go on stage."

"So much for enjoying the party," I sighed dramatically as we stepped past her.

I didn't take more than a few steps across the terrazzo tile, though, for the shock of what I walked into took a full moment to process. The space was amazingly grand in its own right, with matching staircases curving upward to the second story on either side of the floor; an arched hallway beneath the landing led to, among other things, the massive solarium where Rosie spent most of her time when she *wasn't* writing her next bestseller. Above everything was a gigantic crystal chandelier that was original to the space; I had never asked just how much it was worth but presumed each twinkling piece of crystal was valued far higher than my condo. That evening, though, Rosie had leaned into the spookiness that Halloween tended to bring out; the sconces along the staircases had been dimmed to near darkness, and the chandelier, extinguished. In its place were hundreds of LED candles mounted on metal candelabras scattered across the floor; their flickering, watery light immediately made me feel completely uncomfortable. A thick layer of theater fog covered the normally eye-catching pattern of the Italian tile; unseen speakers filled the air with creepy minor-keyed music that had me scanning the room for some deranged individual holding a running chainsaw. Banquet tables were set against either staircase and were filled to overflowing with food; upon closer inspection, though, that, too, had been given a rather ghoulish spin, for there seemed to be no shortage of finger-shaped sandwiches and brain-shaped sponge cakes on offer. Even the punch bowl was in on the act, with small floating eyeballs reminiscent of a particular scene in *Indiana Jones* that had given pre-teen Vasily the willies for weeks afterwards.

I was a little surprised at how my heart was pounding like an animal about to take flight; it took a full minute or so for me to get myself back under control. I thought perhaps I was overreacting, but then Alejandro snuck his arm beneath mine. "Holy *shit*," he breathed. "This is a full on *fucking* nightmare."

"You can say that again," I replied equally as quietly. "When Rosie goes all out..."

"No kidding." Alejandro leaned closer. "So much for being a brave Starfleet officer."

"I'm right there with you," I smiled, despite how my heart was still pounding. "Looks like she's got the dais set up for me over there," I continued, nodding in the general direction of a small stage that had been erected just in front of the hallway arch. "Do you want—"

The unexpected gentle hand at my arm made me jump; I may have even emitted a startled yep. Whirling, I tried to ignore how my hand had immediately gone to where my service sidearm would normally have been snugly pressed against my hip — I'd rather prudently left it locked up in the gun safe at the station before leaving with Alex. Leaning away from me with an expression I presumed was as shocked as my own was young Daniel Kewley; taking a moment to put my heart back into my chest for a second time that evening, I idly noted that the teenager's version of the superhero Arrow was spot on, right down to the green domino mask just barely visible under the hood.

Daniel was the first to speak. "Sorry, Deputy Chief. I didn't mean to startle you."

The kid's British accent seemed to be at odds with his dark Caribbean complexion. I tried to smile, though in truth my pulse was still racing. "I think our host has outdone herself," I said. "This atmosphere seems to have gotten to me."

His toothy smile was partially apologetic. "That might be on us," he admitted. "Ms. Frankenhoffer pretty much told us to make it as creepy as possible, so... we did."

"Leave it to a bunch of horror-obsessed teens," Alejandro said beneath his breath.

"It's quite impressive," I admitted, ignoring my fiancé. "Well done."

"Thank you," he smiled again. "If you really want to be freaked out, you've got to see the Haunted House we put together upstairs."

I glanced around us. "I'm not sure I'm your target demographic," I demurred. "But I'll try to check it out after the auction."

"I hope you can," Daniel replied. "I've got to go start the first round of the Haunted House tours but wanted to make sure you'd gotten the invite for our meeting on Wednesday."

"I did," I nodded.

"Awesome," Daniel smiled. "With Christmas less than two months out, we don't have much time to get the toy drive up and running. I appreciate your willingness to help out."

"I wouldn't miss it," I replied. "Thanks for including me."

"Then we'll see you Wednesday," he replied before disappearing into the semi-darkness.

Once it looked like he was out of earshot, Alejandro leaned over. "Who was that?"

"Daniel Kewley," I said as I started toward the podium. "He's the current student co-chair for KOTO -- Kids on Their Own."

"I've heard of them, haven't I?" Alex asked.

"Yes," I nodded as I went up the short flight of steps. There was a multi-page printout on the podium, which made me frown; even if I'd been able to speak like an experienced auctioneer, the sheer volume of items to get through meant it would be close to the witching hour before the final bid was accepted. "They work with at-risk teens in Rancho Linda ranging from those who are homeless to recent immigrants seeking asylum that were placed with families in the city. There's a particular focus on LGBTQ kids in the community who are struggling for one reason or another."

"Wow," Alex said. "Pretty heavy stuff for a teen."

"Kid's motivated," I replied as I sorted through the list and then located the wireless microphone. "He was born to American diplomats while they were stationed in the UK, so he has a particular affinity for newcomers trying to orient themselves to American society." I looked at Alex. "He's also a 4.0 student looking at a full ride to Stanford when he graduates."

"*Dios mio*," Alex sighed. "I feel like a bit of an underachiever now."

"Says the guy with an Olympic medal," I smiled. "But yeah, I feel the same. The entire group is made up of kids like him; they work out of *The Alternative Way* with Anne's blessing."

Knowing the co-owner of our favorite coffee shop as well as I did, Alex nodded. "High praise if she's accepted him, too. I take it you're helping them out, too."

"Yeah. No rest for the weary," I replied. "RLPD usually has a liaison who works the *Toys for Tots* program; I drew the short straw this year."

Alex's eyes narrowed. "Why do I think you volunteered for the task?"

"Me?" I asked innocently.

"You are a *terrible* liar," Alex smiled. "Count me in if you need an additional hand."

"That I will." I leaned over for a kiss. "You might want to find something interesting to do for a bit. I think I am going to be here a while."

"Don't worry," he smiled, a strange expression on someone made up to look like an emotionless Vulcan. "I won't be far. I might even toss popcorn at you from the front row."

"Lovely," I said before snapping on the microphone and taking up position behind the podium. "Ladies and gentlemen," I began, my voice suddenly booming through the space on those same unseen speakers. "Allow me to welcome you to the twelfth annual Rancho Linda Halloween Gala..."

Two

The Teenager Vanishes

To my great surprise, the evening managed to go by in something of a blur; before I knew it, I was standing beside Alejandro as we watched Rosie close the massive front door of the mansion behind the final departing guest. I didn't need to look at my watch to know it had been a good idea to accept Rosie's offer of a room for the evening; given that it was, essentially, already Tuesday morning, I didn't think either Alex or I were in any shape to make the thirty-minute drive to our condo in Anaheim. At best, I'd be lucky to get a few hours of sleep before having to drag myself out of bed to catch a ride to practice with Rosie; when the septuagenarian suddenly sagged against the dark wood of the portal, I wondered if I was being overly optimistic.

Concerned that she might have overdone it — or worse, her defibrillator pacemaker had suddenly kicked in — Alex and I quickly moved to her and took up position on either side. "Rosie," I asked cautiously as I reached for a wrist to feel for her pulse, "are you feeling okay?"

"Just a little tired," she replied. In the semi-darkness of the foyer, it was hard to tell if her face was as ashen as it looked. "I've been on my feet for more hours than normal, that's all."

I traded a glance with Alejandro; her pulse seemed steady, but it was definitely clear she was more exhausted than she'd been letting on. "Then I think we'll skip the after party you had planned for us in the solarium and get you to bed."

"I'm fine, young man," Rosie replied sternly. "Besides, I had the staff set aside two bottles of Olive Garden wine in the fridge before I sent them home. We can't let that go to waste."

"The wine will be just as good tomorrow," Alejandro said as we helped her straighten up. "Assuming you don't mind us inviting ourselves over for dinner."

"Are you kidding?" Rosie laughed as we helped her over to the elevator hidden beneath one of the staircases. It wasn't lost on me that she didn't lodge her usual protest against using it. "I won't say no to that. You know how I love being doted on by two hunks."

"Who are gay," I reminded her for the millionth time.

"The point remains," she laughed. "Chef will be serving ribeye steaks with baked potatoes; I've also got a cheesecake from that new bakery for dessert."

I glared at her after pressing the button for the elevator. "You were already planning on us coming back, weren't you?"

"Maybe," she smiled again as we entered the waiting carriage.

A moment later, the doors to the elevator opened on the second floor just inside the corridor that led to the various rooms Rosie had renovated into guest suites. She, of course, had pride of place with the multi-room suite at the far end of the hallway; commanding amazing views of the city from the massive windows, I'd often wondered why she used the small space on the first floor as her writing room. I figured the view from her bedroom suite would likely be a distraction when she was otherwise needing to focus on crafting her next book; the former butler pantry did have a nice window, but it looked directly at the craggy hill the mansion had been built into.

Evidence of the Haunted House was at the other end of the hallway, including a small hand-lettered sign pointing the way toward a set of rooms I knew from experience had long been empty. On my first visit nearly two years ago, the cold case I was working at the time had given me the unique opportunity to explore the entire mansion from top to bottom, comparing the place as it currently stood to what the original owner, the former movie mogul Thomas Andrews, had intended. I knew one of the rooms had originally been a private movie theater, complete with a projection room and small concession stand. The gently sloping floor was the only hint of what had existed; that, and the vague smell of popcorn that even the best cleaners Rosie had hired were unable to remove. Based on where the sign was pointing, I assumed Daniel and his team had made use of the unusual space and decided I'd have to poke my head inside to see what they had done before the kids arrived to remove everything later in the week.

We passed the room that Rosie usually made available to us, and the room beside it where Sean had recuperated from his gunshot wounds that spring. It was hard to fathom just how much had happened in the short span of a few months; there were a few low points, to be sure, but the highs far outnumbered them. Glancing toward Alejandro, I felt myself smile a private smile at how he had been more than a significant portion of the *highs* while also helping smooth over some of the worst *lows* I had ever experienced in my life. Every day was a reminder that I had hit the lottery when it came to my soulmate.

Arriving at the door to her suite, Rosie seemed to get her second wind and disentangled herself from the two of us. Smiling a tired smile, she began to untie the ribbon holding her hat to her head. "Thank you again for your help, Vas," she said. "I know how busy you are and truly appreciate it."

"My pleasure," I said. "How much did you raise tonight?"

"Half a million," she smiled wider. "My best event yet."

"No shit," I breathed. "How on earth—?"

Alejandro chuckled. "*Mi amor*, I think you'll be doing this again."

"Me?" I said, head turning toward him. "I didn't do anything."

"Except be you," he reminded me. "Sometimes that's all it takes."

I stared at him for a beat. "Clearly I should have taken that contract with Kellogg's," I sighed.

"After the Olympics? Maybe," Alex laughed. "If only I had been so lucky."

Rosie put a hand out to Alejandro. "Hey," she said softly. "Don't shortchange yourself. I know what you do up there at Cal State Irvine — and how lucky I am that you're willing to be my Christmas headliner."

A slight flush appeared again beneath the greenish makeup. "I'm not Vasily," he said.

"No," she said earnestly, "you are unabashedly *you*, and that is everything."

The flush deepened. "Well," he said after a moment, "we'll see you in the morning."

She nodded before I added: "Good night, Rosie."

"Night." She pulled me into a hug. "You don't know how much this means to me and those kids," she whispered into my ear.

"I think I do," I whispered back before giving her a fond peck on the cheek.

I followed Alejandro down the hall to our room and closed the door behind us; I was slightly surprised when he quickly turned and pressed me to the wall, then planted a sizzling kiss on my lips. Coming up for air — and thinking I knew where he was going, found I was on board with the destination — I hugged him closer and then slowly walked us toward the queen bed by the window. "Someone has extra energy," I observed as I sat him on the edge of the bed and leaned down to kiss him.

"You cannot believe how horny I am right now," he whispered between kisses along the side of my neck. "I always knew you were sexy in uniform," he added as he pulled me to the bed beside him and then ran a hand through my dyed hair, "but this getup takes it to a new level."

"Is this your way of telling me I'll look good as a middle-aged cop?" I asked, narrowing my eyes.

"Yep," he laughed before kissing me again on the lips. "You are going to be one silver-haired devil, *mi amor.*"

"Then I guess I'd better confess: I've always had a thing for Vulcans," I whispered as he pushed me onto my back and began to straddle me. "Something about the way their eyebrows are shaped, I think."

"That makes the plucking—"

The sonorous tones of the doorbell to the mansion suddenly rang out on the floor below us. Startled into silence, it took a second pealing of them before I pushed Alejandro off of me. At his look, I answered his silent question as I headed for the door. "Rosie let the staff go for the night, remember? I'm not sure she'll hear that in her master suite."

Nodding, he followed me back into the hallway and trailed me down the steps; as I reached the massive portal, the doorbell rang out a third time, then a fourth, almost as if someone were physically leaning on it. I drew back the bolt and pulled the door open to reveal a tall Black woman with perfectly braided hair waiting on the patio; she was dressed in a Cal Poly sweatshirt and matching sweatpants and was wearing a worried expression.

"Delores?" I asked, a tentative smile on my face. "What brings you out here at this late an hour?"

"Vas," she replied. "You're not Rosie. Where's Rosie?"

"In bed," I replied, then eyed her for a moment. It was clear she was on the verge of some sort of panic. "What's happened?"

"Daniel is missing," she replied flatly. I saw Alex start at the name. "I mean, he never came back from this party — he missed his curfew. I was hoping she had seen him leave or knew where he went."

"There were a lot of people at this event tonight," I said carefully. "I'm not certain Rosie would have kept track of everyone quite like that. *I* didn't keep track, and I'm a trained investigator."

"Maybe," she said, but her tone told me she wasn't convinced. "Look, this is a large place — is it possible that he got lost? Or locked into a closet?"

I glanced at Alex. "I doubt it. Guests were only here in the foyer—" I said as I waved at the banquet tables and candelabras still set up, "—and upstairs in a few rooms. Not a lot of places to get lost in."

"He never came *home*," she emphasized. "And his phone says he's still here."

My eyebrows went up. "Are you tracking him?"

"Yes," she nodded as she turned her phone toward me. It was a recent vintage iPhone and was showing a small icon against a map; my heart stopped when I saw the avatar attached to it. "His location hasn't updated in hours."

I noted she was correct, based on location timestamp. "You think Daniel is still here?" I asked.

"Yes," she said again. "He *has* to be here."

"Or at least his phone is," I replied evenly. "Are you sure he wasn't going to spend the night with a friend? It *was* Halloween."

"No," she replied, shaking her head to emphasize the point. "He has to be at school in the morning."

I glanced at Alejandro. "All right," I said before looking at her phone again. "Let's eliminate the obvious, then. Why don't you call Daniel's phone and we'll see if we can hear it?"

"I've *been* calling it," she replied, her voice rising an octave. "It goes to voicemail without even ringing."

"That's not surprising," I said, trying to sound light despite a gnawing feeling of dread in my stomach. "The cell coverage up here is pretty lousy; it's also just as likely the battery is dead."

"Can we wake up Rosie?" the woman asked. "I'd like her to allow me to search for my son."

Knowing that I had no authority to allow a virtual stranger access to Rosie's home — and that I was in the unique position of also being a law enforcement officer — I tried to thread the needle as carefully as possible. "Why don't you wait here, Delores, while I get Rosie," I said before looking meaningfully at Alex. "It might take me a few minutes, *mi amor*," I added.

He seemed to get the hint. "I don't think Rosie would mind if I made our guest some coffee while we waited, do you?"

I smiled slightly. "I think we are all going to need some," I said. "We'll regroup in the kitchen."

Alex nodded. "If you would come this way, Mrs. Kewley," he said as he held out a hand. "It won't take but a moment to get something going."

"Thank you," she said but not before looking up the staircase briefly.

"I won't be long," I said, trying to sell my lie with a genuine smile.

Mrs. Kewley nodded and then let Alex lead her toward the kitchen. I waited until they had gone under the archway before I took the steps two at a time to return to the second floor; pausing at the landing that overlooked the foyer, I frowned at the hand-lettered sign that was still standing at the top of the stairs. Looking toward Rosie's room at the far end of the hallway, I decided to follow my gut and instead headed in the other direction. I was immediately met with some sort of wrought iron arbor that had been placed in the middle of the hallway; wrapped around it was several pounds of some sort of fake vine, with small plastic jack-o-lanterns woven into the greenery every few feet. Ducking beneath the arbor, I found myself in a space transformed: bloody handprints were on one side of the wall, and a long streak of red spoiled the tile of the floor, as though a body had been dragged away, unwillingly. Kneeling, I ran a finger through the pool of crimson and discovered that contrary to the glistening surface sheen, it was quite dry; working a nail beneath a section, I pried up enough to confirm it was some sort of plastic resin designed to be easy to remove.

Oddly, that didn't do much for my anxiety.

Confirming the handprints were a similar material, I stood and slowly worked my way down the hallway. Daniel and his team had, indeed, gone to amazing lengths to make the space creepy; I was sure that with the lights off, the plastic body parts randomly placed along the floor (with copious amounts of the fake blood applied) would have seemed just realistic enough to get the pulse pounding. The mannequin at the intersection was a nice touch; I nearly jumped myself when it lunged forward, animatronics clearly triggered by some sort of sensor. I found the side hallway just in front of the former theater crowded with dead shrubs in massive pots, cobwebs strung liberally between the bare branches. They were placed at unusual enough angles that it wasn't a straight shot to get to the double doors of the theater; there also appeared to be plenty of space *behind* each bush for, say, a small teen to lie in wait.

Pulling one of the doors open for the old theater, I found myself digging into the pockets of my costume for my iPhone as I was unsure *where* the light switches happened to be in that room. Tapping the screen, I enabled the flashlight function and then waved it in front of me, revealing a tall wall of hay bales that nearly reached the ceiling. My eyebrows went up, then went up *further* when I found it extended quite some distance to the right before an opening appeared. Turning back toward the wall, I located the bank of switches for the lights and flipped them on only to remain in the semi-darkness. Trying them fruitlessly for a second time, it was clear the circuit for the room had tripped; as I cautiously worked my way back along the hay bales to find the opening, every bad horror movie trope I had ever witnessed suddenly came to mind. It didn't help that I discovered rather quickly the hay had been arranged to create a rather clever maze; about the only help was the fact that the gently sloping floor to the room gave a general hint as to the proper direction, assuming whatever prize awaited me was located about where the projection screen had once hung.

I slowly made my way through the maze, carefully keeping track of each turn I took while also noting just how detailed the kids had been. I knew from having walked the space years earlier that the room was large, but not overly so; the twists and turns from the maze made it seem like something you'd have found on an old family farm. My parents had taken me to just such a spot the year I turned ten, some place out in the Inland Empire where you could pick apples from the trees once you

made it through the labyrinth. Much to the chagrin of my parents —
and portending my future vocation — I'd made short work of the maze
and had been forced to wait for them before moving on to the apple-
picking portion of the program.

Rounding what I was certain was the final corner, my toe hit something on the floor and I paused to shine my iPhone's light on it. A
domino mask was looking up at me, the elastic strap that had been
holding it to the head of its wearer clearly torn from one end. Kneeling,
the harsh light from my phone made the dark green color of the material
seem nearly black; that knot of dread in my stomach tightened when I
recalled that Daniel had been wearing something similar as part of his
Arrow costume. For whatever reason, I found myself shifting into full
detective mode; snapping a few photos, I left the mask where it was and
carefully crept into the open space that was the end of the maze.

A slatted wooden chair was in the center, precariously balanced atop
several short hay bales; if the thick power cables snaking toward it over
the hay weren't enough of a hint, the leather straps on the arms and legs
made a compelling argument for what was supposed to have happened
in the final scene of the haunted house. Though it didn't feel quite
authentic for some reason, I nonetheless felt for whichever teen had
been the one to play the part of electrocution victim, as the chair looked
insanely uncomfortable; the blood-colored resin that had been spattered
along the hay and flooring was at odds with the setting, though, as were
the set of sharp-looking tools far more appropriate to a corn field
massacre. That wasn't the only non-sequitur; holding my iPhone a bit
higher to cast a wider pool of light, I realized the reason the chair looked
like it was teetering was that a corner of the ersatz podium had been
knocked away, taking an entire section of hay with it. The way the hay
had been moved made me think something large had been shoved into
it; stepping back, I tried to gauge how it had been done while trying to
ignore the direction my thoughts were going.

Those thoughts went even darker when my light found the glit-
tering shards of glass on the floor beside the upended hay; following

their trail, I discovered the remains of an iPhone against the wall in the far corner. While I couldn't be sure of the angles, it certainly seemed as though it had been tossed, forcibly, from some spot near the hay bales holding the chair. Snapping more photos on my phone, I retraced my steps and heard an awful *crunch* beneath the sole of the boots I was wearing as part of my costume. Carefully picking up my foot, I frowned when I saw something vaguely tooth-shaped in the light from the flashlight. Kneeling, I felt the frown deepen when I determined it *was* a tooth, though it was hard to know if it was a prop or if someone was genuinely missing a bicuspid. Looking closer, I realized the small pool of dark red around confirmed it was likely the latter; crouched on my haunches, I decided I didn't like the story that I had found was trying to tell me.

Phone tossed in the corner, I thought. *And a tooth likely knocked from someone's mouth? Whoever it belongs to put up quite a fight, and I'm a little worried I know who that might be.*

Standing, I slowly began to scan the floor around where I'd found the tooth; with just the flashlight, I thought I could see a smearing of actual blood moving away from the chair, but it could just as easily been more of the blood-colored resin. Still, I trusted my gut and slowly followed the trail; if my suspicion was right — and I was seriously hoping it wasn't — whoever had lost the tooth would have found themselves with a mouthful of blood. Experience told me that a conscious victim with such an injury would have tried to spit out the foul taste as quickly as they could, but my light was only revealing a few drops of *possible* blood every few feet; an unconscious victim would have had no way to stop it from simply oozing out, but there were no pools large enough for that, either. While it was certainly plausible the victim had managed to dash out of the room, hand pressed to their mouth to keep from getting blood everywhere, someone suddenly missing a tooth would have attracted quite a bit of attention — even in the middle of a Halloween party. Suspecting that wasn't what happened, I retraced my steps and focused the light on the floor, searching for an explanation as to why there was such a significant lack of blood anywhere less nefarious than the one my brain kept coming back to.

When my flashlight failed to turn up anything else, I leaned against the wall where the old projection screen had once been and looked at the back of the chair, unease growing with every passing second. From that particular angle, it suddenly dawned on me why the chair had felt off: there were far more tie-down points than actual leather straps attached to them. I had never been to an actual electrocution — thankfully, California had outlawed capital punishment years before I became a cop — but I'd seen enough pictures while at the justice academy to know that the convicted felon would have been barely able to wriggle a finger when the switch was flipped. Stepping back to the chair, I confirmed my suspicion that this prop version had originally been a faithful recreation, though it was now short an odd number of bindings. My brain suddenly spun into investigative overdrive.

Victim gets knocked out or stunned, I thought, stepping back. *And while they're in their stupor, the attacker further incapacitates them using the leather straps? Maybe they had something to gag them, too? That would account for the lack of blood.* I glanced in the general direction of the entrance to the room. *Shit. That makes no sense — they'd have had to carry the body back through the house, and someone would have* definitely *noticed a bound and gagged victim thrown over their shoulder—*

That strange all-encompassing sense I often got when a puzzle piece suddenly drops into place during any case hit me like a gut punch, for a memory from having reviewed the floorplans to the mansion years earlier popped into my head. Despite purging nearly everything that the prior owner had left behind, Rosie had managed to hang onto the original blueprints for the mansion; that had enabled me to discover a vault hidden in plain sight beneath the cascading water feature of the pool in the solarium and solve a decades old cold case. And, as the cold hand of fear slowly squeezing around my heart was reminding me, there'd been a few other surprises on those plans, too.

Oh shit shit shit shit—

Whirling, I ran the iPhone's light along the wall behind me and felt my blood run cold when I found the telltale seam for the hidden doorway. Running my free hand around the edge, I finally located the pressure point that popped the panel inward; the pungent odor of staleness from a space that had not been used in some time assaulted my nose, but paled in comparison to the gut punch that was the single set of footsteps in the dusty servant corridor just beyond — footsteps leading away from the projection room and presumably toward the other non-public spaces of the mansion the household staff had once frequented seventy years or more earlier.

They didn't have to worry about being seen, I thought morosely. *For they knew — in advance — just how to make their escape.*

The incredible sense of a safe space having been violated in the worst way possible had my hands shaking with barely controlled anger as I tapped at my iPhone; there were a number of terrible phone calls that had to be made before I could return to the kitchen below and begin the process of sorting out exactly what had gone so horribly wrong that evening.

THREE
FULL STOP, FULL SEARCH

Every minute in a missing persons case was critical. I had worked a few in my years in the profession, and nine times out of ten, we generally located the subject within a few hours after they had been reported. Usually, they were older adults with modest to severe memory problems who had lost their way returning home, or on the other end of the spectrum, teenagers who had argued with a parent and decided to camp out on a friend's couch until tempers had cooled. Searching for people who didn't want to be found was almost as complicated as looking for someone who didn't know they were missing, but in both situations, going back to the moment when they were last seen always held some sort of starting clue that allowed us a fighting chance to retrace their movements.

That one in ten case, without fail, was the extreme circumstance when the victim was taken against their will. I had worked a few of those, too; the most common version involved messy divorces with former spouses who felt the courts hadn't granted them sufficient visitation rights and decided to take matters into their own hands. One such case had sent me to Acapulco over a long weekend; while I could never forget the kid I rescued, the steamy evenings I'd spent with the dark-skinned *federales* who had been my temporary partner for the investigation remained seared into my memory. The fling happened during a period in my life when I'd fancied myself as a sort of alpha predator hunting the local gay population while I was, in fact, simply trying to fuck the very thought of Sean Colbeth out of my system. Being raped forced me to reconcile who I had become with the man I truly wanted to be; landing in Alejandro's arms had been all the validation I needed that I had ultimately made the right choice.

Then there was the ultimate subset of that one in ten case, the version that always made headlines whenever it happened: stranger abductions. They were extremely rare — certainly far less frequent than the media tended to portray them — but that didn't make them any less tragic or panic inducing for those caught up in the situation. As I watched the Rancho Linda crime scene technicians slowly carry their equipment into the mansion, it was hard for me not to think about the statistics stacked up against me, especially the glaring one where the chances of *finding* victims of abduction decreased by a measurable percentage every hour after their disappearance. It didn't help that Orange County was uncomfortably close to the Mexican border, nor that I had just happened to have recently seen a bulletin in my email about the spike in human trafficking Southern California had been experiencing. That's why the first call had been to my contact at Homeland Security; the second, to Gina Carruthers, our ace senior crime scene tech. If anyone could discover even a scintilla of evidence telling me where I should look next, I knew Gina and her experienced crew would be the ones to find it.

My third call had been to the Department of Children and Families, for I couldn't rule out that Daniel Kewley was on some sort of watch list and had possibly run away from home before. The night operator hadn't been thrilled about waking a case manager — at least, not until I'd made it *quite* clear we had found evidence of possible violence. While I waited for a call back from DCF, my final call had been to my boss, Chief Michael Gilbert; despite being his number two (and having over the years been traditionally given quite a bit of latitude), when an investigation looked like it was about to tie up significant resources I always liked to loop him in at the beginning. At the very least, it made it easier for him to later sign off on the overtime.

When it felt like all of the possible wheels that could be set into motion had been successfully started, I found myself at the railing of the balcony overlooking the foyer of the mansion. The next step was to talk to the mother, but for many reasons, I was delaying returning to the kitchen to face her. My initial visit after discovering the remains of the iPhone in the former theater space had not gone well; after getting a quasi-positive verification that it had belonged to Daniel, the poor woman had understandably devolved into hysterics. Alejandro and I had finally managed to calm her down enough so I could meet with Gina and her crew, but I was well aware that I was unlikely to get anything substantive from her without the assistance of a trained counselor. I had personal experience as to how good Alex was in such situations but had no desire to put him through that *particular* ringer; only one of us needed to have nightmares about this case, and I'd prefer it not be him.

Tapping my fingers against the railing, I felt more than heard Rosie approach from behind me. I had woken her shortly after finding what I'd found, and then had asked that she remain in her room until everything got sorted. I wasn't all that surprised that her curiosity had ultimately gotten the better of her. Turning, I smiled slightly to see her wrapped in a thick terry cloth robe in off-white; the fuzzy bunny slippers were completely on brand.

"I'm sorry about this," I said when she came to stand beside me. "I have no idea how long they will be here."

"They can take as much time as they need," Rosie said. "How's Delores holding up?"

"About what you'd expect," I replied.

"Which is another way of saying, 'not good,'" Rosie observed.

"Pretty much, yeah," I sighed. "We normally have a veteran social worker on retainer for these sorts of situations, but our regular contact is unavailable. Thankfully, I'm on the good side of the Orange County Sheriff at the moment; she agreed to loan me their counselor for the duration."

"Good." She watched the techs below us as they picked through every last bit of the Halloween decor. "She's welcome to stay here with me if she wants. I know it hasn't been easy for her since Chester died."

I nodded. "It's pretty much why she and Daniel came back from the UK when they did," I said. "Her family is in California; she's already reached out to her sister in Sausalito, actually, though I don't think she'll be able to get here until this afternoon."

"Then she can hang out with me by the pool until then," Rosie said. "I don't think she should be alone until Daniel comes home."

"I agree," I nodded. "Don't take this the wrong way, but I suspect she won't feel comfortable staying here."

Rosie nodded slightly. "She has every right to blame me for what happened; her child disappeared on my watch."

"Rosie," I began cautiously, "you might want to consider talking to a lawyer. This could get a bit ugly."

The writer's eyes widened with dawning recognition. "Criminal or civil?"

"Officially, I can't answer that," I replied, "but as your friend, I'll say you might want to hedge your bets until we've cleared you as a suspect."

She nodded. "Yeah, that's what I thought too." Rosie paused, and her face took on a worried expression. "You don't actually think—"

I reached for her arm and gently squeezed it. "Never in a million years. But we have to do this by the book."

"Yeah," she replied as she put a hand on top of mine. "I suppose you do."

"Do you feel up to a few questions?" I asked. "If not, they can wait until later."

Rosie shrugged. "I'm not likely to get much more sleep. Do you need me to waive my rights?"

I held out my iPhone. "That is totally up to you," I said as I tapped the recording button for the voice memo function. After stating my name as well as the date and time, I recited the Miranda warning for what felt like the millionth time since moving back to California. I took a brief pause to read Rosie's expression before I continued. "This is more of an information gathering chat, but if you would feel more comfortable having representation...?"

"I know my rights, and I waive them," she replied. "What do you want to know?"

"Was it your idea to host the Halloween gala here last night?"

"Yes," she nodded. "As I've done so nearly every year since I moved to Rancho Linda."

"Who helped you decorate?"

"One of the volunteer groups that I've worked with over the decades," she replied. "Kids On Their Own, which uses *The Alternative Way* at the Rancho Linda Mall as their unofficial headquarters. It's a student-run organization that serves at-risk youth in the community."

"How large is the group?"

"Twenty members, I think. Maybe a bit more."

"Were they all here tonight?"

"That I don't know," she replied honestly. "I think most of them rotated through over the few days it took to set up everything, and they'll repeat the process to strike the decorations. Assuming you let me take them down."

"Once the techs are done, I don't think that will be a problem," I smiled.

"Good," she nodded. "The Christmas tree arrives at the end of next week, so I don't have much time."

I felt an eyebrow arch. "Isn't that kind of early?"

"If it's good enough for Disneyland, it's good enough for me," she replied.

That was nearly the same thing Alejandro had said to me while he was flipping through an extremely early holiday catalog we'd received from L.L. Bean. I suddenly felt like I was wholly unprepared for the sort of Christmas season my fiancé was planning for us. "Would you allow me access to the list of invited guests?"

Rosie frowned. "If I had one, sure."

"I thought you sold tickets to the event?"

"'Tickets', yes," she replied, holding her fingers up as air quotes. "It was part of our fundraising to be sure, but we didn't require people to have one in order to get in."

It dawned on me that there hadn't been anyone checking at the door when I'd arrived myself. "So, you have no idea who *could* have been at the gala last night?"

"No. I mean, generally speaking it's mostly people from Rancho Linda, but it wouldn't surprise me if we pulled in folks from the surrounding cities, too. I do a lot of work throughout the county."

"Ah," I said, knowing it meant my job was going to be a lot harder. "Do you have any security cameras?"

"Yes," she nodded. "But before you ask about video, none of them work. They were installed years before I moved in; as you know, I have something of a hate-hate relationship with technology, so I had the system disabled shortly after I arrived." Rosie smiled slightly. "Aside from my books and a ton of Olive Garden wine in the cabinet, there's not much to steal anyway."

I tried not to slap my palm to my forehead. "Lovely."

"Sorry."

"It is what it is," I sighed. "Have you ever used the servant hallways?"

"You mean the secret corridors?" Rosie asked. "No. I know they are there, of course, but I don't have the same early twentieth-century view that staff should never be seen or heard." She smiled slightly. "And since both my housekeeper and chef are part time, they're hardly here enough to need to use those dusty passageways."

"But the corridors aren't locked?"

"I don't think so, no."

I nodded again. "Is the existence of those corridors widely known?"

Rosie shrugged. "Maybe. Probably just to those who have deep roots in Rancho Linda. I think there was an article about the mansion back in the sixties that outlined some of the quirkier aspects of its construction."

"I think I read that article," I replied. "That's how I found out about the water feature in your pool."

"Ah," she smiled.

"How well did you know Daniel Kewley?"

Rosie nodded. "I met him last year, when he was vice-chair of the group and part of the planning committee for the Halloween gala. I was seriously impressed by Daniel and was excited that he was the lead this year."

"Were you ever alone with him?"

My friend looked taken aback by the question but recovered. "No," she replied. "I always met with him and two or three other members of the team. These days, it's a best practice not to meet one-on-one with a minor."

"It is indeed." I looked down at the foyer and thought a bit at how much had happened in the short space of a few hours. "I think that's it. I might reach out again if something comes up."

"Okay." Rosie watched me turn off the phone, then spoke very softly. "Do you think you will find him?"

I thought about that for a long moment. "Honestly? I have no idea, Rosie. I truly don't. If we get a few lucky breaks, maybe, but the statistics aren't on my side this time."

"Shit." Rosie returned the gesture I'd done a few minutes earlier and put her hand to my bicep. "If there is anyone on this godforsaken planet that *could* pull off such a miracle, it would be you, Vas."

I smiled slightly. "Your faith in me might be misplaced."

"I don't think so," she immediately replied. "I truly don't," she added as she turned away and walked back to her bedroom.

I waited for her to close the door behind her before I let myself lean against the banister; questioning a suspect was never fun, and even less so when they also happened to be a friend. I suddenly found myself having even deeper respect for my best friend, Sean Colbeth, for a few years back he'd been forced to interrogate a number of people who were part of his inner circle. It hadn't gone well for him; his cousin had given him the silent treatment for months, and the lingering irritation over his actions within the village had ultimately led to his ouster that past summer. Standards and Practices had very specific policy guidance on such things, guidance Sean had ignored just as easily back then as I had that morning. Sliding my iPhone into my uniform pocket, I hoped I wouldn't pay as hefty a price as Sean had.

The once-empty corridor I had wandered down a few hours earlier was now full of crime scene techs swabbing and measuring and photographing every conceivable item; picking my way around them, I paused at the wide-open double doors to the theater to take my bearings. Tall spotlights had been set just inside the door, and from the brilliance beyond them, it was evident more had been stationed throughout the hay bale maze. Every few seconds, a brilliant burst of white light told me the primary crime scene photographer was likely down by the faux electric chair; having traversed the maze once already, I made quick work of the puzzle and found the familiar form of Gina Carruthers kneeling at the base of the hay bales holding the chair. Despite the hubbub of activity around her, she appeared to have heard my approach and turned her face in my direction.

"Nice costume," she said with a smile as she stood up. "I take it you're watching that new show, then."

"I am," I nodded. "Alejandro and I waited up until midnight so we could watch the second season opener."

"*That* is dedication." She eyed me for a moment. "If you are here for answers, I don't have any for you, yet."

"I'll take vague hints at this point," I replied.

"I don't have many of those, either," Gina said.

"But you have some?" I asked hopefully.

Sighing, she rolled her eyes. "This is all preliminary, okay? Super-*super*-preliminary."

I made a motion of crossing my heart. "I will not put this in my report until you say I can."

"You'd better not," she replied. Looking at the tablet that was always omnipresent in her hands, she scanned the text before continuing. "I'll start with the blood; you're right, there isn't a ton of it, but what we've sampled so far seems to be the same type according to the field test. We'll get a full DNA profile on it back at the lab." She tapped at the screen and then looked at me. "I should also be able to scrape something from the tooth; I'm not a dental expert, but I've worked enough domestic violence cases to know it looks like something from upper jaw."

I nodded. "Roundhouse to the face?"

"That would be the logical conclusion," she nodded. "A damn bloody affair too, since that sort of punch generally lacerates the lip."

"And yet," I said, thinking of Sherlock Holmes, "I feel compelled to point out the lack of blood in the area."

Gina tapped at the side of her tablet. "It's pure speculation on my part but given what you said about the straps on that chair, I'd wager the victim was gagged. If we were to assume they were spirited away against their will."

"That is my view, unless your team finds evidence to the contrary."

"We've barely found anything worthy of being evidence at this point," she sighed. "My team is going to rack up incredible overtime on this one, given the size of this place."

Despite the seriousness of the situation, I felt myself smile. "I suppose it complicated matters immensely that a Halloween gala took place in the same location at the time of the kidnapping."

"You have *no* idea how many prints we are going to lift," she replied. "About the best I can do with a data mountain of that size is to run everything through the databases *en masse* and pray someone kicks out."

"Hope springs eternal," I said before nodding to the open door leading toward the servant hallway. "You already have someone in the catacombs?"

"Yeah," she replied. "So far, they've confirmed the passageways are exactly as shown on the floorplan the homeowner provided. That particular corridor runs between the bedrooms on this floor and leads to a back staircase connecting to the kitchen; unfortunately, it also has an exterior exit into the garage as well."

I nodded again. "No question this was planned in advance, then. Not with such an easy exit away from the hubbub of the party."

"Agreed. There is a lot of real estate to print — literally — but I'm having all the doors on that side of the house prioritized on the assumption our suspect might have been the last one to open them."

"It's worth a shot."

Gina looked up from her tablet. "You really do look good in silver," she said.

"So Alejandro keeps telling me," I replied as I ran a hand through hair I now assumed looked as unkempt as possible. So much for all of those long hours in the chair with Giovanni. "I think it's something I would have to get used to."

"How long are you going to keep it?"

"The color?" I asked.

"Yeah."

"I made the mistake of paying for the good stuff," I said with a slight smile. "So... a while."

"There could be worse things," she chuckled. "I'll regroup with you after we get a bit further. Will you be here?"

"For a bit. Alex has to go to work, so I'll probably duck out long enough for him to drop me at the station so I can pick up my SUV."

"All right. Keep your phone close, then."

"I will. And thanks, as always."

"Of course."

For the second time that early morning, I retraced my steps through the hay bale maze and returned to the hallway; I was still impressed by the level of effort Rosie and her volunteers had put into the Halloween party. Sidestepping another photographer as she snapped an image of something of interest on the wall, I realized I couldn't put aside the base horror of the situation. An actual human being — and one that I knew fairly well — had been abducted from right beneath my nose; the scene behind me indicated a level of violence that made me both angry *and* concerned about the wellbeing of Daniel. Emotions always played a huge part in how I investigated each case; usually, that was a competitive advantage that allowed me to intuit how the suspect viewed the world. As I paused at the railing overlooking the mess in the foyer, I knew this case was going to be a huge challenge in that regard; I was pissed in a way I hadn't felt in years. Pissed to think I had become so comfortable in Southern California that I had let my guard down just long enough to change the course of another life that held so much promise. I knew intellectually it wasn't my fault that Daniel had been taken, but it was also hard not to feel a certain level of responsibility for those under my watchful eye in Rancho Linda.

Something inside me knew that finding Daniel wasn't going to be easy. Finding him *alive* was going to be the longest of long shots I had ever played in my professional career.

Running my hands through my hair again, I tried to push away the growing anxiety that I wasn't moving fast enough. *I need a shower and a massive cup of coffee*, I thought as I started down the long, winding staircase to the foyer. *Or maybe a nice, long workout to exorcise some of this guilt.*

I was so mired in my thoughts that I didn't realize Alejandro was waiting for me at the bottom of the steps until he pulled me into an unexpected but welcome hug. It was a gentle embrace, but one that I didn't realize I'd needed quite as badly as I did. Releasing me slightly, he reached up to brush back one of my long bangs that had finally escaped from the bondage of the hair gel I'd used; his warm smile was like a port in a storm, one that I quickly charted a course toward.

"Hey," he said simply. "How are you holding up?"

"Fine."

Those amazingly erotic dark eyes of his narrowed; like always, he could read me like the open book I was. Still, he decided to ignore my little white lie — for now. "Are you headed in to see Delores?"

"Yes."

"You might want to wait a bit, then. She's talking to the counselor the Sheriff sent over."

I looked toward the hallway that led to the kitchen. "Timing is everything," I replied morosely. "But that did have to happen at some point."

Alex put a hand to my arm. "She's calmed down quite a bit," he said. "Speaking with a professional will center her emotionally, too. I suspect that means you'll get more out of her than you would have earlier."

"Yeah," I nodded with a tired smile. "You're right. I guess I'm just anxious to get this to the next stage."

"Understandable," he smiled again. "I'm going to head back upstairs and pack our things. I presume you want me to run you to the station before I head to work?"

"If you don't mind — otherwise I can catch a ride with one of the officers."

"I don't." He paused. "I had quite a conversation with Delores before the counselor arrived. You didn't mention she'd been the top career diplomat in the UK."

I smiled slightly. "It's not something she talks about regularly," I replied. "Nor Daniel. I think it brings up unhappy memories of her husband."

"Cancer," Alex nodded. "And not the quick variety."

"No," I shook my head. "Like I said earlier, he was the reason they came back stateside. I believe he was enrolled in a clinical trial out of UCLA Medical for a new gene therapy, but it was too little, too late."

"Damn," Alex replied, then looked toward the kitchen. "And now this. No wonder she was so wound up."

"Yeah."

He squeezed my shoulder. "I'll find you when everything's packed?"

"Sounds good."

Alejandro leaned in and kissed me briefly, then hurried up the stairs to our room. His fluid grace as he took the steps two at a time was a subtle reminder of how much time he spent at the pool continuing to perfect a diving talent that had won him accolades on the world stage years earlier; I'd been haranguing him about a pesky wrist injury that was refusing to heal, partly due to his stubbornness at taking any sort of break from his workout routine. I could hardly argue the point, considering I had been quietly increasing my yardage during swim practice to get ready for the Southwestern Regionals slated to be held in Los Angeles in just three weeks. Rolling my shoulder, I decided it was best not disclose to my fiancé just how many things on my own body were currently aching.

Movement out of the corner of my eye caught my attention; turning, I could see Officer Viella had appeared at the end of the hallway and was patiently waiting for me. I'd been impressed with how the young woman had become an integral part of the department, and had recommended her for a promotion to Detective at the end of the year. Her slight nod toward the kitchen was enough to tell me the counselor was wrapping up with Delores; pulling together whatever it was that made me an investigator, I nodded in return and headed toward one of the toughest conversations I knew I would ever have.

FOUR
GATHERING THE THREADS

Like everything else in the mansion, the kitchen had been designed for a time when a full set of staff took care of the family; oversized and bristling with modern appliances, it felt as though it could easily do double duty and support one of the local restaurants down in Rancho Linda proper. Rosie's part time chef tended to prep a few days' worth of meals and then put them into the fridge for the author to warm up if and when she remembered to eat; I had actually only met the gray-haired former restauranteur on one occasion, and had been surprised to learn at the time his father had been the final cook to work with Thomas Andrews, the original owner of the place. It was an interesting connection to the past that was entirely appropriate for a writer who focused on history.

Delores Kewley was sitting at a long table stationed in a small nook just beyond the stove; I had always assumed it was where the staff, back in the day, had taken their meals. Rosie by far preferred to dine at the table she had out in the solarium beside the pool; owing to her many medications for ongoing heart issues, she never felt completely warm unless she was out in the sweltering heat and humidity of the glassed-in space. But every now and then, Alex and I had helped her warm up something in the oven and then snarfed down the always-excellent dishes at the kitchen table, creating some sort of family atmosphere that I knew appealed to my millionaire friend. Without family of her own, the two of us had become her de facto children, a role that we weren't terribly unhappy to play. Despite the recent thawing of my relationship with my mother, I still had issues with my father to deal with, issues that still prevented me casually dining with my parents. Alex's mother had begun to call him more regularly, too, but I also knew it would still be a bit before the two of them traded Christmas cards again. So when Rosie had appeared in our lives and had, quite simply, loved us for who we were, it had created an undeniable bond that was a family of a sort, one that we had no problem becoming a part of.

Officer Viella had followed me in and then taken an unobtrusive position by the long preparation island behind us; I paused at one of the tall ladder-back chairs and took a moment to gauge Delores. She was staring at the cup of coffee in her hands with an intensity I could completely understand; remembering I could use a jolt of caffeine myself, I moved over to the side board where the coffeemaker was and poured myself a mugful.

"May I sit? I asked after I returned to the table.

"Sure," she said without looking up.

I pulled the chair out and then settled into it. Idly, I realized it was of the same variety as the faux electric chair upstairs in the former theater. "I need to ask you a few questions, Delores. I know you might not feel up to answering any of them, and I can completely understand that, but I need you to try."

She looked up. "What do you want to know?"

"When was the last time you spoke with Daniel?"

Delores frowned. "Uh, maybe two yesterday afternoon? He'd come home from school to pick up some last-minute items for the Gala."

"How did he seem?"

"Normal," she answered after a moment. "Excited the event was finally happening. A bit anxious that everything would go off without a hitch." Delores smiled slightly. "Worried about the Physics exam he had the following day."

"Sounds like your son," I replied. "Was he close to any of the kids working with Kids On Their Own?"

She shrugged. "Maybe? He's pretty focused on getting into college, so Daniel hasn't really made a lot of friends since we returned to the States." Delores paused. "He actually spends more time video chatting with the friends he left behind in London." She paused again. "Especially his boyfriend."

I frowned. "Long distance relationships can be hard."

"As he was discovering."

"Was he happy in California?"

"The move here was hard on both of us. Doubly perhaps for him since he lost both his father *and* the life he'd known." Delores looked at her coffee again. "I have to admit, seeing America from his perspective has been something of an eye-opener, Vas. My husband and I left over thirty years ago; what we returned to turns out to be something entirely different than the image we'd been selling to our global friends."

My eyebrows went up. "One slightly aberrant presidential election doesn't change the heart of a country. Especially one that was quickly rectified by the *next* election."

Delores actually smiled. "If you don't mind my saying this, you have a refreshingly optimistic view of this country despite how it has historically treated your community."

"Oh, I assure you I am not some sort of modern-day Pollyanna," I replied. "*Both* our communities have suffered at the hands of those in power; staying *reasonably* optimistic is about the only way I can reconcile what happened to all of us. That, and continuing to believe in the idea that we are a self-correcting society when the need arises."

"Amen to that," she breathed.

"Does Daniel have any other technology?" I asked. "We obviously know about his phone, but did he wear a fitness tracker? A smart watch?"

"A watch, yes," Delores said. "As well as Air Pods. He left both at the house since they weren't part of his costume."

I nodded. "All right," I said before deciding how best to phrase my next question. "Would he have any reason to want to leave home?"

"Yes," Delores said after a moment; she must have seen the surprise in my face because she immediately continued. "Not perhaps the way you meant the question. Part of Daniel's desire to get to Stanford was to follow in my footsteps and go to work for the State Department."

"And land back in London?"

"Yes," she said again. "Though long term, I think he wants to emigrate to the UK."

"Wow," I said. "He really does miss it over there, doesn't he?"

"We both do," she replied after a moment.

I paused again, knowing I was getting into trickier waters. "Were there any adults that Daniel was particularly close to? Anyone he might have sought out if he were in crisis?"

"Besides you?" she smiled slightly.

"Yeah," I nodded, slightly taken aback that Daniel had felt that way. I'd worked with him quite a bit, obviously, but had never considered we had anything other than a mentor-mentee sort of relationship.

"Maybe Anne or Zoe at *The Alternative Way*, I guess. There might be a teacher at the school, too."

"Do you remember their name?"

"No," she shook her head. "I'm sorry, Vas. I've been kind of swaddled in bubble wrap since losing my husband."

"I get it. I'll swing by the school later and ask around," I said, thinking that I might be *persona non grata* with the principal or her guidance counselor. The last time I'd been poking around Rancho Linda High School, a former star pupil had turned out to be a cold-blooded killer — not something I was sure they would want to repeat.

Delores looked at me for a long moment. "Is he still alive?"

While not an unexpected question from a loved one, it was nevertheless not one I wanted to answer, especially since my heart ached to give Delores some sort of hope to cling to. Hell, *I* needed something to believe in, too. I allowed my professionalism to take over and smiled gently before replying. "My team is scouring this house as we speak."

She narrowed her eyes. "That's what I thought," she said, hearing my non-answer for what it was. Delores pushed herself up from the table. "I think I want to go home now."

"Are you sure you don't want to wait here until your sister gets here?" I asked.

"I'll be fine."

"All the same, I'd prefer you not be alone," I said. "Officer Viella will follow you home and hang out until your company arrives."

"Thanks for the offer," she said with a tired smile, "but I'll be fine."

My smile hardened a bit. "I'm not asking," I said firmly. "It's very possible that whoever took Daniel might try and reach out to you. If that happens, I want someone from my team to be there."

Her eyes widened. "I... I never thought about that. You think someone might demand a ransom?"

"I have to keep all of the possibilities open at this point," I said. "As soon as I know anything, I will loop you in, Delores. Now get some rest."

"Okay."

I nodded at Viella who followed Delores out of the kitchen; I remained at the table for a moment jotting down my thoughts in the note app on my phone before standing. The empty kitchen felt unfamiliar and lonely, a strange sensation after all of the warm moments I'd experienced there over the years. The kidnapping had definitely cast a pall over everything, making that anger I'd been feeling burn just a little bit hotter.

There was far less activity in the foyer when I returned; besides a patient Alejandro waiting by the front door, a single lab tech was kneeling on the floor, diligently swabbing something with a long applicator. The windows facing the driveway had the slight glow of sunrise behind them, another visible indicator of just how much time had been lost already; I again felt helpless at how little progress had been made, despite knowing how unrealistic that feeling might be. Looking over my shoulder at the glorious staircases leading up to the second floor, I resisted the urge to dash back to the former theater and ask Gina for an update; she knew how to do her job far better than I did. My anxious presence wouldn't make what was *supposed* to be a deliberate process go any faster than it was capable of going. Feeling world weary, I walked toward Alex and reached for his hand; the gentle squeeze he gave it was welcome validation.

Neither of us felt like talking on the drive to the station; when he parked in the visitor spot by the front door, I leaned over and kissed him. "Thank you for being you," I said simply.

"I can't be anyone else," he smiled, "nor would I want to be. Should I assume you won't be home for dinner?"

"Never say never," I replied as I pulled my swim backpack from the rear seat of the New Beetle. "But it might be a good bet to do something that can sit in a Crock Pot."

"I might have just the thing," he said. "Text me updates?"

"Of course. Have a great day at work."

"I'd wish you the same," Alex said, "but I know it's not going to be much fun."

"Probably not," I sighed before stealing one last kiss.

I waited to watch him pull out before walking around to the side gate that protected the parking lot; fishing my ID out of the backpack, I waved it at the reader and then let myself in. The first rays of early morning sunshine had begun to creep over the horizon, giving the eclectic set of vehicles parked in the lot a far more jovial feeling than they deserved. My Camaro was parked at the far end of the row I happened to be standing beside, looking more brilliantly red than normal due to how the light was hitting it. Shifting the swim backpack on my shoulder, I felt a slight smile appear on my face as I shifted my plans on the spot and began to walk toward the car. After all, I had visiting the high school on my list that morning, didn't I? The fact that the pool I normally worked out at was right next door was pure coincidence.

Whether or not I'd be able to snag a lane was up to who was at the pool when I got there; rule changes a few years ago meant that adults couldn't be on deck when anyone under eighteen was in the water. With the private club there in the early afternoon and the high school competition season not yet started, I was reasonably certain I might have the place to myself at that particular hour. Pulling up beside the aquatics entrance a short time later, I felt validated when the only other car in the lot belonged to the coach of my Masters team. One of the perks of her job was using the facility whenever she wanted; though that didn't normally extend to members of her team, as a former Olympian herself she had in the past slightly bent the rules to allow me to get in some extra laps every now and then. Entering the pool deck, I waited by the edge until she finished a set and saw me standing there like a kid with their faced pressed to the window of a toy store. Smiling, she simply waved me in and then pushed off for another round.

I took care to fold the Starfleet costume into the bottom of my swim backpack before pulling on a favorite pair of purple briefs; the blue swim cap sort of clashed with my look, but at that point I was more interested in getting into the water and trying to calm the noise in my brain that was threatening to overwhelm me. Grabbing my goggles, I locked up everything and then hurried out to the deck and stepped onto the starting block for the lane I normally used; the sunshine sparkled off the pure blue of the water and would have been blinding had I not been wearing polarized lenses. Stretching slightly, I leaned down to grab the underside of the block, then pressed my toes into the surface to complete my racing dive position. Counting down mentally, I threw myself into the air before knifing cleanly into the water, arms stretched out in front of me in a perfect streamline. Three solid dolphin kicks pushed me up toward the surface; getting a breath, I settled into the long, rhythmic strokes of freestyle and allowed my brain to do what it did best.

At the thousand-meter mark, I flipped over and did a few sets of gentle backstroke; there wasn't a cloud in the entire blue sky that morning, a rarity for that part of the calendar in Southern California. The color made me think of one of the first projects I had worked on with Daniel and his group; that had involved reading some of the more popular children's books in various Kindergarten classes and then helping the kids draw out their favorite portion of the story. The five and under set weren't exactly Picassos, to be sure; primary colors seemed to be all that crayon sets seemed to have for that age, anyway, so it hadn't been a surprise that many of the works of art were heavy on blues, greens and reds.

Tapping a hand to the side of the pool so I could swivel into the other direction, I felt myself stop. *Reds... I saw something in red...*

Bobbing there at the edge of the pool, I closed my eyes and thought back to having walked the scene with my iPhone. I'd seen a ton of red blobs, mostly from whatever goop the teens had used for fake blood; it had been everywhere, splattered against the walls—

Holy shit. The handprint.

As I was on the wrong side of the pool from my iPhone, I dove under and did one of my fastest laps of freestyles ever; hitting the wall, I pulled myself smoothly out of the water and popped onto the deck, then dashed across the tiles to the locker room, trailing water in my wake. Skidding around the corner, I slid to a stop in front of my spot and fumbled with the lock for a moment before releasing the latch to the locker. Having left my towel behind on the bleachers, I grimaced slightly as I dug through my backpack to get to my iPhone; holding it with two fingers while trying to ignore how I had just dripped all over the clothes I'd planned on wearing to the office – not to mention the Starfleet costume beneath them -- I speed dialed Gina Carruthers.

"Hey, Vas," she said after picking up on the first ring. "You're not usually this impatient; I told you I'd call—"

"Gina, the handprint," I interrupted. "Did you swab the handprint?"

"The one out in the hallway?" she asked. "I'm sure we did, but nothing has been sent to the lab other than the prints we lifted on the exterior doors by the kitchen. Why?"

"Can you text me a photo of it?"

"Right now?" she asked.

"Yes."

There was a long pause. "Okay, I'll play along," she said. I heard movement as she continued to speak. "Not that I'm doing anything at the moment—"

"If they already sampled it, then trace must have been collected, too," I interrupted. "Has that hit the case system yet?"

"I have no idea," Gina said, her tone now unmistakably exasperated. "Maybe? The data coverage up here is for shit, which I imagine you already know."

"Yeah," I sighed. "Damn."

"What the hell is this about?" she asked. "You only get this agitated when you think you missed something."

"I'll tell you as soon as I see the photo," I replied.

"Shit," she breathed. "Hang on while I take the snapshot."

I waited for what seemed like an eternity, then heard my phone chime the receipt of a text message. Putting her on speaker, I shifted over to the messages system and tapped on the photo. "I've got it," I said.

"Good. Now do you want to tell me what you think you see?"

Pinching the image, I centered the bloody handprint I'd seen earlier on the screen and stared at it for a few moments. "That is not random," I said. "Look at the orientation."

"I don't see what you mean," she replied.

"The thumb, Gina! It's pointed *down*. Almost like someone was pressing themselves against the wall to get up."

There was a long pause. "Or bracing themselves because they'd been thrown against it," Gina added. "Are you thinking this is where the victim was assaulted?"

"The hallway was dark last night," I said. "Daniel would have had to turn the corner from where the theater was and would not have seen anyone hiding on the other side."

"It was plenty dark in the theater, too," Gina countered. "Why assault him *here*? The only benefit is the elevator is just a few feet in that direction, but someone at the party would have seen the kidnapper with this kid over his shoulder."

"I don't think that was the original plan," I said, pacing as I spoke. "I think this started out with the kidnapper trying to talk Daniel out of the mansion and into trouble. Most kidnappings start that way — the abductor tells the victim a loved one is in trouble and needs them. Nine times out of ten it works."

"Oh, *shit*," Gina breathed. "Your victim was that one out of ten and figured out what was going on?"

"His mother works for the State department," I said. "I'd need to confirm it with her, but I would assume all family members were trained to look out for stranger danger. Diplomats and their families are often targets overseas."

"So he doesn't go willingly," Gina continued thoughtfully. "It must have escalated quickly to get to a bloody handprint."

"I'll bet the roundhouse to the face happened there," I said, "and it sent Daniel to the ground. He's a big kid, though; he probably managed to get up and then tried to run."

"*Toward* the theater?"

"Yeah. Unfortunately, the only way out was blocked by his attacker — as far as he knew."

"Well, now that I look at this spot again, there's plenty of red specks here that we also swabbed," Gina said. "You might be right. Maybe the hit loosened the tooth, but it didn't come out until later?"

"Yeah," I said, idly noting I had made quite the puddle in front of the lockers from my pacing. "I still think the blow that stunned him enough to finally be subdued happened in the theater. The tooth probably came out then."

"Makes sense. And also explains why those leather straps were used."

"Daniel turned out to be more of a handful than they expected, so they were improvising — to a point. I still believe they knew about the servant hallway, maybe as a backup plan if they needed a quick exit to avoid raising any suspicions."

"It's a good theory," she said after a moment. "One that more or less fits what we're seeing here. I just don't quite know what it does for the case."

"I'm not sure either," I replied. "But I know someone in Palm Springs that might be able to help on that front. I'll reach out to her and see if she is willing to consult."

"Is that the former FBI profiler you used this summer?"

"The same." I caught my reflection in the locker room's mirror; several silver bangs had escaped from the blue swim cap, making me look a bit like a character from an anime show. "I'm sorry I interrupted. Thanks for indulging me."

"My pleasure. And just to be on the safe side, I'll have a tech go over this spot again."

"I appreciate that."

The phone triple beeped the end of the call, but I continued to pace for another moment; I was dead certain that the placement of the handprint was pertinent, but was at a loss for why I felt that way. Still, every investigator sense I had was telling me I'd stumbled onto something important. As I pulled my goggles back on to head back out to the pool, I hoped further clarity would descend from the heavens.

As if it were that easy.

FIVE

UNWELCOME & UNWANTED

J anice Dolittle did not look pleased to find me sitting in her office.

The principal for Rancho Linda High School was slowly tapping a number two pencil against her scrupulously clean desk, eyeing me as she did so with the air of a person wondering if her day was about to take a serious left turn. I couldn't blame her, for that was generally what had happened each prior time I had appeared in her doorway. While we essentially stared each other down like two gunslingers in an Old West movie, I pondered the rather large and recently added diploma just over her shoulder; despite the hard work that had to have gone into her new Ph.D., I wondered just a bit if she now worried about being confused with the fictional veterinarian.

At length, Dolittle stood from her desk and went to a small Keurig sitting on her credenza. "Coffee?"

"Thank you, yes."

"Is black okay? I don't take anything with mine, but there's cream and sugar in teacher's lounge."

"Black is fine."

Inserting a pod into the device, she pressed the start button and then stared at it as the cycle started. "Why are you here, Detective Korsokovach?"

"*Deputy Chief* Korsokovach now, Dr. Dolittle," I reminded her.

It took a ton of effort not to smile when I said her formal name out loud; since I was reasonably certain I was already on thin ice with the educator, remaining professional seemed the order of the day. I might have subtly undercut that with the windpants-and-muscle-shirt combo I was sporting; stashed for emergency purposes at the back of my locker, it had been the only set of clothing dry enough to wear after I'd dripped all over everything else in my backpack while digging out my iPhone. Then again, it wasn't the first time I'd had my own take on Business Casual during an investigation, though honestly, my badge chafed horribly when clipped to that waistband. Shifting in the plastic chair I presumed was intended to be uncomfortable, I smiled my megawatt smile and plunged in.

"I'm here about Daniel Kewley."

"You know from your prior visits I cannot discuss any of our students without parental consent."

"I'm not looking for any sort of academic information," I said. "Not this time."

The Keurig chuffed to conclusion with a dramatic sigh; Dolittle pulled out the mug and set it aside so she could reload the machine and place a second mug beneath the spigot. Turning, she carried the steaming concoction around her desk and handed it to me, then leaned against the edge with her arms folded against her chest. It occurred to me at that moment I had never seen Dolittle dressed in anything other than a conservatively shaded pantsuit, making me wonder if she'd taken a class on Sartorial Selections for The Discriminating Administrator somewhere along the line. I took a sip at the coffee and decided two things: first, Dolittle was probably far less buttoned down when she was off the clock, and second, I was never buying the store brand K-cups. Ever. Swallowing the distasteful mouthful while trying to look impassive took more effort than snickering over her name had, but somehow, I made it through.

"If not academic data, then what?" she asked. The finger tapping at the side of her sleeve was the only visible indication of frustration over throwing her schedule asunder.

Glancing at the door leading back toward the main reception area for the school, I stood and moved over to it; Dolittle's eyebrows went up slightly when I closed it and then turned to face her. "I presume Daniel was not in class this morning," I said evenly.

Something flickered across her face. "No, he wasn't."

"I'm guessing that is fairly unusual?"

"Yes," she nodded. "Since he arrived in Rancho Linda, he's not missed a single day of class." Dolittle looked at me for a moment. "We tried to reach his mother this morning, but the calls are going to voicemail. Same with Daniel."

"Hopefully Delores is finally getting some sleep," I said as I sat back down in the chair. "It was a long night for her — well, hell, for all of us," I continued as I rolled the mug around in my hands. Despite my better judgement, I took another sip from the brew. It didn't seem quite as bad the second time around; either that, or the first sip had permanently damaged my taste buds.

Dolittle's features softened slightly. "I don't like the sound of that. What happened? Is he okay?"

"Honestly, at this point I don't have the answers to either of those questions," I replied. "Daniel was one of the student volunteers working the Halloween fundraiser last night."

"That's the annual gala up to Dr. Frankenhoffer's place?" Dolittle asked. "I usually attend but had a conflict this year."

"Yes, that's the one," I nodded. "Daniel failed to return home after it ended; my team is currently scouring the venue, but early indications are that someone might have taken him against his will."

The color drained from the principal's face. "Holy shit."

"Yeah," I replied. "Look, I'm grasping at straws right now, but what I need more than anything is a sense of the relationships Daniel had here at the school. Were there any faculty members he was especially close to? Did the janitor detest that he kept smelly gym clothes in his locker? Maybe the librarian was tutoring him on the side? Those sorts of things."

Dolittle looked thoughtful. "That is entirely possible. Daniel is the top student in his class, and as such, is also highly involved in many of the student groups we have. I don't think it would be a problem to share that list with you," she said, before smiling slightly. "Raymond Connolly down in the Guidance Office would be the person to speak with."

I groaned inwardly. On two prior occasions I had been forced to squeeze information out of the balding, overweight guidance counselor; neither had gone particularly well. I hoped the third time would finally be the charm — but wasn't holding my breath. "I'll swing by there on my way out, then," I smiled. "How well do you know Daniel, Doctor?"

"As well as any of my students," she replied easily as she walked back around to the Keurig to get her mug. "I probably saw him more than most due to his volunteering. I knew his father passed away not long ago — cancer, I think?"

"Yes."

"Without getting into specifics, he was a good kid," she continued. "One who never found himself in that chair."

"Sounds like the Daniel I knew," I nodded. "Given his volunteer work both in and out of school, I take it he wasn't involved in any sports?"

"Not that I know of, but Raymond could fill you in on that as well."

"Still pulling double duty as the Athletic Director?"

Dolittle shrugged. "It was easier tossing him some extra salary than hiring someone."

"And more budget friendly, I imagine."

The shadow of a smile appeared. "Yes."

I set the still-full cup of coffee on her desk and then stood. "I'd appreciate it if you'd keep what I've told you in confidence. As I said earlier, we haven't confirmed exactly what happened to Daniel; I'd rather not get the rumor mill cranked up if we can help it."

"Of course," she nodded. "We specialize in discretion around here."

I couldn't tell if Dolittle was being sarcastic. "Thank you for your time," I smiled. "I'll go speak with Mr. Connolly now and then be out of your hair."

"Somehow, Deputy Chief, I suspect that won't be the case."

"Hope springs eternal," I laughed.

Exiting the administrative suite for the school put me into the thick of class change traffic; pressing myself against a wall, I took a moment to chart the currents and then inserted myself into the flow of bodies heading in the general direction of the teacher's lounge. I would normally have had a fifty-fifty chance Raymond Connolly would be there at that moment, but since the clock was inching toward ten, I figured the odds might be better he was stealing a few quiet moments over a cup of coffee before facing the rest of his morning. Pulling open one half of the double doors to the space, I found that save for the addition of a new vending machine, the space hadn't changed all that much since my last visit. A half-dozen circular tables were spread through the rectangular space, each capable of seating five or six staff members; a sink, fridge and microwave were on the far wall, and were all being used at the moment. The bulletin board over the trash and recycling bins had the standard California and Federal labor laws prominently displayed, along with various flyers promoting school events.

No one took particular notice of my entrance, which also wasn't unusual. Despite my attire, it was clear I wasn't a student who had inadvertently breached the sanctity of the lounge; besides, most of the eclectic staff appeared to be absorbed in trying to remember why they had chosen the education field in the first place. More than a few were holding their hands as though they'd been puffing on a cigarette; combined with the still-detectable odor from the years when that had not been illegal, it felt odd that I wasn't wading through a thick haze. Had I not known I was inside a metropolitan high school, I could have easily mistaken the room as belonging to some sort of halfway house for those trying to put their lives back together after dealing with major PTSD.

Raymond Connolly happened to be the one with his head stuck inside the fridge that had to have been at least as old as the school itself was. Oddly, that was the same position I'd found him in two years earlier when I was investigating the death of the school's star tennis player. Hoping that wasn't some sort of creepy foreshadowing of what was to come, I paused a few steps away from his rather rotund backside and loudly cleared my throat; while he'd been portly the first time I'd met him, my particular angle unfortunately provided evidence the counselor had packed on quite a bit more weight. It seemed being athletic was not a requirement for being the Athletic Director.

As he apparently couldn't hear me, I moved a bit closer. "Mr. Connolly?"

In a piece of physical comedy that would have done Lucille Ball proud, Connolly managed to both hit his head on the inside of the fridge while simultaneously dumping whatever it was he was holding all over the floor in front of it. Grabbing at his head, he backed out of the space and started to mumble something close to words no teenager should ever hear before getting a look at who had startled him. The expression of abject terror that appeared on his face was quickly replaced by something closer to pain as he rubbed the rather large bald spot his combover would never cover.

"Deputy Chief Korsokovach," he muttered. "Just when my day was going so well, too."

"I'm sorry to have surprised you," I said as I went to the towel dispenser beside the sink and yanked out ten yards of paper. Kneeling beside him, I mopped up what smelled like cola, a guess that was confirmed when I saw the silver Diet Coke can on its side behind Connolly. "I thought bad days only happened on Mondays?"

"Hardly," he groaned as he continued to rub at his skull. "Are you looking for me?"

I would have thought that was obvious was my initial reply, but I smiled and said instead: "Yes. Do you have a moment to chat?"

He glanced at the massive clock over the double doors. "I've got a student at 10:15, so I can give you six or seven minutes."

How generous, I snarked to myself. "I'll take it," I said.

I tossed the mass of towels into the trash and then waited to wash my hands at the sink; by the time I'd dried them off, Connolly had taken a seat at an empty table as far away from the rest of the staff members as was physically possible. Sliding into a chair opposite him, I felt myself recoil in disgust at the tinny scent of whatever it was he was munching on from a colorful plastic bag; as he chewed, though, I was reminded that I had not actually eaten anything since the night before. Trying to put that to the side, I smiled again and began.

"I understand you work with Daniel Kewley."

Connolly nodded. "He was in my caseload, yes. Full ride to Stanford."

"Was?" I asked, noting the past tense.

"*Is*," Connolly corrected with a slight smile. "Freudian slip, I guess. With students like him, once they are placed there really isn't much more someone like me can offer."

"I see," I replied. "Were any other schools interested in him?"

"Oh, *tons*," he replied. "Even a few overseas. But he decided on Stanford pretty early on."

"I know he was quite a volunteer," I continued, glancing at the clock. "Did he also play a sport?"

"No," Connolly shook his head. He licked something off a finger, which was incredibly unappetizing. "I mean, not as an athlete. I think he was the manager for the soccer team."

"Manager?" I asked.

"Yeah," he replied. "Usually, they're the ones who manage the equipment for the team, or keep score for the coach. In some cases they even do the social media."

I nodded. "I suppose we had someone like that on my swim team, now that I think about it."

"It's usually a role for a kid who always wanted to participate in a sport but wasn't gifted in any way. I also see parents pushing their kids into that role when they want to include such an experience on a college application"

"Can it make a difference?"

"Sometimes," he shrugged. "Depends on the sport and the school evaluating the application."

"What clubs are Daniel part of?"

"A few," he said, his eyes wandering to the clock. "I can get you the list."

"I'd appreciate that," I said. "What kind of work was it, in general?"

"All service or honorary types," Connolly answered before dumping whatever crumbs were left in the bag into his mouth. Crunching the plastic into a ball, he stood. "I've got to go."

"I appreciate your time," I said. "I can't imagine trying to juggle two positions the way you are."

Connolly actually smiled. "The extra money doesn't hurt. And usually it's pretty easy balancing both jobs."

"Usually?"

Connolly shrugged as he tossed the crumpled bag into a trashcan. "We've had a spate of athletic supplies go missing this year. The damndest things — towels, kinesthetic wraps, even a sideline cooler. I've spent the past couple of weeks filling out paperwork for Loss Prevention and dealing with our insurer."

"Sounds like you might have a little crime ring going," I smiled. "Let me know if you need our services; we're pretty good at finding thieves. Even if they are teenagers."

"I think we'll be okay," he replied. "The total amount of stuff missing is under five grand, so the district is likely just going to write it off."

"Ah," I said as I dug my wallet out of my windpants. "Here's my card; it has my official email address on it. Send the clubs list to that if you would."

"Got it," he nodded. He took the card and stuffed it into a pocket, then with more speed than someone of his girth would normally muster, made his escape through the lounge doors.

I waited a moment before following Connolly out of the room. The difference from my last exit into the hallway was like night and day; without the clogged teenaged bodies everywhere, the space seemed positively cavernous. Still, the strange mixture of body odor and cheap pharmacy perfume served as a reminder that the masses were never very far away. I couldn't help but think of my own time in high school; it might have been a different decade, but I imagined most of what I had experienced as a hormonally challenged human had likely remained the same. The cliques, the innuendos, the grind of getting through another day unscathed emotionally all came back in an instant, as well as the additional level of angst surrounding who I seemed to be sexually attracted to. Looking back on it, in some ways having been outed by my boyfriend had actually made my final years far easier; no longer was I trying to hide in plain sight among my peers. No, from the moment it became public knowledge I was gay, it became possible for me to *finally* exist as the person I truly was. No apologies, and certainly no backing down when some homophobic idiot tried to beat me into a bloody pulp in the bathroom. Swimming had given me many things over the years, not the least of which was a body capable of ending anything before it had truly begun. I smiled to think that I *had* sat in just such a chair as Dolittle had in her office, explaining to my principal how the star offensive tackle for our football team had accidentally stumbled into the sink and broken his nose. It had helped, I think, that the principal had been a lesbian — a fact I'd not known until years later, when I'd received a beautiful letter from her after I'd competed in the Olympics as one of the few openly gay athletes.

With the students in the halls, it hadn't been obvious that I'd passed a wall of windows looking out onto a small quad between wings of the building; the grass was a little brown but well tended, as were the squat flower boxes in the exact center. It was a nice touch and one that I was sure the students would never appreciate.

Cynical, I smiled to myself. *Oh, how cynical you are these days.*

At one end of the wall of glass was the standard trophy case that all high schools seemed to have; I'd looked it over during my first case, and as I passed it, didn't think there were any new accolades since the last time I'd been there. The bulletin board beside it *was* vibrantly different, stuffed to overflowing with flyers covering just about anything imaginable. I'd planned on giving it a pass until the recognizable poster for the Halloween gala caught my eye; pausing, I read over the copy that Daniel and his team had come up with, and felt that same pang that I wasn't going fast enough. I was about to turn away when I suddenly turned back; I'd missed it on first glance, but the small section showing the student groups sponsoring the event had been torn at unevenly. Looking closer, I could see that the section had originally been alphabetical, and ended just after one named *Lives Matter*. I wasn't aware of that particular organization, but that only meant it wasn't one that operated out of *The Alternative Way*; I grabbed my iPhone and took a photo of the dismembered poster with the intent of cross checking the names still showing against the list Connolly sent me — and the groups Rosie had invited to help. It may have been nothing, but my gut told me the alteration of the poster had been deliberate, though finding out to what end would be an interesting challenge.

As I slid my phone back into a pocket, thinking about Connolly made me realize we had gone the entire conversation without my telling him why I was inquiring after Daniel Kewley. Pushing out into the warm sunlight of the late morning, I couldn't help but wonder why Connolly hadn't asked.

SIX
COMMAND CENTRAL

Feeling a bit like I was running on fumes, against my better judgment I diverted through the first In-n-Out drive through I passed on my way back to the Rancho Linda Police Department. I tried to make myself feel better about the shockingly poor life choice by ordering the double cheeseburger protein style, but the lack of bread was pretty much offset by the mountain of fries I'd added. Not wanting to be caught with my contraband, I'd pulled into a parking spot and quickly snarfed down the carbs as though my life depended on it. Ensuring I'd not dropped a dollop of ketchup anywhere in the Camaro, I tossed the evidence into the first trash bin I could find and then continued onward to station, somewhat satiated while simultaneously feeling incredibly guilty. Food and I had a complicated relationship, one that I knew would begin to catch up to me should I ever take my foot off of the workout pedal. Alejandro knew better than most how... particular... I was about my body; as I grew ever closer to forty and the inevitable metabolism changes that would come with it, I worried far more than I let on about transforming into an ugly blob of a human he would no longer want to be seen with.

It was nightmare that had propelled me to the pool twice a day for my entire adult life.

Setting aside my personal issues as I turned into the parking lot for the station, I noted as I swiped my badge at the reader most of the spots were full. Considering our current staffing levels, it was a clear indicator that my raft of orders issued in the wee hours of the morning had been implemented, including bringing in anyone off shift willing to assist with the case. While we didn't yet have a place to look, I knew we would use every available hand when the time came that we did; pulling into an open spot, I silently prayed to whatever deity worked with cops that I would soon get a lead to trigger such an effort. Locking up the car, I walked across the lot to the rear entrance and badged my way in; the booking area was reasonably quiet, but the cubicles in the main squad room were, for once, a hive of activity. For just a moment I felt like the calendar had been turned back to a time when the department had three fully-staffed shifts working around the clock to keep the community safe; the reality I'd had to rob *two* of those shifts to over staff the third was rather sobering.

Unsurprisingly, the door to Chief Gilbert's office was open as I unlocked mine; before I could even turn the knob, I heard his voice. "Vas? Got a moment?"

"Sure," I said.

Closing the door, I stepped through his and found him at the large desk he favored; to my surprise, he had his laptop open and was clearly logged into the case system. Several stacks of paper had been arranged on the surface of his desk, which matched many multiples more out on the larger conference room table beside his inner office. As he waved me into one of his guest chairs, he pulled the half-moon-shaped reading glasses from his eyes; they were a relatively recent addition, an unwelcome one according to the grousing I'd been hearing each time he'd donned them.

"Command center has been configured and is operational," he said without preamble as I sat down. "I signed off on your request for seventy-two hours of constant coverage, and might be able to do another thirty if push comes to shove. Although," he sighed as he sat back in his chair, "if it goes beyond forty-eight, you know how bad the odds are."

"Yeah," I nodded.

"I contacted the Feds. Unusually, they want to wait to see what evidence we develop before they weigh in; my peer over there rather candidly told me they've had their hands full with domestic terrorism cells and can't spare anything unless we truly need them."

"That's a first," I said, eyebrows raised. "Normally they rush in and take over this kind of case."

"It's a sign of the times, I'm afraid." Mike rubbed his eyes. "Press office has already put out a release about our missing teen," he continued, referring to the one-woman operation trying to do what a team of ten used to do back in the day. "The tip line went live about an hour ago, and as usual, it's been flooded with cranks who think Elvis took the kid."

"What is this fixation with Elvis?" I asked. "You'd think after all this time, they'd come up with someone more creative."

My boss arched a busy eyebrow. "Like, who?"

"I dunno," I sighed. "Maybe that wrestler dude from ten years ago? The one with blond hair?"

"You mean our ex-governor?"

"No—" I said, then saw him smile. "Ah."

"Anyway," Mike continued, "Linda's scheduled a press conference for eleven-thirty so it can be covered by the noontime newscasts."

I rolled my eyes. "Let me guess who you want in front of the microphone."

Mike eyed my muscle t-shirt. "I hope to God your Class A uniform is in your office."

"It is," I nodded before glancing at my watch. "I have just enough time to shower and change."

"That you do," he replied. "But before you go, where are we at?"

"The very beginning," I answered with a frown. "I've got to go back up to the scene and touch base with Gina and her team; there was, as you can imagine, a ton of real estate to cover at the mansion. I don't expect anything until early this afternoon, honestly."

"Crap."

I shrugged. "On the other hand, I've been running down a bit of background on Daniel. I knew him from my work with *The Alternative Way*, of course, but wanted to get a sense of whether he had any other connections — either at the high school or external."

"Did you find anything?"

"Only more questions," I sighed. "And a tantalizing hint that someone didn't like him or the group he worked for."

"That seems rather vague," Mike frowned. "I was rather hoping you and that famous instinct of yours had already identified a suspect."

"It seems to be failing me at the moment," I replied. "Although I think the administrators at the high school know more than they were willing to say."

"You'd better not be pushing Janice Dolittle's buttons again, Vas," Mike admonished. "The last time you pissed her off, I spent an hour with the council trying to talk them out of firing you."

My eyebrows went up. "I'm union," I reminded him. "They can't do that."

"They did before," he countered. "As they well reminded me."

"Ah," I nodded. "Well, thanks for saving my ass. Again."

"Are you kidding?" he laughed. "No way I'm letting you escape a *second* time."

"Message received," I smiled as I stood. "I'd better go get ready."

"Indeed. And Vas?"

"Yeah, Chief?"

"You might want to think about keeping your hair that color. It suits you."

"Everyone keeps telling me that," I replied. "I think it makes me look old."

"Not old," Mike said. "Distinguished."

I rolled my eyes again. "To-*may*-to, to-*mat*-o."

"Never change, my friend," he laughed as I left his office.

Unlocking the door to my office a second time, I hurried over to the small closet beside my coffeemaker and pulled open the door; thankfully, my spare Class A uniform was hanging there, still inside the bag from the dry cleaners. Pulling it out, I quickly made my way to the locker room and ran through my ablutions as quickly as possible; less than ten minutes later, I was back in my office impatiently scanning the case file for updates while trying to get my tie knotted just right. The last tie I'd worn had been the fancy bow version that came with my tuxedo; for whatever reason, I was finding the half-Windsor insanely difficult in comparison. I was just pulling out another failed attempt when the unique ringtone for Alejandro filled my office. Pouncing on the iPhone, I smiled as I answered.

"Save me, Obi-Wan Alejandro. I can't tie this damn tie."

The chuckle that rose up from my phone chased away some of the weight of the day. "I'm beginning to understand why you always wear a polo shirt."

"It's Southern California," I said. "We're by nature casual."

"Apparently not all the time if you're having trouble tying something."

"The Chief wants me to look my best for the cameras," I said.

"That shouldn't be too hard," Alejandro laughed. "You'd look incredible in anything, even a toga and sandals."

"I don't think I want to be the news story today," I smiled as I managed to finally knot the tie properly. "A toga? Really?"

"Yes," Alex said. "I'll wear one too, if you like, and then you can feed me grapes just like in the movies."

I'd never told Alex about one of my first boyfriends and how *he* had done that very thing to *me* — nor how insanely erotic an act it had turned out to be. Sensing an opportunity, I smiled a bit wider. "I don't think you understand what you're asking for."

"I might," he said with a wicked tone. "Are you up for a challenge?"

"Oh," I said, unable to ignore the sudden pressure below my belt, "I would say that I am."

"Good," he chuckled. "How are things going? I thought I'd check in and see if you wanted me to swoop in and rescue you."

"You can always do that," I replied. "Overall, I feel a bit like I'm just spinning my wheels. We've got the machinery in place to investigate, but nothing to follow up on. Yet."

"It's still early days," he reminded me. "Though I got the impression that time was critical in a case like this."

"Yeah, which is why I feel so useless at the moment."

"You aren't," he said. "And, knowing you, I suspect you already have a few theories percolating in the back of that gorgeous head of yours."

"Maybe," I replied, not quite willing to admit that I had, indeed, thought of a few. "I might have to run up to Palm Springs tonight or tomorrow. I want to talk to that retired FBI psychologist I used this summer. You want to come with me?"

"Does she know you're coming?"

"Not yet," I replied. "She's my next call."

"If you go tonight, are you thinking of making it a round trip?"

I thought about that for a moment. "It depends on where the case is at that point, but I think I'm gonna crash pretty hard after dinner," I said. "If she will see me tonight, I'll probably book in at that Marriott we tried this summer."

"You could probably do with a bit of sleep," Alex replied. "Assuming I'm able to keep my libido in check, that is."

"These are trying times," I laughed. "Let's plan on that — as long as you don't mind skipping breakfast so I can get you to your office on time in the morning."

"Sure," he said. "I can have my assistant cover practice tonight."

"I hate for you to miss that," I said.

"The kid needs to step up," Alex replied. "He's been angling for a bigger role anyway; we'll see how he feels after he's the one herding cats for a few hours."

"I had no idea you were such a sadist."

"I have my moments. I'll head home after work to top off Chat's dishes and then meet you at the station?"

"I'll let you know, but that's what I'm leaning toward right now."

"Shoot me a text, then," he said. "Hugs and kisses."

"Same," I said with a fond smile.

I waited for the triple beeps to signal the end of the call before scrolling through my phonebook to locate the number for Verna Novell; she had been recommended to me during the serial killer case I handled back in the spring by Raphael Gonzales, the National Park Police Officer who I'd first met almost exactly a year earlier. Despite getting off on the wrong foot with each other initially, he'd become a close friend that I spoke to regularly. As my finger hovered over Verna's number, I thought a bit about the last call we'd had; Raphael had made the same sort of romantic leap of faith as Alejandro and relocated to Maine back in August to be with his new boyfriend. While the relationship was still going strong, the boyfriend had unexpectedly tested positive for HIV a week after Raphael had accepted a new position in Bar Harbor. I'd only met Norm Thomas the one time he'd come to Las Vegas with Sean for a case and had really liked him; though it had fallen out of the spotlight, HIV was still a thing in our community, and I'd been devastated to get the news. The antivirals now available were a miracle of modern medicine, and appeared to be doing their job for the young man. Raphael had so far continued to test negative himself, but now that particular elephant was in the room, I knew the two of them were likely dancing a very careful dance. Shaking off a bit of guilt over having had a hand in hooking the two of them up in the first place, I refocused on the here and now and pressed the call button for Verna. To my surprise, it rang but a single time before I heard her voice.

"Hello?"

"Verna, it's Deputy Chief Vasily Korsokovach," I said. "We met over the summer?"

"Ah, Vasily," she replied warmly. "I wondered when you were going to call."

I blinked. "You were expecting me?"

"From the moment I heard about the kidnapping," she said. "As you might imagine, I still have contacts at the Bureau."

Nodding, I smiled slightly. "We reached out to them for assistance."

"I know they rebuffed you, too," she said. "Fortunately, I no longer work for them. When will you be here?"

I couldn't help but laugh. "And here I was thinking I'd have to beg to get some time on your busy calendar."

"You're in luck," she chuckled herself. "I've just had a cancellation and can see you this evening; canasta has been pushed to Thursday."

"Are you sure? I hate to have you miss a session."

"Oh, Beverly can cool her heels for forty-eight hours," Verna replied. "Will you be bringing that other cute swimmer with you?"

"Sean is back in Maine, I'm afraid. But my fiancé was planning on keeping me company, if you don't mind a plus one?"

"Is he a swimmer, too?"

"Diver, actually," I replied. "And *very* handsome. Not that I'm biased in any way."

"Of course," she laughed. "He is more than welcome. Make sure you both bring your appetites, too. I've already started my preparations for your feast."

I glanced at my watch. "Verna, if I'm really lucky we'll get there close to seven. There's no need for you to put on the Ritz."

"Are you kidding? I've not had guests to entertain since the last time you were here. The good tablecloth is coming out this time, I assure you."

"Verna—"

"I'll see you at seven," she replied, cutting me off. "Bring whatever you have at that point and we'll go through it."

Resigned that I was going to need to wake up even *earlier* to work off whatever Verna was cooking, I sighed. "I'm not going to win this one, am I?"

"Nope. You think seven?"

"Six-thirty if I traffic is in my favor. Which it never is."

"Don't you have lights and a siren on that Camaro of yours?"

"No," I said, "but even if I did—"

"Yeah yeah," she chuckled. "Policy blah-blah-blah. No worries, just give me a quick call when you hit I-10. That'll give me enough time to uncork the wine."

Shaking my head, I figured it was good that we were staying over now. "All right. See you tonight, then."

"Until then!" she said. As she hung up, I wasn't sure whether she was more excited over having a case to review, or the fact that she'd be doting over two guests for a few hours. I figured it was probably a mixture of both.

Glancing at my watch again, I had just enough time to book a room at the Marriott we'd tried back in the summer before having to head out and across the squad room to the small space we used for gatherings. Back when we'd had actual *numbers* of people on the payroll, it was often where the shift commander would give their briefing before sending the patrol officers out into the wild; these days, most of that was handled via email or our internal chat system. The remnants of the room's former use remained, however; as I walked in, I could see the ancient projection screen had been pulled down from the ceiling, centered between the flags for California and the United States. Empty cork bulletin boards were on either side of that, places where State and Federal wanted notices had once been posted for all to see. The long folding tables we had once used for staff briefings had been taken down and stored somewhere; the strange plastic chairs that accompanied them were arrayed in even rows and were surprisingly full of attendees. A quick scan of the crowd netted me a few familiar faces from local media; over my time in the department, I'd had more than a few on-and-off the record conversations with reporters and, honestly, had never enjoyed the experience. It was one thing that I'd never had to deal with back in Windeport, largely due to how remote the village was.

Linda Hopwood was standing just to the side of the weatherbeaten podium bearing the official seal for the City of Rancho Linda. She seemed relieved to see me enter the room and motioned for me to join her at the front; as I headed in her direction, I noted that the vibrant purple eyeshadow that was her shade of choice that day was less vibrant than her normal selections. It was also quite close to the color Alejandro had worn as Spock; oddly, I thought the color looked better on my fiancé than the Public Affairs Officer but decided not to share that particular observation.

"Hey, Linda," I said as I looked down at the petite woman. She was *maybe* four-eight, and that was on the days when she wore heels. "I have you to thank for this, I hear."

She smiled up at me. "The press loves someone photogenic," she said. "It'll help get our message out there." Linda eyed my hair. "What the fuck did you do to your hair? It looks like *crap*."

There were times when her refreshing frankness was anything but. "I was Captain Pike for Halloween," I said.

Her eyes went round. "You died your hair for a fucking *costume*?"

"When I commit to a part, I go all the way," I smiled.

"Well *shit*," she breathed. I'd long wondered if her years in the Navy had led to her particularly salty language; what was even stranger was the near-perfect diction and absence of, shall we say, colorful metaphors when speaking as the official voice of the department. "How long before you go back to being blond?"

"I was thinking I'd let my natural color grow out first," I said, putting voice to something that had been percolating in the back of my brain.

"What the *fuck* color is that?" she asked.

I smiled. "It's been so long since I've seen it, I have no clue. I started bleaching it when I was thirteen."

"Huh," she said as she squinted. "Well, then I guess we'll wait to see what it looks like before I retake your official photo."

"That sounds like a plan," I chuckled. Eying the big clock on the wall behind us, I nodded meaningfully to the crowd. "Shall we?"

"I thought you'd never *fucking* ask," she laughed before stepping up to the podium. The ambient conversation died away naturally as she stood there for few heartbeats. Seeing she now commanded the room's attention, she donned the persona that most people associated with the department. "Thank you for joining us this morning. We have a time-critical situation and appreciate any assistance members of the community may be able to render." Linda looked at me. "Deputy Chief Korsokovach will sketch in the major details for you now."

Nodding at her as we exchanged positions, I tried to relax my shoulders a bit and discovered I was far, far more tense than I had realized. Placing my hands on the surface of the podium, I could see Linda had left a copy of the PowerPoint slides currently being displayed behind me. Scanning them quickly to help frame what I was about to say, I looked up at the crowd, tried to ignore the red lights on the cameras at the back of the room and began. "For those of you who don't know me, I am Deputy Chief Vasily Korsokovach," I said. "Please don't try and spell that now — Linda will hand out my card later so you can get it right in your articles."

The slight chuckle from the crowd helped lighten the mood; I picked up the small clicker device that Linda had left on the podium and pressed the advance button. "Last night, between the hours of nine P.M. and midnight, this young man disappeared." I turned to look at the photo Linda had clearly gotten from the Rancho Linda High School yearbook. "This is Daniel Kewley, aged seventeen. He is a senior at Rancho Linda High School and, among other accomplishments, is the current student chair of the charitable organization, Kids On Their Own. Daniel was volunteering at the annual Halloween fundraiser noted author Rosalia Frankenhoffer hosts."

I paused for a moment. "He was last seen at the fundraiser; his whereabouts since are unknown. We are asking for help in determining Daniel's movements after nine last night; any information may be directed to the phone number currently showing on the screen. I must emphasize that no detail is too small — anything brought to our attention may lead us to Daniel."

Clicking the button again brought up a screen of demographics. "Daniel is five ten and one-sixty," I continued, "typical for a male of his age. He was last seen wearing a green archer's outfit in an artificial leather fabric, with matching boots and gloves of a similar color. As he was attending a Halloween party at the time, he also had facial makeup and a domino mask." I paused more dramatically than I'd intended before adding: "The mask was recovered at the party."

The next slide repeated the department's contact information. "I'll take questions now, but given this is a sensitive and active investigation, I may not be able to answer all of them."

Hands shot up, and deciding to bow to the inevitable, I called on Vivian Grandchester from the *Orange County Register*. We had a tense relationship owing mostly to how she had covered my original departure from Rancho Linda. "Vivian."

"Thank you, Chief," she said as she stood. "You've not said this explicitly, but the intimation is that this student was kidnapped from the party. Is that an accurate statement?"

"We're still gathering evidence," I replied. "All I will say at this point is this: we've recovered enough to conclude that Daniel was taken against his will."

"What sort of evidence?"

"I'm not going to get into that," I said. "You, in the back—"

"A follow-up, Chief," Vivian interrupted. "Given it has been nearly twelve hours since this teen disappeared, do you believe he is still alive?"

That is certainly the question of the hour, I thought. "We have no reason to believe otherwise at this point," I said.

"Did you find something at the scene that led you to that conclusion?"

"As I said, I'm not going to get into that today," I repeated, then intentionally shifted my focus to another person in the room. "George, from the *Times*...?"

I managed to get through the next twenty or so minutes without spilling any secrets, much to the chagrin of the reporters who had attended; as the crowd broke up, though, I realized a rather tall and burly specimen who had been leaning against the rear wall had never raised his hand. He was wearing a baseball cap backwards over what looked like close-cropped hair, and had an unopened spiral notebook in his hands; with several days' worth of dark stubble, he didn't look like a typical beat reporter. As Linda generally handled most of our PR, I leaned back toward her and nodded in the direction of the guy as he headed for the exit.

"Who's that?" I asked quietly.

Linda looked where I'd nodded. "Damned if I know. He's not one of the regulars; he must be from out of town or saw one of the bulletins I put out."

Alarm bells started to go off in the back of my head. "Maybe we should find out," I whispered. "Were the cameras on when we did this little dog and pony show?"

Linda nodded. "Standard procedure," she said. "Why?"

"I'll tell you when I know myself," I said.

SEVEN
MANSION ON A HILL

G ina's text came in while I was shucking out of my Class A uniform and pulling back on my far more comfortable workout attire. Asking if I could rejoin her at the mansion for her walkthrough, I let her know I would leave immediately and (traffic willing) be there in under thirty minutes. As I exited the locker room, though, the strange reporter from the press conference continued to weigh heavily on my mind, enough that I detoured to the surveillance office before departing. The young officer currently working the vast wall of monitors covering every square inch of the Rancho Linda Police Department quickly agreed to pull the footage from the meeting room and send it to the Orange County Forensics Office; Gina had long wanted to dip her toe into the AI facial recognition packages out there, but our perennial budget woes had continually thwarted her. Fortunately, our friends in the Sheriff's Department apparently had money to burn and the willingness to lend a hand whenever we needed it. I feared that their beneficence was a prelude to a more hostile takeover, but so far, it had yet to come to pass.

On my way out to the Camaro, I dialed Alejandro with the expectation of leaving him a voicemail; to my surprise, he picked up right away.

"*Mi amor*," he said. "I was just having the most wonderful daydream about you."

Pushing through the door to the parking lot, I felt an eyebrow arch. "Oh? Was it PG-rated?"

"Hardly," he laughed. "You caught me between appointments which is when my mind tends to wander anyway. Are we set for tonight?"

"Yes," I replied. "I've got to run up to the mansion but should be back to the station no later than five. I want to be back on the road by six, can you meet me by then?"

"If I push, yeah," he said. "My last appointment is at three-thirty; I'll sneak out the back door so I can get a head start on traffic, but it will be close."

"Don't break any laws," I laughed as I unlocked my car. "I'm not leaving without you."

"That was a given," he replied. "Do you want me to grab anything from the condo?"

"A clean change of clothes would be nice," I said.

"I can do that. Anything else?"

"Maybe a few of those banana-flavored condoms...?"

"Someone is feeling frisky," he chuckled. "Will we have time to, uh, use them?"

"I'll make the time," I replied.

"Then condoms are going into the bag," he confirmed. "Ah - there's my one o'clock now. Gotta run. See you this evening."

"Love you," I said.

"Love you *more*," he replied warmly before the call ended.

I started up the Camaro and pulled out of my spot, momentarily buoyed by the conversation. No matter the context, chatting with my beloved always seemed to raise my spirits; I had no small amount of hope that Gina might do the same once I arrived at the mansion. Traffic outside of the station was of the midday variety making it reasonably easy to navigate; the only hiccup I faced was a portion of the main drag through town that had been reduced to two lanes due to some sort of water main break. I'd seen the alert in my inbox at some point but was just tired enough that I'd forgotten to tack around it. Sitting in traffic was never a favorite pastime of mine; by the time I had finally crept past the open hole in the ground, my patience had worn thin enough that I knew I was likely to bite the head of the next person I spoke to. Thinking that might not be wise, I pulled into the first Starbucks I found and ordered one of those insanely sugary frappe-style drinks I normally purchased for Dr. Marguerite Pembroke. While I wasn't a fan of the liquid treats I always provided to the Chief Medical Examiner, I knew I was running on caloric fumes myself and needed the instant shot in the arm the tall plastic container full of fluff would provide. Sipping at the chocolate concoction as I pulled away from the drive-thru, I decided it would be best to never admit that I actually liked that particular flavor.

It wasn't until I was halfway to Rosie's that I realized a Ford pickup had been following me. Having been stalked by the guy who ultimately assaulted me, I'd taken on a habit of being particularly observant of my surroundings. I knew that was entirely due to the lingering sense that the *one* time I'd let my guard down had led to my being tied, spread-eagled, to the bed in my condo; nearly dying as a result of my failure to listen to my inner senses was a mistake I was never going to repeat. Sipping at what was left of my drink, I drove past the turn I should have made and watched as the truck, now several cars behind me, did the same. Slowing, I signaled to make a left into a smaller neighborhood; the truck followed me, but remained far enough back that I couldn't get a good look at the front license plate.

Setting the drink down into the cup holder, I tapped at my phone and quickly brought up Apple Maps; while I was reasonably familiar with most of the major areas in Rancho Linda, each individual subdivision tended to be a voyage of discovery. Trying to simultaneously keep my eyes on the road, the truck and the map was a bit of a challenge, but ultimately I found what I was looking for just up ahead.

Glancing at the truck in my rearview mirror, I eased off the accelerator and then slowly pulled to the curb beside a set of mailboxes for the townhouses I was driving past. Parking, I got out of my Camaro and walked to the aluminum doors, looking for all the world as though I were checking my mail; sliding my iPhone from my pocket, I activated the video function and then held it in my hand upside down and facing the street.

Fishing my car keys from a pocket, I acted as though I were inserting my key for the locker at the station into a door just as the pickup truck slowly drove by. Pivoting quickly, I brought the camera up and tried to film the bumper just as the driver deduced what I was doing; in squeal of rubber, the truck shot away from me and veered around the curve in the neighborhood. Sprinting back to my Camaro, I slipped behind the wheel and gunned the engine; I felt the car leap to the task around me, and in moments I was careening around the same corner, the Ford just a handful of yards in front of me.

Mindful I was still in a residential neighborhood, I kept my eyes peeled for a stray pedestrian wandering into the path of our vehicles as I chased the truck; just in case my phone hadn't gotten a clear enough shot of the plate, I accelerated a bit more and squinted so I could commit the number to memory — and then nearly rammed into the truck's bumper as it came to an abrupt stop. Stomping on my brakes, I twisted the wheel to avoid hitting the Ford and at the last minute realized that had been the intent all along; as I skidded to a stop on the sidewalk, the truck roared to life once more and sped away, leaving me quite literally in the dust I had kicked up.

Knowing there was no way to catch up at that point, I reached for my phone and swiped to the videos; to my everlasting relief, I'd caught a break and had a clear shot of the plate. Tossing the phone back down into the small well between my cup holders, I put the Camaro into reverse and backed onto the street. Aside from a long streak of rubber from my hard stop, it didn't appear I'd done any damage to the sidewalk or my car; counting my blessings, I shifted into drive and then resumed my trek to Rosie's, all the while looking for a shadow that fortunately didn't return.

As I pulled around the circular driveway in front of the entrance for the mansion, I wondered a bit at who my shadow had been. I didn't think it was one of the reporters I'd just spoken to, but couldn't rule it out, either. I had been rather vague about parts of the investigation, so I wouldn't put it past one to try and scoop the rest. Still, pickups weren't exactly their vehicle of choice. Shutting down the Camaro, I queued up the video again and then emailed it to Gina; one of the whizzes on her team would be able to run the plate for me and confirm who owned the truck in question. Then I might also have the name of someone I'd very much want to question.

I found Gina just inside the door. The foyer looked exactly as it had when I'd left hours earlier, save for the fact that the two of us were alone in the space. "You're a bit late," she said as she held up her phone. "Can I assume this is why?"

Smiling at the paused image of the truck, I nodded. "I had a shadow on the way here."

Her eyebrows went up. "Really? That changes things a bit, doesn't it?"

"It depends on who was driving that truck," I said. "Can your team—"

"Already forwarded it," she replied. "Answers will be forthcoming."

"Cool." I nodded at the mess that still needed to be handled. "Is Rosie still here?"

Gina nodded. "Out in the solarium. She asked that you say goodbye before you take off."

"I can do that."

"Since we're here, let's start in the foyer," she said. "Although honestly this foyer is the size of a minor ballroom."

"You noticed that, did you?" I chuckled.

"My team did," she replied. "They had to measure every angle. It wasn't fun."

"I'm sure."

"I won't give you the count, but we found a number of prints down here," she continued. "All of them are being processed by the computer back at the lab now, but the most I might be able to offer is a random hit from a prior offender."

"Or someone with an outstanding warrant."

"That, too," she said. "For what it might be worth."

"Could be a lot," I said. "Depending on what their crime happened to be. Especially," I added despite my desire to do so, "if they are a registered sex offender."

"That has been in the back of my head this entire time," Gina replied. "Given the age of the kid."

"Yeah. Got to keep it top of mind."

"There are times when I hate my job," Gina said.

"Me, too."

"Anyway, we found no blood down here — though there *were* some interesting biological samples taken from what I presume had been one of the darker corners of the space last night."

My eyebrows went up. "What *sort* of samples? Semen?"

"Oh yes," she nodded as she pointed to a spot beside the left staircase. "And a schmear or two of spermicide."

"A dropped condom," I said as I slowly nodded. "Rosie's not going to like that. This isn't that sort of party."

"So she thought," Gina said quietly. "But it *was* dark and there were a ton of people here; it's entirely possible no one would have noticed two people going at it in the corner." She paused. "We also fished several condoms out of the guest bathroom toilet on the second floor. This seems to have been quite the happening place."

I knew I had a look of disbelief on my face. "As mixed an audience as it was, I can't believe all that was going on."

"Halloween brings out the best in people," Gina replied. "Some masks come off while others go on."

"No kidding. I presume all of that will be run for DNA?"

"As we speak, though the toilet condoms are likely not going to have much in the way of viable samples. But you never know."

I glanced at the small dais where I'd conducted the auction. "I can't believe all of that was going on while I was here."

"These are strange times, Vas. Strange times." She looked at the tablet that always seemed to be in her hands. "That's about it for the foyer, including these staircases that look like they are from some sort of Hollywood set."

"Anything else on this level?"

"We printed every surface in the kitchen and the doors on either side of the servant's stairwell. And before you ask, no joy on those prints; the interior of the kitchen came back to Rosie and an unknown, which we presume is a member of her staff. A completely different unknown owns the prints on the exterior door."

"Well, that's something."

"There's more: that unknown print on the exterior door also matches prints we lifted upstairs on the door in the theater."

"Encouraging, though I am somewhat surprised our suspect wasn't gloved."

"I thought the same thing," she nodded. "We'll know more after those are run against the rest of the prints collected." Gina started up one of the staircases, and I followed her. "The handprint you wanted me to check out typed to O positive. While that matches our victim, it's also the most common blood type, too."

We turned the corner and walked down the hall toward the theater together. It seemed oddly quiet without the techs working. "It's enough for me," I said as we stopped in front of the bloody print on the wall. "How about the blood spatters on this floor?"

"Save for one sample we took, all type O. We'll run the DNA on them to confirm it's the same donor, but it seems obvious from the scene it was."

"Okay."

Gina waved at the hallway. "About a hundred more prints were taken here, same story as downstairs in that they are all percolating through the database at the lab as we speak."

"A fair majority will match ones from downstairs, I would think."

"Agreed. But you never know."

She led me away from the print and around the corner to the theater; I followed her inside and then through the hay maze. With the regular overhead lights now on, it seemed rather silly walking through them. Gina paused at the hay bales that had once held the chair. "We took the chair to the lab," she said, seeing my questioning look. "Far easier to try and get prints off of it there than here. Interestingly, that uncovered this little beauty."

Gina produced a small evidence bag from her pocket and handed it to me. I held it up to the light and saw a small irregular piece of fabric. "Clothing?"

"I think so, yes. Ensnared by one of the clips that had been holding those leather straps." She pointed to where the hay had dimpled below the chair. "This is where we found that outlier sample of blood. It was rather significant; I thought perhaps it was from the tooth being spit out, but now I'm not so sure."

I knelt. "Why?"

"It was B positive."

"That's rare, isn't it?" I asked as I stared at the spot.

"Depends on the stats you cite, but generally, yeah. Only about ten percent of the population has it."

"Huh," I said as I stood. "Maybe our suspect opened a knuckle or something when they hit Daniel that final time?"

"Maybe," Gina nodded. "Only flaw in that theory is we didn't find any more blood *anywhere*, including the servant corridor."

"Perhaps our suspect had Band-Aids on them?" I smiled before I was struck by another thought. "I suppose it's more likely they borrowed the gloves our victim had been wearing."

"The victim had gloves?" Gina said, frowning. "We were able to lift a pretty good set of whorls from that hand print."

"He may not have had them on at the time," I said. "It was the end of the party, maybe he'd taken them off and stuffed them into a pocket." I frowned myself. "However if they *were* wearing gloves that would mean our fingerprints might not be those of the suspect."

"A definite possibility." Gina pointed to the floor with the edge of her tablet. "Your suspicion some portion of the altercation happened in this area seems spot on. Once we cleared away the hay from the floor, we found scuff marks here and here; they match similar scuff marks closer to the doorway."

"Our victim being dragged away?" I asked as I knelt down to take a closer look at where she had been pointing. While faint, twin streaks of black against the tile of the floor were definite. "These seem parallel."

"You said the victim was wearing boots, right?"

"Yes."

"The width of each streak is about average for a heel for someone wearing a size eleven," she replied. "I don't have enough to tell you what kind of boot, but it's damn close to several in the database. And if you measure the gap between the two streaks, consistent with our assumption the legs were bound."

I traced the lines with a finger. "These are too even. The victim wasn't struggling when these were made."

"I agree. They had to have been incapacitated in some way; the tooth and blood has me leaning toward having been knocked unconscious, but it's also entirely possible Daniel was bound in such a way he would have been unable to move."

Standing, I dusted off my hands. "Both are possible," I mused. "I don't see him willingly allowing someone to tie him up, not with the handprint out there in the hallway speaking to his attempt to escape."

"A A gun might have been involved. That tends to make people more compliant."

I nodded. "Perhaps. But having a gun in one hand makes it pretty difficult to tie someone up with the other."

"Good point."

The door to the servant's corridor was slightly ajar; I walked over and pushed it open, then stepped into the cramped space. Gina followed me in. There was just enough illumination from the old-fashioned incandescent bulbs hanging from the ceiling that I could make out additional footprints in the dust; oddly, the pungent odor of the chemicals the techs had used to detect blood was a marginal improvement from what I had smelled initially. Slight traces of the dust used for fingerprinting were here and there, underscoring just how thorough the team had been.

"I only saw the one set of footprints when I opened the door," I said, looking at Gina. With her standing beside me, the space felt incredibly cramped.

She nodded. "That's all we found — one set leading away from the theater and toward the steps. The trail was a bit fuzzy at the bottom of the stairwell."

I gauged the height of the hallway and then partially crouched; pantomiming throwing someone over my shoulder, I started down the corridor. "The ceiling is relatively low in here, so if our suspect literally carried our victim out, they wouldn't have had a lot of clearance."

"I hesitate to point out you're not actually average height, Vasily," Gina said. There was a trace of humor in her voice. "However, given the weight of our victim, you may not be wrong in assuming the suspect is a larger-than-average person."

Stopping a few feet away from her, I straightened up and turned to face Gina. "That's the only explanation that makes sense. Without evidence of some other way of carting off Daniel, our suspect has to be somewhat athletic."

Gina tapped her finger against the side of the tablet. "Don't discount the possibility that one or more of the straps they took from that chair may have been used for a sling; not all of them would have been needed to immobilize Daniel."

My eyebrows went up. "Excellent point," I said. "So much for narrowing down the subject pool."

"I aim to please," she chuckled. "For what it's worth, I think the stats support your theory more than mine."

"Thanks for throwing me a lifeline." I turned and looked at the hallway again. "Getting down that staircase with a struggling human slung over your shoulders couldn't have been easy."

"It wasn't," Gina replied as she slipped past me. "And I think I have proof for you of that."

Intrigued, I followed her down the long corridor. Idly, I wondered a bit at the rooms each of the doors we were passing opened into; the next time we stayed as guests of Rosie, I was going to search our room top to bottom to find the secret entrance I presumed was there. Gina stopped just as we reached the narrow and very steep staircase, then pointed to something on the wall. I leaned in for a closer look.

"Streaks," I murmured. "Just like the ones back on the floor in the theater?"

Gina nodded. "Given the height of our victim, I think the suspect carrying him had to turn slightly to get down these steps. That allowed Daniel to press his boots against the wall." She pointed downward. "The smudge extends all the way to the door."

I smiled. "Damn. The kid left us a trail."

"That he did — as much as he could." Gina rifled through her pockets again and came up with another small bag. "This was just outside the door."

I took the second bag and held it up to the weak light. "It looks like a wedding band," I said.

"We'll confirm that in the lab, but I think it is, too. There was some blood on it as well, but not enough to make it easy to sample here in the field. I'll have the lab test that, too. We might get lucky and also find some skin cells on it."

"This wouldn't have been Daniel's," I said, arching an eyebrow. "And Rosie has never been married."

"I would also point out that the guests didn't access this part of the mansion during the party," Gina added. "One other thing to note is the current staff don't use this entrance either, at least according to the owner."

I looked at the ring again. "It would be the wildest stroke of luck that the suspect lost their ring during all of this."

"That it would. Which is why we'll run it through all the tests we can think of."

I handed it back to her. "Your lab geeks are going to have their work cut out for them."

"Don't they always?" she laughed. "I'll make sure the case system is updated with everything we found here today and let you know once the more involved tests come back. Will you be at the station later?"

"No," I said as we walked back to the theater. "I'm off to Palm Springs to get a better sense of whoever it was that abducted Daniel. I'll be back in the morning."

"And I thought my to-do list was difficult," she chuckled. "May you find the answers you seek."

"Amen to that."

EIGHT

PALM SPRINGS PSYCH

Alejandro rescued me from the mountain of paperwork that had appeared on my desk courtesy of the tip line; after my press conference, the blizzard of tips that came in had literally snowed the team under hundreds of possible leads, all of which needed to be triaged and then followed up on. The top ten percent had reached my desk for final approval, and though that seemed like a small percentage, in truth it turned out to be more than seventy pages that had to be carefully gone through. I had become so enmeshed in the work that I didn't realize he was in my office until the first kiss was planted ever so gently along the base of my neck; startled back into reality, I turned directly into a smoldering kiss that, under better circumstances, would probably have led to some bedroom antics. Briefly returning the favor, I reluctantly pushed my fiancé away with a rueful smile.

"Feel free to interrupt me that way anytime," I said as I turned back and packed up my laptop.

"I'm glad that worked," he said as he trailed a finger along my shoulder. "I've been here nearly ten minutes."

I turned back to him. "Really? Shit. I'm sorry—"

He put a finger on my nose. "When you focus on something, it's all in with you," he said before leaning down and lowering his voice to a whisper. "As I know from personal experience."

I smiled slightly. "So you do," I said. "I just need my gun and then we can go."

Alejandro looked at me. "And where are you planning on storing said gun?" he asked, his eyes glancing meaningfully at my workout gear.

I pondered that for a moment. Technically, while on duty my sidearm was supposed to be on my person at all times, but I'd pretty much ignored that all day due to my attire. Still, policy was policy — especially since I was heading into another jurisdiction altogether. Pulling open a drawer, I yanked out a shoulder harness that I truly hated, then stood and shrugged into it. Alex gave me the gimlet eye as I retrieved my Glock from the locked safe below it and carefully slid it into the harness.

"Seriously?"

I shrugged. "It works. Come on, let's see what Southern California traffic is going to throw at us. I hope you're hungry, by the way."

Alex rolled his eyes. "I'm *always* hungry. It comes with being an athlete. Why?"

"Our host is planning on fattening us up tonight," I replied enigmatically.

"Oh, lovely," he sighed as we pushed out into the cool evening air of the parking lot. "And just after I managed to shed those five pounds from Las Vegas."

I paused in the lot. "You have never been overweight, my love."

"Eye of the beholder," he smiled.

As I unlocked the Camaro, I wondered a bit at his comment. I knew we both struggled with body image issues, something that was not uncommon among athletes of any stripe; I knew in our case, though, it was exacerbated by an ingrained desire to remain alluring enough to our partner so their eye wouldn't wander toward greener pastures. I couldn't deny a large reason I spent so much time in the pool was to maintain the form Alejandro had fallen in love with; I knew my lover well enough now to understand his endless hours atop the diving tower were for much the same purpose. In an incredible moment of clarity, I realized we were each subtly pushing the other to maintain an ideal that, with age, would be increasingly difficult to maintain.

I turned toward Alex. "*Mi amor*, at the risk of quoting Fred Rogers, I love you just the way you are. I'll love you whether you're thin or fat; I'll love you in a felt-tipped hat."

A smiled quirked at the edge of his mouth. "You're mixing a few genres in there, Vas."

I shrugged. "I've been up for more than twenty hours, so my inner Seuss is coming out. But the point remains," I continued as I gently placed my hand against his cheek. "You are a beautiful human being, inside and out. A few pounds either way isn't going to change that for me."

Alex flushed slightly. "Ah," he said softly. "I was hoping you'd forgotten that little admission I made at the tux rental place."

"I hadn't," I said as I turned the car on and pulled out of the lot. "Especially since I struggle with the same thing all the time. I was a gym rat long before you came into my life; I can't deny I stepped it up a bit *after* I fell into your arms."

"As did I," he whispered quietly. "I live in fear—"

"Alex," I said firmly, "that will never happen." I reached over and tapped the ring I'd given him months earlier. "This is supposed to be a daily reminder of that. You own my soul, lock, stock and barrel. Nothing — and I mean *nothing* — is going to change that."

He held my hand for a moment. "We are fucked up a bit, aren't we?"

"No more than any other couple," I smiled. "Comes with the territory."

We lapsed into a comfortable silence while I navigated the messy traffic getting onto the 57; a few miles out from merging onto the 60, Alex cleared his throat and rocked my universe. "I almost forgot to tell you, there was a FedEx package for you at the condo. It looked like it was important, so I tossed it into my backpack for you."

Groaning inwardly, I realized I'd been so focused on the case, I'd forgotten about the package I was expecting from the Fairy Tale Weddings department at Walt Disney World; it contained the final paperwork for the über secret surprise ceremony I'd been quietly plotting with the help of Sean's girlfriend, Suzanne Kellerman. Keeping it off the radar of my fiancé had been a huge challenge, especially after I'd casually told him I was thinking of taking us to Florida for a few days in January; when he stopped reminding me that we'd not set a date for our wedding shortly after the reservations for Orlando were confirmed, I'd become convinced he suspected I was up to something. My only hope now was that the package I'd failed to intercept didn't have anything remotely incriminating on the outside.

Smiling slightly, I tried to find out how much damage had been done. "Oh? Who was it from?" I asked lightly.

"You know, I didn't really look at it," he said. "Were you expecting something?"

Being an investigator, I had heard my share of rehearsed answers and immediately felt my heart sink. "I was," I replied, trying to keep my tone light. Not being a good liar — okay, I was a *terrible* liar — I decided to skirt the truth. "I was checking into what it would cost to get married at Disney World."

There was a long pause. "You... you *were*?" he said, emphasizing the past tense. There was a note of disappointment in there, which gave me a slight sense of relief.

"Yeah," I continued as I fought to get to the carpool lane. "I called a number I found on the website and spoke to someone. It started off sounding magical, but by the time we were finished, the price tag wound up reflecting that. Still, I agreed to check out some material if they sent it to me." I glanced at him. "You can look it over if you want," I added, hoping he'd say no.

"Nah," he sighed. "What a bummer, though. It would have been nice."

"Yeah," I nodded soberly while secretly dancing for joy on the inside. "Anyway, tell me about your day...?"

We chatted companionably for the next hour or so, allowing the miles to pass far faster than they normally would. At length, we turned into the retirement neighborhood where Verna lived; the first time I'd been there, it had been during the daytime and the houses had all seemed quite grand. At night, deep in the heart of the desert, they felt even more dramatic under the dark night sky; many had landscaping lights shining against trees or flowerbeds, giving the street a sort of Disneyesque feel. The stately home where Verna now resided had a semicircular driveway that ended in a detached garage; I pulled up and parked just beyond the tasteful front door, then killed the engine.

Alex followed me over to the front door, which was pulled open just as we arrived. "Vas," said the short woman clad in denim overalls just behind it. Her hair was up in the most elegant beehive I had ever seen, topping, perhaps, the *last* one she'd worn when I'd been there that spring. "How very good to see you again."

"Verna," I smiled as she stepped forward and unexpectedly hugged me. I returned the favor before nodding toward Alex. "This is my fiancé, Alejandro Ortega-Cortez."

To my everlasting delight, Alex went into full Don Juan mode and placed one hand behind his back before executing a half-bow to reach for her hand. Kissing it gently, he looked up at her. "*Señora*, a pleasure."

I couldn't be sure in the half light of the front porch, but I thought Verna's face had colored slightly. "Such luck getting *three* Olympic medalists to visit me in the span of a year."

Alex's eyes widened. "You know who I am?"

"Of course I do," she smiled as she stepped back and waved us inside. "Silver medal on the ten meter in Beijing, if my research is accurate. Current record holder in Southern California for highest marks on a dive, including that set of perfect tens you received in August." Her eyes twinkled slightly. "What I didn't know was how tall, dark and attractive you were in real life."

Despite everything we had talked about on the drive up, Alejandro, like me, tended to get embarrassed when objectified. The color creeping up his sculpted cheeks was adorable, as was his barely audible mumbled response. "Thank you."

"This way, gentlemen," Verna said.

As she led us through the decidedly cozy interior of her home, it seemed much like it had before; as we passed the living room, though, something caught my eye and I backed up. Staring at a painting on the wall, I frowned. "Did you do this one?"

Verna doubled back. "Oh that? No, I bought it online."

"It looks familiar," I said as I stared at the work. Tall mountains shrouded by mist were in the background, and a small field of green, the foreground; a barn-like structure stood at the edge of the painting, with a waterwheel.

"I'm not surprised," she chuckled. "It's an original Bob Ross."

I heard Alex choke. "The guy from PBS?"

"One and the same," she replied as we continued toward the rear of the house.

"I had no idea those were for sale," Alex said. "Where did you find it?"

"You're going to laugh when I tell you," she said as we entered the modest kitchen. The smells wafting from the oven were mouth-watering. "In my past life at the FBI, I worked with a reformed art fencer. He knew of my hobby and sent that piece to me for my birthday."

My eyes widened. "Verna..."

"It's on the up-and-up," she laughed. "He runs an estate auction business these days and cleared out a place in Indiana. The garage was full of artwork, including the one now hanging on my wall."

"Wow," Alex said. "Just... wow. Those have to be incredibly rare."

"My insurance agent said the same thing," she sighed. "The rider for my homeowners is a bit of a headache, but worth it. Now, I hope you brought your appetite! Everything is ready on the back patio; I just need to get the lasagna out of the oven. Go on out and get settled." She paused. "It's a bit chilly for my tastes, so I've turned on the space heaters — if it's too much, let me know and I'll go get a sweater."

"I'm sure it will be fine," I replied.

Alex followed me out into the backyard; as before, Verna had pushed a portable cart overflowing with food beside a small conversation area comprised of a long wicker couch and two smaller wicker chairs. Unlike before, a tall metal space heater was just beside the couch, the red-yellow flame flickering with a slight crackle. The pool beyond had the underwater lights on, giving the entire area a nice resort-like atmosphere. I pointed to the plates carefully stacked next to the veritable buffet we were standing in front of; the intake of breath from my fiancé underscored the cornucopia of food ranging from sliced roast beef with gravy at one end to a casserole that smelled very much like it contained both sweet potatoes and no small amount of orange liqueur. A giant Caesar salad sat in a massive bowl in the middle, piled high with thick slices of parmesan cheese; a far smaller bowl holding what I suspected were hand-made butter rolls was beside it.

Considering how little I had actually eaten that day, I only felt marginally guilty for piling my plate high with what was on offer. By unspoken agreement, Alex and I took the couch and dug in. A few moments later, Verna slid open the patio door and carried out a colorful ceramic dish; the air immediately smelled of oregano and tomato sauce as she moved to place the dish on the low table between the couch and the chairs.

"Wine?" she asked. "I just opened a nice Fess Parker red."

My forkful of roast beef paused in mid-air. "Not *the* Fess Parker?"

"Well, the poor guy passed a while back, but yes, it's his family winery in Santa Barbara. I get a case every now and again. Interested?"

"Yes, please."

"Alejandro?"

"Sure."

"Okay - I'll be right back."

Alex leaned over to me and lowered his voice. "Who's Fess Parker?"

I saw Verna coming back through the door with a bottle of wine. "I'll tell you later."

Once drinks were poured, Verna settled in on one of the chairs across from us and began munching on a plate that was, to my eye, barely a third full. "So," she said between bites of her salad, "what sort of criminal mastermind are we looking for this time?"

"Kidnapper," I said without preamble. "Someone who apparently blends in with the rest of us."

Verna nodded thoughtfully. "I read the APB your department put out. It was a teen taken, right?"

How the retired forensic psychologist was able to be so well connected was a question I didn't care to dwell on for too long, especially since it short circuited a ton of background conversations. "Yes. Daniel Kewley was a senior at Rancho Linda High School; full ride to Stanford was in his future."

Putting her plate down on the small table, she reached to the side of the chair and retrieved a three-ring binder that I'd not seen sitting there. Opening it, she ran a finger over something. "Average height and weight for a kid of his age; academically gifted, but not inclined athletically. Member of multiple service organizations, including one of the ones running the charitable party where he disappeared."

"Yes."

She looked up at me. "It's clear from the photo the kid is Black," Verna said. "Are you suspecting a racial motivation?"

"I don't know *what* to suspect," I sighed. "Racial is likely, I guess, but it almost seems trite."

"Not under the current social climate," Verna replied. "I don't know if you've been keeping up on Homeland's annual assessments, but the number of domestic terrorists being tracked quadrupled after the last presidential election."

I blinked. "I did see those," I admitted, "but I wrote them off as Federal-level budget posturing."

"There's some of that, to be sure," she smiled slightly, "although in this case, the numbers are deadly serious. I had to book a full-day spa treatment after I read the initial draft just to get my blood pressure back into normal range."

My eyebrows went up. "Shit."

"Yeah, exactly. So we keep racial as a top reason this kid is missing," Verna said.

I thought about that for a moment. "He's also gay."

Verna scribbled something on a page of her notebook. "Then we'll add that as a factor to consider. Tell me more about where the abduction took place."

"It was a big mansion on the outskirts of Rancho Linda," I said. "The host was the famous author Rosalia Frankenhoffer, and it's one of many charitable fundraisers she does throughout the year. This particular one has been held at her home for years now, all without incident."

"Until this year," Verna noted.

"Right."

"What was different this year?"

"I have no idea," I started. "I've only helped out for the last two or so—"

"You hosted," Alex interrupted.

My head turned toward him. "What?"

"You *hosted*," he repeated.

"I did," I said, feeling confused. "I mean, I suppose that was a difference. Otherwise it ran as it always did."

"Who normally hosted?" Verna asked.

"I think Rosie always did," I replied after a moment of thought. "Like I said, I've only helped for a few cycles."

"Hmm," Verna said. "And you work with the groups that she was fundraising for?"

I rolled my eyes. "This is not connected to me. Not in a million years. This is about a kid being taken by some crazy idiot—"

"Don't be so sure," Verna replied quietly. "Triggers for people who kidnap come from many angles. Maybe this one abhorred a change to established norms; perhaps the group Daniel worked for rubbed them the wrong way. It wouldn't be the first time homophobia ruled the day, either; hell, I can't discount a weird combination of any of that." She paused. "Do you work with Daniel's group?"

"Yes," I replied. "They are one of several that are hosted out of a small safe space in the Rancho Linda mall."

"*The Alternative Way*," Verna nodded. "I've heard of it. They have great coffee."

"That they do. And the owners have hearts as big as the Grand Canyon."

"I've heard *that*, too," she smiled. "How big is this mansion?"

"Big," Alex replied. "I think Vas told me it used to be owned by a Hollywood producer."

"So big enough for someone to hide in plain sight during a big party?"

"Yes," I said.

"Is the staff large enough that — what did you say her name was?"

"Rosie."

"Ah, right, Rosie. How big is the staff running her house now?"

"Two," I said.

Verna nearly choked on her wine. "*Two*? When you said she was a famous author, I assumed she was living like one."

"Hardly," I laughed. "And the two people on staff are actually part-time," I added. "I was thinking the same thing you are, though, that our suspect inserted themselves into the household to get a sense of the floorplan. The idea has merit given how unique the knowledge of the escape route was."

"Yeah," she nodded, "but two? No way a third person doesn't stick out like a sore thumb."

"Exactly. I suspect now whoever did it found out about the servant corridors the same way I did — the public material available at the library."

"Still," she mused, "that requires a level of preparation. I'm not thinking this was a spur-of-the-moment abduction."

"No."

"And there hasn't been a phone call demanding cash?"

"No," I shook my head. "The kidnapper has yet to reach out to the family." I paused and then shot a glance at Alex. "Although, I *did* have someone tail me earlier today."

The fork dropped from my fiancé's hand and loudly clattered across the concrete of the patio. "Say *what*?"

"It was nothing," I replied airily, but I could see from his expression it was anything but.

Verna sliced right through my deflection. "You think that was the suspect?"

"Yeah," I said after a moment. "However, it could also have been a reporter from the press conference I had just led prior to spotting the tail."

She looked at me. "You don't truly believe that."

"No," I replied.

Alex put his plate down on the table and continued to stare at me.

"So. Party in a big mansion at the edge of town; huge guest list?"

"There were a ton of attendees, yes," I answered. "There were tickets to buy for the event, but they weren't required to get in the door. We did use them later for a drawing, though."

"It might be worth checking who bought tickets," Verna said thoughtfully. "As well as any strange patterns to the purchases."

I frowned. "I don't know if that will net us much. Most of the sales were word-of-mouth."

"But you do have a list of who bought them?"

"Probably," I said. "I'll ask Rosie. Honestly, I never thought about them in terms of evidence."

"Then that means you didn't drive all this way for nothing," Verna smiled before looking at the paper again. "Kids On Their Own? What can you tell me about them?"

"It's a small student-run group that serves at-risk youth in Rancho Linda," I replied. "Like any city, we have a homeless crisis that seems intractable. One area of focus is ensuring teens in that situation have a place to escape the streets for a few nights; they also offer a pathway to short- and long-term foster situations. There's a particular emphasis on children who are immigrants since they tend not to be eligible for other more mainstream help."

"Hmm," Verna said again. "Another connection."

I frowned. "To what?"

"Daniel is Black. He works with a group that helps immigrants," she said simply.

That little aurora of recognition went off inside my head. "Minorities and immigrants," I sighed. "It cannot be that simple."

"Most likely not," Verna replied. "But it's probably the mix that triggered this suspect."

"I'm sorry," Alex said, interrupting. "I know I'm not really part of this conversation, but are you suggesting that this *teenager* was targeted for being a champion of a needed social cause?"

"Yes," Verna replied. "Among other things."

"That's fucked up," he said before putting a hand to his lips. "I'm sorry."

"Don't be," Verna said. "You're absolutely right, but if this suspect is the kind of person I think they might be, your kidnapping victim is in grave danger."

"I'm hoping he's still alive," I said. "I'm also pragmatic enough to think he's not."

"Oh, he's alive," Verna said, though the way she did gave me goosebumps. "He has to be in order to satisfy whatever retribution the subject is trying to wreak — but only for a few days at most. After that…

well," she looked down at the paper, "then this becomes more of a recovery operation, doesn't it?"

"There was evidence at the scene that Daniel put up a bit of a fight," I said. "And got bloodied in the process."

Verna looked up. "That could work in our favor," she said. "First and foremost, the suspect will want to break your young victim; if he seems feisty, that will extend the process. However, once it goes too far, the end will be rather swift."

"You're not making me feel any better," I said, putting my own plate down on the table. My appetite, once ravenous, had suddenly disappeared.

"I wasn't trying to, but you know that too," she smiled. "Okay, I think I have what I need. I'll work on this and get something to you by the morning."

My eyes went wide. "We're on borrowed time, aren't we?"

"Yeah," she said softly. "Which means I'm not going to offer you coffee or dessert this evening..."

NINE

DOWNTIME

The short drive across Palm Springs to the Marriott I had booked us into passed in utter silence. For my part, I was dealing with an increased level of anxiety over what Verna had said; until she'd dropped her little bomb into our lap, it had been a bit academic as to whether Daniel would be alive when we found him. Now I had concrete reasons to worry why that wouldn't be the case. Furtive glances at Alex told me he was *seriously* pissed I'd not told him about the little matter of having been tailed earlier in the day; his displeasure seemed to deepen further as we handed the car over to the valet and entered the ornate lobby. He waited with his arms folded tightly against his impressive chest while I checked in, and remained silent as we rode the elevator to our floor; when I unlocked the door to the room, he grabbed his suitcase and made a beeline for the bathroom, appearing some minutes later stripped down to his boxer briefs.

It was hard not to get mixed messages, for part of me — a significant part, it seemed — thought that might be a prelude to breaking out the banana flavored condoms, but that notion died a horrible death when he yanked back the sheets on his side of the bed and slid beneath them. I thought snapping off the light and leaving me in the dark was a nice, albeit dramatic, touch, but the message was nonetheless received: my partner was closed for business.

Carefully making my way to the bathroom, I closed the door behind me and stared at my tired reflection. Given the number of times I had nearly died since he'd known me, I was well aware of how he felt about me being in any sort of jeopardy. I thought we'd gotten to a good place about it — I mean, I *was* a cop, after all — but clearly finding out I'd been tailed by someone who might have also been crazy enough to kidnap a teenager had brought back all of his fears. While I intellectually didn't think I was the particular type this psycho was looking for, I also knew there was no way to tell Alex that without him getting increasingly worried. Running my hands through my mass of silver hair, I sighed and wondered what the fuck I was going to do about any of it. I was tired and emotionally spent and had zero business asking the partner I had inadvertently hurt to help me back out of the hole I seemed to have fallen into.

As world-weary as I felt, I suddenly had no interest in getting the silent treatment; unzipping my suitcase, I grabbed the Speedos I always packed and my flip-flops, changed, and then quietly escaped the room. The lobby was fairly quiet for that hour, but it was a Tuesday, weeks prior to the high season. Nodding at the clerk behind reception who seemed rather enthralled by the guy striding across the tile in nothing but a swimsuit, I pushed out the rear doors and into the large resort pool area; according to the sign, the lifeguards had already gone off duty, but the pool and amazing lazy river we had made liberal use of the first time we were there remained open until midnight. Not particularly feeling the need for getting any laps in, I grabbed a towel from the rack and then circled the faux lagoon in search of a jacuzzi; while there were several to choose from, I found one that seemed more secluded from the rest with a squat row of bushes between it and the main deck. There was a small cabana on the other side, marking it as a spot that was normally reservable during the daytime hours; while I didn't expect to be inter-rupted at that late hour of the evening, I also wanted to be alone, so it suited my purposes perfectly. Tossing my towel onto the comfy looking recliner in the cabana, I kicked off my flip-flops and then descended into the gloriously bubbling warmth. The tub was surprisingly deep; by the time I reached the bottom step, the water was up to my pectorals, which was saying something considering my height. Wading over to the side, I felt for the bench and was pleasantly surprised to find it had smooth tile — nothing to snag my rather expensive swimsuit. Sitting down, I adjusted my angle until two of the jets were more or less kneading the knot that had formed between my shoulders; closing my eyes, I tried to put the case out of my mind for a few moments only to find to my horror it refused to be relegated to the back seat.

Fine, I sighed.

Reluctantly, I allowed myself to review the day and what I had learned. Admittedly, I didn't have much; I knew the broad outlines of what had happened to Daniel, understood perhaps a bit of *why* he had been taken, and now knew the ticking alarm clock I'd been feeling from the beginning had been well founded. Talking to Verna had been helpful, and any profile she came up with would certainly be useful, but deep in my gut I felt like I already knew the sort of person we were looking for. I was reasonably certain Daniel was targeted specifically; this wasn't a random abduction where the first kid the suspect encountered won the worst lottery imaginable. Assuming that to be the case meant there was something about the kid that had attracted the suspect's attention — or, perhaps more specifically, their ire. I couldn't discount the racial component, for Daniel *was* of Afro-Caribbean heritage; his accent might lead some to assume he was an immigrant, but that was just a byproduct of having grown up in London.

Perhaps of more import was the work he was doing with *actual* immigrants; public sentiment had downshifted into the negative territory when it came to those new to America, something I was personally deeply ashamed of. For a country that prided itself as having been founded as a cultural melting pot (albeit initially a white-bread one), the severe backlash that had developed over those who were seeking a better life was mind numbing. The hypocrisy of those who were descended from earlier waves slamming the door behind them was hard to take — especially since we were supposed to be far, far more enlightened than our forebears. Still, the thought that someone out there targeted a seven-teen-year-old because he had been handing out new socks to kids living on the street made me physically ill; how could that *possibly* be recon-ciled with some sort of nationalistic focus-on-the-homeland mentality? The simple truth was, it couldn't.

The harder truth was that those who were preaching such tenants truly didn't believe them, either.

Sinking lower into the bubbling water, I realized that instead of calming down I was becoming even more agitated; closing my eyes, I tried to focus on my breathing in an attempt to push out the waves of anger and frustration that were threatening to overwhelm me. My thera-pist had recommended both yoga and meditation as part of my ongoing healing from the assault; while I'd never quite gotten around to the yoga part, I had looked up some popular mediation videos on the internet and found a few to be relatively beneficial. Focusing inward, I let the small sensations of sitting there in the tub begin to make themselves known; first, it was the temperature of the water. Then, slowly, I felt the small bubbles from the jacuzzi as they moved against my skin; next, the rough surface of the spa pressed against my bare foot, followed by the gentle current washing around my body. My breathing deepened, and eventually, the small warming sensation I always felt deep in my chest appeared, the sign that I was truly beginning to let go; taking another deep breath, my senses began to become far more acute. There was a bird a few feet from me, chirping about something; off to my left, the gentle burbling of the water in the lazy river reminded me of the marvelous day Alex and I spent slowly circumnavigating the area. Stray chords from the hidden speakers by the pool came and went, painting in bits and pieces of songs I knew; the hinges on the gate by the entrance to the hotel creaked, and then creaked again as the door closed.

The sound of flip-flops drew nearer, and as they did, I realized I recognized the cadence of the steps. Opening my eyes and turning in that direction, I saw Alejandro as he made his way across the pool deck towards me; he was wearing the tiniest briefs he had in his collection, the ones small enough to show the tan line from the *normal* ones he wore each day at the diving well. Under the lights, his various tattoos and piercings looked incredibly dramatic; pausing at the side of the hot tub, I could see he had his whale-tale pendant on, a stroke of bright white against his dark skin.

"May I join you?" he asked.

"Always," I smiled as I held my arms out.

Kicking off his flip-flops, he slowly descended into the hot water and then waded over to me. Snuggling into my side as he sat down, he put his head on my shoulder and then quietly spoke. "I hate it when you do that, you know."

"I know," I said as I pulled him close to me.

"And I hate my reaction to it even more."

"You wouldn't be human otherwise," I replied. "I should have told you sooner."

He looked at me. "So I could have been angrier, longer? *Fuck* no."

"Good point," I smiled. "Still, I *am* sorry."

"For what?" Alex asked. "For my being a useless pile of worries each time you leave the condo? That's on me, not you."

The smile I had faded into a look of concern. "Alex, please tell me you don't feel that way. We've talked about this—"

"I know we have," he said as he sunk lower into the hot water. It lapped against his chin as he spoke. "And, intellectually, I've accepted the fact that you might not come back someday. But emotionally?" Alex shook his head, sending mini waves across the surface of the jacuzzi. "I don't think my heart is capable of understanding and might never be."

I pulled him into me. "Shit. I wish you'd said something sooner."

"It's not easy for me to admit," he said quietly. "I've been paradoxically worried you'd go into full Protect Alex Mode and quit your job if you found out."

"I would," I said instantly. "If it meant keeping you happy."

"I know you would," he said with a gentle smile, "and I won't have that. You belong exactly where you are doing the work you're doing. I'll get through this." His dark eyes searched mine. "I hope you don't think any less of me for my fears."

"Hardly," I smiled.

"Good," he said, then swallowed. "I... I've decided I might need to see someone professionally. To get over this little hurdle of mine."

I put my forehead against his. "*Mi amor*, someone wise once told me it takes a ton of courage to admit you need help, and even more to seek it out."

Alex smiled slightly. "Do I know this person?"

"Maybe," I said. "He's tall, dark and handsome with a mountain of curly black hair. And," I continued, lowering my voice as I did, "he's got the most exotic eyes I've ever encountered."

Those same eyes narrowed with humor. "I see."

I sunk a hand below the surface and gently pressed it against his insanely sculpted abs. "He also has a ripped body, too," I said as that hand snaked lower.

Alex's eyes widened momentarily when my hand ghosted across the front of his briefs. "This might not be the *best* spot for what you seem to have in mind," he said after glancing back toward the hotel.

"Oh?" I asked as I leaned a bit closer. My hand might have accidentally brushed the now slightly bulging front of his suit as I did so. "Was I doing something?"

Those beautiful eyes narrowed. "I see," he said before he took a longer moment to confirm (as I already had) that we were utterly alone at the moment. His eyes then moved to the cabana, then upward suggestively to the privacy curtains that were currently tied back.

My eyebrows went up. "Seriously?"

"Dude," Alex replied, a sly smile appearing on his face, "you should *never* have told me about those two lifeguards. As soon as I saw the cabana..."

I rolled my eyes; he was obliquely referring to the case Sean had helped me with back in February. Since it was the *same* case that had landed my best friend in intensive care with a gunshot wound, the details were never very far from my thoughts — including the two high school seniors who'd been having poolside sex when they were *supposed* to have been prepping for the day's guests. Their coupling had produced a child that wound up leading to the murder of a noted radio host back in Maine and his twin brother.

Shaking my head slightly, I felt myself frown and tried to ignore another part of myself that seemed *very* interested in what Alex was proposing. "That story was meant as an object lesson in what *not* to do," I reminded him. "Not a guidebook for illicit behavior."

Alex leaned closer. "It's dark, no one is around and we can close the drapes."

I glanced back at the hotel again, more than slightly concerned about what might happen if we were caught. "I'm a cop," I replied weakly. "If this goes south—"

A sudden *crunch* from behind the cabana had us both turning in that direction; a tall figure was standing in the shadows, backlit by the landscaping floods but clearly facing the jacuzzi. When they made no move to melt into the darkness of the evening, training immediately took over; quickly placing my body in front of Alejandro's, I tried to commit the image of what I was seeing to memory, then felt my pulse quicken when whoever the watcher was continued to stand there. Instinctively I knew we were not in *immediate* danger, that this was instead some sort of non-verbal threat; that it was the same person who had tailed me earlier in the day seemed to be a given. Whether it might also be the individual who had taken Daniel was an open question, although for the life of me I couldn't understand why they would take an interest in the lead investigator.

That question was partially answered when I saw the metallic reflection of a handgun as it was raised in our direction.

Alex felt me tense up and seemed to understand we were in some danger; still, he remained where he was, presenting a somewhat united front. I was pressed so close to my lover that I could feel how his heart rate had elevated; for my part, a surge of adrenaline coursed through me as I tried to expand my torso to cover Alex. The longer we faced off, the more certain I was that this was intended as a message — a visceral reminder that I had been caught unawares and completely helpless with no real way to protect someone I cared about.

Willing someone from the hotel to appear out of nowhere netted me nothing, so instead, I carefully waded away from Alex and toward the edge of the jacuzzi closest to whoever our antagonist was. "Why did you take him?" I asked, my voice steady.

The gun waved around. "People like that need to disappear."

"People like *what*, exactly?" I asked.

"Immigrants," came the flat reply. I thought I could detect the hint of some sort of accent, but it was hard to place.

"Daniel is an American," I said as I moved a bit closer to the edge.9

"He can't be. No one with skin that color is a native." There was an ominous pause and the gun shifted again, this time pointing toward Alex. "Just like that brown fairy you were about to fuck."

It was hard to tamp down my anger. "That is a rather outdated term."

"Oh, my bad," was the reply, though the sarcasm was heavy. "I suppose you prefer something more progressive? *Mexican-American fairy, maybe?*"

I felt my blood run cold; it was clear this guy — and I was convinced it was a guy — had done his research. "You seem to have us at a disadvantage."

"In more ways than one."

"Where is Daniel?"

"Right where he belongs," was the answer just before the figure took a step backwards and then disappeared.

I immediately pushed myself out of the hot tub and crashed through the bushes behind the cabana; there was a poorly lit maintenance path there that appeared to run the perimeter of the pool area. Just beyond it was the wide-open golf course for the resort; scanning the darkness as best as I could, I was unable to see a figure fleeing in any direction. Not that it mattered; I wasn't in much of a position to pursue whoever had accosted us, nor, with my phone back in the room, could I call for any sort of backup. Anger had to have been coming off me in palpable waves when I picked my way back through the brush and found Alex standing at the top of the steps to the jacuzzi.

"Gone?" was his one-word question.

"I think so," I nodded before pulling him toward me. "That was more excitement than I needed tonight. Shit."

"I'll second that," he nodded. "I think I'd like to get back to the room now, if you don't mind."

"Not in the least," I replied.

TEN
WATCHFUL WAITING

Unsurprisingly, our mutual libidos had cooled significantly once we'd returned to the room. We went through the motions and changed for bed, but neither one of us felt like sleeping, either. Somewhere close to two, I shifted my position on the pillow to look at Alex and saw he'd been staring at me already.

"Let's go home," I said.

"Works for me."

I changed into my swimming gear, tossed on some warmups and packed up everything else while Alex used the bathroom; he took an extra moment to gather his things, and then the two of us headed to the lobby. Having been caught with my pants down once already, I might have overcompensated by continually scanning our surroundings as we walked, worried that I had missed something that was hiding in plain sight. Save for the night custodian washing the marble floor close to the reception desk, the space was completely deserted; similarly, no one was lurking next to the valet stand while we waited for the Camaro to be retrieved. It was something of a relief not to find anyone hiding in the backseat of the sportscar, though the saner portions of my brain chided me for thinking my new nemesis would do something so predictable. Still, as I pulled away from the cheerful lights of the entrance portico, I found myself continually checking the rearview mirror for headlamps trailing us; I began to feel extremely foolish when I merged onto I-10 and nothing remotely nefarious had appeared.

Alejandro was drumming his fingers on the arm of his seat, something of an insight into the state of his psyche. I caught glimpses of his expression as we rolled beneath the highway lights as we passed exits, and what I could see confirmed my suspicion that he remained unsettled about our encounter at the jacuzzi. Seeking to comfort him — despite how troubling I found the episode myself — I reached a hand over to his and squeezed it.

"I'm going to find Daniel," I said with more conviction than I felt. "And then I'm going to find the bastard that ruined what was shaping up to be an evening of mad, passionate love making."

"Oh, I know you will, and heaven help them when you do," he said with a rueful chuckle.

I felt an eyebrow go up. That wasn't the response I was expecting. "You sound angry," I observed.

"Damn right I am," he replied before turning toward me. "I don't deny I'm a little tense over the idea that a possible lunatic tracked us down miles away from the crime scene, but I've learned a thing or two from having a police officer as my lover." He smiled slightly, the white of his teeth flashing in the darkness. "One of them is that you don't give these jerks what they want."

My eyebrow went up further. "And what does this guy want?"

"He wants us to be afraid," he replied simply. "To be constantly looking over our shoulders and jumping at the slightest sound. Putting us so completely off balance we won't see the truth before it's too late."

I felt myself nodding. "There are days when you sound like a counselor, Counselor."

"I keep telling you, *mi amor*, I'm not *that* kind of a counselor."

"Like hell," I smiled.

"I do want to know how he found us, though," Alex continued. "The threat part I get."

I nodded again. "I don't know if it would help Verna we've confirmed this dude *is* a homophobe, but I'll pass it on all the same." I paused. "Alex, while I don't think he's actually coming after you or me, I'm going to take precautions all the same."

"My love," Alejandro said as he squeezed my hand back, "that's exactly what this idiot wants. I refuse to live inside a locked box until you've captured him."

"Then I will stay by your side—"

"Absolutely not," Alex shook his head. "You've got a kidnapper to catch. I can take care of myself — more so, now that this *zoquete* has tipped his hand. I won't be stepping into any stranger's cars or walking down darkened hallways if that's what you're truly worried about."

"I am," I replied. "But it might not be easy to spot—"

"Vas," Alejandro said softly. "I am a gay Mexican-American who spent more time than he cares to admit hiding that fact from the world. I can read the room better than most. Trust me on this."

"Alex—"

"I'm going to work this morning, and so are you," he interrupted firmly.

I felt my other eyebrow go up to join the first. "Is that your final answer?"

"Yes, Regis Philbin," he laughed. "Now, tell me how you're going to catch this fucking asshole."

"Before or after I get that sex you were promising me?" I asked with a sly smile.

Alex smacked his forehead. "I'm trying to be serious here."

"So am I. You left me rather hot and bothered back there."

He looked through the slits of his fingers. "Seriously? The only thing on your mind right now is getting laid?"

I shrugged as I sped up to pass a semi. "Can you blame me? I'm in love with a Greek god."

"*Caramba,*" Alex sighed. "I didn't realize what I was uncorking."

"Shame on you."

He glared at me. "Might I remind you of the numerous occasions your office interrupted us at, shall we say, a delicate moment?"

"Those aren't my fault."

"Right," Alex laughed. "Even if I said *after,* there's a massive flaw in whatever plan you are developing: my car is at the station. You're gonna have to wait until tonight, sweetie."

"Shit," I said. "I'd forgotten about that."

Alex leaned over and kissed me on the cheek. "Sorry. Then again, I can tell you from experience that there is some ecstasy to be found in the agony you are currently inflicting on yourself."

I glanced at him. "You're enjoying this, aren't you?"

That impish smile that always melted my heart appeared. "Immensely."

We chatted amiably as always until I felt myself flagging; that was rectified with a quick detour through the first all-night coffee shop Apple Maps was able to locate. I pulled into the Rancho Linda Police Station parking lot just a hair before four; after giving Alex a farewell kiss, I took just enough time to watch him start up his New Beetle before I reversed out of my spot and headed over to the high school pool. I wasn't surprised to find the gate to the pool once again unlocked and open, despite it being well ahead of our normal five A.M. start time; Coach appeared to be the only one on deck and simply nodded at my appearance before continuing her efforts to get the pace clocks synchronized.

Opting for expediency, I dropped my bag into the lowest bleacher and simply pulled off my warmups; digging through my backpack netted me my goggles and swim cap, and a few moments later, I was absorbed in the first of what would turn out to be ninety grueling minutes of laps. As unsettled as I'd become, it was the only way I knew how to reset my emotions so I could refocus on the work ahead of me that day. Somewhere about halfway through the session, I relaxed enough to realize Alex had been right: the suspect, whoever he was, had overplayed his hand. Trailing me all the way to Palm Springs (setting aside for the moment exactly *how* he had done that) and then threatening us was a cover for something — or an attempted distraction from something important. Rolling around the evidence I knew we had collected already from the scene, I wondered if a seemingly innocuous item was in fact more of a key to the case than we'd realized initially.

But what could it have been? I pondered as I hit the wall with a particularly violent flip turn, propelling me an easy fifteen yards underwater before I had to even think about kicking. *Was it the blood, the tooth, the cloth or the ring? Or was it possible we'd actually* missed *something? Something small enough to be overlooked, but with an outsized importance?*

I hit the wall at the other end and pushed off even harder; I was nearly halfway down the lane before I surfaced for my first stroke — something that would have been highly illegal had I been competing. *Damn — is why he was following me? To try and find out if we had collected whatever it was? How the Hell would he have figured that out? It's not like I was carrying a sign saying I was following up on evidence.*

Hitting the wall again, I did a triple somersault and came up to the surface, struck by a thought.

Or maybe I was, I thought as I treaded water. *I went back to Rosie's, didn't I? And my next stop was Palm Springs — holy Hell, if he looked up who I was visiting, he'd know I was talking to a profiler. Shit.*

Flipping on my back, I stroked for the wall, turned, and pushed off again, staying on my back. *I don't think Verna is in any danger; she doesn't fit the profile of someone he might harass — not unless he escalates. Which is possible. Damn. I'll call my contact up there and see if we can't at least get someone to drive by her place a bit more regularly for the next few days.*

Grabbing my board at the other end, I started to kick rhythmically. *Alex, on the other hand, is another issue altogether. I'll have someone surreptitiously keep track of him because every instinct tells me this dude is coming after him as a way to get to me. Maybe Jenna won't mind the overtime... she thinks he's kind of cute, anyway, even if he is already spoken for...*

Turning yet again, I started to kick for the wall once more. *I think we missed something,* I mused. *As crazy as it sounds that Gina's crack team overlooked a clue, that's the best explanation of why this guy wound up harassing us at the jacuzzi. There is something at the mansion. All I have to do is find it.*

Tossing my kick board back onto the deck, I reached for my flippers and suddenly froze.

It's not inside, is it? It's outside! Outside the damn door he exited. Damn!

Glancing at the clock, I could see it was barely five-thirty; the other lanes were now churning with swimmers working through the normal practice that had started at the top of the hour. Feeling a bit more energized than I had when I started, I smoothly pulled myself out of the pool and nodded at Coach before yanking my towel out of my backpack and quickly drying off. Not wanting to waste a moment more, I pulled on my warmups once more and hurried off the deck and back to my waiting Camaro; tossing my backpack into the rear seat, I started up the car and roared out of the parking lot. As I turned onto the main drag for Rancho Linda, I chanced the ire of Gina and speed-dialed her.

I wasn't terribly surprised to hear a bit of crankiness in her voice. "Vas, it's not even six. Please tell me you don't need me to roll anywhere — I was on a callout last night and barely got an hour of sleep."

"That's more than me," I chuckled.

"Shit," she sighed. "Where's the body, then?"

"Nothing quite like that," I said. "I'll tell you the details a bit later, but I need to ask you about the search we did at the mansion."

"Sure," she said. Her yawn was loud enough it came through the line.

"I know we dusted that rear door for prints," I started. "Did your team do anything in either the garage or the rear driveway?"

"I don't have my notes in front of me," she replied, "but I believe we did a cursory review. Nothing turned up. Why?"

"Maybe we didn't find anything because it was missing," I said thoughtfully. After another moment, my heart started to beat faster when I began to realize I might have an inkling why. "That's what it is. Shit."

"That's what *what* is?" Gina asked.

"I think our suspect knows there's something at the mansion that we overlooked," I answered.

"Overlooked?" Now Gina sounded a bit annoyed. "My team is pretty thorough, Vas. If there was something to find, we would have located it."

"Exactly," I said.

"Okay, now I'm confused."

"So was I," I confessed. "Any chance you can meet me at the mansion?"

"Right *now*?"

"Yeah, I'm headed there as we speak."

There was a long, long sigh. "It's a damn good thing I like you, Vasily."

"Me?" I asked. "Or my cute ass?"

"Well, if you must know, it's those rock-hard abs you insist on displaying regularly," Gina replied.

"Aww, you noticed."

"Hard not to in those tight polos you favor," she said. "I suppose, given our sexual harassment protocols, I'm not allowed to say anything about the fantasies I've derived from them."

"Probably not," I laughed. "Then again, does it really apply in my case?"

"Let's not find out, shall we," Gina replied. "I'll grab some coffee and get there as soon as I've woken up."

"I owe you big time."

"I'll just put it on your already sizable tab," she chuckled tiredly. "See you in a bit."

I let the connection end and returned my focus to the road; at that still-early hour, crossing the city wasn't as difficult as it would be in less than forty minutes, so it didn't take long before my headlights washed across the two golden lions guarding the end of Rosie's long driveway. Slowing as I climbed toward the front door, I let my instinct take over and turned away from the grand semi-circle and instead drove down the narrower driveway that curved around the side of the mansion. Ultimately, it widened out to accommodate the multi-car garage that had to have originally housed quite a collection of high-end vehicles under the reign of the prior owner. These days, the vast space held only Rosie's Oldsmobile Cutlass Calais that was only slightly younger than me. Pulling to the side of the garage door where she normally parked, I popped open the glovebox and pulled out my industrial flashlight, and then after a moment of thought, opened the gun safe and retrieved my service Glock.

Turning off the Camaro, I stepped out into the damp morning and snapped on the light. Being such a frequent guest at the mansion, Rosie had given me a clicker for one of the other bays, and I reached back into the Camaro to press the button on the device hanging from my sun visor. My designated door chuffed open, allowing the light on the opener to flicker into life; carefully wandering inside, I noted from the empty spot where the Oldsmobile was normally parked that Rosie hadn't yet returned from swim practice. Stopping in the dead center of the garage, I lifted the flashlight and then slowly began to rotate, methodically using the beam to search. As I suspected, there wasn't much to find given how Rosie lived alone; a small set of shelves beside the door that opened directly to the kitchen were bare, but spoke to a time when the chauffeur might have stored supplies for keeping the family limousine in tip-top condition. I presumed whomever was now taking care of the massive lawns and several flower beds for Rosie was bringing in their own gardening equipment, for none were in the garage.

I walked toward the door to the kitchen and tried the handle; unsurprisingly, it was unlocked, and I pushed it open to step into the short hallway. The overhead light was off, so I lifted the flashlight a bit higher and then began to look for the secret door to the servant staircase I'd not known had emptied out into that space. Although the mansion was no longer an active crime scene, the tape the tech had used to frame the door during the initial search was still there, so I pressed gently at an edge and heard the door click open. Pushing it open slightly, I waved the light up the steps that appeared and nodded; pulling it closed, I turned and looked at the hallway again.

If he was carrying Daniel, coming down that staircase wouldn't have been easy. Less so if the kid was struggling. I looked at the framed in door again and frowned. *Even if he were trussed up as tightly as possible, it would have been like having a wriggling caterpillar over a shoulder. Unless he had been stunned more than I think he was by that shot to the jaw.*

I felt myself already discounting that as I shook my head.

Chloroform would have taken too much time to subdue him, but that's one possible explanation. If there was no fear of discovery, maybe he knocked out Daniel after tying him up. It would have been far easier to have done that after for sure - no way for him to avoid the cloth pressed to his face. That's pretty old school, though. And a relatively hard substance to get under the radar — but far easier than other sorts of drugs that would do the same thing far quicker. Another thing to check into, I guess.

Running the flashlight across the floor and then up to the wall across from the doorway, I felt that little frisson of excitement when the beam caught the long, dark groove in the wall. I knew it wasn't from anything that had happened the night before as I'd found it a full two years earlier when sleuthing around the mansion on the first case I'd ever worked for Rancho Linda. The groove was the result of the luggage cart Rosie owned being regularly parked in that spot in the hallway; while it might have originally helped the household staff move suitcases around the mansion, I knew Rosie and her staff tended to use it to shuttle groceries from the garage to the kitchen. I also knew from that very first investigation that the somewhat tarnished golden colored device had allowed Rosie to move a dead body from her solarium to her writing room in what had been a poor attempt to stage a robbery of a manuscript she'd been reluctant to turn into her publisher.

Turning back toward the hidden door, that frisson turned into something closer to an adrenaline rush. *The cart would have been right here,* I thought. *Perfectly positioned for easily moving a dead weight you could no longer carry...?*

Pulling the door to the garage open again, I stepped out into the space and confirmed the luggage cart wasn't out there, either. Following a hunch, I continued back out onto the driveway, and then slowly made my way along the pavement. Although not quite as grand as the one leading to the front door, the asphalt looked well-tended to; several portions had a small, raised bed along the edge, creating a decorative barrier between the lawn and the pavement. Flowering bushes had been cut back for the season, but I had been there during the spring and knew from experience how beautiful the purple flowers were. I ran my light over the raised beds as I walked, not really expecting to find anything but hoping I might; slowly, I walked the perimeter, which included a small turnout area at just about the spot where a car from the garage might do a two-point turn to reverse their direction. I'd used it myself and knew that it was just deep enough for a sedan; fill had been used to keep the driveway level with the mansion, so that had resulted in something of a steep falloff along that side of the pavement due to the property's geography. Though pretty to look at, the plantings served a more practical purpose by denoting just how far one could go before literally plunging over the edge.

As I ran the flashlight over that portion of the planting, something glinted in the beam. Focusing my attention on the spot, I crouched and found a metal plate buried in the dirt, centered in a groove. Turning the light slightly, I felt the beginning of a smile appear when I saw a similar track at just the right width; digging around the plate, I pulled a dark metal wheel out where it had become embedded in the soil. Holding it up into the beam of my light, I could see how the screws that had originally held the wheel to the base of the luggage cart had been sheared off and felt myself slowly begin to nod.

Standing up, I peered over the edge of the flowerbed and shined the light down into the small valley that was behind the driveway. The gentle curves of the luggage cart twinkled in the beam far below. Pushing my way through the same slight opening the kidnapper had to have used, I skidded down the slope and landed next to the cart. It was on its side in the grass, perpendicular to the bushes above in the exact orientation I would have expected it to be in had someone more or less kicked it over the edge. Squatting next to it, I ran the light over the metal of the cart and confirmed where the wheel had come off; standing again, I slowly circled the cart as though it were a whale that had washed ashore along the beach in Santa Monica, a million thoughts running through my head. I was so busy sorting through how to update my theory of the escape of our kidnapper, I nearly missed the small square of fabric that appeared to be caught beneath the front edge of the cart. Pausing, I crouched and held the light above the swatch. The tiny portion visible had a slash of dark red against the fabric; leaning closer, I took a cautious sniff and immediately sat up when I got the first whiff the sickly-sweet smell indicative of chloroform.

Hot damn.

Eleven

Telling Clue

"Well, I suppose that means I need to get a new one."

It was hard not to smile as I stood there at the edge of the driveway with Rosie, looking down on what was left of her luggage cart as techs from the crime lab went over it and the immediate area with a fine-tooth comb. "I'm surprised you didn't get rid of it after the first time it was used to transport a body."

"Not after as long as it took to get the blood off of it," Rosie replied. I was a bit surprised at the churlish tone, especially since she'd essentially been interfering in my investigation at the time. "Truth be told, it's pretty much sat there in the back hallway since then." She looked at me, and I realized she was still pained over how her former housekeeper had died. "Seeing as it remains a poignant reminder each morning of how to be a better human being, I think."

"You didn't notice it was missing?" I asked. "I assumed you were using it to move groceries from the car."

Rosie arched an eyebrow. "I am still perfectly capable of carrying my shopping into the kitchen," she said. "Though I don't do a lot of that these days, either. Most of that is delivered biweekly per Chef's instructions."

"But you walk past that spot each morning on the way to practice," I pressed. "As you must have done yesterday, and again today."

"I don't know what to say, Vas," she replied. "While I might not use it myself, the staff *do* from time to time; I just assumed one of them had pressed it into service during the Halloween party and didn't give it another thought."

I nodded; while it was a reasonable explanation, I couldn't help but feel like we'd lost precious time as a result of not discovering its absence. "I'll need to have your staff provide their fingerprints for elimination," I said. "We, uh, already have yours on file."

"So you do," she chuckled. "You think Daniel was actually moved out of the house on that?"

"It's a distinct possibility, but we won't know until it's checked over thoroughly."

"I thought you said he'd been carried down from the second floor?"

I looked at Rosie. "Someone has been talking," I said with a slight smile. "For I don't recall telling you about that little tidbit."

The author colored slightly. "I may or may not have been chatting up the techs the first time they were here."

"Rosie, you know you shouldn't do that."

"It's my damn home," she replied indignantly. "I want to help, and I can't do that if you keep me in the dark."

"You've been a part of way too many of my cases," I reminded her. "Keep this up and I'll have to put you on the payroll."

Her eyes widened. "What does it pay?" she asked. "Maybe I can quit being an author."

"Not a wise career choice," I smiled as I leaned over and gave her a quick peck on the cheek. "Go have your breakfast. And then you can join Alex and I for dinner tonight and get the full scoop."

She eyed me. "You're supposed to come over *here* tonight."

"That wouldn't be the best idea, since this is an active crime scene and all."

Sighing, she rolled her eyes. "So much for the short ribs I'd had planned."

"Have Chef stuff them into a Crock Pot," I said. "While they warm up, I'll pour you some wine and lie to you about the case."

"All right," she smiled. "Then I will see you this evening."

I nodded and then watched as Rosie walked up the driveway and disappeared into the garage; Gina Carruthers appeared to have been watching my conversation from where she'd been standing beside the open door and took the opportunity to head in my direction. Considering she'd pulled an all-nighter just ahead of my call, she looked reasonably pulled together; about the only tell she might be pushing it a bit were the dark smudges beneath each eye. I smiled as she came to a stop just beside me.

"Seems like it was only yesterday I was dusting that very luggage cart for evidence of a murder," she said as she peered over the edge with me. "How time flies."

I glanced at her. "Were you on that case?"

"I was," she replied. "Though not as senior tech. My promotion came through the week after you solved the case." Gina smiled. "Or three, right? Two deaths and a missing film reel?"

"Yep," I replied. "I hear the new version of that movie will be out next spring."

"About damn time." She glanced at her tablet. I could see she was holding a plastic evidence bag beneath it that appeared to contain the rag I'd found. "I've got some stuff if you have a moment."

"For you, always."

Gina smiled tiredly at me. "I can't tell if you are being sarcastic or not."

"For you, never."

"Ah," she smiled a bit wider. "I think I needed that. So, as you might have been expecting, there were plenty of prints on the cart." She tapped at the tablet. "Through the magic of modern technology — and a 5G hotspot — I was able to send them back to the computer at the office."

"Please tell me you've got a hit on *someone*."

"At least two," she nodded. "Unsurprisingly, Rosie was one of them; the other matched one of the unknowns we took from the second-floor theater." Gina paused. "And the door to the garage."

"Making those a good bet for our kidnapper," I said.

"That's my thought. We also swabbed several samples of blood from the cart; the field test for the majority of them come back to our victim, but we have an unknown donor for a spot just beside the missing wheel."

My eyebrows went up. "Someone cut themselves?"

"I'm guessing a toe," she nodded. "Without the wheel, whoever pushed the cart through the flowerbed probably tried to nudge the thing with a foot."

"And got injured for their troubles," I said. "Nice. Do you have enough for a DNA sample?"

"Yes," she replied. "If I'm lucky, it will match other samples from the mansion."

"I'll keep my fingers crossed."

Gina produced the bag she'd been holding. "I didn't dare sample the blood on this, but our electronic nose confirmed the chemical traces for chloroform. I also think I saw some other staining when we pulled it from beneath the cart — probably saliva from the victim if the rag had been held over their mouth and nose. I should be able to pull DNA from that."

I shook my head. "Chloroform takes way too long to do its thing," I said. "It's not like it would have incapacitated Daniel after a single inhalation. Our kidnapper would have needed time to do it."

"Agreed." Gina looked at me for a moment. "Have you considered that Daniel might have been unconscious when he was carried out?"

"That doesn't jive with what we found in the hallway," I reminded her. "Or the idea that Daniel was trying to leave us a trail."

"Maybe not," she replied. "On other hand, I don't see your kidnapper carrying a struggling teenager all the way to the garage, and *then* using chloroform on your victim before wheeling him out to a waiting car."

Slowly, I began to nod. "Yeah, I don't either. We might want to revisit the second floor then and see if there is anything we overlooked."

"Already in progress," she smiled. "Do you mind if I send a tech to Daniel's home? We're going to need something to compare the DNA to."

"No," I replied, "but I'll take care of that. I still need to sort through his personal affects to see if there is anything there that might tell me who the *hell* had him in their sights."

"Okay. Bring it to the Lab as soon as you can."

"I will. Anything else?"

"Yes," she smiled. "We're a full-service shop, so I've also taken the liberty of sampling the fluid that must have come from the getaway vehicle."

"The *what?*" I asked as I looked down. Squinting, I couldn't see anything.

"Motor oil, actually," she continued, pointing to a spot just behind where I was standing. Squinting even more, I still couldn't see anything against the dark asphalt and started to wonder if I'd waited too long to get an updated prescription for my contacts. "I'll be able to tell you more once we run that back at the lab, but I thought you'd want to know that whatever vehicle we are looking for, it seems to have sprung a leak."

"Like about nine hundred thousand other vehicles in Southern California," I sighed.

"I'll be able to narrow it down a bit," she reminded me.

"God, I hope so."

"I'm going to take the cart back with us," Gina said. "I don't expect to find much else, but you never know."

"How much longer will you be?"

She shrugged. "I don't know what we are looking for upstairs," she said. "Why? In a hurry to arrest our suspect?"

"Always," I smiled, "but I think you need some rest, as does your crew."

She smiled tiredly again. "We're running on coffee, admittedly, but the team is fine."

"All the same, finish up here and then go get some sleep. I'll make sure Rosie keeps the mansion buttoned up until you return."

Gina nodded. "Then we'll be back in the afternoon, barring any other emergencies."

"Let me know if you find anything."

"Don't I always?" she laughed.

"That you do," I smiled. "Now, go get some rest."

"Aye, aye Deputy Chief," she replied.

I laughed as I turned and headed for my Camaro; knowing what the tech team would be bringing, I'd driven it around to the front of the mansion and had parked it beside the fountain. Glancing at my watch, I was surprised to note it was barely seven-thirty; the slight rumble that issued from my stomach at that moment reminded me I'd been off schedule since the shadowy figured had appeared next to the jacuzzi in Palm Springs. Knowing that I still needed to speak with the owners of *The Alternative Way*, I decided to kill two birds with one stone and grab breakfast while I was at the bookstore/café. The sudden thought of biting into a freshly baked croissant had me picking up the pace; I'd nearly made it to the car when my iPhone went off. Pulling it out of the pocket of my sweatpants, I frowned when I saw the number was an out-of-state area code. Taking a chance that it wasn't a telemarketer, I tapped the answer button.

"Deputy Chief Korsokovach."

"Oh!" was the startled voice at the other end. "I'm sorry, I might have the wrong number."

"It happens all the time," I replied. "Who are you trying to reach?"

"A... Vasily? Did you say your name was Korsokovach?"

"Yes," I said. "I'm Vasily Korsokovach. Who is this?"

"Dieter Grauffman," was the immediate reply.

Something at the back of my brain said the name was familiar, but I was having a hard time placing it. "And what can I do for you, Mr. Grauffman?"

"I'm with Fairy Tale Weddings," he said.

I blinked. "At Walt Disney World?" I asked.

"Yes," Dieter answered. "I'm the coordinator for your wedding?" he continued. "We've spoken over email about your plans...?"

It occurred to me at that moment I was probably just as worn out at Gina. "My apologies, Dieter; I've not had my coffee yet. I didn't recognize your name."

He laughed a bit nervously. "I'm just now realizing what time it must be out there in California."

"It's all good," I replied as I leaned against the Camaro. "What can I do for you, Dieter?"

"I wanted to make sure you received the packet we overnighted to you," he said. "And then to confirm you still wanted that specific date you selected."

"I did get the packet," I said, glancing at my backpack in the rear of the Camaro. "I'm afraid I've not had a chance to review it quite yet."

"That's fine — you still have a few days before the deposit is due."

"And as for the date — that is the best one for our mutual schedules," I continued. "My fiancé will be on break from his university, and it's a slow time for me at the department."

"Ah." There was a pause. "I need to confirm one other item," he continued. "Your fiancé is Alejandro Ortega-Cortez?"

I felt myself frown, for I wasn't sure I liked where this conversation was going. "Yes, Alejandro is my fiancé," I said, subtly emphasizing the gender. "Is that a problem?"

"Maybe, though it's a rather delicate issue," Dieter said. His discomfort was almost palpable.

"I was under the impression that same sex weddings were welcome," I replied icily. "My partner and I were already on the fence about coming to Florida. If you are about to tell me—"

"No, no that's not it at all," Dieter hastily interrupted. "It's just that — well, there's no easy way to put this—"

"Then just say what you need to say," I sighed.

There was a long pause. "Mr. Ortega-Cortez has, well he's actually *already* booked the specific slot you'd been planning on," Dieter replied. "And listed *you* as *his* fiancé."

"I'm sorry — *what*?"

"I would have called you sooner, but I only just found out," Dieter continued in a bit of a rush. "I was working with my colleague to reserve the space on the date you wanted and discovered the issue. I... I thought it might be best to let you know and then have you decide what you want to do with Mr. Ortega-Cortez."

"Wait — he's already booked us?"

"Yes," Dieter confirmed. "We've received the deposit, so the reservation is on the books."

That sneaky sonofabitch—!

"I appreciate you reaching out," I said as calmly as I could though my thoughts were racing. "I'm going to have to get back to you. Is this a good number to reach you?"

"Yes. I'll be here until five Eastern, and then back tomorrow starting at eight."

"It will probably be tomorrow," I said. "I'm up to my eyeballs in... work... at the moment."

"I completely understand." He paused again. "I'm so sorry you had to find out this way. If it helps, it happens more than you might think."

"In a weird sort of way, it does," I replied. "We'll speak soon."

"Thank you."

The phone triple-beeped completion of the phone call and I pulled it away from my face and stared at it as though it had a hand in the strange situation I now found myself in. I'd spent months plotting with Suzanne every last detail of what was supposed to be the trip of a lifetime for my soulmate; I had gone to amazing lengths to keep Alex from finding out, for I'd planned on springing the entire surprise on him at

Christmas. Oddly, knowing that he'd been planning the *same* thing — with likely the same reveal — didn't take away from all of that clandestine planning, but I was worried about how my investigator instincts had failed me in this particular instance. Smiling slightly, it occurred to me that Alex might have had some help in keeping me blissfully unaware; unsure of how to proceed, but also having a good sense of who the guilty party was, I tapped a particular speed dial and pressed the phone back to my ear.

Sean Colbeth's warm baritone always made me smile when I heard it. "Morning, Vas," he said cheerfully. "You caught me on the way to a call."

My eyebrows went up. "Nothing major, I hope?"

"That remains to be seen," he laughed. "I never know what I'm getting into these days," he added, an oblique reference to his new position as Commander, Major Crimes for the State of Maine. "What's going on in California? Did I miss our usual check in?"

"Not yet," I replied, then carefully chose my next words. "No, I wanted to touch base. I just heard from Fairy Tale Weddings."

His response was as smooth as I'd expected it to be; it wasn't for nothing Sean was considered one of the top investigators in the country. "Fairy Tale Weddings?" he asked. "That sounds vaguely Disney-esque."

Sighing, I decided I didn't have time for games. "Sean, you grabbed my date."

I could almost hear the light bulb go off over my friend's head. "Oh, fuck," Sean swore after a long moment. "You were planning the same damn thing, weren't you?"

"Yes."

The rueful chuckle from the other end took a bit of the sting out of the situation. "I should have seen this coming. I warned Alex we'd have trouble keeping this from you anyway – especially after we bought the plane tickets."

"Yeah," I smiled. "He can't lie worth shit. I've suspected something for a while now. Just not this."

Sean thought about that. "I suspect I know who was helping you."

"Suzanne," I replied simply.

"Suzanne," he sighed. "She mentioned that she was working on some kind of special Christmas present you were getting Alex and swore me to secrecy."

"Much like I swore *you* to secrecy?" I asked, my eyebrow arching.

"Shit, shit, *shit*," he breathed. "I couldn't tell her about the plane tickets."

"Something tells me there are *four* sets of plane tickets out there," I sighed. "Holy hell indeed."

"Well, this is fine mess we're in, isn't it?"

"No kidding," I sighed. "What are we gonna do?"

"Confront it, I suppose," Sean replied. "I can talk to Suzanne."

I thought about that for a moment. "Let me deal with Alex first," I said.

"That sounds ominous," Sean chuckled. "You're not thinking of burying him in the desert, are you?"

"Hardly," I said. "I think—"

My blood suddenly ran cold.

Shit. Dear lord, that's why he was in Palm Springs, wasn't it? Not to follow me...!

"Vas? Everything all right?"

"No," I replied honestly. "I think you might have accidentally told me where my victim is."

"Your *victim*? What the hell kind of case are you working?"

"Kidnapping," I said. "And I've got to run. I'll call later if I can."

"I'm going to hold you to that," Sean said.

I hung up on Sean and then immediately flipped through my contacts for Verna Novell. She picked up on the second ring. "Hello?" said the rather sleepy voice that answered.

"Verna, it's Vas. I'm sorry to call you at such an early hour, but I need your help."

"Of course," she replied. "If you're looking for that profile I promised, I'm almost done with it. I should be able to get it to you later this morning."

"That would be awesome," I replied. "Actually, I'm wondering if I am recalling something you told me the first time we met — it was a case you handled that dealt with a serial killer and a golf course?"

"I think you're referring to the one where the victims were buried in the sand traps," she said.

I nodded, though she couldn't see it. "Were the victims alive when they were buried?" I asked.

"Not in that case, no," she answered. "Why do you ask?"

"Don't ask me why, but I think our victim might be buried alive somewhere in the desert," I replied. "Possibly in or just outside of Palm Springs. Would doing that fit this case?"

There was a long pause from the former FBI profiler. "It would, actually," Verna ultimately answered. "I won't quote statistics to you, but it's far more common in cases where a ransom is being demanded."

"Right," I nodded as I pulled open my car door and slid behind the wheel. "Once the money is delivered, in theory GPS coordinates are provided to locate the victim. Except the victim is usually already dead by then."

"Not always," Verna replied. "You think that's what's going on here?"

"Maybe a variation," I said as I started the Camaro. I waited for the Bluetooth to cut in before continuing. "We've not had a ransom note or call or anything. But I have this weird sense that we're supposed to *find* Daniel — that this is part of some twisted scavenger hunt."

"Dead?" Verna asked. "Or alive?"

"Probably the former," I sighed. "I'd prefer the latter. Let me ask you this: why go to the trouble to kidnap Daniel and then drag him out into the desert to die? Why not just kill him *here* in Rancho Linda?"

"If your suspect is the kind of person I think they are," Verna replied, "then terrorizing the teenager would have been part of the plan from the beginning." She paused. "You can't get more terrorized than waking up in box with no idea where you might be." Verna paused again. "Part of that would also include keeping Daniel alive long enough for the fear to become nearly overwhelming."

I pulled out of the mansion's driveway and onto the road leading back to Rancho Linda. "That is the first good news I've heard today," I said. "Offset by what I suspect you are about to tell me."

Verna laughed wryly. "You already knew you were on the clock, Vas. I can't add much more to that."

"I suppose not."

"I'll wrap up the profile now and send it to you within the hour," Verna said. "I hope it helps."

"It already has," I said. "Believe me."

TWELVE
LATE MORNING COFFEE

"I could work up some models for you, but all of them would be grim."

"*Anything* would help, Peg," I replied. "I need a sense of how much time I might have left." *Or if it's more realistic for me to shift into a full-on murder investigation*, I added mentally, not wanting to give voice to my actual fears.

The Chief Medical Examiner for Orange County sighed audibly over the phone. "It's a crapshoot, Vas. There are too many variables."

"Just give me a ballpark figure," I said. "Some way to figure out where to start looking."

"Shit, Vas," she said as she blew out a breath. "Tell me again what you're thinking?"

Taking a moment to gather my thoughts, I swirled the cup of coffee I'd bought when I'd first arrived at *The Alternative Way*; the steam was still slowly wafting away from the surface. I was sitting at what had become my de facto remote office in the bookstore/café, a small table nestled between two bookcases but with an unobstructed view of the stage. There was rarely live music in the café during the day, but the house piano quartet was apparently rehearsing a new set that morning the owner had told me would debut Friday evening. From what little I had heard already, I'd decided to try and pop in for the full show — assuming, of course, I had successfully wrapped the case by then. Considering how little progress I felt I had made, it seemed like the odds were longer than they normally would be.

"I think our victim is buried in the desert close to Palm Springs," I explained to Peg. "Assuming our suspect did the speed limit, that's between sixty and ninety minutes of driving time, depending on where they ultimately stopped. Further assuming that our suspect would find it easier to handle our victim while he was still comatose, I'd need to also factor in how long a kid like Daniel would have been under." I paused. "That might narrow down how long they would have been driving, or how far off the beaten path they might have gone."

"Gina said you think it was chloroform?"

"We found evidence to support that," I confirmed.

"Just off the cuff, whatever dose your victim got at the mansion would have worn off fairly quickly. Unlike more modern drugs, chloroform would need to be re-administered at regular intervals. It's essentially an anesthetic, though not one widely in use today."

I felt myself frown. "That had been in the back of my head," I said. "I'm obviously unsure of how much of a dose Daniel would have gotten; if our suspect is experienced in these matters — and I hope to God they aren't, for that opens up an entirely *different* can of worms — I agree with the notion it was enough to keep him insensate for loading into the vehicle."

"I don't think you're wrong about wanting to have him under once they arrived wherever they went," Peggy said. "It wouldn't be hard to press a cloth to the kid's face again while he was in the trunk."

"Yeah," I replied. "I imagine Daniel wouldn't have willingly gone into whatever container our suspect was using." I paused again, caught by a thought. "Oh, hell. Maybe he was put *into* the container at the mansion? Then it wouldn't matter about keeping him under, and, I would imagine, easier to handle him later."

"Other than the air situation, no," Peg said. "That also tells you a bit about the vehicle used, though, doesn't it?"

"It does — probably not a sedan. More likely a van or a truck."

"I'd think that a truck or van pulled to the side of the road would be memorable," Peg said thoughtfully. "More so than a sedan. You might get lucky on that."

I toggled my laptop screen over to the online traffic incident database. "I'll sort through any CALTRANS reports on Halloween and the day after. Someone might have seen something; it could narrow down our search."

"All right. While you do that, I can have our whiz kids do the math — assuming you are still wedded to this theory."

"I am — and if I'm right, that makes it all the more critical to know how long he would be able to survive if he were buried alive," I said. "Would it be fair to assume that both the location and the container were picked out and ready to go in advance?"

"That might be more a question for your profiler," Peg replied. "The container, for sure, especially if Daniel was stuffed into it at the mansion. Which also speaks to a hefty malice aforethought."

"No kidding."

"Okay," Peg replied, then paused. "We've had a few of these cross my exam table over the years, Vas. None of them ended well; in just about every case, the victim was buried in a box and suffocated within hours. If Daniel is in a similar situation, I can already tell you that his air would have run out a long time ago."

"I think he's still alive," I replied stubbornly. "Our profiler tells me that this suspect might get a kick out of thinking our victim would be alive long enough to know no one could find them. And," I added after a moment, "the thrill of knowing *we* are aware of how powerless we might be to prevent such a horrible ending."

There was a longer pause. "That's just sick."

"Agreed."

"So a finite source of oxygen, then? We had one case about six years ago where the victim was buried with scuba gear; between what was in the tank and the volume of the box, we think they survived almost a full day." she said. "In that particular situation, it was carbon dioxide poisoning that ultimately claimed the victim. If you are right about the suspect's motivations—"

I frowned. "I'll cross check that with Verna, but I think I am. Daniel has to be alive."

"—then that would presume some way around the carbon dioxide and oxygen issues, which takes far more planning than just burying a box in the desert. And for that matter, why go the trouble of driving all the way out to Palm Springs? There's plenty of desert here in Orange County."

"I don't have an answer for that quite yet," I confessed. "Other than my gut telling me there's a connection between Palm Springs, Rancho Linda and our suspect.

"Ok." I heard tapping at a keyboard. "I've got the bio/demo data on your victim, we'll use that to create the parameters for survival. It may help that he was sleeping for a significant part of the ride, but Vas," Peg paused. "I've got to be realistic. You should probably assume the kid's dead."

I glanced across the café toward where the owner, Anne Dawson, was speaking to the barista behind the counter. "I can't accept that. Not yet."

"All right," Peg said. "Let me see what we can do, and we'll get back to you."

"I appreciate it," I replied. "Call me as soon as you have anything."

"Will do."

As the call ended, I put my iPhone down beside my laptop and stared at the coffee mug for a few moments. Ever since my epiphany with Sean, the unsettled feeling that had dogged me from the moment

Daniel disappeared had grown far more intense; despite my best efforts, I also couldn't help falling into the trap our suspect had created, for thoughts of the teenager being trapped in a coffin-sized space beyond my reach were never far from the surface. The level of malevolence behind what was happening to Daniel spoke to a deep animosity that I found hard to fathom; in a multiracial society, it wasn't uncommon for the fringiest of fringe players to blame their perceived ills on those deemed to be *other*. Sipping at my coffee, I tried not to think about how I'd been on the receiving end of such vitriol at various points in my life; while I couldn't perhaps fully appreciate what it was like to live as a racial minority in America, I had a decent sense of being considered a pariah. My own experience hadn't been pleasant in the least, which was, perhaps, something of a guide; recent societal evolutions had made people like me more acceptable, but it also seemed to wildly vary based on where you lived. Years ago, I had hoped that by the time I'd gone to the great swimming pool in the sky *everyone* would finally be treated equally and with respect; the closer I got to forty, the more it felt like we were regressing to a point where gay men would once more be treated as some sort of aberration in humanity.

Dour thoughts, dude, I sighed as I sipped again at the coffee. *You are in a bleak place today. Which is understandable.*

Putting my mug to my lips again, I realized it was completely empty; sighing again, I started to stand up to retrieve a refill when I felt a hand on my shoulder. Turning, I saw Anne had appeared as if by magic, holding a thermal carafe. Having told her about Daniel upon my arrival, I could tell I'd inadvertently muted her usual joyful demeanor.

"Refill?" she asked.

"What will it cost me this time?" I asked with a slight smile, playing the usual game with my friend.

"It depends," she said as she reached around and nabbed my mug from my hand. "Do you still have the Starfleet uniform you wore to the Halloween party?"

"It needs a good cleaning, but yes," I nodded.

"Good," she smiled as she handed me back my mug. "Can you be here next Thursday? I've got a group of kids interested in science and you are the featured speaker."

"Okay." I took a sip from the mug, and then cocked my head. "Usually you want me to come as Spidey and talk about being yourself; Captain Pike isn't exactly in the same league as a teenager grappling with superpowers."

"They're closer than you think," Anne replied.

"I can't see how. And I'm not exactly a scientist."

"Aren't you?" she asked. "You spend half your time in the crime lab, and the rest going through data forensically."

"Well, sure," I nodded. "But that's not *science* science."

"Potato, po-TAH-to," she laughed. "Can you be there?"

"I'll put it on my calendar," I said, "with the optimistic hope this case is done by then."

Anne put her hand on my shoulder again. "You'll find Daniel."

"God, I hope so," I breathed. "His group meets tonight, doesn't it?"

"Yeah," Anne nodded as she came around and took the seat across from me. "Every Wednesday. I've not figured out what to tell the rest of the kids."

"Be honest," I advised. "The truth will serve them better than a polite lie."

"I don't know," Anne said. "I've known many of those kids for years; a polite lie might be easier."

"Would you mind if I crashed the party, so to speak?" I asked.

"You've mentored that group many times before," Anne replied. "Given the circumstances, I'm sure you'd be more than welcome. I expect they might have some questions only you can answer."

I smiled slightly. "As much as I can. I figure they know Daniel far better than I do, assuming they are up to my questioning them."

"I'm sure they will be. The group meets at eight."

"I should be here," I nodded. "How close are you to Daniel?"

"Fairly," she smiled. "He's one of those purely on the volunteering side of the house, lending a hand with many of the causes we support. So few people will do that if they are not personally affected by a particular issue; it's a rare trait, especially in one so young."

"He's only known a life of service," I said. "His parents have been with the State Department longer than Daniel's been alive. I imagine it's baked into their DNA."

"Probably."

"What did you think of him?"

"As a person?"

"Yeah."

Anne looked thoughtful. "Thoughtful. Compassionate. Driven," she said. "I never had any qualms about asking him to take on a project for any of our groups, for I knew it would be in good hands." She paused for a moment. "His passion for social justice and equality was a bit unusual in someone so young. It was also rather infectious; he was one of our best volunteer recruiters."

"I could see that," I said as I sipped from my mug. Running a hand through my hair, I absently realized I'd never put any styling product into it; as long as it had become, my natural body meant it probably looked a bit like I'd just rolled out of bed. "Did he have any friends?"

"That I couldn't tell you," Anne replied. "I would assume so, if not among the groups he belonged to then back at the high school."

I frowned slightly for I'd not thought to ask that particular question of Dr. Dolittle when I'd been at the school. "I'll follow up back at Rancho Linda High on that," I said. "I understand he was also the manager of the soccer team."

"I believe that's true," Anne replied.

"How on earth did Daniel have time to do all that he did?" I asked.

Anne arched an eyebrow. "You of all people should know the answer to that, Mr. Olympian."

"I suppose I do," I smiled wryly. "When you believe in something and are driven to do it, you kind of figure out how to manage your time.

Or you are forced to, if you have a maniacal coach that wants you in the pool twelve hours a day."

"Twelve hours? Seriously?"

I smiled a bit wider. "Maybe not twelve. But there were days when it felt like that, I assure you. I can remember falling into my bed at the dorm at the end of those long days, exhausted, only to have to haul myself back out again in the wee hours of the morning for practice. It was a grueling existence."

"Do you ever miss that?"

"The life of an Olympic swimmer?" I asked.

"Yes."

"Every day," I replied instantly. "More, I suppose, as I get older."

"I never pegged you as someone who lived in the past," Anne said.

"Oh, I don't miss it for that reason," I replied. "I know my glory days are behind me. Don't get me wrong, I enjoyed my moment in the sun; I think what I miss most about those days, though, is the freedom to just focus on one thing — and being the best I could possibly be at it."

Anne looked at me askance. "Doesn't sound all that different than what you do today as a detective, Deputy Chief."

I blinked. "I hadn't much thought of it in those terms," I said. "I suppose you are right."

"I usually am," she smiled.

"I wouldn't dare to dispute you," I laughed.

"That is wise," Anne said as she stood. "As much as I'd love to keep chatting, I've got to go check on some pastries; we're baking extra so we can feed the masses tonight."

I smiled slightly. "A definite perk of meeting here."

"Oh yeah. Want another croissant?"

I looked down at the crumbs of the one I had demolished. "Sure."

"Okay," she said as she topped off my coffee. "Back in a moment."

Struck by a thought, I reached for her arm and arrested her departure. "Anne, one quick question before you go."

"Sure."

"Do you have many groups from the high school that meet here?"

"Independent from the ones we sponsor?" she asked.

"Yes," I nodded.

"A few," she replied. "We're a bit selective about who we allow, given how we want to maintain the café as a safe zone."

"Could you share that list with me?" I asked.

She looked at me for a long moment. "If it were anyone other than you, I'd say no right out of the gate. What is it you really want to know?"

I sighed. "It's nothing but a long shot, Anne," I replied. "A hope that I might see a name on one of your lists that I've seen elsewhere; some way to narrow in on where I should be looking." I sat back in my chair and ran both hands through my hair. "Maybe with more data, I'll finally see a pattern."

Anne nodded. "All right. That's fair. And to be honest, it's only two groups at this point. We had to kick out a third a few months ago when we realized they had misrepresented who and what they were."

A tiny twinge hit my stomach. "Lives Matter?"

The owner of the café blanched. "How the *hell* did you know that?"

"Why, *exactly*, did you kick them out?" I asked instead.

Anne glared at me for a moment, then sat back down before lowering her voice. "The leader of the group contacted me back in April saying they'd lost their regular meeting space," she began. "It was the usual sob story I hear from many of the groups we ultimately take in and sponsor: someone gets a hair up their ass over what the group is doing and boots them to the curb."

"I can see that with LGBTQ+ affiliated groups," I said. "But this one sounds like it's more on the religious spectrum?"

"Oh, it sure is," she replied as she frowned. "They told me they were a social justice group dedicated to harmonious living in a color-blind world; who could resist that kind of a pitch? Though I have to admit, I did find it odd such a group had lost their space."

"When did they start meeting here?"

"Early May," Anne replied. "As you know, we have two meeting rooms out back, and often use the café itself as a third on busy nights. Lives Matter wound up here on the same night as Kids On Their Own."

That twinge became a bit of a knot. "I'm going to guess there was some friction there?"

"You could say that," Anne said as she blew out a breath. "It started small — the leader of Lives Matter waited until June to request the bigger space out here in the café even though they had — at most — ten people attending the weekly meetings. After a bit of musical chairs, we managed to accommodate them; then they complained about being interrupted when the *other* groups had to walk through the café to get to our meeting rooms."

"That would seem to have been an obvious downside to being out here," I replied.

"It was kind of the point of them moving, as it turns out," Anne said. "They asked — demanded, really — that the other groups stop coming on the nights they were here."

My eyebrows went up. "Bold from a group that got booted from their original home."

"It gets better." Anne nodded toward the bookcase behind me; until that moment, I'd not realized it was the section on gender issues. "A week after we refused their request to cancel the other groups, I had a half-dozen moms appear as I was unlocking the gate; they claimed to have kids attending the weekly Lives Matter meetings, and wanted to express their concern with our allowing *other* groups to meet at the same time."

"I don't think I like where this is heading."

"I didn't either," Anne smiled wryly. "Without a shred of evidence, a mom claimed someone from Kids On Their Own had made unwanted advances to more than one of the kids attending the Lives Matter meeting. They more or less gave me an ultimatum: clear the space for the group or they were going to go to the police about how *The Alternative Way* had become a front for grooming youth."

It was hard not to frown deeply at what had become an all-purpose term generally used by some to besmirch the reputation of others. While the potential always existed for inappropriate conduct in any group situation, *The Alternative Way* was very specifically set up to be the antithesis of such environments. Accusing Anne and her partner of somehow turning kids into something they weren't would be like saying Fred Rogers had been using his television show as a recruiting tool for the Presbyterians. (He wasn't.)

I couldn't help the eye roll that followed the frown. "You're not serious?"

"Completely."

"Kids On Their Own isn't an LGTBQ+ group," I said. "Unless grooming means something other than how it's currently been bastardized."

Anne smiled wryly. "Apparently advocating for progressive causes counts."

"Dear Lord. What about the other group?"

"Hardly — unless learning to play chess in Japanese counts," Anne shook her head. "Call it a gut instinct, but I purposely scheduled Lives Matter with groups I thought would have something in common with them. In retrospect, I think I suspected they had left a word out in the name of their group."

I nodded slowly. "*All* Lives Matter?"

"Exactly," she replied. "My gut told me they might not mix well with my more marginalized groups."

"Apparently that was a solid call."

Anne shrugged. "For all the good it did. They still managed to stir things up a bit."

"That must have been quite the conversation."

"It was." She smiled. "I knew I wasn't going to get anywhere with the moms that morning, so after they vented to me — and I do mean *vented* — I told them I would look into it and speak with the group leader."

"Who is that?"

"Blake Dolittle," Anne said.

That frisson of excitement that always hit me when a clue dropped out of nowhere made itself known. "*Dolittle*? Any relation to the principal, Janice Dolittle?"

"He's her son," Anne nodded.

My investigator brain went into overdrive. "Huh. What a coincidence."

"I thought you didn't like those."

"I don't," I nodded.

"Here's another, then: Blake is a star soccer player for Rancho Linda."

"The same team that Daniel is the manager for?" I asked. "Huh."

"Probably," she replied. "Blake's a senior and the team captain."

"Was Janice one of the moms you saw?"

"No," Anne said. "Though she *was* name checked a few times."

"Did you confront him about the allegations?"

"I did," she nodded. "He had nothing to add to them other than not feeling 'safe' meeting in our space while the other two groups were here. Blake was extremely uncomfortable with the KOTO kids."

I thought about that for a moment. "How monochromatic are the members of Lives Matter?"

"You can't get any whiter than they are," she replied.

"Shit," I whistled. "Lives Matter indeed. Were they burgeoning racists?"

"Maybe," Annie said after considering me for a moment. "More like a youth version of the Oath Keepers or the Ten Percenters. I allowed them to meet that final night and then kicked them out."

"A new generation of jackbooted thugs? Now that is a rather scary thought," I said. Images of what had happened at the Capitol after the last Presidential election flashed in my brain. "I feel a bit like we are living in a strange new world."

"You're not wrong," Anne replied, then smiled sadly. "History teaches that with each leap forward in progress, we tend to also see a temporary period of setbacks. But in the end," she added as she stood once more, "what is *right* I ultimately prevails."

"May we both still be alive to see that when it happens this cycle," I murmured.

"Amen, brother," Anne said. "Now let me get you that croissant."

Thirteen
Seeking Guidance

I wasn't entirely certain why I returned to Rancho Linda High School after finishing my second pastry at *The Alternative Way*; Raymond Connolly had dutifully emailed me the list of student groups sponsored by the school, along with a second list noting which of them Daniel had been involved with. Aside from being amazed at how thin he had been stretched, each of the societies to which he'd been affiliated had a heavy community service bent, totally in keeping with the sort of volunteer-minded teenager I knew. The only anomaly was his membership on the soccer team; I was having a hard time fathoming why Daniel would willingly give up time he would otherwise spend helping out at, say, a soup kitchen for toting soccer balls across the field or washing jerseys for the players. I could *maybe* see him doing it as a resume building effort — a notion that Connolly himself had hinted at — but now that I fully understood just how busy Daniel had been making Rancho Linda a better place for, frankly, *everyone*, it just felt... wrong, somehow.

So, I could almost convince myself that was my motivation for striding back through the front door of the school looking once more for answers. Except that I also had enough self-awareness to understand that my attention was more focused on another square peg trying to fit into a round hole, one by the name of Blake Dolittle. Pausing in the main lobby for the school, I pondered how best to proceed; walking into Dr. Dolittle's office and confronting her wasn't going to get me anything other than being tossed out of the building on my ear, so I opted for a slightly less aggressive play and made for the Guidance Office.

The empty hallways told me I had serendipitously hit the school while classes were in session; opening the door to the Guidance Office proper, I found my luck continued to hold. Not only were all of the uncomfortable looking chairs in the waiting room empty, Raymond Connolly happened to be behind the small reception desk, thumbing through some sort of thick paperback book. He looked up at the sound of the door being opened and frowned when he saw who it was that had appeared on his doorstep; trying to put him at some sort of ease, I smiled my megawatt model smile as I closed the door behind me.

"Mr. Connolly," I said jovially, "I'm *so* glad I caught you. I wanted to take a moment to thank you in person for sending me those lists last night. They were incredibly helpful to the case," I added, laying it on a bit.

It had the desired effect, for the frown on the counselor's face shifted to one of surprise. "Were they?"

"Yes, quite."

"I'm glad to have been of service," he said, still sounding amazed.

I took an intentional look around the empty waiting room. "Slow day today?"

"Oddly, yes," he replied. "Normally I'm booked solid, but every now and then, I get a bit of a breather." He tapped at the book he was flipping through. "Gives me a chance to catch up on some reading."

"What is that?" I asked. "It looks a bit like a tourist guide to some place exotic."

Connolly laughed, although it sounded a bit like water gurgling. "You wouldn't be wrong," he answered. "It's the listing of the top four hundred public and private universities. Everything you would ever want to know about them, from their academics to whether the student recreation center has a lazy river."

My eyebrows went up. "That's a thing?"

"Oh yes," he nodded. "I've had a student or two make their final choices based on something like that."

I found myself beginning to fear for the future of our civilization, but put that away for the moment, for Connolly had inadvertently given me an entrance for why I was there. "I imagine it also lists what sorts of scholarships are available, too?"

"Yes," he nodded. "Both academic and athletic."

"Can't that all be found on the internet now?" I asked, eyeing the book. "Print seems so last millennium."

Connolly actually looked sad for a moment. "As it happens, this is the final edition of the book. Next year it will be completely online." He looked down at it. "The end of an era, I guess."

Momentarily torn between handing Connolly a Kleenex and pursuing what I was after, I waited a moment or two for him to process his grief and then plowed onward. "Speaking of scholarships, you told me the last time we spoke that Daniel had been playing on the soccer team. Was he looking for a full-ride spot somewhere?"

Connolly's eyes came up to mine again. "I thought I said he was the manager of the team."

I smiled weakly. "Did you? I had a hard time reading my notes when I was typing them into the case system. My handwriting has gone to hell since college anyway."

"I can relate," he smiled. "No, he wasn't looking for an athletic scholarship — he already had multiple offers for academic ones, though."

I made as though it was the first time I'd heard that and nodded solemnly. "I see. I suppose being a manager wouldn't have qualified him for one, anyway."

"No," Connolly said.

"Rancho Linda High seems to have had a number of stellar athletes, though," I continued, priming the pump slightly.

"We do," he replied with a trace of pride. "Six seniors this year alone, including Dr. Dolittle's son."

I tried not to react at the mention of Blake. "Really? What sport does he play?"

"Soccer," Connolly replied. "He's a damn good striker; I wouldn't be surprised if MLS recruits him and he skips college altogether."

"Do you have his stats?" I asked casually. "They must be pretty impressive."

"I do, actually," Connolly said as he pushed his bulk out of the reception chair. "Hang on while I get them..."

I watched Connolly disappear into his office and then heard the sounds of someone rustling through paper; unsure of how long it might take the guidance counselor to locate whatever it was he was hunting for, I wandered away from the reception desk and idly perused the items posted on the bulletin board over the waiting room chairs. All of the usual suspects were there, including an announcement that another round of ASVAB testing would be taking place next weekend; being a college-bound student athlete had meant that my focus had been primarily on getting through the insane workload that was my Advanced Placement curriculum, so I'd never really given a career in the armed forces much of a thought. Eyeing the extremely attractive sailor that was pitching this year's version of the ASVAB had me wondering if I might have liked a life at sea, though it was rather sobering to remember that gays had not been allowed to openly serve in the military when I'd been of age to do so. It was clear, however, that the Navy seemed to be trying to make up for lost time.

There was a square window comprised of glass blocks embedded into the far wall, and to my surprise, I discovered a rather eclectic collection of small potted plants thriving in the light from outside. Leaning down slightly, I had no idea what I was looking at, botanically speaking, but it was very clear that someone in the office had a green thumb. Seeing the flowers reminded me that Alejandro had mentioned wanting to grow something on our balcony; he'd had success with window boxes back in Maine while he'd been living in a small cottage along the shore in Windeport, and had hoped to replicate that in our new home. I'd blessed the endeavor with the caveat that I had zero clue how to keep anything alive; Alex had assured me he'd find something that was nearly indestructible. That seemed too good of a challenge not to pursue.

The slamming of a lateral filing cabinet returned my attention to the office door on the other side of the room; a moment later, Connolly wobbled out of his office holding a three-ring binder. Wandering back to the reception desk, I suppressed a smile at how the poor man looked more and more like one of those roly-poly bottom-heavy toys toddlers were unable to knock over each time I saw him. Tossing the binder down on the desk, he groaned audibly as he sank down into the chair on the other side; I had to look twice to verify that the effort he'd expended in making the round trip to his office had produced a flushed complexion and a sweaty brow. I resisted my impulse to reach for his wrist to rule out he was having a cardiac arrest in my presence, but just barely.

"Stats for the soccer team," he said between great heaving gasps of air. "For this year and last," he added as he slid the binder toward me. "Since Blake transferred in from St. Frederik's Prep as a junior, so you'd have to talk to them if you wanted anything on him prior to that." He took another long moment to try and catch his breath, which seemed like a losing effort. "I... understand from my colleague up there he was their leading scorer, though."

"Blake was in private school?" I asked, arching an eyebrow.

Connolly nodded, which seemed to be easier for him at the moment.

"That seems unusual, given his mother works for a public school."

Taking another gasping breath, he wiped at his brow before speaking again. "St. Frederik's... specializes in churning out student athletes for Division One colleges. We focus mainly on... academics."

I had my own opinion on that particular breakdown, but let it pass. "Why did he return to Rancho Linda, then? Were there academic issues?"

Connolly eyed me. "I couldn't really say," he replied after a long moment. "Student privacy and all that."

I nodded, for it seemed his non-answer had, in fact, been an answer of a sort. "I imagine Dr. Dolittle wasn't entirely upset to have her son around, then."

"Probably." Despite the room being relatively temperate, rivulets of sweat had begun to roll down his face; Connolly grabbed for a Kleenex from the box on the desk and dabbed at his skin.

"Are you okay?" I asked, worry finally trumping my professional manners. "You look like you've run a marathon."

"I just need to catch my breath," he said.

"Ah," I nodded, though I had my doubts.

Turning the binder in my direction, I flipped the cover open and revealed what appeared to be a professionally done full color publication for the soccer team. The photography was phenomenal, with action shots of the soccer team overlaid with data from their seasons. I moved past the first few pages that seemed to be mostly group achievements and then got into the meat of the piece: each player on the team had a two-page spread, with a large solo photo on one side, and their stats on the other. Save for the goalie, each player was standing on the field I knew was just behind the pool at the high school, one foot on a soccer ball, staring at the camera with a *I am the best player on the team* look on their face. I did a cursory scan of each one I came to, but then did a more thorough review when I finally found my quarry.

Blake Dolittle appeared to be every inch of the six-foot-five height the bio demo stats indicated; his frame otherwise had that lanky but solid build soccer players all seemed to have, the result of the intense cardio fitness required to be able to run up and down the field for up to ninety minutes at a whack. His dark brown hair was sporting the current fad in styling, which was shaved sides nearly to the crown, with a strange tuft of hair that flopped to one side. A hint of a tattoo of some sort was peeking out from beneath the short sleeve of the uniform top; I wondered if it was a thematic match to the very large bald eagle that was featured prominently on his left thigh. Considering California had some pretty strict laws regarding minors getting ink, I rechecked the bio demo section and confirmed that Blake had turned eighteen in the spring. That made me look up at Connolly.

"Blake seems older than his teammates," I said, warily eyeing the counselor. His face had gone pallid, and, oddly, was still breathing quite hard.

"Kid has ADD, and wound up repeating kindergarten," Connolly said after a moment. "Although I probably shouldn't have told you that."

"I'll forget you said anything," I smiled. "Are you certain you're okay?"

Connolly waved at me. "Yeah, fine. I just need a moment."

I returned my attention to the photo, which was intentionally making Blake look like some sort of all-American teenager. The wide smile featured perfect teeth, and if I looked closer, I could see the outline of well-defined abs being hugged by the technical fabric of the uniform top. Biceps that would have been impressive on a far older college student were also present, hinting perhaps at just how much time the kid spent in the gym. Rounding out the package were legs that had been perfectly sculpted for bursts of speed; in short, he looked to be the perfect specimen of a player. Eyeballing the stat lines below his demographic information, I discovered he was (unsurprisingly) the leading scorer on the team, and had been for most of his career at Rancho Linda. I wondered a bit at how the coach was going to plug the very big hole Blake would be leaving when he departed for college at the end of the academic year.

"These stats are something," I murmured more to myself than Connolly.

To my surprise, Connolly agreed. "He—he's especially proud of having at least fifteen goals each year for the past four years," he managed to get out between great heaving gasps.

"No one else seems even close," I observed as I ran my finger along the stats.

Knowing that Connolly was watching me rather intently, I flipped the page again and then went through the remaining players as fast as I could without looking like I was simply scanning them. The final page of the publication had a short message from Principal Dolittle, expounding the achievements of the team over the years — and making the entreaty for the reader to donate to the boosters in order to continue the success. That last part made me smile, for I had worked a case surrounding the former booster society that used to support all sports at the high school; it had opened my eyes to the incredibly aggressive politics that went on within such groups, which in that case had led to my exposing a multiple-year embezzlement scheme. I'd wondered how the fundraising had been handled after that; judging from the slick package I'd just read, it seemed they had it well in hand.

Closing the book, I pushed it back toward Connolly. "Some team."

"Yeah," he said. "Yeah."

I managed to get around the desk just as he clutched at his chest and began to slide out of the chair; his bulk hit me like a ton of bricks, but I managed to ease him onto the commercial linoleum. The bluish tinge that had appeared on his lips matched the nonexistent pulse I was barely able to find after pressing my fingers to his carotid; yanking my iPhone from my pocket, I dialed 9-1-1 and then pressed it between my cheek and shoulder as I tore off Connolly's tie and then ripped apart his dress shirt. Buttons flew away in three directions, though I was oblivious to how they ricocheted into the depths of the room as I leaned closer to determine if he was still breathing; not seeing the massive expanse of his chest move in the slightest, I started to scan the room for any sort of medical kit, hoping beyond hope I wouldn't need to give the guy the kiss of life. Oddly, my brain also took that moment to remind me just how often I'd been around people who suddenly had health emergencies. Shaking off the strange feeling some higher power seemed to always be ensuring I was right where I needed to be at any given moment, my eyes hit on the brilliantly colored AED cabinet hanging on the wall beside the door just as the operator answered.

"9-1-1. What is your emergency?"

"This is Deputy Chief Vasily Korsokovach, Rancho Linda PD," I said as I pushed myself off the floor and dashed across to the AED. "I'm at the Rancho Linda High School, Guidance Counselor's office; apparent heart attack in progress," I continued as I ripped open the front of the cabinet. A screeching alarm began to sound as I yanked the small box out. "I need immediate medical assistance at this location."

"Okay, Chief," was the calmly professional reply. "Rolling an ambulance to your coordinates now. Do you have a pulse?"

"No," I said as I dropped to my knees and pressed a free finger to Connolly's neck. "Also no breathing."

"All right. Do you want me to walk you through CPR?"

"I have access to an AED," I said as I rapidly scanned the outside of the device. "Do I want to use it, or should I start CPR?"

"AED first," was the immediate reply.

"All right," I said. "Hang on, I'm putting you on speaker."

I tapped the speaker button on the iPhone and then placed it next to my thigh; returning to the AED, I pressed the on switch and then began to slide the package holding the pads out from the slot at the back of the device as the small display lit up. We'd done a round of CPR certifications at the department back in the Spring, but I was just hazy enough on how to use the technology that I wasted precious seconds waiting for the device to begin to speak to me.

"Adult. Take out pads," the device intoned mechanically.

"Already did that, dumbass," I muttered as I ripped the plastic container open and then yanked out the folded pad.

Deciding to ignore the device as it slowly began to tick off what to do, I unfolded the peculiarly shaped pad and lined it up as per the diagram on the outside; Connolly had a rather hairy chest, so I worried that the adhesive on the rear of the pad might not hold, but when I pressed it onto his clammy skin, it pretty much stuck in place. Checking one last time to make sure I had lined everything up properly, I turned and pressed the *shock* button on the front of the AED; the mechanical voice had been in the middle of telling me how to place the pad but immediately shifted into all business mode.

"Stay clear of patient. Analyzing."

I wasn't sure, but I *thought* I could hear sirens in the distance.

"Shock advised. Deliver shock now. Press flashing button now."

Smashing the button a second time, I heard the high-pitched whine of the device revving up and then watched with some amazement as Connolly came up off the floor slightly. I waited impatiently for the device to reset and tell me the next step.

"Analyzing. Begin CPR."

Crap, I thought.

I shifted to straddle Connolly; his girth was large enough that I felt a bit like I'd tried to sit down on a barrel. Interlacing my fingers, I lined them up over the massive cross at the center of the pad from the AED and forcibly began to plunge my fists down into his ribcage. The unsettling *crunch* I felt beneath them told me that the recovery time from this particular incident had just been elongated — assuming I managed to keep Connolly alive long enough for the EMTs to take over. Beside me, the AED began to click like a metronome, telling me the exact rhythm I needed for compressions; it took just a moment for me to synchronize and then I was off to the races. Somewhere in the back of my head, I recalled an instructor telling me that the proper number of compressions per minute was close to the base line for the classic 1970s Bee Gees hit, *Staying Alive*. While not a huge fan of Disco era music, I had ventured into more than a few gay bars that catered to those who were back when I was a foolish twenty-something, so I was quite familiar with the song — enough that the lyrics began to pop into my head as I labored over Connolly.

No one tells you during CPR training just how painful the experience can be, both for the person administering the CPR and the victim on the receiving end. My arms first began to ache, and then started to burn with the effort required on each compression; sweat started to roll down into my eyes, but I knew I dared not stop long enough to wipe at my brow. Trying to blink away the stinging sensation, I felt my own heartbeat begin to rise and my breathing become more labored.

"Increase compressions."

"Shit shit shit," I yelled aloud, for I could tell I'd slipped slightly behind the clicks from the AED.

Gritting my teeth, I pushed through the vague feeling I might not have enough in the tank to keep up the grueling pace being set by my electronic master. The tingling along the inside of my arms was a precursor to the onset of a massive cramp, but I kept on going knowing a life depended on it. Droplets of sweat began to fall from me and dampen the paper of the pad still glued to the massive chest beneath me; stars at the edge of my vision were a warning of another sort. I began to gasp as though I'd done a hundred meters underwater; the intake of $CO2$ made my vision swim enough that I forced myself to take a deep breath, then another, all the while still maintaining the aggressive compressions mandated by the AED. Time became meaningless as I pushed myself well beyond the limit; my world narrowed to the singular *down-up-down* motion, then narrowed further to the strange freckle that appeared to be growing just of the centerline of Connolly's breastbone.

Just as the stars began to overtake my vision completely, I felt a set of hands at my shoulders; intrinsically understanding, I did two more compressions and then rolled off Connolly as smoothly as was possible and crumpled into a heap on the linoleum beside him. Closing my eyes, everything seemed to ache as though I had run several marathons; as I lay there, gasping, I felt gloved fingers at my wrist, followed by someone prying open an eyelid.

"How do you feel?" asked a female EMT as she flicked some kind of light at me.

"Don't worry about me. Deal with him," I managed to say.

The slight glance away from me told me everything I needed to know.

Oh, shit.

FOURTEEN
DATA

Whatever else I had wanted to do that day pretty much got sidelined as I dealt with the aftermath of Raymond Connolly's unexpected passing. I was mildly surprised by how much bureaucratic paperwork was involved, considering that both the school district and the Rancho Linda public safety departments were all part of the same city; in the end, the wrangling seemed to be mostly about assigning the appropriate amount of liability to the proper department. Part of that assessment required me to go through an extensive interview with RLPD's Internal Affairs officer, followed by a second, equally as intense session with the risk manager for the school district. For the most part it was mundanely routine; save for losing almost six hours in the process, my actions were deemed sufficient and appropriate with no need for further follow-up.

All the same, as I finally exited the high school just as dusk was beginning to fall, I felt incredibly frustrated to have been waylaid by procedural issues while in the middle of my own very time-sensitive investigation. Glancing at my watch, I couldn't help the exasperated eye roll; I'd tried to postpone the interviews until after I'd closed my case, but had been the victim of more than one California statue that had necessitated the delay. Not even my well-connected boss, Chief Michael Gilbert, had been able to extract me from the requirement that I participate fully with the onsite investigators; in the end, I'd opted for expediency through cooperation, though it hadn't truly netted me much.

Unlocking my Camaro, I slid behind the wheel and frowned deeply at my reflection in the rearview mirror. Despite having connected some dots with Connolly, being forced to cool my heels while the investigators determined whether I could have actually saved the poor guy had successfully interrupted the thin investigative thread I'd developed. Tapping at the steering wheel with some irritation, I found I didn't truly know what to do next. Fortunately, the universe chose to have my iPhone interrupt me at that critical moment; pulling it from my pocket, I smiled when I saw it was Alex.

"Hey," I said after answering. "I am insanely late for dinner."

"Not quite yet you aren't," came the reply with a warm chuckle. "Rosie called and said she was delayed slightly; she had to hire a new editor and her meeting was going long. How far out are you?"

"I'm still in Rancho Linda," I replied. "I got held up at the high school."

"Hmm," Alex said thoughtfully. "I might turn the sauce down a bit then."

"You've already made dinner?" I asked. "I thought we were going to do it together."

There was another chuckle. "When you didn't reply to my text messages, I figured something was up and made an executive decision," he said.

"I am so sorry," I replied, startled that I'd essentially ignored him. Tapping at my phone, I saw the list of messages from him and felt my heart sink. For whatever reason, it seemed wrong telling Alex about Connolly; even so, I felt *terrible* about the fact that I was routinely late whenever we had plans.

"Honestly, I figured this might happen, given you are on a case and all," Alex said. "Believe it or not, I've started to adjust to having a cop as my fiancé."

"Somehow, that makes me feel even worse about being late," I said.

"Don't," he said, his voice warm and full of love. "How is the case going?"

"Slowly," I said as I started up the Camaro. "Very, *very* slowly."

"I'm sure it's better than you are making it out to be," he said.

"I wish," I sighed. Looking out of my windshield at the school, the angular architecture of the building sported some unusual periwinkle highlights as the sun slowly sank behind the hills of Rancho Linda. "Tell me your day was good."

"Well," Alex said brightly, "it was, actually."

Something in his tone had me straighten up. "What happened?"

"I think I'd rather wait for you to get home before I tell you," he said.

I felt an eyebrow arch. "You sound too cheery to have been fired."

"Definitely not fired," he laughed.

"Then what?"

"When you get home, *mi amor.* I want to share the news with you in person."

"You sure know how to pique my curiosity," I said.

"I do," he replied. "Maybe you'll get home just a bit faster as a result."

"Quite probably," I chuckled. "I need to swing past the office, then I am on my way."

"You might well get here just as Rosie arrives."

"Stranger things have happened," I said. "Hugs and kisses and may you be naked and waiting for me in bed when I return."

There was a startled chuckle at the other end. "I'm not sure I would be a very good host for our guest if I were to do that."

"I feel like she would understand."

"You know what?" he replied. "I think she would. Nevertheless, I will *not* be doing that."

"Damn."

"However," he added, a sly tone to his voice, "I may or may not be wearing the Speedos you love under my shorts."

"That might be just enough to keep me going," I said, feeling the slight pressure in my groin as confirmation.

"I figured. Hurry home."

"I will."

Backing out of my spot, I pulled around to the exit for the school and then turned in the general direction of the station. Traffic was at its rush hour worst, which for a small city like Rancho Linda meant what would normally be a five-minute jaunt stretched into fifteen. I'd lived in California long enough to normally just roll with the punches, though that afternoon, my impatience began to get the better of me. I could feel my blood pressure was up a few notches by the time I turned into the gated entrance for the lot at the station; tapping my ID against the reader, it went up another point or two when the gate refused to open. Smashing my ID to the reader a second time — and then a third — the damn thing finally chugged into motion; as I pulled through and then drove toward my usual spot, I mentally made a note to speak with Facilities to see if there was an issue with the system again. As with other budget savings measures the Chief and I had been forced to implement, we'd been able to save quite a bit of money by merging our security software into the same system used by the Orange County Sheriff's Office. At least, that had been the plan; from the moment we'd cut over, we'd had a series of glitches that had kept the tech nerds busy racking up thousands of dollars in overtime. Idly, I'd wondered if it was their way to remind all of us that we'd literally be unable to function without them.

Locking up the Camaro, I adjusted my work backpack over my shoulder and then headed for the rear entrance; the booking desk appeared to be deserted as I passed through, though the cubicle farm that was our squad room was bristling with activity. I didn't know how much longer I'd be able to keep the spigot of unlimited overtime open, but as I paused at the edge of a carpet-covered wall, seeing officers hard at work in a space that was normally as desolate as the moon's surface made me smile.

Miles Guernsey chose that moment to appear in the intersection between aisles of the farm and noticed me standing there. Smiling slightly after taking in my outfit, he headed in my direction. "You should just chuck the dress code altogether, Chief," he said.

"Do we even have a code?" I asked with a slight smile.

"We do."

"I must not have seen that part of the personnel manual," I deadpanned before nodding at the blue folder he was holding. "Please tell me you have something."

Miles frowned. "Nothing in particular," he said. "Other than a teenager who's had one too many moving violations."

My eyebrow arched. "You got the results back on the plate for the truck that followed me?"

He nodded as he tapped the folder against the palm of his hand. "Registration was for a mid-2000s Ford F-150; according to the title history, it was purchased via a private sale a year ago by one Blake Dolittle." Miles paused when he saw my expression. "I take it you've heard that name already."

"I have," I nodded. That frisson in my gut appeared again. "He's the star of the Rancho Linda soccer team and son to the principal. And," I smiled slightly, "he happens to lead a student group that had issues with the one run by Daniel Kewley."

Miles frowned. "What sort of issues?"

"They had the audacity to advocate for marginalized kids."

Miles frowned deeper. "Holy shit. Maybe this *is* something."

"I'm not entirely certain he was the one who tailed me," I said. "I didn't get a good look at the driver, just the vehicle."

"It would be one hell of a coincidence that he would have let someone borrow it."

"Indeed," I smiled slightly. "How new was that truck?"

"New enough that it has a GPS tracker built in," Miles replied, correctly intuiting where I was going. "I'll write the warrant when I get back to my desk."

"Route it to Judge Spenser," I said. "And then give Gina's group the VIN."

"Are you *that* sure he'll grant our request?" Miles asked.

"I think so," I nodded. "Especially if we dangle the notion that the flatbed would have been extremely useful in transporting our victim."

"You're thinking Blake is our suspect?" Miles asked. "Isn't he a bit young to be into kidnapping?"

"Age is not a qualifying factor in crime, Detective," I replied.

"True."

"It also won't hurt if you mention on the warrant request the truck was tailing *me*, specifically."

Miles smiled slightly. "No fair leaning into how he likes you, Chief."

"I was thinking more along the lines of reminding him a cop was in personal jeopardy," I replied, slightly worried about how my colleagues were reading the relationship I had with Spense. While the jurist was indeed gay — and had also made no secret of how he felt about me — he was well aware that my heart was already spoken for.

"Of course, Chief," Miles replied, though the way his eyes were dancing with merriment, I wondered if he thought I was covering for the judge. Knowing Miles as well as I did, I wasn't overly worried about how he viewed either of us, but I wasn't as sure about the rest of the department. Realizing I needed to warn him to be slightly more discreet before harm came to either of our reputations, I made a mental note to call Spense and clue him in.

"While we're at it, let's pull everything we can get our hands on for Blake," I said as I started to walk toward my office. "And peel off someone to do a deep dive into a group called Lives Matter; I want to know who they are underwritten by and where they met before they landed at *The Alternative Way* earlier this year."

Miles nodded. "Can do. Anything else?"

"Yeah," I said as I pulled my keys from my microfiber shorts and unlocked my office. "I need a confirmation that Blake had a full-ride scholarship lined up."

"You want a financial workup on the family?" he asked. "That could be a tougher sell to the judge; I don't think we have enough probable cause for that."

I pursed my lips. "No, no we don't," I agreed. "Send someone back to Rancho Linda High School and have them retrieve the press book for the soccer team. Raymond Connolly was showing it to me before he decided to shuffle off this mortal coil; I suspect it's still on the desk where I left it."

"I'll send Jenna," Miles nodded. "How long are you going to be here?"

Glancing at the clock over my door, I frowned. "I needed to leave ten minutes ago."

He smiled. "Then I'll make sure everything is updated in the case system so you can review it tonight."

"A little light reading before bedtime," I smiled. "Perfect."

Miles nodded and bowed out of my office; I sat down and flipped through the mail that had been stacked up on the corner, tossing most of it into the trash. After having had a serial killer mail their list of intended victims to me earlier in the year, I'd been far more vigilant going through my physical inbox. Putting my backpack down on the floor, I pulled out my MacBook and quickly logged into the network to check the virtual equivalent; to my surprise, there was a note there that Peggy's nerds had come up with a number. Frowning at the intricate formula I was seeing, I decided to go to the source directly and dialed the number for the Orange County Morgue.

"Chief Medical Examiner's Office, this is Dana," was the prompt answer after the first ring.

"Dana, it's Vas. Is your boss around?"

"Hey Vas," Dana replied. His warm baritone still held a hint of his native North Carolina. "I think I saw Dr. Pembroke going into the break room a moment ago. Hang on and I'll see if she's free."

"Appreciate it," I said.

I waited a moment on hold before Peggy's voice came on the line. "Got my email, I take it?" she asked somewhat curtly.

"And good afternoon to you, too," I laughed.

"Sorry," she sighed. "It's been a rather long day. I got pulled into an unexpected PM on a high school counselor that apparently dropped dead in his office today."

"Raymond Connolly?"

"Yeah," she answered. "How did you know?"

"I'm afraid I'm the one responsible for his broken breastbone."

"Oh, fuck," she breathed. "I guess your day was as good as mine."

"Hardly," I replied. "Not that it's germane to why I'm calling, but what was his cause of death?"

"Massive cardiac arrest," she replied. "I've rarely seen as much blockage in the major vessels as this guy had, Vas. If you're concerned about not reviving him, there was nothing short of a heart transplant that would have saved him."

"I *was* a little concerned," I admitted. "It's not easy having someone go like that."

"Yeah." She paused for a moment. "So, you're probably trying to figure out what that equation was my nerds gave you."

"I was, yes. Despite having passed calculus, I can't make heads nor tails of it."

"That's why they included a spreadsheet," she said. "It has various scenarios built into it so all you have to do is adjust the variables."

My eyebrows went up as I toggled back to the email. I'd missed the attachment, and quickly clicked into it; as promised, an Excel spreadsheet appeared with somewhat opaque instructions. Scanning them quickly, though, I began to nod as I realized how it worked. "This is rather cool."

"Isn't it?" she replied. There was a trace of pride in her voice. "Anyway, the first tab has their thoughts based on the data you originally provided."

I clicked the link and saw a set of numbers. "This looks like it goes from best case to worst case scenario," I said.

"We wanted you to have a range," she replied, "but for all practical purposes, it would probably be best to focus on the worst of them."

"I don't like this number," I said, tapping at the table with a finger.

"That doesn't change the fact that your kid is probably dead," Peggy replied softly. "I told you earlier it was highly unlikely someone buried in the desert with a limited air supply would last more than a few hours. Our model supports that theory with science."

"Shit," I said, feeling a bit of anger welling up inside me. "Just. *Fuck*."

"Have you considered that your theory might be wrong?" Peggy asked gently. "Maybe the kid is just tied up in the basement of a house somewhere in Rancho Linda."

"I have," I replied. "My gut tells me that's not the case."

"Well," Peggy said after a moment, "your gut is rarely wrong. But—"

"There's a first time for everything," I said quietly. "Yeah. I've thought about that, too."

"I'm sorry, Vas."

I looked at the numbers displayed in black and white on my screen, and couldn't resist going to the median; my heart refused to give up on Daniel still being alive, that the suspect would want him to stay that way for a while. *He's alive*, I thought stubbornly. *But even the median number tells me I'm running out of time...*

"Thanks for this," I said.

"Glad we could help, such as it is. By the way, did you see the results on the DNA test we ran for Gina?"

I blinked. "No," I said, flipping back to the case system. "Which DNA?"

"It was on a ring recovered from the scene. Gina listed it as a wedding band, but it's more akin to rings sold used by those attempting to break a porn addiction."

"Say *what*?" I asked, feeling a bit like we had shifted gears, hard. "Porn addiction?"

"Exactly," she replied. "I can't give you the specifics of what this particular ring represented, but the computer kicked out seventeen support groups online that sold something similar. All of them purport to help keep the subject focused on *not* viewing porn, or if they do, reminding them of their commitment to not do anything about it."

"Is that the modern equivalent of snapping a rubber band against your wrist each time you have impure thoughts?" I asked, feeling my eyebrow arch.

"Pretty much. Though far more expensive, from what the nerds told me."

"Shit," I breathed. "What was the ring size?"

"Ten and change," she replied. "There was a handful of skin cells on the inside of the ring, which is what we collected the DNA from. It came back to a male suspect, no match to anything in our databases. Except," she said with a dramatic pause, "the blood collected at the scene that was *not* your victim."

"Holy hot fuck," I exclaimed. "A god*damned* actual connection to the suspect."

"I would agree," she replied. "Details are in the file. Find someone good and send in a swab."

"I already have an idea in that department," I replied. "I just need to ensure my probable cause stands up."

"Knowing you, I'm sure it will," she chuckled. "Good night."

"Nite," I replied, "and thanks."

"Of course."

I put the handset back into the cradle for my desk phone and stared at the laptop for a moment. After going what felt like an eternity without any movement on the case, suddenly leads were piling up faster than I could process them mentally. Fighting back a yawn, I figured that might have more to do with the fact that I'd been up since two; yielding to the inevitable, I closed down my MacBook and shoved it into my backpack, turned off the lights and locked my office. The cubicle farm was still a hive of activity; despite wanting to check in again and see if they'd developed anything further from the tip lines, I knew my team would reach out the moment something appeared that was actionable. Instead, I made my way back out into the parking lot and my waiting Camaro; the sun had completely set by that point, leaving the task of illumination to the soft white of the sodium lights evenly spaced across the asphalt. As I approached my car, I smiled slightly at how it seemed as though the light I had parked under was acting as a spot; the candy apple red of the paint scheme was rather muted under the watery light, though it did emphasize some of the dings and scratches I'd picked up over the years. Frowning, I slowed down as my eyes went to a particular spot close to my bumper where the paint had been scraped away to the underlying base coat. Crouching to get a better look, my eyes widened when I recognized what I was actually seeing. Pulling out my iPhone, I took a few photos of the spot before texting them to Gina.

Predictably, she called me right back. "Why are you sending me pictures of an Air Tag?" she asked.

"Because it's glued to the back of my Camaro," I replied.

"Holy shit," Gina replied. "*That's* how they tracked you?"

"To a point," I answered. "Isn't the range on these things a bit finicky?"

"It depends. A direct Bluetooth connection can be made when the phone the tag is paired to is within, oh, thirty meters, give or take? Beyond that, a less accurate position estimate can be established if the Air Tag can connect to the Find My network."

I frowned. "That would require Apple devices to be nearby, right?"

"Exactly." Gina laughed. "We *are* in California, though. The odds are pretty good in that department."

"True. Are you still here? I'm in the parking lot at the station."

"I'm not, but I've got a tech on site still. Why?"

"I want to know who planted it," I replied. "And whether it's still active."

"Just pop it off and bring it to our inner sanctum," she said. "It will take a few hours, but we can definitely backtrace it."

"Then they would know I found it," I said. "I want them to think I am blithely ignorant."

There was a long pause. "I'm on my way."

FIFTEEN
NIGHTS OF WINE & ROSIE

As expected, Rosie beat me to the condo and was already settled in at the breakfast bar enjoying a glass of wine when I finally came through the door. Alejandro's only response to my tardiness was a slightly raised eyebrow before I kissed him; coming around the island, I hugged Rosie and then stepped back. Even Chat presented himself for inspection, weaving between my legs with enough fervor that I felt compelled to kneel so I could scratch beneath his chin. Satisfied I had recognized him sufficiently, he sashayed toward the middle of the living room and flopped over to clean a paw, eschewing both the cat tree beside the couch and the small cat-shaped pillow Alex had left in front of the sliding balcony door. Standing, I wondered if it was finally time to tell my fiancé it was time to reevaluate the cat furniture strewn throughout the condo.

"I'm sorry to be so late," I said. "Let me freshen up and then we can have dinner."

"Take your time," Rosie smiled. "Alex has been slowly getting me drunk on the theory I won't press you for details on the case you're working."

I glanced at my fiancé, who reddened up slightly. "He would never."

"I think he would," she chuckled.

"Then I'd better chastise him," I said before glancing toward the bedroom meaningfully.

"Don't be too rough on him," she replied. "He's only trying to help you."

"For all the good it will do," I sighed.

"There's that," she laughed as she held up her quite full wineglass. "Take your time chastising him. Alejandro says he has four bottles of the good stuff; the way this week has gone, I intend to make a dent on at least two of them."

"Rosie—"

"Besides, the ribs haven't entirely warmed up yet," she continued as though I'd not tried to interrupt. "We weren't sure when you were getting here and didn't have them up high enough."

"They need another thirty minutes," Alex said meaningfully. "At least."

My eyebrows went up. "I see," I replied, suddenly understanding what was truly going on and knowing I might have my fiancé to thank for it. "Then I'm going to take a quick shower. I have to get back out to the *Alternative Way* later so I can meet with some students."

"Don't hurry on my account," Rosie smiled.

"We won't," Alex replied under his breath. I resisted the impulse to slap him.

I headed for the bedroom with Alejandro close on my heels; the door had barely closed before his hands were grasping the base of my t-shirt and yanking it over my head. "Hey now," I said as those same hands quickly started to untie my shorts. "What happened to taking our time?"

"The fuck with that," he replied as the fabric slid from my waist to the floor in a quiet *whoosh*. Alex took a moment to appreciate what the vibrantly colored Speedos that had been revealed were framing before shifting those deliciously dark eyes to my face. "You've been on my mind from the moment you told me you were frisky."

I took that as an excuse to look meaningfully at the slight bulge that had appeared in his microfiber shorts. "I can tell," I deadpanned.

I gently reached to his waist and repeated his maneuver, first with the muscle t-shirt and then with his shorts. Pulling him to me, I felt the moment sizzle between us as the fabric of his swimsuit brushed up against my skin; it was nearly electric when he bent his head slightly and drew my nipple into his mouth. The sensation sent a bolt to my groin and in mere seconds, the pressure against the Spandex was nearly intolerable. Deciding there was some merit to continuing to mirror Alex's actions, I shifted slightly so I could graze the surface of his erect nipple with my tongue; the shudder and slight moan the act elicited spurred me forward. Running my hands down the smooth skin of his torso, I began to untie the cord to his Speedos while at the same time beginning to kiss my way up from his pectoral toward a particularly sensitive spot along his neck.

Not to be outdone, I felt Alex's fingers at my belly button and assumed he was following my lead; to my surprise, he simply slid a hand between the waistband of the suit and my skin, then gently wrapped it around my erect cock. The stimulation from him rubbing me into the fabric of the suit was surprisingly intense and had me at the edge nearly instantly; despite my Herculean attempt to focus on my partner, I quickly realized I needed to slow everything down if we had any hope of properly using the full thirty minutes Alejandro had conspired to give us.

Reluctantly, I stepped backwards, then gently pulled his hand out from my suit. At his puzzled expression, I simply nodded toward the master bath and the glassed-in shower visible through the door; his smile appeared when he understood my meaning. Interlacing my hand in his, I pulled him into the bath and, just to provide a little more sound dampening, closed *that* door behind us as well before reaching into the shower and twisting the knob on. Plumes of steam immediately began to fill the small space, threatening to overwhelm the ceiling fan charged with keeping the area from becoming moldy. I stepped into the shower and turned to have my back against the spray from the shower head; Alex stepped in behind me and the slid the glass door closed. The steam immediately fogged it over; with some mirth I watched as handprints on the interior appeared, a leading indicator that the shower figured prominently in our sex life.

The intensely warm water cascading over me immediately soaked through the Speedo, constricting the fabric further and quite literally revealing how eager I was to continue. Alex stepped beneath the flow and pressed his body to mine; the heat from his passion was nearly equal to that of the water, burning with an intensity that never failed to melt my heart. Running a hand through his rapidly matting mound of black curls, I pushed his bangs back enough that I could kiss above a sculpted eyebrow, then beside the strange piercing he'd added at his temple shortly after Labor Day. While he'd decided not to replace the nose ring he'd once had, that hadn't stopped him from considering ever more exotic locations; I'd cringed when he'd mentioned wanting one in an *extremely* intimate location, a reaction that had apparently prevented him from going through with it. I still had nightmares about it, though I loved him enough that I would support him should he ultimately go through with it.

A squeeze at my cock focused my attention enough to realize that somehow both our suits had landed in the corner of the shower; unsure of how I had lost track of time, I caught a sly smile on my fiancé's face and immediately knew that this, too, was part of the plan. Alex had a knack for understanding when I'd become too enmeshed in a case and always seemed to have just the right distraction planned. My heart leapt once again at the thought I would be spending the rest of my life with this amazing man; shifting into alpha mode, I swiveled him against the wall and pressed my lips to his with a vengeance. He returned my passion with passion, grinding his hips against mine as his hands roamed my abs and then shifted to my ass so they could press me even closer.

My pulse began to pound in my ears just as that strange twinge from deep inside appeared; toes curling as my body began to spasm, I managed to keep my eyes open long enough to catch the look of total release when it passed across Alex's face at nearly the same moment. We shuddered against each other a number of times before I found myself with my palms against the tile on either side of his head, breathing as though I'd just swum a fifteen-hundred butterfly. Alex had that satiated expression I had come to know, the one that said his first serving at the buffet had been good, but that there was room for a second helping. Smiling slightly, I devilishly licked a few droplets from his nose with the tip of my tongue before pulling back.

"Hold that thought," I said as I reached for my shower gel. "I do actually need to shower before I head back out."

"Then let me help," Alex replied as he took the sponge from the small alcove and held it out. "It'll go faster with two hands," he added as his eyes danced.

I had my doubts about that, but before I could object, Alex had taken the bottle from my hands and then exquisitely slowly squeezed an amount onto the sponge. It was such a surprisingly erotic motion that I felt myself beginning to have those familiar stirrings; giving myself over to him, Alex slowly began to scrub every square inch of my skin, slyly avoiding the one area that was demanding his immediate attention. By the time he *did* focus on that spot, it took barely a touch of the sponge before my world went white once more, leaving me a spasming, gasping mess with my forehead pressed against the tile.

Turning to face him, I saw he'd pressed his hand to his mouth and was trying hard not to laugh. Frowning, I arched an eyebrow at him. "What on earth is so funny?"

Removing his hand, he rinsed out the sponge as he replied. "You remember that ball gag you joked about making me wear?"

I nodded. "It was a joke for Sean's benefit," I replied. "So you wouldn't make any noise when we made love."

Alex was losing the battle against a bubbling up of laughter. "You... might want to consider something like that in the future," he chuckled. "I'm assuming you have one in your size."

I felt the color rising on my cheeks. "I might," I replied, wondering about the sudden left turn dealing with my brief foray into BDSM with a boyfriend back in Windeport. About the only thing I'd enjoyed about the experience had been the skintight outfits we'd used; being trussed up like a Thanksgiving turkey hadn't turned me on in the least, a realization that had been driven home in the worst way possible during my assault. "Why?"

"Let's just say Rosie might have a good idea about what we were *really* doing in here," he said as he reached around and turned off the water.

The heat on my cheeks felt like it was visible from space. "Fuck."

"I had no idea you could be so *loud*," he teased as he slid the door open and handed me a towel.

"When the mood strikes," I replied weakly.

"I'll say," he chuckled as he toweled off and then wrapped his around his waist. "I'll go do some damage control while you get that hair of yours under control."

I glanced at the fogged over mirror, but it didn't matter; I knew it would take a massive amount of gel to get it back into shape. "Maybe I'll just wear a ball cap tonight."

"Like Hell," he said before adding thoughtfully. "Are you wearing workout gear to your meeting?"

"Maybe."

Running a hand through his damp curls, Alex stepped across to the door and disappeared into the bedroom, returning a moment later with one of my technical fabric headbands. "This would look very sexy," he said, "especially if you allow a bang to hang over the edge."

"I'm not trying to pick up a teenager," I replied, eyeing the stretchy fabric.

"No, but you *are* trying to win their trust," he answered as he held it out to me. "This will help."

"All right," I nodded as I took it from him. "Say, what was your news?"

Alejandro smiled. "I had an unexpected phone call today from the Dean of the Business College," he replied. "She's asked if I would consider being Director of their Career Center."

My eyes widened. "Holy *shit*," I said as I pulled him into a hug. "That's insane! Congratulations!"

"Don't congratulate me yet," he replied. "I still have to go through the competitive interview process. And there are other candidates in the pipeline."

I looked at him askance. "Dude, if she called you directly—"

Alex nodded. "I know, but it would be best not to get my hopes up. I might well just be the diversity interview."

"Since you're Latino?" I asked a bit more harshly than I'd intended. "Or because you're gay?"

"Either," he replied, "or both. Who knows? Higher education is a strangely political place that has its own set of rules."

"That much is true," I said. "Still, your reputation must be somewhat solid for her to even make the call in the first place."

He smiled slightly. "I may or may not have been responsible for her kid landing his dream job."

"There you go," I laughed. "You've got this gig in the bag, then."

"Maybe," he smiled slightly. "I'm torn between excitement and terror, though."

"Why?" I asked as I wrapped my towel around my waist. "You're damn good at what you do."

"I am," he nodded with no trace of ego. "I've just never managed anyone, let alone an entire organization."

I put my hands on my hips. "Seriously? And what do you call coaching a diving team?"

"That's not quite the same as professional staff," he countered.

"How can you say that?" I asked, somewhat exasperated. "Getting teens all on the same page has to be at *least* as difficult as herding cats. Adults are far easier." I smiled slightly. "Trust me on this — I've been a manager, in some form or another, for a long time now. It's not entirely different than what you have to do to goad someone up the ladder of a ten meter."

"Well, you might be right," he replied, though I could still hear the self-doubt.

"You'll be brilliant at it," I said as I put my hands on his shoulders.

"It will mean some late nights every now and then," Alex said. "And some travel."

"As long as you get to bring your husband on the trips," I smiled as I turned back to the now less-foggy mirror, "I'm all in. I've seen some of the destinations you academics like to go to. Orlando. Honolulu. Phoenix. Far better than our police conventions."

"Are they, now," he said. I could see his white teeth as he smiled.

"Oh yes," I replied as I dug my pomade out of the drawer and started to massage it into my unruly hair. "Last year we were in Seattle, remember? During the rainy season."

"Must have been cheaper," he chuckled. "Nice to know I have at least one vote of confidence."

"You have far more than that," I replied, looking over my shoulder. "I hope you know that."

His eyes went soft. "Yeah," he nodded. "I do. I'm gonna find some warmups to change into and get back out to our guest."

"I'll join you shortly."

Alex eyed my hair. "I think not. But hurry if you can."

My heart did that little pitter-patter it always did when he smiled his special Vas smile before ducking out of the bathroom; I returned to my task and, unfortunately, discovered my partner was right as always for it took way longer than I would have liked to transform back into street-appropriate Vasily. While I didn't miss the hell that had been the long ponytail I had worn for years, the amount of effort it took to make my hair look casual and carefree had me pining away for the simplicity of gathering up my long hair and quickly tying it into a flip. I had to admit the sliver-gray coloring was beginning to grow on me; I still had a few weeks before I returned to the salon chair and had to decide whether to bleach it back to my usual surfer persona, or to continue to keep it in Captain Pike style. Shrugging, I decided it was the least of my current problems before wandering out into the master bedroom to find a clean set of workout clothes for my evening sojourn. In the end, I opted for a pretty standard running outfit: microfiber shorts over my favorite electric blue compression tights and a muscle t-shirt in a complimentary shade. I wasn't entirely sure *why* I wanted to convey the impression that I had popped into the student meeting on my way to the gym, but as Alex had correctly intuited, I *was* trying to downplay my role as a police officer in the hopes they would talk more freely. Strictly speaking, I was enough of a regular at *The Alternative Way* I suspected the effort was unnecessary, but then again, it couldn't hurt to at least appear more approachable than the average police officer.

When I rejoined Alex and Rosie, they were leaning across from each other on the breakfast bar and had apparently just shared some sort of comedic moment. Alex caught my arrival and straightened up quickly. "Wine?" he asked.

"Please."

He reached over to the bottle that appeared to be half-full and poured a nice quantity into a glass that he pushed across to me. "Ribs are ready; I've got about six minutes before the rolls will be done. Rosie's chef also provided us with fresh coleslaw, a tossed salad, potato salad and enough barbecue sauce we'll never need to buy another bottle."

I didn't need to look at our guest to know she had that twinkle in her eye indicating it likely hadn't been the chef that had insisted on the extras. There were times when I felt like her latent mothering instincts came out with the two of us. I nonetheless turned and arched an eyebrow.

"Rosie, there is enough food here for the entire swim team," I accused.

"You can put the leftovers in the fridge, right?" she asked.

"That's not the *point*," I said. "How on earth—"

"Besides, given the number of calories the two of you burn through daily, I imagine you could use some extra snacks after your workouts."

I couldn't help but glare at her. "Wait, are you actually trying to fatten us up?" I asked.

"Hardly," she smiled as she took a sip at her wine. Rosie's eyes dropped meaningfully to my midriff. "I need to maintain the view at all costs."

"I'm not sure that isn't worse," I sighed. While I knew where we stood with the millionaire author, every now and then I wondered if she appreciated us *more* as eye candy.

Alex cleared his throat. "If you're finished worrying about your waistline, dinner is ready."

I rolled my eyes. "Seriously? I'm not worried about my waistline, my love."

"That," he said as he leaned across the counter to kiss me on the cheek, "is the first lie you've told me in our relationship."

Subconsciously pressing my hands against my abs, I felt my cheeks warm slightly. Despite all of my efforts and now nearly two years of professional help, I still had body image issues that were a key reason *why* I spent so long at the pool. And the gym. And on the running trails around Rancho Linda at lunchtime. So, in a sense, Alex was right — as usual. His dark eyes narrowed slightly as he saw the realization in mine, and I sighed again.

"Those ribs smell divine," I said as I pointedly took a plate from Alex and pulled out a portion with the tongs. "Thanks for dinner."

"Of course," Rosie said.

I'd not purchased the condo with the intent of entertaining guests, so unlike other floorplans in the building, there really wasn't space set aside for a dining room table of any kind. That had been driven home when Sean and Suzanne had stayed with us back in February; while they'd been more than comfortable on the pull-out couch, mealtimes had pretty much meant all four of us had hovered around the breakfast bar, snagging whatever space we could. It had been a bit of a godsend that Sean had spent much of his recovery at Rosie's, for it had become quite evident my single-bedroom unit was exceptionally crowded with that many adults. When it was just Alex and me, it was simply cozy, even after adding Chat to the mix. And, honestly, I'd never thought about hosting *anyone* before Alex came into my life; between his family and my extended one, there were now more than a few people interested in spending a long weekend in Anaheim with us, making me think seriously about finding a larger replacement for my beloved condo.

The three of us chatted companionably over the excellent food and made good progress decreasing the inventory of Olive Garden wine; knowing I still had to drive back to Rancho Linda forced me to limit myself to a single glass that I carefully nursed. To my everlasting delight, though, Alejandro seemed to be in a celebratory mood and matched Rosie glass for glass. He rarely got drunk, but when he did, seemed to become this cute teenager version of his personality, one that smiled twice as much and didn't believe in personal space of any sort. By the time we wound up on the loveseat with slices of the Key Lime pie that had been snuck into the bottom of the proverbial picnic basket, Alex was essentially in my lap with one arm draped across my shoulders. It was a tough position to actually eat anything, but then again, that didn't truly seem to be the point.

Rosie had, oddly, continued to sit on one of the barstools for the breakfast bar, though she'd turned around so she could lean her back against the counter. As she sipped from her glass again, she got that look she always wore when she was about to interrogate me over a case; groaning inwardly, I realized far too late that though she may have been matching Alex glass-for-glass, she was in no way inebriated enough to be distracted from her mission.

"I was talking with one of the crime scene techs today," she began, watching me carefully as she spoke. "Seems like I might get my house back by tomorrow — or Friday at the latest."

I nodded. "It feels like we've found everything we're gonna find at this point, but don't hold me to that," I replied. "Evidence may suddenly pop up that requires us to revisit the scene. You might want to hold off on having your staff clean for a bit."

"Duly noted," she said. Swirling her quarter-glass of wine around in a slow circle, she seemed to be considering her next words carefully. "If you need it," she ultimately began, "I know someone at the LAPD that might be useful to you."

My eyebrows went up, for it was completely out of character for my friend to question my investigative chops. "Rosie, I don't think I need outside help."

"But you might need a thermal imaging camera," she replied.

I felt Alex shift. "Thermal *what*?" he asked, his words a bit slurred.

"Thermal imaging camera," I replied softly, keeping my eyes on Rosie. "How the *hell* did you find out about our working theory?"

Rosie simply sipped at her wine, wearing a devilish smile. "I've already made the initial inquiries, the helicopter can be ready to go in under an hour."

"I'm lost," Alex said as he slipped off my lap and onto the cushion beside me. "Why would you need a thermal thingie? Is someone sick?"

"Not quite," I said, slightly ignoring my fiancé. "The department can't afford that," I replied to Rosie. "And even if we could, I have no idea where we would use it."

"It's taken care of," Rosie said. "And I have faith that you will soon know."

"Will *someone* please explain what the *fuck* we're talking about?" Alex demanded angrily. At least, he was *attempting* to be angry; the way he was slightly swaying as he spoke made it hard to take him seriously. It seemed prudent to pull the plate of Key Lime pie from his hands before it slipped to the rug and set it on the end table. "Why the *fuck* would you need a thermometer? On a helicopter?"

"A thermal imaging camera can be used to chart variations in temperatures," I said evenly. Alex's glassy eyes were a bit unfocused, but he also seemed to be hanging on my every word. "Rancho Linda PD doesn't have one, but larger departments—"

"Like the LAPD," Rosie interjected.

I glared at her. "Like LAPD often have them. Usually, they are used to detect victims in a building collapse after an earthquake, or lost hikers in one of the state recreational areas. Their body heat will stand out on such a scanner against the concrete or the trees."

Alex frowned. "You're not investigating a lost hiker."

"No," I nodded before glaring at Rosie again. "But as Rosie seems to have figured out, there is a chance that *my* victim is... somewhere in the desert."

Smiling smugly at the revelation she was right, Rosie looked at Alex. "And if the camera is mounted on a helicopter, someone could conceivably fly over the desert looking for the victim."

"Exactly," I sighed.

"So, could you use a thermal imaging camera?" Rosie asked.

"You *know* I can," I replied testily. "Otherwise, you wouldn't have gone to all this trouble. Who the *fuck* told you?"

Rosie shrugged. "I know people. And I know how to *talk* to people."

"That is true," I said before narrowing my eyes. "It was someone at the Coroner's office, wasn't it? Outside of myself and the Chief Medical Examiner, they're the only ones who know about our working theory."

"I'll never reveal my sources," she replied as she put the wineglass down on the counter and stood. "My ride back to the mansion will be arriving shortly," she added as she carefully bent to retrieve her purse from where it was leaning against the breakfast bar. Unzipping it, she fished out a business card and held it out to me. "Call this number when you are ready."

Still annoyed, I nonetheless stood and went over to her; taking the card, I jammed it into my shorts without looking at it. "Thanks again for dinner," I said pointedly.

Rosie's expression changed slightly, and with it the seeming realization that, despite our deep friendship, she might have overstepped for once. "My pleasure," she replied easily, though I wasn't sure if she was referring to the dinner or the offer of thousands of dollars of police equipment and time. "I can see myself out."

"I can walk—"

"No," she said, cutting me off. "See you at the pool in the morning?"

"Yes," I said after a moment.

"Good," Rosie said. She seemed to be on the brink of saying something but thought better of it and instead looked over at Alex. "Good night."

"*Buenas noches,*" he replied cheerfully.

And with that, she was gone. I went back to the couch and sat, then leaned my head back against the cushion of the couch, squeezed my eyes closed against the headache that seemed to be forming and blew out a breath. I'd gratefully accepted help from Rosie on multiple occasions; why was I so upset about *this* particular offer? I rubbed at my grainy contacts and slowly began to chuckle.

She outfoxed me, I thought. *Outfoxed me in a way that I should have seen coming. And that is why I am so annoyed; it's her nature to lend a hand — besides, the fucking kidnapping happened in her home! No wonder she's so plugged into my investigation. I should have seen it coming — I have to be far more tired than I realized.*

"Shit," I sighed loudly. "I think I could have handled that better."

The soft snores coming from beside me in response had me turn toward Alejandro; he'd somewhat impossibly curled into the arm of the loveseat and was dead to the world, his face had that untroubled angelic expression I loved waking up to each morning. Chat, ever the opportunist when it came to snuggling, had managed to sprawl luxuriously along Alejandro's side and was similarly fast asleep. Slightly jealous that our feline fur baby had temporarily supplanted me, I nonetheless resisted the urge to slide him off my fiancé and instead re-evaluated just how much wine Alex had to have imbibed. As he'd not been all that tipsy during our escapade in the shower, it was clear that in that brief period before I'd reappeared in the kitchen Rosie had rather devilishly ensured my partner was thoroughly and completely sloshed. Arching an eyebrow, I wondered slightly if that had been intentional; she had actually tried to refill my own glass a number of times during the meal, but I had waved her off due to my having to drive back to Rancho Linda.

She wasn't trying to get Alex drunk, I thought with a slight smile. *Rosie knew I wasn't going to like her suggestion and was trying to soften me up for the delivery. Poor Alex wound up being caught in the crossfire.*

I sighed again, for if past were prologue, I'd be grabbing a blanket from the closet and letting Alejandro sleep it off on the couch; waking him just to move him to the master bedroom was out of the question. Besides, I had a suspicion I was going to need some of my own cuddling once I returned from the mall; the loveseat had proven to be quite the spot for such activities. As I carefully surveyed Alejandro's amazing body, I felt myself begin to react physically and tried to tamp down some of my more lecherous thoughts; draping myself over his slumbering form was likely the best I was going to get that evening.

Guess I won't be talking to him about our conflicting Disney World wedding plans tonight, either, I thought with a wry smile. *Though maybe I need to take a page out of Rosie's book on that — it may be easier to discuss after he's had a few glasses of wine.* Fingering one of the earrings that had appeared after the shoe had been on the other foot, I felt the wry smile turn a bit sly. *It wouldn't be the first time one of us had agreed to something while three sheets to the wind, now would it? Fair is fair, mi amor.*

I gently kissed Alex on the forehead, carefully slid off the couch and then headed out for my meeting at *The Alternative Way*.

Sixteen
Meet the Teens

The last dregs of rush hour made getting across Anaheim and onto the 57 something of a drag, but once I was on the freeway, traffic was flowing far freer than normal. Enough that I felt somewhat safe in answering Gina Carruthers when her name popped up on my display. Eyeing the clock on my dashboard as I triggered the Bluetooth function for the Camaro, I felt myself frown when she came on the line.

"Shouldn't you be home?" I asked.

"I could ask you the same," she laughed in reply.

"Our work is never done, is it?"

"Never," she agreed. "I thought you might want an update — additional lab results trickled in this afternoon, and I noticed you weren't haunting the file the way you normally do."

"I was... distracted," I replied, feeling my face heat up yet again at the particular nature of the distraction in question.

"By a tall, dark and handsome diver?" was the instant reply, making the heat on my cheeks a bit more intense. "Who wouldn't be?"

"Indeed," I said gamely. "What came back?"

"I think Peggy already called you about the DNA from the ring," she started. "And how it matches what was in the second sample of blood taken from the scene."

"Yes," I replied.

"Then I'll skip to the good stuff. The motor oil we collected on the driveway was unremarkable save for the fact that it is a brand typically used by used car dealers."

I felt myself frown. "That's not especially *good*."

"I'm not done yet," she chuckled. "This particular brand is a no-name repackaging of a far better known national brand; it also happens to be one used in vehicles more than ten years of age."

"All right, but still not seeing the *good* here," I said. "There have to be thousands of vehicles in that category in Orange County alone."

"What if I told you it was the right viscosity for pickup trucks?" she said. "And that we traced this *particular* motor oil to Red's Fair Deals of Orange, who happens to have gotten a gonga deal on a few barrels of the stuff last year."

"I'd say you saw my BOLO for Blake Dolittle's wheels in the file," I said as my eyebrows went up. "Assuming that's where he bought his Ford?"

"Yep," she replied proudly. "Red's Fair Deals was listed as the seller on the sales agreement."

"Well, shit," I said. "Can you tie that specific motor oil to the pickup?"

"Find me the truck and we'll test what's in the engine against the sample at the scene," she said. "Assuming he's not had an oil change yet."

"I'm guessing he hasn't if you matched the oil to the dealership."

"Your suspect appears to be the typical teen driver," Gina said. "All about the wheels while ignoring the maintenance."

"Let's hope. Thanks, Gina — the truck just moved higher on my to do list."

"We aim to please," she laughed. "Talk later."

The ending of my call with Gina corresponded with turning off of the 57 at my usual Rancho Linda exit; coasting down the off-ramp, I shifted lanes and turned in the direction of the Mall. I was a little surprised at how full the parking lot was, given it was a random Wednesday in early November; we were still a few weeks away from the crazy shopping season kicked off by Black Friday, so I was somewhat curious as to what had drawn the attention of so many people. Finding a spot, I locked up the Camaro and half-jogged across the pavement to the entrance I favored for *The Alternative Way*; it led directly to the food court, a place that I usually found during my morning sojourns to the café was usually overflowing with silver-haired senior citizens enjoying breakfast after making a few circuits in their sneakers. That night, the court seemed packed with an incredible number of elementary school-aged kids; every table was full, and there were lines six to ten people deep for each of the fast food counters. Pausing at the pony wall that was essentially the demarcation between the walkway and the seating area, I scanned the crowd trying to make sense of what was going on; I was no nearer to figuring it out when I heard someone chuckle beside me.

"Quite the sight, isn't it?"

I turned to see Janice Dolittle standing there in black yoga leggings and a pullover sweatshirt bearing the Rancho Linda High School logo. "It is," I said. "Do you have any idea what's going on?"

"Middle School Perfect Attendance Night," she said, nodding to the crowd. "Usually it's later in November, but the way Thanksgiving fell this year forced the boosters to move it."

My eyebrows went up. "A celebration, then? For, what, the first quarter?"

"Exactly," she answered. "The boosters give each eligible kid a ten-dollar gift card, then work with the food vendors to mark down the meals slightly just for the evening."

"Wow," I said. "The best I got was a paper certificate with a star-shaped sticker affixed to the front."

"Times change, Chief," she laughed. "These kids want more tangible awards."

"Apparently," I smiled before glancing meaningfully back at the kids. "Is one of yours in that melee?"

She nodded. "My youngest son. He's in seventh grade."

"How many kids do you have?" I asked.

"Just the two," she replied. "Blake and Edward."

I wondered for a moment if that was some sort of joke, and realized it wasn't. "Well," I smiled again, "kudos to you for raising them. Being a parent these days seems to be quite the challenge."

"Not interested in having kids of your own, Chief?"

"Nope," I replied, before I realized it was a conversation I'd never fully had with Alejandro.

While he'd been an only child, I was aware that his extended family was rather massive; it had led to some discussions about who might be left off the guest list of our wedding. I wondered if he might feel some pressure to add to the family line in a way that I didn't, and worried slightly that other than a few stray comments here or there, I had no clue what my fiancé might be feeling on the subject. *Having* children as a gay couple was a bit more of a challenge, of course; still, it wasn't entirely uncommon now — especially in Southern Cal. I made a mental note to bring it up before turning my focus back to Janice.

I must have had an attentive enough expression despite checking out for a moment for I quickly found she'd continued to chat amiably. The woman standing beside me seemed a universe apart from the cool professional I'd frequently encountered at the high school; was that even a hint of a smile I was seeing as she related some story about how her kids had captured a frog in their backyard years earlier? If I'd never encountered her as a school principal, I'd have assumed she was a typical soccer mom, waiting for her kid to finish up before whisking them away in the minivan to the next stop on the schedule that evening. It was hard reconciling the two personalities; she saw some-thing on my face in that regard, for she paused in her story about

Blake "washing" the car with a can of black Rust-Oleum and smiled slightly.

"Expecting the suit, were we?" she asked not unkindly.

"Frankly, yes," I replied honestly. "How much effort does it take to not bring Principal Dolittle home each night?"

"Thirty minutes on the treadmill," she laughed, "and a large glass of Pinot."

"I can actually relate to that," I replied.

"The wine?" she asked with a smile. "Or the workout?"

"The workout," I nodded.

Dolittle eyed me for a moment. While I'd seen plenty of men undress me mentally, it always felt a little odd when I saw a woman do it; more so when the woman in question was a school principal. I sorted through our various conversations over the years and realized with a start she might not actually know I was gay; that was confirmed when she spoke again. "Based on those muscles, it seems safe to assume you spend a *lot* of time unwinding from work."

Slightly unsettled that she appeared to be hitting on me, I smiled my model smile to hide my discomfort. "I never stopped doing the work-outs that landed me in Beijing," I replied. "My fiancé has the same prob-lem, though as a diver, I happen to think his routine is far more demanding than mine." I noted how her eyes widened slightly at the pronoun I'd slipped into the sentence. "You should see the drawer of athletic bandages we have. The two of us are a matched set."

"Clearly," she laughed, though the mirth seemed a bit forced.

Curious why she had taken her particular tact, I looked back at the crowd and phrased my next question carefully. "Do you share custody with your husband?"

I felt her stiffen slightly beside me. "No," she replied after a long moment. "He moved to Washington, D.C. to take a position with the Education Department. Shuttling Blake and Edward back and forth didn't make any sense, so I have full custody."

"Then I am even more in awe," I said as I turned back toward her.

"Raising two teenage boys *and* handling a school full of hormones? There has to be some sort of award for that."

Dolittle smiled slightly. "One can hope."

"Is Blake here with you tonight?" I asked casually.

"No," she replied.

"Oh," I said. "I thought the social group he was part of met at the *Alternative Way* on Wednesday?"

Something washed across her face. "It did, yes."

I arched an eyebrow at the past tense and feigned ignorance. "No longer?"

"No," was her terse answer.

I nodded. "That's too bad," I continued. "I volunteer there regularly; in fact, that's why I'm here tonight." I paused. "I'm speaking with one of the groups there and assumed it was Blake's."

"They were kicked out some time ago," Dolittle said. "I don't think they've found a new spot, so the meetings moved to online."

"Now that is a bummer," I said. "It can't quite be the same."

"It isn't."

"What happened? If you don't mind my asking."

Dolittle continued to look out across the food court while she considered her words. "I think there was a misunderstanding between the owners and Blake's group," she said.

"Over what?"

"No clue," she replied shortly. All traces of the flirtatious version of Dolittle had been subsumed beneath her normal principal persona. It would have had more effect were she not dressed so casually. "At the end of the day, despite appearances it turned out *The Alternative Way* was far from being open and affirming."

"That seems harsh."

Dolittle shrugged. "I don't think those women wanted their worldview challenged in any way. Removing Blake and his group kept their little pinko utopia intact."

It was a significant challenge to keep my expression neutral at her casual slander of the safe space my friends worked so hard to maintain. "Did you try and talk to them?"

"What would be the point?" she countered. "It's a private establishment. They can have who they please and bar who they don't."

"True," I said after a moment. "I'm sorry it didn't work out."

"I'm not," she said. "Nor is Blake."

"I understand Blake might be a top prospect for Major League Soccer," I continued. "That's quite an achievement."

"That's the hope. He's worked pretty hard to stand out to the scouts."

"I'll bet," I replied sagely. "I only had one team I needed to stand out to when I was trying to make the Olympics. I'm glad I had a coach who understood the environment and could guide me."

Dolittle seemed to thaw ever so slightly and nodded. "His travel team coach is the same guy who ran the school team at St. Frederik's Prep," she said. "It helps to have those contacts in the league."

"St. Frederik's Prep?" I asked, feigning ignorance again. "I don't think I've ever heard of them. That's not here in Rancho Linda, is it?"

"No," she shook her head. "It's on the fringes of Palm Springs."

"Now that must have been one hell of a daily commute," I smiled.

"He stayed on campus during the school year," she replied. "Home on holidays, of course."

"Of course." I frowned slightly. "Why did he return to Rancho Linda?"

"The school wasn't a good fit for him," she answered quickly.

"That happens. It must be nice to have him back home."

"Yeah," she said. The lack of enthusiasm spoke volumes.

"Speaking of Blake, maybe you can help me out," I continued casually. "Was he at the Halloween party up to Rosie Frankenhoffer's place on Monday?"

Dolittle's reaction to my question — or attempt to *not* react — also spoke volumes. "I have no idea. He's eighteen now and doesn't really need my permission to do anything."

I smiled. "Ah. The freedom of young adulthood."

"I suppose we all remember those first steps into responsibility," she said.

"Not me," I laughed. "I was pretty much either in the pool or doing homework."

"Mm-hmm."

"I didn't even have a car until I was out of college," I added. "And my first one was a beat up Civic. Nothing like the pickup Blake has."

"It was a gift," Dolittle replied absently. "From his father."

"Nice," I said. "A bit of parental guilt in that, I'll bet."

"Yeah," Dolittle said.

"Any idea why he used it to follow me around Rancho Linda?"

Dolittle's head snapped in my direction. "I'm sorry?"

I let my expression harden slightly. "You heard me."

"Are you accusing my son of something?"

"I'm just asking questions," I replied.

"I wouldn't know," she replied after a moment.

"Fair enough; he is eighteen, after all, and a *legal* adult," I said, watching her face carefully. "I imagine your answer would be the same if I were to tell you he appeared at my hotel in Palm Springs yesterday."

Her face betrayed her shock. "Palm Springs? Why on earth would he be *there*?"

"To send a message," I said simply.

"A *message*?" she asked, incredulous. "You're making Blake sound like some sort of mafia enforcer."

"I'd not thought of it in those terms, but that's an accurate analogy. He was rather effective, I have to admit."

"You're not making any sense," she replied. "What the hell are you talking about?"

I stepped a bit closer and dropped my voice. "If you see Blake tonight, please let him know that I will be speaking with him soon." I paused and let an edge into my voice. "Very, *very* soon."

"Is that some sort of *threat*?"

"No," I said as I started to turn toward *The Alternative Way*. "Just a courtesy warning."

I left Janice Dolittle more-or-less spluttering behind me. I rarely took satisfaction in needling people in that manner, but something in the way she had nearly defended the actions of her son had rubbed me the wrong way. It wasn't good that it had also goaded me into over-playing my hand slightly, but as I walked down the curving mall corridor to the bookstore/café, deep inside, it had felt like the right move to make. Up to that point, we'd been playing by a warped set of rules governed by what I assumed was a troubled teenager; turning the tables slightly might force Blake to make a move that he wasn't prepared for, one that might *finally* give me the edge I needed. And as I came to the entrance for the café, I was increasingly convinced that Blake was my guy.

Pausing at the entrance for a moment, I replayed that evening at the Marriott in Palm Springs and tried to put the face I'd seen in the soccer yearbook to the shadowy figured who had threatened us. The build had been right, but neither Alex nor I had gotten a good look at our stalker. Shaking my head, I continued into the store, my gut telling me it didn't really matter at that point. I had the scent of blood in my nose now, and nothing was going to stop me from following the trail.

Anne was standing at the coffee bar and waved me over; the rest of the bookstore was deserted, save for a few patrons perusing the magazine rack. Heading in her direction, I smiled when I saw the ceramic mug appear on the counter, paired with a chocolate eclair I knew her partner had likely baked just for that evening. I shook my head as my eyes watched the steam rise from the mug.

"Like I really need that," I sighed.

"You burn off more calories in one workout than Zoe and I do in a week," Anne chuckled as she pushed the goodies across to me. "The kids are in the second meeting room."

"Thanks," I said as I lifted the mug from the counter with one hand, and then took the small plate in the other.

I carefully made my way through the aisles to the door leading into the inner sanctuary that was the heart of *The Alternative Way*. Pushing through the curtain, I smiled as I heard the muted voices wafting toward me from further down the hallway; Anne and her partner had carved out a series of safe spaces from their stockroom, allowing their sponsored groups a privacy they wouldn't enjoy anywhere else. Wandering down the hallway, I passed the pair of small dressing rooms where Anne had magically removed the last of the eye makeup that had been part of Sean's costume for the comic book convention we'd been attending; I'd not had the heart to tell him that the sunglasses hadn't been hiding it in the least. Beside that was the actual office Anne and Zoe used to do the administrative work for the store, and then at the very end, the actual storeroom for books destined for the floor. Two doors with translucent panels were on the other side of the hallway, each guarding a small conference-room sized meeting area; the light was on behind the second, which I stopped in front of before gently knocking.

The door opened immediately, revealing a high school aged Latino whose hair had been shaved nearly to the scalp; earrings dangled from either ear, which, oddly, were a compliment to the surprisingly full beard gracing the angled face. Sharp eyes looked me over before they moved back to my face.

"Deputy Chief?" they asked. The voice was deeply masculine, but considering where I was, I was loathe to make gender judgments without additional cues.

"Yes," I nodded. "I'm a bit late — my apologies."

"It's all good," they said as they pulled the door wider and motioned for me to enter. "Please, make yourself comfortable."

I stepped inside and scanned the room; like everything else about *The Alternative Way*, the space was warm and welcoming, featuring comfortable couches and a few padded armchairs. A low coffee table was in the center of the room and was filled to overflowing with baked goods accompanied by two tall thermal carafes presumably containing Anne's special blend of coffee. I made my way over to an empty armchair and sat down, then placed my eclair on the small side table next to me before looking back up at the set of expectant faces. I'd spoken to this particular group a number of times, of course, though aside from Daniel, the names of the rest of the members hadn't taken up residence in my brain. Fortunately, they were all wearing small name badge stickers that evening.

"Thank you for allowing me to stop by this evening," I said as I carefully made eye contact with each of them. "I'm sure by now you are all aware of the situation. I'm here to answer any questions you might have and to assure you that we are doing everything we can to locate Daniel."

Several of the members shifted uncomfortably, but no one spoke.

"Let me begin by telling you a bit about where we are in the investigation," I continued. "I will try to be as frank and forthcoming as I can, but remember that I'm not going to be able to disclose every aspect of how my Department is working the case."

There were some nods; the teen that admitted me seemed to be watching me with special interest; glancing quickly at their name badge, I realized it bore the name of the person Daniel had mentioned was the vice-chair of the group, Francisco. "Daniel Kewley was taken against his will during the Halloween party close to midnight on Monday night. We have evidence to suggest that he might have been overpowered by his attacker; I also suspect strongly that Daniel is no longer in Rancho Linda."

"Is he still alive?" a young girl asked. Her dreadlocks shifted as she spoke.

"I believe there is a chance he is," I replied. *One that is fading with every hour lost.*

"Where is he, then?" she pressed.

I took a sip of my coffee. "Does this group have any sort of connection to Palm Springs?"

Francisco spoke up from where they were leaning against the wall. "It's outside of Orange County," he observed. "But we have a companion organization up there and often assist each other with our community service."

I nodded. "How long has the relationship existed?"

Francisco shrugged. "Before my time, man. Long enough that we are *familia*."

I smiled. "I get the concept. What was the last event the two groups worked on jointly?"

"St. Frederik's took in a group of teens who crossed the border in San Diego," a smooth-skinned teen replied. With long hair, painted nails and tastefully applied makeup with complimentary eyeshadow, I suspected they were either trans or bi. "We did a fundraiser down here and then used the money to purchase clothing and other necessities for the migrants."

"St. Frederik's?" I asked, feeling another connection snapping into place.

The teen nodded. "It's one of the larger Catholic parishes in the area, so it usually does the most in the community."

"Doesn't it also have a school attached to it?"

"Yeah," Francisco interjected. "A prep academy for aspiring sports stars. They charge exorbitant tuition to the rich and well connected, and use the funds for their mission work."

My eyebrows went up. "That's an interesting take on 'help thy neighbor.'"

"It's quite effective," the teen with the painted nails smiled. A small stud became visible in their lower gum when they did, which made me wince internally. "Anyway, once we had all of the items, several of us drove up to the church and gave them to the nuns running the shelter."

"When was that?"

"Two weeks ago," Francisco said.

"And Daniel was the lead?"

"Yes."

"And that was in addition to the normal service you do here?"

"Yes," Francisco replied. "We have a dedicated shift at the halfway house St. Elspeth's runs — usually on Saturday evening — where we help the nuns in the kitchen."

"That's the one for teens in recovery?" I asked.

"Not only them," the young girl who'd spoken earlier replied. "They have their fair share of undocumented migrants as well." She glanced at Francisco quickly. "In fact, the migrants outnumber residents two to one these days."

My eyes widened. "I knew the situation was bad," I said, "but not *that* bad."

"Between the cartels and the economy, there's not much hope for a normal life south of the border," Francisco said. "Parents pay an unbelievable sum to send their kids on a risky journey to a possibly better future."

I thought a bit about the odd juxtaposition of people like Janice Dolittle paying top dollar to send their kids to a sports prep academy so their children could get a leg up in the world versus the more desperate position the migrant teenagers were coming from — and how much, not just in money, it was costing their family. Right behind that was the strange realization that Blake had to have gotten into some serious shit to get sent back to his mother in Rancho Linda. Making a personal visit to St. Frederik's seemed like a logical item to add to my to do list, if for no other reason than to confirm it was the very elite school I thought it was. Getting anything out of the administrators up there about Blake would be difficult; getting a warrant, nearly impossible given the school was well outside of my jurisdiction.

Something else was hovering on the periphery of my brain, though. *There's a connection between Daniel and Blake,* I thought. *And it intersects at that school. Damn! Wasn't there something in that profile from Verna about the suspect righting old wrongs? I've got to get to that school!*

I realized Francisco had been talking and focused on him again. "— thought there might be trouble," he was saying.

It took a moment for me to understand the context. "Between KOTO and Lives Matter?"

"Yes," he nodded.

"I take it meeting at the same time didn't work out particularly well."

"Not in the least," he nodded again. "Their leader — Blake Dolittle — is a racist homophobe intent on ridding this country of anyone that doesn't look like him."

"Lives Matter," the teen with the eyeshadow snorted. "Only if you're white and cis."

"Did they threaten you? Any of you?" I asked, looking around the room.

Slowly, almost all of them nodded. Francisco waited a moment before speaking. "All of us go to Rancho Linda High," he said. "Crossing Blake wasn't an option, not with his mother protecting him."

My eyes widened. "What did he do?"

Francisco looked at the teen with the eyeshadow; they sighed and then reached into the small purse they had on the couch beside them and pulled out a small packet of makeup remover wipes. Pulling one from the pack, they made quick work of wiping away their makeup. I tried not to react when the bruises were revealed, including the remnants of what had to have been one hell of a black eye.

Vibrating with anger, I worked at keeping my voice steady. "When did that happen?"

"Two weeks ago," they said as they crumpled up the wipe and tossed it across the room to the trashcan.

I nodded slowly. "After you delivered the care package to Palm Springs?"

"Yes," Francisco said.

"Who else?" I asked, slowly looking around the room. Multiple hands went up, increasing my anger. Looking back at Francisco, I watched him fold his arms against his chest. "Even Daniel?"

"Yes," he nodded.

"Was this brought to *anyone's* attention?" I asked. "A priest? A teacher? Anne or Zoe?"

"We didn't want Anne to know," Francisco said. "She was already in enough hot water. That group of moms is suing *The Alternative Way* over Lives Matter being kicked out."

"Shit," I said, wondering why Anne had left that little fact out.

"We did have a plan," he continued, before shaking his head. "Daniel had pulled something together and had an appointment with Dolittle on Tuesday."

"Tuesday," I sighed. "The day *after* he disappeared?"

"Yes," he nodded. Francisco paused again. "Do you think that's why he was taken?"

"Among other reasons," I replied softly.

I glanced at my watch and realized the chances of getting home that evening — let along grabbing a few hours of sleep — were bottoming out around zero. Looking around the room again, I felt the anger just beneath my breastbone beginning to bloom again, and I let a tiny portion of it out into my voice.

"This is not acceptable behavior in our society," I said. "Not under any circumstances."

"We're not exactly in a position to make it stop," the teen who had wiped their eyeshadow off said dejectedly.

"No, but I *am*," I replied. "If you ever feel threatened again, come to me directly. There are legal avenues to correcting this that my department is able to take."

"Cops don't tend to protect people like us," Francisco observed. "Or the people we are trying to help."

"More of us do than you realize," I said emphatically. "This is not twenty years ago."

"It doesn't always feel like that," Francisco said.

I pushed myself out of the chair, somewhat sad that I'd not eaten the eclair. "That changes today, then," I said as I headed for the door. "Thank you for your time."

"You're going to get Daniel, aren't you?"

I paused at the door, and turned toward the girl with the dreadlocks who had asked the question. "Yes," I said.

"And the person that took him?" Francisco asked.

I smiled the sort of smile that a predator might wear when they realize their prey is in sight. "Oh yes," I said as I reached for the door handle.

"I'm not sure I would want to be them," he observed.

"Me either," I laughed darkly.

SEVENTEEN
HIDE & SEEK

I wasn't surprised when my call to Alejandro went directly to voicemail; I left a message telling him the case had taken a turn and that I didn't know when I'd get back to the condo, then pulled out of my spot at the Mall. Driving all the way to Palm Springs hadn't been on my agenda when I'd left my fiancé that evening, and as a result, all I had was the emergency overnight duffel I kept in the trunk of the Camaro. It wasn't outside the realm of possibility that I might somehow manage to get back to the condo in the wee hours of the morning, but the chances were slim enough that I'd gone ahead and booked back into the Marriott where Blake had accosted us. Partly that was a nod to the reality of the situation, but there was also an angle to be played, as well; having left the Apple Air Tag on my bumper, there was a *better* set of odds I might once more be visited by the teenager. I wasn't entirely certain why, but my gut was telling me it was going to happen; just the possibility made me happy that Alex was safe and sound at the condo sleeping off his wine.

That he would be pissed I'd ventured into harm's way again was something to be dealt with later.

Turning onto the main drag of Rancho Linda, traffic was light enough in the city that I quickly found myself on the 57 headed North; at the interchange for the 60, I scanned the vehicles around me, fruitlessly attempting to gauge whether my shadow had indeed taken the bait. Returning to Palm Springs at such a late hour *should* have attracted Blake's attention and made him wonder if I had uncovered something; catching a glimpse of his pickup would be far more likely when the highway reduced to two lanes a few miles ahead, but that was a long shot I wasn't willing to bank on. Tapping at my iPhone, I speed dialed Miles back at the department, hoping my version of divine intervention was about to intercede.

The detective picked up on the third ring. "Hey Vasily," he said. Miles' voice sounded as tired as I felt.

"Pulling a double?" I asked.

"And then some," he replied. His yawn came through clearly before he continued. "What can I do for you at nine-thirty in the evening?"

"Please tell me the warrant for the suspect's truck came through," I said as I changed lanes and sped up slightly. "Specifically the access to the GPS tracker."

"It might have," he replied before yawning audibly again. "Damn. Sorry — I think I'm having a rebound from all the caffeine."

"I'll investigate getting IV drips installed," I chuckled.

"That might help next time." I heard him typing something on his computer. "Damn," he swore again. "I'm more tired than I thought. It came back an hour ago; I'm sorry I missed it."

"We have a lot going on," I said easily. "Can you punch up the pickup's current location?"

"One second," he replied. "Let me change systems... all right, keying in the VIN now."

I tried to keep my impatience in check, but it was impossible to do. "And?" I prompted.

"It's almost up," he replied. "I'm in."

"Give me the quick history of the past ten days, would you?"

"In other words, did the truck make a recent round-trip to Palm

Springs?" Miles asked with a slight chuckle. "Most definitely. There are at least four visits in that window, though one of them is somewhat odd."

"In what way?"

"The tracking for a trip late Monday/early Tuesday morning ends at an approximate location that has a twenty-five mile margin of error. Overlaying the trip with satellite imagery only confirms that the truck essentially drove into the desert somewhere south and west of metro Palm Springs." Miles paused. "Based on the other trips the system logged, this one is a bit of an outlier, Vas."

"You might have found my victim," I replied. "Can you give me the coordinates?"

"All I can do is get you in the ballpark," he said. "Sorry."

"I'll take what I can get," I sighed. "No — wait a minute. Can you ping the current location of the truck?" I asked, playing a gut feeling.

"Sure. One second... pinging it now."

I tapped at my steering wheel with a finger and sped up even more; my instincts were telling me time was of the essence, even if I was being shadowed.

"The pickup is stationary at the moment," Miles reported a moment later. "The coordinates place it just outside of Palm Springs — fairly close to where it went into the desert, actually." Miles paused. "Is that what you were expecting?"

I veered around a slow-moving truck. "Yes," I said with a sudden certainty.

There was a long pause. "Shit. The suspect is with the victim? Right now?"

Suddenly wishing I'd driven the SUV — and would therefore have the use of my lights and sirens — I stomped on the accelerator and watched the speedometer leap closer to the century mark. "I believe so. Can you cross reference those coordinates with the street atlas? I need to know if I'm going where I *think* I'm going."

"Got it," Miles said. All traces of fatigue were gone from his voice, presumably driven away by a jolt of adrenaline. "I can't be entirely exact, but it comes back to a parcel owned by the Catholic Diocese of Greater Palm Springs. Specifically, it seems to house a cathedral, private school and other supporting structures for St. Frederik's."

And there it was. "What is the truck closest to?" I asked, but the way my heart was beating told me I already knew the answer.

"The school — I think," Miles said. "There's some uncertainty given how the GPS is tracked."

"Wake up whoever you need to in Palm Springs and get me into that church," I said. "Alert whatever LEO covers that part of the area and tell them I'm on the way."

"Will do." Miles paused. "You're not going to wait for authorization, though, are you?"

"Probably not."

"I'm sorry, you broke up just then," Miles said, before adding quietly: "Good hunting."

"I'll call when I get on scene," I said before the connection went dead.

I made it to Interstate 10 in record time and careened around the exit Siri indicated on what felt like two wheels not long afterward. There were some benefits to owning a sportscar, one of them being nearly unlimited amount of horsepower when needed. I was forced to slow down substantially when I hit the surface streets and had to pay closer attention to the directions Siri was spitting out at me; as many trips as I had made to Palm Springs over the years, I was going ever deeper into a section I had not visited before. It was clearly one of the older portions of the valley, though that was more of an impression than an observation; not really being in the tourist mode, I pretty much kept my eyes on the road and turned when told to do so. Ultimately, I found myself along a rather desolate divided highway that appeared to lead toward the mountains; I couldn't be sure, but it felt like multiple subdivisions had been planned at one point and then somehow arrested. I sailed through intersection after intersection guarded by stoplights that had no need to change, for the cross roads they were protecting were nothing more than short stubs leading nowhere. I'd encountered many an area like that in California, ghostly reminders of the massive real estate crash that happened in 2008.

The darkness was broken by a bright swath of lights some distance away from me; as I drove closer, it resolved into the soaring arches of a cathedral, lit by massive floodlights in a warm tone. I was somewhat surprised at how far away the church was from civilization, and wondered if the founding members had assumed the suburb would ultimately reach them. From the barren wasteland I'd passed through, that assumption seemed rather flawed. Slowing, I turned into a large parking lot abutting the church; perpendicular to the cathedral was a single-story school-like structure, and beyond that, a second three-story building studded with irregularly lighted windows. I circled the lot once looking for the pickup truck belonging to Blake Dolittle; it was a fairly quick search given there were no other vehicles beyond my own in evidence. I assumed that there was a separate lot elsewhere for staff members but didn't want to take the time to look for it, so instead, I drove to the front of the school building and parked the Camaro in one of the visitor spots. Unlocking the gun safe, I grabbed my Glock and slid out from behind the wheel; checking to make sure I had a full clip, I slid the weapon into my holster and started across the pavement to the front entrance for the building.

As dark as the building appeared to be, I wasn't surprised that the doors were locked and no one responded to my repeated bangs against the glass. Stepping back, I hunted for and found a walkway that went around the side of the building and carefully started in that direction. The shocking lack of outdoor lighting forced me to use my iPhone as a flashlight; save for the floods against the cathedral and the faint illumination from the dorm in the distance, the space was essentially inky black beneath the moonless night. Glancing upward, I thought astronomy students — if they had any at St. Frederik's — likely appreciated the lack of light pollution from being so far out of metro Palm

Springs. For my part, I was wishing I had my high intensity standard issue flashlight; like all the rest of my standard equipment, it was in the back of my departmental SUV, currently parked at the station. While my trusty iPhone was certainly up to the task, I was rapidly beginning to second guess my decision to drive the Camaro up to Palm Springs.

The path widened a bit and was bordered by multicolored gravel that sparkled under my iPhone's light. Given the school catered to athletes, I wasn't surprised to see fencing appear, cordoning off the green of either a soccer pitch or a football practice field. I paused long enough to locate the locked gate before continuing onward; the gentle whirring of an industrial strength pool filter hinted at what the ghostly presence of a diving tower ultimately confirmed, namely that aquatics were also on the sports menu. Just behind the pool, I found a sizable shed large enough to house several massive pieces of equipment. Beyond the shed was a far smaller parking lot, forming something of a border between the athletic fields and the dorm at the other end. A smattering of cars were visible in shadow only; they were silent confirmation that I'd located the staff parking area, though it wasn't immediately obvious how one actually drove to that lot. Walking to the edge of the pavement, I squinted into the darkness and tried to divine whether Blake's pickup truck was among the vehicles present. Sighing, I realized it would be impossible to discover short of actually walking up and down the aisles; something in the back of my head told me it was irrelevant in any event. Blake was there, somewhere; the only question now was how to smoke him out.

Turning slightly, I saw that the desert surrounding Palm Springs was essentially the far border beyond the athletic fields. Pulse suddenly pounding, I felt like I was close — insanely close — to finding Daniel, as nutty as that sense might be. For a long moment, I wondered if I should dig the business card out of my pocket and call the number Rosie had provided; having air support, especially one with thermal imaging capabilities, would certainly be handy. And yet, something told me it wouldn't be necessary. Slowly spinning a full circle, I took in the entire campus and began to see it in a different light.

I wasn't a student here, but Blake was, I thought. *He knows the grounds far better than I do, including places that the faculty wouldn't normally monitor. If I were a student here, where would I feel safe keeping things I didn't want them to find—*

My eyes shifted immediately to the shed.

That's too obvious. Or is it?

Gravel crunching beneath my feet, I hurried back toward the shed and began looking for a way in. There were two large garage doors on one side, and a small standard-sized doorway facing the pool. I tried the garage doors and found them to be locked, but the handle to the door turned freely beneath my touch. Knowing that was not a great sign, I extinguished the light on my phone before stuffing it back into my pocket, then slid the Glock out of my holster. Holding it up, I leaned a shoulder into the door and tried not to wince when it opened with a loud groan.

Letting my eyes adjust to the darkness, I carefully stepped inside the space and was immediately accosted by the smell of decaying grass mixed with the acrid strains of fertilizer. Landscaping tools hung on the walls, reflecting what little light was getting through the door; tall stacks of bags of something were against the far wall, and the shadow of a mower was right behind one of the two garage doors. There were plenty of places for someone to hide, but that strange sixth sense I always had when I was clearing a scene told me I was alone. Still, I remained wary as I slowly worked my way through the space. Sidestepping the mower, I was surprised to see the second bay was empty; it was large enough to hold a second mower, or something slightly larger, like a small tractor. Shifting my gun, I pulled my iPhone back out and snapped on the light once more then wafted it over the concrete. Twin dark lines where tires had been repeatedly driven were spaced wide enough to indicate equipment far bigger than the mower I had passed; turning the light against the rear wall, I smiled grimly at what appeared to be a large maintenance workbench, above which were several shelves holding bottles of hydraulic fluid.

Turning, I nodded slightly. *What good ground maintenance crew doesn't have a small backhoe?* I asked myself. *And I would be willing to bet if I search long enough, I'll find a trailer that attaches to it that would be capable of carrying whatever it was Daniel had been loaded into.* I stood there for a long moment. *I might have the answer as to how Daniel was buried, though when the Hell did Blake learn to operate one? And how did no one here at the school notice it was being used? I have some real concerns about security in this place...*

The light of my iPhone caught another door at the end of the bay, and I walked toward it. Slightly ajar, I pushed my toe through the small gap that had been created and opened it enough to reveal some sort of office. Pushing the door open wider, I immediately got the feeling I was no longer alone; edging inside, I slowly moved the iPhone's flashlight from one end of the office to the other, revealing a typically claustrophobic space that might have been the domain for an administrative assistant responsible for keeping the vendors in line.

Taking another step into the office, the sense someone was hiding in that cramped space became nearly overwhelming; I slowly washed the flashlight over the space again, this time with the gun raised defensively. Besides a desk dating back to the Eisenhower administration holding an incongruently modern flatscreen computer, there weren't a ton of options for cover; there was a beat up couch in the corner and a set of four full-sized lockers on one wall. A second, smaller door beside the lockers was fully open; my light reflected off the ceramic of a toilet. The lockers seemed like the most obvious option, but just for form's sake, I made a point of looking beneath the desk and behind the furniture before taking up position in front of the lockers.

"I'm a police officer," I said loudly and clearly. "I'm not going to hurt you."

The silence in response felt heavy.

"I just want to talk," I continued as I carefully moved toward the locker at the end of the row.

The way the slots of the metal were angled, it was impossible to shine my light in to see if anyone was inside; although it was against my better judgement, I had to use the edge of my gun to lift the latch and pull open the door. It swung open with enough of a metallic screech that it nearly masked the sound of sneakers squeaking on the concrete floor behind me; I managed to get my gun up as I turned but was unprepared for the linebacker tackle that shoved me into the cramped interior of the locker. My head slammed against the rear hard enough that I immediately saw stars; when I reflexively tried to stand up, I smashed into the small shelf above where you normally hung things. The second impact brought a hint of darkness to the edge of my vision and the warm trickle of something down my face; dazed as I was, I managed to keep a tight grip on the Glock — for all the good it did. The same couldn't be said for my iPhone; the tinkling of shattered glass as it hit the concrete floor coincided with the flashlight immediately going out.

So much for the device's vaunted resilience.

A rapid punch to the gut had me double over into a cross to the jaw; stunned a second time, I sagged back into the cramped interior just as the door was slammed shut. Plunged into complete darkness, the acrid smell of body odor emanating from whatever garment I'd become entangled in revived me enough to lean forward and try to push the door open. It was a fruitless effort, for I quickly discovered what any bullied high school student could tell you, namely that the latch was not designed to be opened from the inside — a key fact that would have been nice to have had a few minutes earlier. Anger bubbled into action as I twisted my six-foot-plus frame around just enough to ram my feet into the metal door several times in a vain attempt to kick it open, action star style. The effort netted me little more than a serious calf cramp and a blood pressure reading likely well above heathy levels.

Bowing to the inevitable and the mountain of paperwork that would come with it, I shifted my position again so I could get a better angle on where I thought the latch was and brought my Glock to bear. Blinking away a massive headache that might well have been the early warning sign of a concussion, I took a deep breath and squeezed the trigger; in such an enclosed space, the sound of my firearm going off immediately set my ears to ringing, but the effort had the desired effect when the door popped open. Trying not to grimace as I unfolded myself from the embrace of the interior, I kept the Glock trained on what turned out to be an empty office.

Wiping at something sticky on my forehead, I moved to the bathroom and felt the glass of my iPhone crunch beneath my shoes as I went. Pressing myself to the wall, I took a breath and then whipped around the edge of the frame to find the alcove of a walk-in shower directly behind the wall for the locker. I mentally castigated myself for not properly clearing the space while simultaneously agreeing to leave out certain portions of the evening's activities when I finally related them to Alejandro. He was already going to be pissed that I had gone to Palm Springs alone; telling him I'd let the suspect get the drop on me would land me on the couch for the rest of my adult life. Assuming he didn't walk out on me.

Pivoting, I ran through the darkness of the office and into the main portion of the maintenance shed; the door I had entered was wide open, bumping slightly in the night air against its hinges. I hurried across the space as best as I could given I had no light beyond what little was coming through the door; bursting out into the night, I sprinted around the edge of the building and down to the parking lot, arriving at the edge of the payment just in time to see a pair of red taillights disappearing behind the bulk of the dormitory.

Despite still feeling a bit woozy, I jammed the Glock back into my holster and sprinted back up past the athletic fields, playing the odds that whatever access road Blake was taking fed into the main parking lot for the school. Rounding the corner, I dashed past the front of the school and made it to the Camaro just as the pickup came roaring around the far side of the lot. Sliding across the hood of my car, I threw myself behind the wheel and started it up, then backed out of the spot before properly buckling up. Spinning my tires on the pavement, I launched the Camaro directly across the empty lot, eyes firmly locked on the tailgate of the pickup as it sped toward the exit. Stomping on the accelerator, I managed to narrow the distance while simultaneously avoiding any of the plantings designed to slow people like me down; Blake squealed around the corner and somewhat surprisingly managed to shoot away from me and toward I-10. Twisting the wheel, I managed to go over the edge of the concrete curb and fishtailed slightly before I was able to come back up to speed. Being out in the middle of nowhere worked in my favor, for it was just the two of us roaring down the four-lane divided highway.

Cursing that my iPhone was in pieces back at the school, my options were somewhat limited in terms of reaching out for assistance. Once more I found the choice of using my personal vehicle coming back to haunt me, for the SUV had the standard two-way radio along with a bevy of other goodies that were currently unavailable to me. It didn't help, either, that I was loathe to do anything that might so much as scratch the finish; placing the Camaro in the path of the pickup was definitely not happening, but that meant somehow cutting off Blake from the escape that I-10 represented would be a hell of a challenge. Pressing the accelerator to the floor, I made up the distance quickly, the engine of the Camaro purring as though it ran at those speeds regularly. Blake had to have seen my headlights closing in on him, for a cloud of smoke issued from the pickup's tailpipe as he attempted to pick up the pace. Smiling slightly, it occurred to me that not only had the pickup been a used car purchase, the teen had likely never had it serviced; a plan began to form, one that saw me push the Camaro closer to the century mark so it could be just a few yards off the pickup's bumper.

Swerving slightly one way and then other, Blake telegraphed the panic he must have been feeling with me so close to his heels; unfortunately for him, I had the edge police training provided, anticipating his moves while creeping slightly closer to him with every mile. Intersections whipped by at speeds not recommended by the local authorities, but I kept my focus on the truck and its increasingly erratic movements. When the sign appeared noting I-10 was less than two miles ahead, I apologized to my car and shifted to the left lane, then smoothly pulled the edge of my front wheel even with the rear wheel of the truck. Turning the wheel, I immediately closed the distance to the truck and grimaced slightly as the edge of the Camaro kissed the side of the truck; it was a classic PIT maneuver, though truth be told, I'd never done it in a sports car.

Time slowed down for me as I watched the truck slowly begin to spin out in front of me; turning the wheel, I steered out of hitting the truck and onto the verge, allowing the antilock brakes to bring me to a sudden stop. Throwing open my door, I yanked my Glock from the holster and dashed over to where the truck had come to rest against the landscaped divider; my prayer that the gently sloping center median would prevent the truck from rolling over had been answered, though the speed at which it had been going had forced it up and onto the gravel. One rear wheel was spinning from where it hung over the pavement, and the tailgate had dropped open, revealing a bed containing multiple shovels and a long crate. Setting that aside for the moment, I slowed to a trot and trained my gun on the driver's side door.

"*Get out of the fucking truck!*" I yelled as I planted myself a safe distance away. "*Get the fuck out with your hands up!*"

I waited a few heartbeats for a response, idly noting that it felt like my pulse was throbbing in my forehead. When there was no answer from the truck, I took a step closer and repeated my instructions.

"*Get out of the truck with your hands up!*"

After not getting a peep for the second time, I cautiously stepped to the driver's side door and saw why Blake hadn't responded. The remnants of the airbag hung over the steering wheel, but it appeared to have hit the teenager squarely in the nose; if the effusive blood running down his face hadn't been enough of an indicator, the mangled mass it was running from spoke to how horribly broken it was. I imagined the pain had to have been insane, given how Blake's head was lolling against the headrest, his eyes more than a little unfocused. I had to admit, I took a momentary pleasure in the fact that maybe, just maybe, the airbag had meted out equal justice for having slammed me into the locker back at the school.

Not trusting he was completely out of it, I kept my Glock trained on him as I opened the driver's side door. An iPhone tumbled out as I pulled it toward me and landed face-up; my eyebrows went up when I saw the contact that was at that very moment on the line. Crouching slightly, I picked up the phone with my spare hand and held it to my face.

"Dr. Dolittle," I said, "I'd like to see you at the Rancho Linda Police Station tomorrow morning. Could you be there at nine?"

EIGHTEEN

ROADSIDE ASSISTANCE

The massive headache didn't seem to want to fade despite the rather strong analgesic the EMT had given me. It had been even *more* difficult to get rid of the concerned healthcare worker who seemed convinced the egg-shaped bump on my head warranted being sent to the Emergency Room at Eisenhower Health. I had ugly memories of the *last* time I'd been in an ER — namely, after the assault that nearly took my life — so I had little desire for a repeat visit. Instead, I'd simply used the damp cloth they'd given me to wipe clean the worst of the blood from me and then shrugged off any further care. Getting myself completely checked over could wait until I had Daniel's location, though it seemed wise not to mention to the EMT that I was occasionally seeing double.

Two fire trucks, a pair of ambulances and a single patrol vehicle from the Riverside County Sheriff's Office had responded to my 9-1-1 call; with all of the flashing lights about, it felt like dawn had come early to the desert. As I made my way over to the young officer sitting against the hood of his SUV, I watched the tow truck slowly drag Blake's pickup truck onto its flatbed. Chief Gilbert — after reaming me a new one for going off script in the most spectacular way possible — had reached out to his peer in Riverside County and already made arrangements to have the pickup sent to the crime lab in Orange County; while not one to raise his voice in anger often, I wasn't sure if the ringing in my ears was left over from my shooting out the latch in the locker or Mike eloquently expressing his fury. I wasn't looking forward to my one-on-one with him once I returned to Rancho Linda; on second thought, maybe heading to the emergency room wasn't such a bad idea after all.

The Latino kid leaning against the SUV looked more to me like a teenager cosplaying a police officer than an *actual* law enforcement agent, especially as it appeared as though he'd not yet begun to shave. I reassessed that slightly once I drew close enough to see the slight shading of stubble along his jaw, though it seemed more like it had been carefully landscaped to look like it hadn't. It went with the pitch-perfect spike haircut far more appropriate to a beach cop than one working the night shift in a retirement community. While not exactly scrawny, he nonetheless didn't have the bulk I normally associated with cops; I was sure that without the obligatory bulletproof vest, he was probably less than 150 pounds dripping wet. I knew Riverside County couldn't have less stringent physical requirements for the position than its peers in the LA-area, but it did make me wonder. Smiling as I came up to the cop — and trying to ignore the pain in my jaw as I did so — I nodded toward the scene behind us.

"Sorry to disturb the peace this evening," I said.

The kid smiled. According to his name badge, his last name was Olson. "We don't get this much action in a month around here," he laughed. "Feel free to visit Palm Springs any time you like, Deputy Chief."

I figured Olson was also making an oblique reference to the small crowd of techs that had recently departed; I'd given the lead tech my statement while the rest had gotten busy taking photos and measurements of the scene before moving on to St. Frederik's. I knew there would be a mountain of paperwork for me to go through when I returned to Rancho Linda, but felt confident my probable cause argument for the high-speed chase would hold up. I wasn't quite as sure how to justify shooting out the locker's latch, though that might have more to do with not wanting to admit to having been locked inside.

"I'm not sure my Chief would appreciate that," I chuckled as I reached for his hand and shook it. "And please, call me Vasily."

"Paul," he nodded as he released my hand with a smile that accentuated his teenager look. If he'd been interested in Hollywood, Olson could have totally been one of those actors who played a decade younger than he actually was. "All the same, this is the most excitement I've had on the graveyard shift in months."

"I suppose the geriatric set doesn't get into car chases that often."

"Hardly," he smiled. "Though, in fairness, we have plenty of residents below the eligibility age for Medicare."

"Good to know," I laughed.

"How are you feeling?"

"Fine," I lied. There was a peculiar twang to Olson's speech, but I couldn't quite place it. "Now that they've patched me up, I'd like to talk to my suspect."

Olson nodded to the second ambulance. "I figured as much and had them hold transport until you were ready. Paramedics say his injuries are minor, all things considered, so they weren't in a rush to get him to Eisenhower anyway."

"I'll want him sent to Rancho Linda once he's been checked out."

"Your Chief made that clear to the Sheriff," Olson replied. "Someone is already headed up to retrieve him."

I nodded. "Good. Did the crime scene techs pull anything from the truck?"

"Quite a bit," Olson said. Pushing off of the hood, he went to the rear door for his patrol car and opened it; a moment later, he returned with a plastic tub holding a number of evidence envelopes. Without any sort of consideration for the finish of his vehicle, he plopped it atop the hood of the patrol car and then stepped back. "Kid seems to have been an odd sort of magpie."

I moved to the hood and began rifling through the bags. Blake's iPhone was in a small, clear bag, and tapping at the screen through the plastic showed me eighteen missed calls from his mother. I smiled slightly as I set it aside; I had to admit I was looking forward to interviewing her back at the station. Several bottles of pre-mixed protein drinks were in another bag, the sort of off-the-shelf nonsense that true athletes never actually used; a third held a half-eaten protein bar. Aside from being a marvelous source of DNA, I found myself questioning the soccer player's nutrition regimen — or the coach that had recommended it to him. Setting those on the hood, I dug down further and found a rectangular folding leather case with a built-in card holder sized for the iPhone; easily visible through the plastic was Blake's driver's license and the top edge of a credit or debit card just behind it. In what was becoming an increasingly cashless world, I imagined the kid probably used his phone more often than not to make a payment, eliminating the need for a traditional wallet. It was funny how quickly things changed; I still carried what I thought of as a billfold, though it pretty much just held my ID, health insurance card and any paper receipts I might still get while shopping. Alejandro, just a few years my junior, carried only his iPhone; he'd cheered when California had announced a digital version of the driver's license and had quickly signed up for the pilot. I'd been forced to remind him that his physical ID was still required when driving — once a cop, always a cop — so he'd reluctantly slapped a small holder to the back of his phone case that fit the license rather nicely. I wasn't entirely certain I'd be comfortable with a digital-only version of my ID, especially since I knew just how fragile our information technology systems were writ large; still, I could read the writing on the wall and found myself resigned to what was coming.

Toward the bottom of the tub was another small bag. Holding it up to the strobing light of the patrol car's flashers, I eyed a half-dozen of the round Apple Air Tags; most still had the keychain fob attachment, but one had apparently become detached, with the small plastic connector rolling around as I shifted the bag. I felt myself frowning as I stared at the tracking devices, for it was an elegant if not inexpensive way to stalk someone — and, with what little I knew about Blake, felt like a non sequitur. I held them up to Olson.

"You ever use these?" I asked.

Olson shook his head. "I'm an Android guy," he said.

"We can never be friends, then," I chuckled as I put the bag back into the tub.

"I take it you've been brainwashed by the Cult of the Fruit?"

"It happened slowly years ago. My first Chief is the one responsible for my addiction."

"There are support groups for that," Olson laughed. "And cheaper phones."

"I'm afraid I've already sold my soul to the devil," I smiled as I sorted through the remnants in the tub.

There was a complete soccer uniform in one bag, and muddy cleats in another; clearly, doing laundry after a workout wasn't high on his list. Several other bags contained the various brick-á-brac any teen might have, ranging from fast food wrappers to unopened strips of condoms. Fingering the brand Blake seemed to favor, I found it hard to believe he was in a relationship with anyone — or rather, that anyone would *want* to be in a relationship with him. Putting the condoms on the hood, I wondered if he was more of the one-night-stand kind of guy, and then began to reassess that when I picked up the second to last bag.

Enclosed in the plastic was an extremely dog-eared paperback; turning it over, my eyebrows went up at the artwork on the cover. To say it was X-rated would be to put it mildly; the extremely interesting position the couple were using to make love to each other was one I'd never considered, though in all honesty, it was probably more appropriate for hetero couples anyway. My eyebrows went up further when I saw the sticky globs across the bottom of the bag; from the streaks of dampness on the cover, they'd clearly migrated there after being bagged.

"So much for the ring," I said.

"Ring?"

"We think the suspect was wearing a ring to prevent him from, well, doing this," I answered, pointing to the bag. "You can buy them online. They're hugely popular with the super-religious sect."

"And clearly don't work."

"It's all a matter of what you believe in, I guess. At least I won't need to ask for a cheek swab now."

"No," Olson replied, a slight smirk tugging at his lips. "Your suspect seems to have provided plenty of DNA already."

"Must be quite a read," I said as I put it on the hood.

"I wouldn't know," Olson said, then paused for a moment before adding: "Weird he had a book though. I would think porno is cheaper on the web these days."

The comment struck me. "It is, isn't it?" I murmured. "And easier to get anonymously."

"Exactly."

"He must have found this somewhere," I said thoughtfully.

"Is it significant?" Olson asked.

"Maybe," I nodded before glancing at the bottom of the tub. A small caliber gun was in the final bag. "Where was that?"

"Glove box," Olson replied. "Doesn't look like it's been fired, nor did we find any bullets to go with it."

Thinking about how Blake had waved it at us back at the Marriott, I nodded. "More for show, then."

"Possibly."

I repacked everything into the tub. "All right, let's see if this bastard can tell me anything."

Olson chuckled as we started to walk toward the ambulance together. "And here I was going to ask who was going to be playing the bad cop."

"Sorry to disappoint," I smiled. "I hope your note taking skills are solid; I usually record interviews on my phone, but it's in pieces back at the school."

Olson brought out his godforsaken Android phone. "Got you covered."

"Good," I replied. "Follow my lead."

"Will do."

The rear doors for the second ambulance were still open, revealing the stretcher holding Blake Dolittle. He was sitting up slightly, and it looked like a massive napkin had been wedged up his broken nose; a slight purplish discoloring had begun to appear beneath his eyes, underscoring how hard the airbag had hit his face. I'd never had the privilege of experiencing an airbag go off, but had seen plenty of evidence over the years; it wasn't pleasant. Stepping up and into the back of the ambulance, I caught the eye of the female EMT who was rolling up some bandages. She understood my unspoken request and quickly disappeared. Olson took up position on one side of the stretcher, and I took the spot on the other side.

Blake had watched our entrance with some interest, but the slight glazing to his eyes told me the IV going into his arm wasn't just saline. I tried not to frown, for there was plenty of legal precedent throwing out incriminating statements when a suspect was interviewed while under the influence. Nodding to Olson, I waited until he tapped the recording button for the voice memo function before turning my full attention to the teenager.

"My name is Deputy Chief Vasily Korsokovach," I said. "Rancho Linda Police Department."

Blake ran his tongue over his swollen upper lip. "I know who you are," he said. The words were slow, but not slurred; hope bubbled up that I might not be on as shaky ground as I feared. "You're the fairy who got raped."

My eyebrows went up slightly. "I've been called many things, but fairy is not one of them," I replied easily. "I'm not sure you understand the demographics of the gay community, Mr. Dolittle."

"I understand enough," he said before shifting his eyes to Olson. Moving his head seemed rather difficult; it might have had something to do with the restrictive plastic neck brace the EMTs had strapped onto him as a precautionary measure. "I see Palm Springs hires illegals now."

"That would be against the law, sir," Olson said. "Not that it matters, but I'm actually from Green Bay."

I looked at Olson. "That explains the accent."

Olson smiled. "I've tried for years, but can't quite shake it."

Blake glared at both of us. "Whatever."

"Before we get started, Officer Olson is going to read you your rights," I continued.

"Am I suspect in something?" Blake replied. The sarcasm was nearly palpable.

I let the comment go and instead nodded to Olson. "If you would, Officer?"

"Blake Dolittle, you have the right to remain silent..."

I watched Blake carefully as Olson recited the phrases from memory, and was impressed that he didn't so much as flinch. The kid was going to be a hard one to crack, but I'd gone up against people far more self-assured than him, and had come out on top. Blakes eyes shifted between the two of us once more before landing back on me.

"Do you understand these rights?" Olson asked.

"Yes."

I took a moment to let the silence weigh on Blake. The bleeping of the machine pumping the IV into him merged into the rhythm of the heart rate monitor for a moment, making an unusual soundtrack for the interview. "Since you are eighteen, you are legally an adult and capable of making your own decisions. I will need you to think long and hard about how you answer my next question."

Blake rolled his eyes. "I've seen the cop shows. I don't have anything to say."

"Do you consent to speaking with us without legal representation?" I asked.

"Sure."

"Are you *positive* you don't want to call anyone?" I pressed.

"I'm good." The defiant look had returned to his face.

"All right." I looked at the wave rolling across the heart monitor and realized it had ticked up a few beats. It was rather handy having access to how he was responding to me. "Why were you at St. Frederik's this evening?"

"I wasn't there."

An eyebrow arched as I responded. "We've got techs there now swabbing every surface for DNA," I said. "Lying to me isn't going to help your cause, Blake."

"I'm not lying."

"I suppose now you're going to tell me it wasn't your pickup that I followed from there to here?"

"I don't have to tell you nothing," he said.

I was a bit surprised at his lack of language skills, considering how long he'd been at a private school. Then again, it was more likely he'd spent much of his time on the soccer pitch instead of the classroom. "Let's try another tact, then," I smiled slightly. "Where is Daniel Kewley?"

"Who?"

"Don't waste my time, Blake," I said before leaning closer to him. His eyes widened slightly as I lowered my voice. "I've been up for nearly twenty hours and have zero patience for games at this point. *Where* is Daniel?"

"I have no idea who that is."

"Strike two," I sighed as I straightened up. "Want to try a third time?"

"Not especially."

I turned to look at the amazingly well-organized shelves built into the side of the ambulance, and ran a finger along a drawer labelled *analgesics*. The way my head had truly begun to throb made me wonder if downing the entire contents would help. "You kidnapped Daniel from the Halloween party on Monday," I said as my eyes ran over the rest of the shelves.

"Why would I do that?"

I wonder how much it costs to stock all of this? I thought idly before turning back to Blake. "I suspect it has much to do with a difference of opinion on things like multiculturalism," I said evenly. "Or maybe it was something as simple as the fact that you were upset that the group he helps to run, Kids On Their Own, exists."

"You mean that stupid organization that kicked us out of the lesbian bookstore?"

"My understanding is that you kicked yourselves out," I said.

"Whatever." Blake smiled slightly. "We didn't need the space anyway."

"That's fortunate. Especially since you now won't have to associate with kids like that." I moved back to the side of the stretcher. "Gays, Blacks, Latinos, trans — I'm sure each one of those groups offended you."

Something flickered across his face. "Wackos, all of them."

That eyebrow of mine arched again. "Why, exactly?"

"Why, what?"

"*Why* are they 'wackos,' to use your term?"

"They are not natural. Normal. Part of the rest of us."

"Oh?" I asked, a dangerous tone dripping into my voice. "Because they're not *white* and *straight*?"

"It's more complicated than that."

"Enlighten me."

Blake looked at me funny. "The lights are already on."

Jesus. "Explain to me *why* you consider anyone not like you aberrant," I said, then amended when I saw his brow furrow again. "Wacko."

The teen actually looked like he was trying to think. For the first time, I realized I was dealing with the rare but stereotypical jock that made the rest of us look terrible. Tapping my fingers along the raised metal bar designed to keep Blake from tumbling off the stretcher, I waited impatiently for the kid to assemble his explanation.

"There is only one pure race," he ultimately said, drawing out his words.

Once it became apparent that was all I was going to get, I closed my eyes and tried not to swear out loud. Opening them again -- and blinking away the duplicate image of Blake and Olson I immediately saw -- I decided to cut to the chase. "Whatever your motivation was," I said, "you kidnapped Daniel. And because you wanted to extract some sort of retribution from a teen that hadn't done anything, you brought him up here and stashed him away somewhere no one would find him." I paused. "At least, not easily."

The slight smile that appeared fleetingly told me I'd hit the right approach. "Maybe he had it coming."

"Maybe," I nodded. "Getting him up here was a challenge; knocking him out was a good first step, then loading him directly into the box you were going to bury a solid second." I glanced in the direction of the school. "Since you appear to have had access to the storage shed at St. Frederik's, you were able to use the tractor to drag the box out to the desert."

Blake shrugged. "Hopefully he's not claustrophobic."

I stared at the teenager. Something in my face must have alarmed Olson, for I saw his eyes widen; it was enough of a warning for me to tamp down the first ten things I'd wanted to say and instead go for number eleven. "Let me put this in real terms," I said as I leaned closer again. "The box you will be in could be the same size if we don't find Daniel alive and well. There is a huge difference between kidnapping and murder in the eyes of the law."

Blake started to turn his head away from me; I put my hands to either side of his face and forced him to look at me. He brought his hands up to try and fend me off, but was restricted by the cables fastening him to the equipment; he had even less success twisting out of my grip. I held him there, holding his gaze for an uncomfortable few heartbeats. For the first time, I saw a flicker of panic in those eyes that had been so sullen earlier.

"You *own* this," I said. "You and whoever helped you get to this point. Start talking and maybe I can salvage something of your life; clam up and I guarantee you'll never see the outside of a jail cell."

He swallowed. "You've got nothing on me," he said, but his haughtiness was offset by the sudden increase in both respiration and heart rate on the monitor above his head.

I released his head and then started to tick items off on my fingers. "I've got your blood at the scene of the kidnapping. I've got the GPS records proving you were at the Halloween party. Those same records show you driving to Palm Springs on the night Daniel disappeared," I added, though in truth I'd not actually seen that data yet. Based on how his eyes were beginning to dart between me and Olson, though, I was certain I didn't need to. "I've got you running from the possible crime scene here in Palm Springs. And," I finished with a flourish as I picked up his hand, "I've got your ring."

Blake stared at the faint discolored portion of his ring finger that I was pointing to; as he raised his hands, I'd caught the streak of a not-quite-healed wound from where the jewelry had been forcefully yanked off. His eyes couldn't have gotten any rounder when they turned back toward me; I was impressed when he tried one last round of bravado.

"What ring?"

"All I need to do," I said as though he'd not spoken, "is match your DNA to any *one* of these items and you are toast. The only question you *should* be asking yourself right now is whether you've fucking pissed me off enough that I toss you into the county jail up here and forget about you for a month. Or two." I glanced at Olson. "I hear you're overcrowded right now, too."

Olson picked up on my thread. "We've been arresting migrants in waves this month," he said with just enough seriousness to sell it. "They outnumber the locals two to one."

"The *white* locals?"

"Yeah," he nodded solemnly. "What are left of them; we lost two this week alone. Stabbed in the back with a sharpened toothbrush while taking a shower," he explained, looking at Blake.

"Creative," I said with no trace of irony.

"Seems the Latinos don't really like the whites," Olson said. "A sorry state of affairs."

"Clearly," I nodded sagely. "But don't worry, Blake," I said soothingly. "I'm sure they will consider you part of their 'pure race,' right?" I paused for a long moment before figuratively going in for the kill. "Except, of course, they won't. They will be every bit as close-minded as you; if you are lucky," I added after lowering my voice enough that the recording might not pick it up, "you'll be dead before you realize that."

"You're fucking crazy," Blake said loudly. "You can't do that!"

"I can," I said before leaning away. Turning to Olson, I sighed dramatically. "I'm sorry to add to your woes, Officer."

"I'm sure we can squeeze in one more body," he said.

"Indeed," I said as I stood and began to leave the ambulance.

"My mother will make sure that never happens," Blake said. "You've got nothing to hold me."

I looked over my shoulder. "Life is not like television, Blake," I said. "There will be no eleventh hour reprieve here." I nodded to the stretcher. "Your injuries will be treated, and then you'll land in the Riverside County jail general population until we sort this out in front of a judge. Your mother will be more than welcome to visit you, of course, but even if she has the best lawyers in California, the soonest she'd be able to get you out would be, oh, Saturday?"

Olson helpfully stepped in. "At the earliest. We're short staffed on top of everything else."

That seemed to unsettle the teen, so I stepped back toward the stretcher. "Or," I continued, "you can tell me what I need to know and instead be our guest in Rancho Linda until your arraignment." I shrugged. "Honestly, I don't really care one way or the other. But if you throw me a bone, I might be disposed to return the favor."

Blake looked at me, then at Olson. "You're just bluffing."

I shrugged again. "See you in court," I said as I jumped down to the pavement.

Olson followed me out and we walked about ten feet toward the parked patrol car before we heard Blake begin throwing epithets at us; I was somewhat impressed at the mix of racial and gay slurs he managed to pack into the few sentences he uttered before the EMT climbed back into the rear of the ambulance and closed the doors. Leaning my back against the hood, I folded my arms and watched in dismay as the ambulance started up and pulled away, taking with it whatever leads I'd hoped to wrestle from the teenager.

"Shit," I said aloud.

"I take it that didn't quite go the way you wanted," Olson said. He'd taken up position beside me, and to my horror, had produced a vaping device and begun to puff away at it. The cloud of white smoke nearly obscured his face as he spoke.

"Not entirely, no," I sighed. "Usually the fear of getting placed into the general population is enough to rattle someone like Blake. He's either smarter than I thought or truly thinks law enforcement is exactly what he sees on *Law and Order*."

"I highly doubt the kid has seen that," Olson replied. "Maybe that nasty remake of *Hawaii Five-O*, though. That seems more his speed."

"They should never have tried to replace Jack Lord," I said. "Or his hair, for that matter."

"I'm with you on that. You still want us to transfer him to Rancho Linda?"

"Yes," I nodded. "But make sure he sweats a bit before we claim him."

"Can do. I'll text the booking Sergeant." He paused. "What now?"

"Now I go back to the school and hope there is a clue back there," I sighed. "One that didn't get trashed in my haste to catch up to the suspect."

Taking another hit from the device, Olson considered me before blowing out another billowing cloud of faintly-mint smelling smoke. "Could you use another hand?"

"I'd hate to pull you away from your normal duties."

"As scintillating as it would be to hide behind the billboard and catch drunken drivers this evening, I feel like I could be more help at the school."

I looked at Olson. "'Scintillating?'" I asked before narrowing my eyes. "Where the Hell did you go to school?"

Even in the minimal light of the flashing strobes, I thought I could see a slight shading to the kid's cheeks. "Berkeley," he admitted after a moment. "My undergrad is in Engineering."

"Why the fuck are you a cop?" I asked. "You should be out designing spacecraft or something, not sitting here with me during the graveyard shift."

"Would you believe me if I told you I didn't want a normal nine-to-five?" he asked.

"Not in the least," I replied. "What happened?"

"The short version is my life as a white collar worker sucked. I wanted something where I felt like I was making a difference."

My eyebrow arched. "And you're finding that on the overnight watch?"

"Low man on the totem pole," he laughed. "But I'll be a Chief like you soon enough."

"Dude," I smiled, "it took me *years* to get here. And I'm just a *Deputy* Chief."

"Who is, essentially, running the whole department," he countered. At what must have been my rather shocked expression, he continued. "My roommate at the Academy was hired by you, so I know a bit about what goes on down in Rancho Linda."

"Harrison Jenkins?" I asked, for the list of people I had hired over the last year plus was pretty short, given our budget problems. "He was your roommate?"

"Yep," Olson nodded.

"Wow." I thought about that for a moment. "You must be the guy he keeps telling me we need to poach. Except your resume has never crossed my desk."

"I'm not finished in Riverside," he said. "But when I am, you'll be the first to know."

"Good," I smiled. I watched as the last of the fire trucks pulled away, leaving just my Camaro and the patrol car. "Ready to find a kidnapping victim?"

"Lead the way, Chief."

I nodded and walked over to my car, and then took the painful moment to look at where my front bumper had kissed the truck. The edge had predictably crumbled, though it looked like the headlight hadn't been damaged; still, I knew it would cost a pretty penny to get the Camaro pristine once more. I also knew it was likely the last time I'd be allowed — officially — to use it for police business. As I got into the car, I thought perhaps it would be a fair trade if it meant the safe return of Daniel Kewley to his mother.

NINETEEN
SEARCHING FOR ANSWERS

Gina Carruthers's peer from the Riverside County Sheriff's Department was taller and far more gregarious, presuming such a thing was even possible. She greeted me as I exited the Camaro from where I had parked it just behind the maintenance shed, her mountain of hair barely held back by a pair of precariously perched reading glasses. Her wide, toothy smile reminded me of someone who was likely a favored aunt at gatherings, one who told fantastic stories and then quietly slipped extra candy to the kids before leaving. I'm not sure if that was why I intrinsically knew I was going to like her in that moment.

I extended my hand to her gloved one. "Vasily Korsokovach, Rancho Linda Police."

"Florence Chambers," she smiled as we shook.

I nodded toward Olson, who'd taken up position a half step behind me. "I think you know Officer Olson?"

"I do," Florence smiled. "A bit more excitement than normal, eh Paul?"

"No kidding," he laughed.

Florence looked back at me. "It's a pleasure to meet you in person. Gina has told me all about you."

My eyes widened. "Has she, indeed?"

"Oh yes," Florence laughed. "I know all of your secrets."

I felt a tiny flush grace my cheeks. "*All* of them? Good lord."

"Crime scene investigation is a small, tight knit community," she chuckled. "It doesn't take much for someone like you to ripple out across the network."

"Is that a good thing or bad?"

"All I will say is that Gina has never complained about working one of your cases," she replied. "Everyone calls me Flo, by the way."

"Then Flo it is," I nodded. "Please tell me you've located a clue or two?"

"It depends on your definition of 'clue,'" she answered before handing me a pair of gloves from a pocket. Her eyes flicked down to the table she was holding, something I was beginning to think might be a job requirement for people in her position. "We're just about halfway through the maintenance shed, nothing exciting there other than the biologics we lifted from the office." Flo looked up at me. "I assume some of that blood was yours?"

I nodded. "Around the locker, for sure; I probably dripped all the way out to my car when I gave chase, too."

"Yeah, you did," she replied. Flo smiled slightly. "I take it you were stuffed into a locker?"

The flame on my cheeks felt warmer, especially at the slightly shocked expression on young Olson's face. "Something I never experienced in high school," I confirmed.

"Nice work taking out the lock. I'll need to compare the bullet we found lodged in the concrete to your sidearm, though."

"I'll have Rancho Linda send up the gun barrel," I said. "We have the images on file for all active officers. Unless you want to fire a test bullet."

"The image will be fine for now." Flo started toward the shed, and I fell in beside her. "We found prints in the bathroom, but no other trace aside from your blood," she continued. "I'll have the lab run it against your suspect."

"I presume it was in the shower?" I asked as we rounded the corner of the building. The garage doors had been opened and all of the lights turned on; it felt like an entirely different place than the one I'd entered less than ninety minutes earlier. "That's where I assume he was hiding."

"Yes," she nodded. "Based on where the fingerprints were."

"Lovely."

Flo stopped at the edge of the light spilling out from the building. "Did he get the drop on you, then?" she asked carefully. "That's how I've been reading the scene."

"Essentially," I nodded. It seemed best not to go into specifics unless she asked a more pointed question.

She looked at me for a moment and read enough between the lines that she simply nodded. "We woke up the head of maintenance, and he's been going over what's supposed to be in the shed," she continued. "It appears a very expensive tractor is MIA at the moment," she added, nodding to the empty bay.

"One with a backhoe attachment?" I asked.

"Yes," she nodded.

"Well, shit," I said. "I suppose it *was* too much to ask that the kid dug the hole by hand."

"Gina sent up the file," Flo said. "It had your theory that the victim is buried somewhere in the desert?"

"Yes," I nodded. "I saw shovels in the back of the suspect's truck and hoped he'd had to dig by hand; since the truck isn't of the off-road variety, I presumed he would have picked a spot easy to drive through." I eyed the empty stall. "If he drove a tractor, especially one that has a digging attachment, that changes things."

"We might be able to help there," Flo said. "The missing tractor is expensive enough it has the equivalent of a LoJack system."

My eyebrows went up. "Seriously?" I asked.

Flo nodded. "Which begs the question why someone here taught your suspect how to use the backhoe."

"That will be one of many questions I ask the people running this school," I replied. "*After* I've found my kidnapping victim. Do you have access to the LoJack data?"

She smiled slightly. "We persuaded the groundskeeping manager it was in his best interest to log into the system for us. It's up on the computer in the office right now."

I followed her through the shed and past the small fleet of professional-looking techs carefully sorting through every last item in the space; entering the office, I made a point of not looking at the locker where I'd briefly been imprisoned and instead turned my attention to the balding man sitting at the massive desk. He'd turned at the sound of our entrance and smiled at Flo.

"Good timing. I've just located the tractor's GPS unit."

"That was fast," Flo said. "This is Deputy Chief Korsokovach, from Rancho Linda. You know Paul, of course."

The guy simply nodded at us and then pointed to the display. "Looks like it's about a half-klick from here, due East," he said before looking at Flo again. "The telemetry indicates the thing ran out of gas."

"No shit," I breathed as I looked at the map on the screen. It was fairly easy to see the small cross indicating the position of the tractor. Looking at Flo, I felt that familiar feeling when a case was about to come to an end. "We have a direction."

"And a place to search," Flo said. "That can't be the location where your victim is buried, though?"

"Get me out there and I'll tell you for sure," I said before turning to Olson. "Would you grab the suspect's phone from the evidence tub?" I asked.

Olson smiled. "You think he planted an Air Tag with the kidnapping victim, don't you?"

I nodded. "How else are you going to know where you buried it?" I asked.

Flo looked at me. "The cell coverage out in that part of the desert isn't great," she said after a moment. "You'd have to be right on top of it to find a signal from a tag."

"Within thirty meters," I replied. "Less, if my victim is buried well below the surface."

"I'll be right back," Olson said before literally running from the office.

I turned back to Flo. "Got anything that can drive out there?" I asked.

"Maybe," she replied, looking thoughtful. "Assuming the terrain isn't too rough, my SUV should be able to do it."

"Better than my Camaro," I smiled.

Flo looked at the guy at the computer. "Text me the coordinates?"

"You bet."

Feeling like I was finally on the scent, I turned on heel and hustled out of the office; Flo managed to keep up but put a hand to my arm once we were standing in front of the open garage doors. "My SUV is over there," she said, pointing to a late model Ford painted with the Riverside departmental colors.

I felt an eyebrow arch. "Are you *sure* that can get us out there and back?"

"Yes," she said as Olson appeared on the run around the corner of the shed. "And if not, I know someone with a helicopter than can save us."

"Good," I replied, a smile quirking at my lips. "Hopefully it won't come to that."

Olson handed me the phone. "Dispatch let me know Dolittle arrived at the hospital; his exam will take about an hour, and then he'll be transferred to the jail."

"Good," I repeated. "Want to go for a ride?"

"I thought you'd never ask," he laughed.

The three of us loaded into the old SUV; Flo snapped her tablet into a stand that looked as though it were growing from her cup holder and tapped at the display. It took a moment, but then a map appeared with a route for her to take to the current GPS coordinates of the tractor. Turning the key for the ignition, the truck shuddered into life in such a way that I began to consider preemptively calling in for a rescue. Twisting a few knobs and pulling a lever on the floor, Flo put the SUV into gear and slowly pulled away from the shed.

"The four-wheel drive feels a little tight," she remarked as we rather capably trundled over the concrete curb and out into the desert. I revised my estimates upward accordingly.

Flipping on the high beams and then activating the auxiliary light bar atop the roof, Flo threw the desert into sharp relief and deftly began navigating around anything too large to go over. We were low enough that the predominant flora tended to be small scrub bushes and cacti; it didn't take long, though, for us to discover that the route we were being directed upon was some sort of right-of-way for a pipeline buried a few feet below us. The going was smooth enough that Flo risked increasing her speed; for my part, I realized I'd not been far off in my original theory.

"Blake's pickup truck could navigate this, right?" I asked.

"Probably. It's designed for maintenance vehicles for the gas company," Flo said. We had to speak up over the whine of the SUV going a bit faster than it should in four-wheel mode. "Getting over the concrete back there is the worst part, especially if his wheelbase is similar to mine."

"Yeah," I nodded. "That explains how he got the box my victim is in out here, then."

"And the shovels," Olson interjected. "You might be right — he planned on digging it by hand originally."

"I bet that changed quickly after the first few shovels," I said. "My guess is he left my victim out here, drove back to the shed and borrowed the backhoe to finish the job."

"Wow," Flo said. "I would not want to be your victim. That had to have been a special kind of torture."

"Yeah," I replied. I noted that Flo had managed to increase our speed a bit more. "How far?"

She glanced at the tablet. "Quarter of a mile."

We lapsed into an uncomfortable silence as the yards dropped away. I'm not sure I'd realized I'd been holding my breath until the faint shape of a tractor appeared in the lights from the SUV in the distance; sitting forward, I watched it paint into full relief as we closed in on it before turning to look at Olson over my shoulder. "Moment of truth."

"I hope he's close," Olson replied as Flo pulled up to the tractor and put the SUV into park.

We exited the SUV *en masse*, then headed as a group toward the tractor. It was about what I'd expected, larger than anything you could purchase from a home improvement warehouse but smaller than what a utility might have in its maintenance arsenal. Pulling back on the plastic gloves Flo had given me, I leaned into the driver's seat and saw the fuel gauge sitting at zero; a quick scan of the controls told me that it had been designed specifically for someone with no training in how to use such a piece of equipment. The handles to control the backhoe currently curled beneath the rear of the tractor were extremely straightforward, as were the knobs and other dials controlling the rest of the hydraulic system. Ten minutes would have been all it would have taken to figure out everything — even for someone like Blake, who I was starting to suspect wasn't exactly heading into Rhode Scholar territory when he graduated from high school.

Stepping back from the tractor, I eyed the right-of-way beyond it and began to think aloud. "Blake drives out here, digs a hole, fills it back in and then tries to drive back," I said as I stepped around the backhoe and began to wander West. Olson and Flo were right behind me. "I'm willing to bet he never checked to see how much gas was in the thing before he left — or, maybe he did, but had no idea what sort of fuel economy a tractor might get."

"Especially crossing the desert," Olson chimed in.

"Especially crossing the desert at high speed," Flo added. "These things are not truly designed to be driven."

"No, they're not," I said as I pulled the plastic bag with the iPhone from my pocket. Tapping at the screen, I came up with the PIN screen and frowned. "Damn."

"What is it?" Olson asked.

"This was unlocked when I used it the first time," I said. "I neglected to get Blake's PIN before we sent him away."

"You might not need it," Flo said as she came up beside me. "If you get close enough to the Air Tag, the lock screen will pop up with a notification."

"It would be faster if I triggered the location software," I sighed. "I wish—"

Staring at the screen, something in the back of my head clicked and I heard what were nearly the last words out of Raymond Connolly before his massive heart attack.

He's most proud of the fact he's scored fifteen goals each year for the past four years.

"It couldn't be that easy," I said.

"What?" Flo asked.

"His code," I muttered as I quickly tapped *1-5-4-4* into the numeric keypad. To my amazement, the main screen of the iPhone appeared. "Well, shit."

"How the *hell* did you guess that on the first try?" Flo demanded.

"I read the kid's soccer stat sheet earlier today," I explained. "He appears to have been a bit narcissistic about his achievements."

Flo eyed me. "You'll need to explain that."

"Later," I smiled. "Over a nice glass of wine, when this is all over."

"I'm going to hold you to that." She nodded at the phone. "Let's hope this works."

I tapped at the *Find My* icon on the screen and was rewarded with a whole series of devices Blake was apparently tracking. My eyes widened at the number of Air Tags present, which appeared to have been planted on far more people than I'd anticipated — assuming the names on them were accurate; whatever agenda the teen was following, he had bigger plans than just kidnapping Daniel Kewley. Each tag seemed to have a moniker denoting how Blake felt about whoever it was he had planned on targeting; most of the appellations were eye-poppingly racist, underscoring his true motivations. I was silently thankful that, for now, he was safely tucked away behind bars. I scrolled through the extensive list until I found one that made my heart stop.

Shithole Immigrant Daniel, it said. *Last position: 0.25 miles due west.*

"This way," I said as I began to run in the direction indicated.

Flo and Olson were close on my heels as I flew across the gravel; the light from the SUV was bright enough in the moonless night that I could easily make out the path while still keeping half an eye on the small dot on the phone. I slowed to a walk when it looked like we were within the circle the phone had designated for the Air Tag; while I'd hoped to get something more specific, I knew we were close.

"Fan out," I said. "Start with this as point zero and do a standard circular spiral. Look for evidence of the soil being turned up recently — or tracks from our tractor—"

"Like these?" Olson said. He had snapped on his flashlight from his phone and had it pointing down on parallel tracks leading off the maintenance path and into the desert below.

"Well done," I said as I hurried to his position. "I think—"

I must have suddenly gotten within range of the Air Tags, for the phone in my hands suddenly pinged with an alert. Interrupting myself, I read the message and felt the first vestiges of relief wash over me. "Ten feet in this direction," I said as I followed the arrow on the screen.

The three of us carefully picked our way through the scrub, though Blake had done a pretty decent job of using the tractor as something of a bulldozer. Planting strobe lights along the edges of the route wouldn't have done much more to indicate that the slight mound we ultimately came upon was our destination; I paused at the edge of the roughly rectangular plot of desert that had clearly been dug up, my heart sinking with the realization that there was a real chance someone was buried beneath the umber colored earth.

"I've got flashlights back in the SUV," Flo said.

"Any chance you have a shovel?" I asked as I knelt down and dug into the soft surface. "This isn't very compacted, we might be able to dig ourselves."

"I might have an emergency one," she replied before putting a hand on my shoulder. "It would take too long with that," she added softly. "I'll use the radio in the SUV to call for some proper tools."

I began to scoop out the dirt, my impatience with the universe in general finally overwhelming me. "Tell them to hurry," I said. "And bring me that damn shovel."

Flo had the good sense not to say anything further and instead took off at a good clip toward the SUV. Olson dropped to his knees beside me and wordlessly began to scoop out the light sandy soil; I barely noticed it when Flo reappeared and set up a series of small lamps around the edges of where the ground had been disturbed, but did gratefully accept the small emergency shovel when it was handed to me. As small as it was, it still doubled the capacity of what I was removing; my world shrunk to the repetitive motion of displacing the soil one frustrating cubic foot at a time. Sweat began to roll down my face, and the throbbing of the headache I'd been trying to ignore all evening became so intense as to be physically painful. Still, I kept at it, removing first one layer, then another from what I was hoping wouldn't turn out to be a shallow grave.

Time became meaningless as the three of us worked to expose whatever it was that Blake had driven out into the Palm Springs desert. More than a few cactus thorns found their way into my hands, but the tingling pain served only to focus my motivation further. To our credit, we had managed to remove almost a foot of soil before I became aware of more people in my periphery vision; a gentle hand to my shoulder forced me to shift out of the way, replaced by one of the techs I had seen back at the maintenance shed. He quickly went to work with a long-handled spade, removing earth far faster than we'd been able to do with our bare hands. Sitting back on my haunches while simultaneously trying to blink away the stars from the headache that just wouldn't quit, my breath caught when I saw the half-dozen techs, all with shovels of various shapes and sizes, get down to work as a nearly perfectly synchronized team. Mounds of dirt began to appear all around us, and the hole in the middle steadily grew deeper. Feeling revitalized slightly, I picked up my emergency shovel and got back to work myself, adrenaline chasing away the worst effects of fatigue.

When the metallic *clunk* of a shovel hitting something echoed out across the empty desert, all of us immediately froze. The hole was *maybe* three feet deep at that point, perhaps underscoring how little time Blake had felt he had to complete the job. I set my shovel to the side and slipped down into the hole, then knelt again; brushing away the slight layer of soil, my hand felt a hard but irregular surface. Wiping away more soil, I motioned for a light and was immediately rewarded with pool of bright white illumination just in front of me; my heart sank when I saw the mascot for Rancho Linda High School just above the logo for Yeti, a company well known for its thermal coolers.

Shit.

Vibrating with anger, I swept away the dirt in long, vicious movements; I was quickly joined by multiple other hands, and in what felt like hours (but was likely just a few minutes) the entire surface of the cover had been revealed. The overall cooler was barely five feet in length and by my eye slightly less than two feet wide; designed to hold a game's worth of sports drinks for the team, it was ill suited for how Blake had repurposed it. Shifting my position, I dug around one latch and heard someone doing the same at the other end. Glancing to my side, I saw Olson there, face grim and hands hovering just above the release button.

At my nod, we both flipped the latch upward, then gripped the edge; the cover held firm for a moment before swinging upward. The stench of what was inside immediately came with it, along with a wave of recriminations for not getting there sooner; I waited until someone brought the light up a bit higher before admitting to myself, finally, that we were far, far too late.

Crammed into the cooler at an incredibly unnatural position was the body of Daniel Kewley; his head was at one angle, his torso, still clothed in his costume from the Halloween party, at another. It took me a moment to realize he looked a bit like a rag doll that had been haphazardly stashed into a trunk by a child no longer interested in playing with it; while an unsettling analogy, I felt it quite apt given Blake's obvious antipathy toward Daniel. Since the cooler had been airtight, decomposition had been somewhat arrested, so other than the nausea-inducing way his head was twisted, the teenager looked much like I had seen him that one final time. His nose appeared broken, though, and the eye black he'd used behind the mask had run; the hint of what had to have been a massive bruise on his chin was peeking out from beneath multiple layers of athletic tape that had been tightly wrapped around the teen's head and used as a gag. One of the straps from the faux electric chair had been cinched about his torso, binding his arms to his sides; another had been used at his ankles, augmented by additional bands of athletic tape above and below the knees as well as around the wrists. It had been an intentional job, one that would have rendered any sort of movement nearly impossible — as well as make it far easier to carry a struggling victim. I'd have to wait for the postmortem to know if the neck had been broken as a result of being dumped into the cooler, or if it had happened prior; either way, it spoke to the violence that had landed the teenager there in the desert. The eyes were wide open and staring at nothing in particular; I resisted the urge to reach down and close them, knowing the medical examiner would want to review Daniel *in situ.*

Frustrated and angry and having no idea what to do about any of it, I hauled myself out of the hole and stood at the edge; Flo appeared at my shoulder. "I'm sorry."

"So am I," I said, my eyes still on the body down in the hole. "And now we know what happened to all of the athletic supplies, too," I murmured, more to myself than anyone else.

"Sorry?"

I looked at Flo. "I was just thanking you for your efforts."

"Of course." She nodded at the hole. "We'll set up here next and do a thorough once-over."

"You said Gina gave you access to the file?" I asked. My head had begun to pound again, but I tried to ignore it. Rubbing at my temple didn't seem to help, oddly.

"She did, and we'll update it accordingly." Flo paused. "Are you okay?"

"Far from it," I sighed. "No offense, but I'm going to want my ME to do the postmortem on the victim."

"I think ours will understand," Flo replied. "I'll make the necessary arrangements."

"I appreciate it," I said before looking at Olson. "I'm going to head back. Do you mind taking charge here?"

"Not at all," he replied.

"Thanks," I said as I started back toward the right-of-way.

"You want me to drive you back to the school?" Flo asked.

"No," I said as I continued. "I think I could use a bit of a walk just now."

"Are you sure?"

I paused and looked back at the hole and nodded. "Now more than ever."

TWENTY
COLD, HARD FACTS

Despite the increasingly frequent episodes of double vision and a headache that was threatening to split my cranium in two, I rather amazingly managed to follow the morgue van from Palm Springs all the way to the Orange County Coroner's Office in Santa Ana without driving into a ditch. As I pulled into the empty parking lot a tad after four in the morning, I was hard pressed to remember when I had last slept — or snagged a cup of hot coffee, for that matter. Locking up the Camaro, I wasn't shocked to see Dr. Marguerite Pembroke standing just outside of the loading dock as the van backed up to it; I *was* rather surprised to find she was holding a cardboard tray with two tall Starbucks takeaway cups, one of which she pointed to me as I came up beside her.

"This one is black," she said without preamble.

"I'm sorry the roles are reversed this morning," I said as I gratefully pulled the mug from the embrace of the cardboard carrier.

Peg smiled slightly; the way the light was hitting her face from the loading dock made it look a tad scary. "I think I owe you a mugful or two, considering how regularly you bring me the flavor-of-the-month."

"It's my never-ending Catholic guilt over trying to jump the line on my first case," I said as I took a tentative sip from the steaming brew. The jolt of caffeine induced me to take a second, longer gulp; oddly, I felt the warmth of the coffee as it moved into my stomach, a warning perhaps that there wasn't much else down there at the moment.

"I didn't know you were Catholic," Peg said as she took the other cup and tossed the cardboard carrier into a trash can beside the rollup door that led directly into the morgue freezer.

"I am, more or less," I replied. "It's been years since I attended Mass, or Confession for that matter." I smiled sadly. "Until the Church fully accepts gay parishioners — and allows same sex marriage, for that matter — I'm pretty much just holding the faith in my heart."

"Didn't the Pope just make some sort of pronouncement about that?" Peg asked. "I thought I saw something about it in the *Times*."

"Change is coming," I nodded. "Probably not fast enough for my tastes, but it *is* coming."

"You could change faiths," Peggy observed.

"And risk eternity in purgatory?" I laughed. "I think not."

Peggy raised her eyebrows. "You are a complicated man, Vasily."

"So Alejandro tells me." I nodded at the two techs who were carefully rolling a stretcher out of the morgue van and into the building; the odd shape of the cooler was evident through the plastic body bag they'd wrapped it in. "Thanks for doing this, especially at such an ungodly hour."

"I know you want some answers," she said before putting her hand to my bicep. "We'll get them."

"If anyone can, it's you," I said.

"Be sure to let the Sheriff know you said that," she laughed as she turned and began to follow the stretcher. "My performance appraisal is coming up; I could use a few testimonials."

"I'll sing it from the rooftops if it would help."

"It might."

I had rarely entered the morgue from the loading dock; as most of the corridors were the same industrial tile and drab paint, and perhaps owing to just how tired I suddenly felt, I realized I had no idea what part of the building I was in and simply trusted that Peg knew where she was going. Eying the signage along the walls didn't seem to help, for the letters kept changing position as I tried to read them; blinking hard, I managed to settle them down long enough on one placard to see I was near the men's locker room.

"I'm... going to change," I said as I headed toward the door and started to press it open.

"Not in there, you aren't," Peg chuckled. "Unless you've suddenly become very fluid in the gender identity department."

My eyes shifted to the icon on the door, which may or may not have been dancing. Squinting for a moment, I realized it was the classic symbol for the opposite sex; smiling at Peg, I redirected to the door a few yards beyond it. "I must be more tired than I realized," I said.

A look of concern creased the medical examiner's face for a moment. "It's going to take a moment to get set up," she said. "You've got enough time to wash that desert dirt off before you join me in Exam Seven."

"I wouldn't mind that at all," I said before looking down at my dust-encrusted khakis. "I didn't bring a change of clothes with me, though."

"I think we can spot you a pair of scrubs," she laughed. "See you in fifteen?"

"Sounds good."

I pushed my way into the locker room and randomly picked the first locker I came to; pulling it open, I quickly shucked out of the workout gear I'd carefully selected what now seemed like a lifetime ago and hung them inside, then closed the door and grabbed a towel from the rack beside the showers. Pulling the curtain closed behind me, I twisted the dial as far to hot as I could and stepped back to avoid the initial cascade of water from the shower head. Tepid as always, I tried to repress a shiver as I plunged beneath the lethargic stream and ran my hands through my hair. The shock of the cold water revived me somewhat, but not enough to avoid a sudden return of the double vision I'd been trying to ignore; it took two shots to work the dispenser for the industrial strength shower gel the morgue had on offer, and that was after using both hands to try and stabilize its location. As I began to scrub away the dust and dirt from the desert, I felt as though the tile beneath my toes had begun to tilt away from me; placing a hand against the cold wall behind my back did little to stop the waves of vertigo suddenly washing over me.

Gasping slightly as the world started to spin out of control, I found myself clinging to the long grab bar as though my life depended upon it; squeezing my eyes shut didn't do much more than accentuate the vertigo. Slipping down to my knees, I pressed my forehead to the cool surface of the tile and blessed it for being there. The respite was short-lived, however; bile suddenly rose in my throat, and I felt what little I had in my stomach — namely, the coffee Peggy had given me — come rushing forth. In moments, it was painfully clear my gut was trying to turn itself inside out; powerless to stop it, I sagged back against the tile beneath the dial for the shower and just let it happen, all the while acutely aware that something wasn't quite right with me at the moment.

I have no idea how long I sat there, the tepid water pelting me as it washed away the worst of the vomit. It was apparently long enough that Peg had begun to wonder what had happened to me; her voice, calling from the entrance to the locker room, managed to roust me from whatever stupor I'd descended into.

"Vas? Are you okay?"

It took a few swallows before my voice wanted to work; it still felt raw from the bile, and to my ear, sounded a bit ragged. "I'm fine — just finishing up now."

"Well, good thing we don't back charge for the facilities," I heard her chuckle. "Not that anyone has ever taken an hour-long shower before."

My eyes shot to my Apple Watch and I groaned; even if there were, oddly, two watches on my wrist, both showed I'd been out of commission for nearly sixty minutes. "First time for everything," I said gamely as

I reached for the grab bar and tried to haul myself to my feet. "Out in five."

"I'm going to hold you to that," Peg said.

Focused for the moment, I managed to successfully start over and scrub away both the vomit and the desert dust before toweling off and donning a pair of green scrubs. I spent a long moment looking in the mirror to ensure I'd not put either the pants or the shirt on backwards, then hurried out of the locker room, intent on trying to get back on track. The little voice in the back of my head warning me it might have been a bad idea to eschew the medical checkout the EMTs had offered in Palm Springs was easier to ignore the closer I got to Exam Seven.

Pushing through the swinging metal doors, I felt the cool embrace of the chilly space against my exposed cheeks, though for once I didn't shy away from it. As I tied the mask across my face, I surreptitiously squeezed one eye shut so there would be just a single exam table to head toward. Peggy was standing in her usual position next to the rolling cart that held her computer — at least, one of her was; the second one was a good few feet to her right, though the doppelgänger was wearing the same frown as the original when I came up beside the table.

"You look a bit peaked," Peg said as she came around her computer desk. "Are you sure you're okay? Did you pick up a bug while digging around the desert?"

I waved her off — or tried to wave in the general direction I thought she was. "I've been on my feet for nearly a day and a half," I said. "It's catching up to me."

"Clearly," she said, but the tone of her voice told me she wasn't convinced.

Trying to throw her attention from me to the matter at hand, I nodded toward the exam table. Even with my vision as wonky as it seemed to be at that moment, I could tell that Daniel had been removed from the cooler and laid out along the table; squinting slightly, the fact I had been in the shower for an eternity was underscored by the standard

Y-shaped incision across the chest having *already* been sewn shut. "You seem to have made some progress."

"I did," Peg replied. "The easy stuff first: DNA testing confirms this is our missing teenager, Daniel Kewley. It also confirms that multiple samples taken at the mansion were from him. We'll go through the standard identification protocol later this morning once the rest of the world is awake."

I couldn't help the sigh. "Damn."

Peggy put a gloved hand to my bicep; the warmth of her touch bled through the thin fabric of the scrub. "We both knew this was the likeliest outcome," she said.

"It still sucks."

"No question."

I leaned over the body of the teen; the wounds he had taken in an attempt to defend himself from Blake were clear smudges against the ghostly white pallor. "He put up a fight?"

"Evidence speaks to that," Peg nodded. "Broken nose, fractured right occipital bone and several missing teeth tell me it was a losing battle." She twisted me to look at her. "Not that it helps how you feel, but you should know I think he was dead long before he made it to the desert."

"Say *what*?" I asked, my tone incredulous.

Peggy released my arm and walked to where Daniel's head was, then placed her hands to either side of it. "I don't know how it fits with the way you read the scene, but it's quite clear the kid's neck was broken," she said as she carefully tilted it sideways. Pointing to something that wasn't entirely visible to me, Peg continued. "I see this injury ten times in a thousand; your victim came down, hard, on the back of his neck *here*."

I felt a frown form. "Was he pushed into something?"

"Or down *onto* something," she nodded as she repositioned the head again. "Those ten times in a thousand I mentioned? They tend to be people who fell down a flight of stairs."

Thinking back to the screening room at Rosie's mansion, I started to nod slowly. "Could you get that sort of damage from hitting a hay bale?" I asked. "We found one that was off-kilter at the scene, but assumed it had been bumped into as part of the fight."

"*Anything* can cause this injury," Peg replied. "You just have to hit it at just the *right* angle." She nodded to Daniel. "Unfortunately, this kid hit the wrong kind of lottery."

"Yeah," I replied sadly.

"The only good news is that it would have killed him within moments." Peg looked at me. "He wouldn't have suffered."

"Save for the whole dying part."

"Well, yeah." Peggy came around to stand on the side opposite me. "Other than that, your victim was in perfect health. Not even a filling."

"Somehow, that makes it worse," I sighed.

"We pulled trace from beneath the fingertips," Peg said as she picked up a limp hand. "It looks like your victim managed to scrape some epithelial cells from his attacker; I woke up the on-call lab tech and she's running it against everything we've got." She paused. "I know you have DNA coming in from your prime suspect; once it arrives, we'll of course test it against that, too."

"Just wait until you see the sample," I said, smiling slightly. I looked at the nails on Daniel's hand. "How deep a scrape?" I asked.

"Enough it might have left a mark," she replied.

I nodded again. "There is evidence on my suspect that a ring was forcibly removed," I said before looking at Daniel's face. "My take is that Daniel was trying to leave us a clue."

"He may well have," she nodded. "That ring is already in our inventory, right?"

"Yes."

"Then we'll test the DNA we pulled from the ring against that from beneath your victim's nails," Peg said. "It won't hurt to have another match."

"No, it won't," I said. "Peg—"

The room chose that moment to begin to slowly spin around me; I tried to reach for the side of the exam table to keep myself steady, but misjudged the distance and found myself grasping at air as my legs buckled. Down I went, face first into the side of the exam table; I hit it hard enough that stars immediately flooded what was left of my vision. Flailing a bit like a fish out of water, I crumpled backwards onto the icy coldness of the industrial linoleum and hit the back of my head right where I had rammed it into the top of the locker. Darkness immediately overwhelmed me, blotting out the bright light hovering over the exam table that I had been staring into.

Moments of lucidity came and went.

I felt something warm and wet trickling down my face, followed by gloved fingers at my carotid. I thought about saying something, but honestly, I was so *damn* tired; lying there on the morgue floor, I tried to think about how long I had been awake. It wasn't the first time I'd worked around the clock on a case; now that there was no longer a reason to do so on *this* one made me think I could steal a few moments to regroup. I didn't need much, really; Peggy was enough of a friend she'd probably let me stay there for a bit anyway.

Slipping back into oblivion, I surfaced again when it felt like I was being lifted off of the linoleum; for some reason, I felt infinitely sad, for no place had seemed quite as comfortable. Oblivion came back for me again, only to part slightly when I felt a stinging sensation at my temple; a part of me recognized it as a wound being tended to, but it was hard to understand exactly *why*. The reason seemed to be just out of reach of my comprehension; that in itself seemed odd, for didn't I pride myself on figuring out things people couldn't?

Something is wrong with me, a voice that sounded very much like my own was saying. *I think I need help.*

Swimming upward again against the pressing weight of oblivion, I felt as though I were about to break through when this warm sense of peace settled about me. Once more, the part of me that seemed to understand such things recognized the signs of a sedative taking hold; no longer wishing to fight it, I simply relinquished control and melted away into the bliss it offered.

TWENTY-ONE
ALEX LAYS DOWN THE LAW

T he alarm from my iPhone seemed to be blaring in my ear, though as I pushed away the tendrils of slumber, I quickly realized I had no alarm on my phone that sounded akin to a heart monitor. Cracking open an eye, it took less than a moment to recognize I was in some sort of hospital room, despite my vision being extremely blurry. Blinking a few times confirmed that my contact was missing; carefully opening the other eye simply underscored a nurse had followed protocol and removed both of them when I'd arrived. Wherever that *was*, of course.

Knowing this was likely the fallout from having, essentially, passed out in the morgue, I assumed I was a guest of the Orange County Medical Center yet again. Closing my eyes, I wondered idly if I had finally matched Rosie's record in terms of the number of emergency visits to the hospital; it wasn't exactly the kind of competition I'd wanted to engage in, honestly. Lying there against the surprisingly comfortable pillow, though, I oddly felt more at peace than I had in days — a side effect I was sure of whatever drugs they were pumping into my arm. The overwhelming sense of well-being felt a bit like being wrapped within a cozy blanket; whatever worries I might have had were secondary to enjoying the moment. Aside from a tiny tingling at my temple and a strange itchiness on a portion of my scalp, the world seemed pitch perfect. Taking a deep breath, and then another, the temptation to snooze once more was quite strong; the only thing that stopped me was a gentle hand against my cheek and the very recognizable cologne that appeared with it.

I blinked my eyes open once more and found myself staring at the handsome face and beautiful eyes of my fiancé; dark smudges beneath those eyes and a heavy shading of stubble along his chiseled features told me exactly how long I'd been there, upping the level of guilt I was already awash in. Those amazing eyes searched mine for a moment before a slight smile revealed his perfect teeth. I matched it as best as I could, though given the drugs I was on, I figured it looked closer to goofy than loving.

"Hey, beautiful," I said, my voice sounding strangely light.

"*Buenos días, mi amor,*" he whispered before leaning down and brushing his lips against mine. Pulling back, he looked at me again. "How are you feeling?"

"Relaxed," I admitted. "More than I have I right to be."

Alex smiled wider. "I'm not surprised. The doctor has you on something that's unpronounceable," he said. "You needed some rest."

"Clearly," I said. "How long...?"

"Let's just say Rosie's a bit annoyed you missed *Thursday Night Football*," he replied.

My eyebrows went up; a burst of adrenaline chased away some of the effects of the IV. "Shit. It's *Friday?*"

"Yes," he nodded. "Friday *afternoon*, to be specific."

I could hear the heart monitor start to tick up. "I've got suspects to interview," I said as I struggled to push myself up. My muscles felt a bit rubbery and the cords tying me to various machines in the room didn't help, either. "Where's my phone? Oh shit – I need a new phone. Still, I need to call Chief Gilbert—"

Alex gently, but firmly, pressed me back into the bed. "You're not going anywhere."

"Alex—"

"Vas," he interrupted, "you're recovering from a severe concussion and injuries sustained from that little swoon you did in the O.C. morgue."

The tingling at the side of my head suddenly made sense; I reached up and felt the bandage, and beneath it, the set of thin stitches it was covering. Alex must have seen my frown, for he took my hand into his and held it. "Stitches?" I asked.

"Yeah," he nodded. "Three at your temple and four on the top of your head."

I wouldn't have been surprised if the monitor behind me had registered how my heart dropped like a stone when I realized what the itchiness meant. Almost as though I were in a trance, I ran my hand over what was left of my hair and felt the new buzz cut I appeared to be sporting; my fingers located the second bandage right where I expected it, evidence of how hard I'd hit the locker in Palm Springs. Dropping my hand to my lap, I wasn't sure if I was taking the fact I was now virtually bald *worse* than having been sidelined for two days from my investigation.

"If it helps, you look sexier than ever," Alex said.

"I've never had it this short," I replied. "*Ever.*"

Even without my contacts, I could see a slight flush on Alejandro's cheeks. "That, uh, is my fault," he said quietly. "They had to shave around the wound, and I, uh, figured you'd rather have it all be the same length." Alex paused. "Instead of, you know…"

"Having a bald *spot* in the center?" I finished. "Probably."

"Well," he smiled slightly as he ran his fingers over where my bangs *used* to be, "the doctor did warn me it might make you a bit more sensitive."

Even with the drugs, I couldn't deny the electric sizzle from his touch. "The jury's still out," I said.

Alex eyed me for a moment. "Right," he said, seeing through me like I was a thin piece of paper.

I tried to keep my tone serious as he continued to run his fingers across my now *extremely* sensitive pate; knowing what little I was wearing beneath the sheet, I shifted as best as I could to hide what he was doing to me. "I really need a phone, Alex," I said. "I've got to check in."

"No, you *fucking* don't," Alex replied with an intensity that surprised me. Pulling back his hand, he stayed leaning against the side of the bed just close enough to ensure I could see his face clearly. "It's my turn to go into full protection mode, *mi amor*. Maybe you didn't hear me earlier, but you suffered a serious *concussion*. The last thing you should be doing is working that brain of yours; not for another few days, at least."

"I have a case in progress," I protested. "Suspects that we were about to arrest—"

"That can *wait*," Alex interrupted. "Your staff can handle that for you."

"It can't," I said firmly. "There are laws surrounding how much time I have to bring charges against people; if I've been in this bed as long as you say I have, I'm dangerously close to giving their lawyers a massive get-out-of-jail-free card."

Alex pressed a finger to my lips to silence any further protests. "Only you would be more worried about how the case is going than your own wellbeing," he said. Those dark eyes were flashing dangerously, which was as good an inducement as any for me to keep my mouth shut. "Setting aside for the moment how you *yet again* placed yourself into mortal peril — a subject we will discuss far more thoroughly at a later date, I assure you — this is one time where you truly need to be a tad bit selfish."

I started to say something only to have him glare me into silence.

"No arguments," he said. "This is serious, Vas. For a guy who relies on what Poirot calls 'his little grey cells,' you don't seem to get the fact that you may have seriously injured them."

"Alex—"

He glared at me again. "You hit your head pretty hard, *mi amor*. Not once but *twice*. From what the doctor tells me, it might take days or weeks or even *months* to truly know how much damage was done."

"I feel fine—"

"Sure you do," he interrupted. "Given the drugs you're on, I'd expect nothing less."

Alex slipped off the bed and began to pace along the side of the bed; despite my not being able to see him clearly, his body posture spoke volumes about how he felt. "Chief Gilbert tells me that you have a significant amount of sick time, more than enough to recover from this properly." He whirled around and leaned down again. "And you *will* recover, because I'll be damned if we miss our *fucking* wedding in January because you've turned into a *fucking* mental vegetable that can't remember what day of the week it is."

I swallowed, unsure if I should — or could — respond. When Alex simply continued to glare at me, I decided he was actually waiting for me to speak. "Am I that stubborn?" I asked with my best *aw shucks* smile.

"Dude," he rolled his eyes. "Do you even have to *ask*?"

"Ah," I coughed. "I had no idea I was becoming my father."

Alex smiled slightly. "Well, you're not that far gone. Yet."

"I trust you'll keep me on the straight and narrow from now on?"

My diver fiancé sat back on the edge of the bed. "Oh yes," he replied. "Assuming you don't wear me down with that soulful teenager routine of yours," Alex added. "It melts my resolve every single time you use it."

"I will only use my powers for good," I said, before cocking my head. "Wait — how did you know about January?"

Alex smiled again. "The same way you do," he replied. "My rep at Fairy Tale Weddings called when you tried to book the same weekend."

"Shit. So much for surprising you."

"Ditto," he laughed. "Sean and I have been working on those plans for *months*."

"As have Suzanne and I," I admitted. "Wild. What do we do now?"

"Oh, we're still going," he said as he slid onto the bed completely and curled around me. "Once you get out of here, we'll compare the two packages we picked and pluck out the best parts. I already paid my deposit, so I'm afraid you're stuck with the balcony overlooking the geyser at the Wilderness Lodge for the ceremony."

"I think I can live with that," I said. "Though the wedding pavilion *did* have a nice view of Cinderella's Castle."

"I suspect we'll have plenty of time to see it after the ceremony," Alex said.

"Really?" I asked. "I assumed we'd be... busy."

Alex shifted his head and gazed into my eyes. "I had no idea you were such a traditionalist," he smiled.

"I just want to see you wearing nothing but mouse ears as we drink champagne and make mad passionate love to each other."

"We could do that now," he observed.

"Somehow, it wouldn't be the same," I sighed.

"True," he laughed before leaning over to kiss me. "I am serious about this, Vas. You need to step back a bit and heal."

I looked at my fiancé and felt compelled to say what he wanted to hear, but I knew deep down it would be nothing more than a lie, or an irrevocably broken promise. "How about this," I said instead. "Let me wrap up this case — with help from my staff — and then I'll take all the time off the doctor requires of me."

Alex frowned. "This isn't a negotiation," he said.

There was a slight uncomfortable cough from the doorway that had both Alex and I looking in that direction; as fuzzy as my distance vision was, the lines of a standard duty uniform for a police officer were hard to miss. "It might have to be," came the very recognizable voice of Chief Michael Gilbert.

"Oh *fuck* no." Alex rolled off the bed and took up a defensive position beside me. "Chief, Vasily's not exactly up to par at the moment," he said with a surprisingly firm tone. "Whatever you want will have to wait."

"Actually, it can't," Gilbert replied. "May I come in?"

"If I said no, would that make any difference?" Alex responded.

"Probably not."

"Then by all means, come in," he said with an exasperated sigh before moving to stand against the wall. I wasn't surprised when he folded his arms rather tightly against his chest; even with the drugs I was on, I could feel the waves of anger as they radiated off his finely toned body.

"Chief," I said once he was close enough that I could see the salt-and-pepper hair.

"I'm glad you're awake," he replied. Hooking his hands into the uniform belt, it suddenly struck me that Batman had far fewer items hanging from his. "How do you feel?"

"Fine," I said before hearing Alex snort.

"He's drugged up to his gills," Alex interjected. "Take whatever he says with a grain of salt."

"Noted," Gilbert chuckled. I saw him half turn toward Alejandro. "Alex, could I have a few minutes with Vasily?"

For a long moment, I thought Alex might force the issue and stay, but ultimately he nodded; only someone who knew him as well as I did would have caught how he was struggling to keep his anger in check as he wordlessly slipped out of the room. If the door hadn't been on a pneumatic hinge, I suspect he might have slammed it closed behind him. I waited a full heartbeat or two before looking at Gilbert.

"Don't be angry with Alex," was the unexpected first thing out of my Chief's mouth.

"I'm not," I replied defensively.

"Oh yes you are," Gilbert chuckled again. "You think he's trespassing into forbidden territory."

"Well, he doesn't understand the importance of what's going on," I blurted out before realizing I had, essentially, confirmed what Gilbert had accused me of.

"No, he doesn't," Gilbert replied. "Any more than my wife does. Or any significant other attached to a member of our department."

I stared at Gilbert. "You've had the same conversation with your wife?" I asked with dawning realization.

"Oh yes, many years ago," he nodded. "Contrary to what the new recruits think, I wasn't always Chief; there was a time when I was just as young and brash as you." He looked around the room for a moment. "I may have also landed myself in the emergency room a few times as a result, too."

"Huh," I replied, my fuzzy brain trying to reconcile that image with the man who was now my boss. "I can't see you with my same devil-may-care attitude."

"Sorry to destroy the picture you have of me," he smiled. "Anyway, I'm ordering you onto medical leave effective immediately. You're to recover fully before returning to the station."

I began to protest. "Chief—"

Gilbert held up a hand to silence me. "With one caveat: there are some loose ends that need to be tied up before you start your leave — including interviewing our lead suspects in the Kewley case."

I blinked. "I can't do that from this bed," I said.

"I don't think you'll be here much longer," Gilbert replied, "but even if you were, there is this newfangled technology called a 'video conference.' Maybe you've heard of it?"

"Very funny," I said. "And that is a terrible way to gauge a suspect's reactions. I'd far prefer it to be in person."

"You'll have to make it work," Gilbert said. "The doctor won't sign off on you going back to the office, but he has agreed to a *limited* number of hours of remote work."

"Including the interviews?"

"Exactly," he said.

"Is it even possible to interview them still?" I asked. "You had to have released Blake Dolittle by now."

"Oddly, no," he smiled. "The techs got enough of a DNA match to tie him to both scenes; that allowed us to charge him with both kidnapping and murder. I'm happy to report the teen has been cooling his heels in the Orange County Jail awaiting his arraignment."

I cocked my head slightly. "Which has been slow walked, I presume?"

"The court calendar is quite full at this time of year," Gilbert deadpanned. "Or had you forgotten?"

"I guess I had," I smiled. "What about his mother?"

"We didn't have anything to hold her on, so we released her as soon as we heard about your collapse. However, that didn't stop us from keeping a close eye on the principal."

"Good."

Gilbert looked at me for a moment. "You gave all of us a scare, Vas. *Again.* We're going to have to talk about your penchant for running into burning buildings alone."

I smiled slightly. "Too many comic books as a kid, Chief. I'm just channeling my inner superhero."

"I'd prefer if you didn't, moving forward." His statement was made with a fatherly smile, but had the force of an order behind it.

I nodded. "Of course, Chief."

"All right," he continued. "I'm going to go out there and tell your fiancé what the deal is and then let him take his frustrations out on me. However, I have a feeling he's every bit as pissed with you right now as my wife was back when I did something this bone headed." Gilbert paused. "You've got a keeper there in Alex; don't mess this up by pushing when you don't need to."

"Roger that, Chief."

"Good," he smiled again before turning and moving toward the door. "Now, wish me luck."

"You're going to need more than luck to convince Alex to let this happen."

Gilbert paused at the door. "I can be persuasive when I need to be."

I thought about that for a moment. "God help us all."

The Chief laughed as he pulled the door open. "Amen to that."

TWENTY-TWO
THE END OF AN ERA

Not for the first time did I find myself thinking a second bedroom would have been rather handy in our cozy little condo; Sean had jokingly made the observation that things were rather... snug... when he and Suzanne had crashed on our pullout couch, though at the time I'd reminded him that the cost of housing in California made upsizing somewhat problematic. As I sat at our breakfast bar logging into the Rancho Linda Police Department's virtual private network, it occurred to me that I'd never had a space to use as a home office. I knew Sean's cottage back in Windeport had a den that he'd transformed into his personal sanctuary, and before that, he'd used a spare room in the apartment for the same purpose. Despite the long hours I had put in while working as his *de facto* number two, I'd been happily content to work cross-legged on my bed or leaning up against the couch in the living room; I'd pretty much repeated that pattern in Anaheim, though with Alex in my life, that had morphed into using whatever space he *wasn't* at the time. Both of us were the typical white collar professional, putting in oodles of unpaid overtime just to ensure the job got done in a timely manner; without kids, I'm sure we were working far longer hours than our contemporaries with families. It was part of the reason I never felt guilty about ignoring my email when we did get a few hours — or, heavens, an entire *weekend* — to ourselves.

Switching over to the video conferencing software we used at the department, I was privately thankful that Alejandro had opted to go into his office that day, despite it being Sunday; I'd spent another night in Orange County Medical before the attending physician had grudgingly allowed me to go home, capping off a very long week where Alex had taken way too many personal days to see to my recovery. That had left him with a ton of work to catch up on, including prepping for some sort of seminar taking place on Monday morning — something best done in the small classroom the Career Center had versus our bedroom. Fortunately, that also meant he wouldn't be around to overhear any of the interview, either; we were already on thin ice doing a remote interrogation of a suspect, so having a civilian on hand during questioning was an added complication we truly didn't need.

It took longer than I thought it should before the logo for the department disappeared from the video window, replaced by a very close shot of Miles Guernsey; from what I could see in the image, he was sitting in the small control center where we housed all of our surveillance technology. "Hey, Vas," he said. "How are you feeling?"

"Better," I replied. "Sorry to have left you guys in the lurch."

Miles shrugged. "Your notes were exhaustive, as always, so it wasn't difficult to pick up the threads."

"It helps to be surrounded by good people, too," I smiled. "Thanks for keeping the case moving forward — especially given the extensive digging the team has been doing."

"Our pleasure," he replied. "I'm only sorry we have to pull you in for this step."

"Probably best for me to close it out this way," I said. "Who's up first?"

"I've got Dr. Dolittle on ice in Interview Two," he answered. "I had a feeling you'd want to talk to the mother before tackling the teen."

"Good guess."

"It may have also had something to do with the fact that the van from the county jail is stuck in traffic and will be arriving late."

I laughed. "Not the first time we've had to roll with the punches."

"Nope. Ready?"

"Yes."

"Switching over to Interview Two. Remember, this will be a party line."

"I will."

The screen shifted back to the Rancho Linda Police Department Logo; while I waited, I glanced over the short list of questions I'd scribbled on our Mickey Mouse-themed grocery list pad. Though I was feeling far better, I had grudgingly admitted to Alejandro that my mind was still not completely capable of the laser-like focus I once enjoyed; while not uncommon in those who experience a concussion, for me, it was like being a superhero down a critical superpower. The notepad had been his idea, one of many subtle ways he'd once again been helping me recover.

A trill from my laptop brought my attention back to the screen, and a moment later the interior of one of our interview rooms appeared. Janice Dolittle was sitting across from the camera and staring into it with an intensity that spoke to how she likely treated truculent students at Rancho Linda High. I frowned slightly, for I couldn't for the life of me remember if there was a monitor bolted to the wall displaying my image; then again, it wouldn't make sense for us to use an interview room that wasn't conference capable, would it?

Dolittle saw my frown and misinterpreted the meaning immediately. "I'd rather not be here, either, Deputy Chief Korsokovach," she intoned. "Especially after being made to wait hours before someone had the courtesy to tell me you'd cancelled our appointment."

"That's on me," I smiled graciously. "I'd not planned on digging up a dead body when I'd made our appointment. Nor had I realized I'd soon be a guest at the Orange County Medical Center, either."

Dolittle's face shifted slightly. "You were... in the hospital?" she asked.

I nodded, and found it curious that was the part she'd keyed in on. "Yes. I suffered some injuries in the course of trying to arrest a suspect," I answered. "I'm actually on medical leave right now."

"Medical leave? I guess that explains why I'm here and you're not. Again."

"I hate to leave things unfinished," I said. "Once I wrap up this case, I'll get back to recuperating."

"And what case would that be?"

"We spoke of it in your office a few days ago," I replied. "Daniel Kewley? The student from your school who was kidnapped?"

"Oh, right," she said, feigning a sudden recollection. I had to admit, her acting skills were pretty good. "Did you find him?"

"We did," I answered amiably.

"Then why am I here?" she asked. "It would seem I can't add much more to your case."

"Did you tell your son that Daniel had booked a meeting with you?"

Dolittle looked at me. "I'm sorry, what the *fuck* are you asking?"

Such language from an educator, I thought with a mental *tsk tsk*. "I understand that Daniel wanted to meet with you," I explained. "I believe he had an appointment for the day after he disappeared."

"That's news to me."

"Are you sure?" I asked with a smile. "You do know I can easily get access to your calendar, right?"

"Not without a warrant."

"That would be true in most cases," I said. "Except the Rancho Linda School District is part of, well," I smiled slightly, "Rancho Linda. Meaning your systems are considered part of the city's infrastructure and subject to the same central IT oversight."

The color started to drain out of Dolittle's face. "Are you essentially saying you are *legally* entitled to view my calendar?"

"Pretty much," I replied as I reached for a sheaf of paper just off camera. Alejandro had laughed when I'd asked him for anything I could use a prop, and then had pulled a package of resumes from his backpack; it had been a very visual reminder of how much work my beloved did for the students at Cal State Irvine. Holding it up to Dolittle, I shrugged. "I'm happy to pour through this, plus all of your emails, but you could save both of us a lot of time and just tell me what happened."

Dolittle looked at the paper for a long moment, then shifted her attention to me. "Daniel made the appointment last week," she finally said. "Beyond saying it involved allegations of bullying and the theft of supplies from the soccer team, he was rather cryptic about why he needed to meet with me and not the vice principal."

"Daniel didn't mention your son by name, then?"

"No," Dolittle replied quickly — too quickly.

"I see."

I looked away for a second as though I were thinking about something more significant than what Alex was making us for dinner that evening; the delicious smell of what he had already prepared before leaving for work was still hanging in the air of our condo, making my stomach rumble in anticipation of savoring his not-quite-secret-family-recipe for enchiladas. Sadly, I still had a few more days of the concussion drugs left, so the usual accompanying pitcher of margaritas had been shelved in favor of iced tea. Convincing Alejandro to make his dish had been more of a challenge than I'd expected; fortunately, the gay equivalent of the strange position I'd seen on the cover of the porn novel we'd recovered from Blake Dolittle's truck had proven to be exceptionally intense, rendering poor Alex far more amenable to my request. Unfortunately, my wily partner had made me promise in return that we try the position again that evening — but in *reverse*. Unwilling to deny him anything — especially when his enchiladas were involved — I had happily agreed to his terms.

Glancing back at my laptop screen, I could see Dolittle was getting a little anxious over my continued silence; playing up the notion that she'd not answered me as I'd anticipated, I pulled off my rimless glasses and rubbed at my eyes. While the double vision hadn't occurred in quite some time, my doctor had recommended not wearing my contacts for a few days in order to give my optical nerves a bit of a rest. Between the loss of my hair and having to wear the thick lenses, I was beginning to feel very much like I was suddenly middle-aged.

Putting the glasses back on, I looked at Dolittle directly. "When did you tell Blake about the appointment?"

Dolittle shifted in her chair. "I'm not sure what you're asking."

My eyebrows went up. "Seems pretty straightforward to me. Did you tell Blake that you had a meeting with Daniel Kewley? Yes, or no?"

Her eyes finally betrayed her when she looked away from me. "What difference would it have made if I did or didn't?"

I shrugged slightly, hiding my satisfaction that she had, indeed, answered my question already. "When did you tell him?"

"I sometimes talk about work in vague terms when we make dinner," she replied. "I don't speak in specifics of course as he can't know who I'm talking about due to student privacy."

"Of course. So you were making dinner on, what, Friday night?"

Dolittle sighed. "Thursday," she finally admitted. "It had been a helluva day and I was down to making hamburger goulash for dinner. Blake wasn't happy about it — he wanted pasta, since the team had a game Friday — and pressed the issue; I'd had about enough of it and told him he was going to eat what I made and *like* it."

"And did he?"

"Hardly," she sighed again. "Blake can be just as pig-headed as his father, something I reminded him of that evening." Dolittle looked at me. "I am aware that my son has a reputation for bullying kids on campus; it's what got him sent back to Rancho Linda from Saint Frederik's. I've not been able to do anything about it because *none* of the kids being bullied have been willing to step forward."

I nodded. "Daniel was your chance to do something?"

"Formally," she nodded. "I can read between the lines as well as you can, Chief. I knew what Daniel was coming to see me for; Connolly had already passed on that he thought Blake was stealing from the team, though he wasn't able to prove it." Dolittle looked away again. "Daniel was going to be the final straw; he just didn't know it when he approached me."

"So you told Blake?" I asked. "To, what, scare him straight?"

Dolittle's eyes came back to mine. "Something like that."

"What happened after that?"

"I don't know, for sure," she replied. "He left, angry, with a promise of getting real food. Now that he has his own vehicle, I can't really do much to stop him."

"You could take away the keys."

"He's eighteen," she reminded me unnecessarily. "An adult in the eyes of the State. As his mother, I'm reduced to feeding and sheltering him now."

"When did he return?"

"After school on Tuesday," she replied. "He will often crash on the couch of one of his teammates, so that's not unusual. I keep tabs on him based on his phone's location."

I tried to remain impassive. "What did you think when it showed him in Palm Springs?"

Dolittle started. "I... know he still has friends up at Saint Frederik's," she answered after a moment. "I assumed he was visiting them."

"All weekend?" I asked, seeing if I could confirm a hunch I had about the timing.

"Yeah."

"But he was back in town on Monday?"

Dolittle's face flushed slightly. "Yeah," she replied quietly.

"And you didn't think it was strange he was at the Halloween party?"

Now completely caught, Dolittle's mouth started to open and close like a fish out of water. It took a moment for her to regroup. "I assumed he was volunteering there," she said. "His group was one of the sponsors for the event."

"They were," I nodded, thinking back to the poster I'd seen in the school. "How closely do you follow the movements of your son, Doctor?"

"As close as any mother," she replied.

"And you really didn't think it was odd that he *returned* to Palm Springs on Monday night?"

"No," she replied quickly. "Blake's snits often last a few days; he returns home when his temper finally abates. Or he runs out of money."

"I see." I tapped at the breakfast bar with a finger. "At some point, I'm going to want to know *why* you didn't mention any of this the first time — or the second time — we spoke."

"You can see how it looks," Dolittle replied.

"Yes," I nodded. "And it looks about the way it might if Blake were involved in what happened to Daniel Kewley."

Dolittle started to protest, but something in what I had said finally registered with her. "Hang on a second — is Daniel dead?"

"Yes," I said.

"My son didn't have any part in the disappearance of that kid — or his death."

"I'm afraid that's not what the evidence is telling me," I replied. "By your own admission, Blake was at the mansion at the time Daniel was kidnapped, and then later, was in Palm Springs when we think the body was being buried."

"I didn't say any of that!"

"Maybe I paraphrased for you," I said. "Not that it matters, for we have the GPS records supporting Blake's movements. You've simply provided more context for the data we had."

"I've done nothing!" Dolittle huffed a bit. "And you can't hold me responsible for anything Blake *allegedly* did."

"True," I nodded. "I can't. As you so eloquently pointed out, Blake is eighteen; he'll be handling this on his own."

Dawning realization appeared on her face. "I want to speak to my son," she said. "*Now.*"

"I'll let him know when I see him," I smiled. "Now, if you don't mind holding there for a bit, I need to get to another interview before my doctor barges in here and makes me go back to bed."

"I demand to see him!" she said as she stood from the table. Banging against the door to the interview room, she started to yell. "Let me out of here *right now!*"

"An officer will be by shortly," I said sweetly as I reached for the button to disconnect. "It's been fun chatting; have a wonderful day."

Dolittle glared over her shoulder at me. "You *motherfucking-gay-son-of-a—*"

"Bye now," I smiled as I killed the connection.

TWENTY-THREE

GOTCHA

It went against my better judgment, but the doctor had been pretty specific about laying off of the caffeine while I healed; knowing I would be rather cranky about that, Alejandro had made a special trip to a boutique market just outside of Palos Verdes that specialized in rare and unique foods, and had returned with two bags full of decaf that, frankly, didn't taste like decaf. Brewing what had to have been my fourth cup of a Kona blend that appeared to have come directly from Hawaii, I had to grudgingly admit I might be warming up to the concept of decaf forever — not that I would ever admit it to anyone. Leaning against the counter as I waited for the Keurig to finish chuffing, I glanced over at my waiting laptop; the traffic jam that had delayed Blake Dolittle's transport from the Orange County Jail was far more serious than we'd originally known, requiring the van to detour significantly east before being able to return to Rancho Linda. After hanging up on Janice Dolittle, I'd called Miles and been informed that my suspect was still about ten minutes out, plenty of time for a quick trip to the bathroom to, er, deal with the first three cups I'd downed.

Pulling the mug from beneath the spout, I removed the K-cup from the holder and debated whether I wanted to go through the trouble of separating the grounds from the plastic. Alejandro had, in his own quiet way, begun to hint that perhaps my prized coffee maker wasn't exactly the best option, environmentally speaking; considering how many of the small pods were usually in the trash by the end of the week, I couldn't really argue the point. To my great embarrassment, I'd not known that it was possible to recycle the pod until I'd begun to, in typical Vasily fashion, dig into the issue; the only problem had turned out to be my unwillingness to consistently do what was necessary. I left the pod on the counter with the intention of cleaning it out after my interview, but knew as I rounded the corner to reclaim my spot on the barstool it would just as likely be snuck into the trash later.

Tapping at my MacBook, the screen woke back up and allowed me to log back into the system; a message was waiting there from Miles telling me Blake had been made comfortable in Interview 13. I smiled a bit at that, for by design, comfort was one of the many things the small rooms lacked; I also wondered why he'd stuff the teenager in the worst one of the lot. I was certain it was one of the original spaces from the initial brick building housing the department; the air conditioning never seemed to work properly, and facilities had never been able to completely eliminate a slight musty odor that pervaded everything. Smiling a bit wider, I realized it was probably the *perfect* space for a suspect who had proven to be a handful already.

Shifting screens on the laptop, I logged back into the conference system and launched my connection to Interview 13. As with everything else in that room, the web camera was a bit older and took a moment to focus on Blake; the teenager was slightly slouched in the seat on the other side of the table, though his posture was hampered by having his handcuffs attached to the loop in the center of the Formica. Since he was alone in the room, it wasn't strictly necessary -- but it would help to ratchet up the tension just a bit. Dressed in the standard burnt orange jumpsuit of a guest at the Orange County Jail, he looked far less the soccer star than some sort of street thug we had pulled in for questioning; the dark stubble accentuated this sense, and reminded me that puberty hits everyone differently. The black eyes from the airbag had faded a bit, but his nose was still a massive disaster area; the file had said that the medical staff at the jail had done what they could until Blake was able to see a specialist. Seeing the slight curve where it had broken, I suspected that look was about as good as it was going to get; depending on how the next few minutes went, Blake's odds of having access to healthcare outside of the State Penitentiary System were pretty low.

Eyeing me, Blake shifted in his chair — as much as the handcuffs would allow. "You again," he said, nearly as standoffish as his mother had been earlier.

"Yep," I nodded. "Good to see you too, Blake,"

"How's the head?" he asked, managing a bit of snark despite the way his voice sounded incredibly nasally. "I heard you hit it pretty hard when you fainted."

I smiled a bit at the innuendo. "I have good days and bad; thanks for asking. That nose looks pretty awful, though."

"I'll get it fixed as soon as I'm out." Blake glared at me. "Among other things."

I cocked my head slightly. "You're not *actually* threatening me, are you?"

"Take it however you want."

"Seriously, dude," I sighed. "You really need to learn when to quit."

"Not in my nature."

No kidding, I thought. "I'll just add it to your tab, then."

"Whatever. My lawyer will get this all dropped anyway."

I looked at Blake. "Didn't you waive your right to having representation when you arrived at the station?" I asked as I toggled back to the intake screen on the case system. The fact that Miles' note to that effect was pinned to the top of the file told me I wasn't going crazy, but I had to be careful; the last thing I needed was a lawyer bursting in on the interrogation at the wrong moment.

"Yeah."

"Have you changed your mind? Do you want someone present before we continue?"

"No."

I nodded while also wondering if Blake truly understood what was going on; based on his conversation with me in the ambulance, I was willing to bet he was still seeing the entire process through the lens of a television prime-time drama. "All right," I began as I made a show of shuffling the same stack of paper I'd used as a prop with his mother. "We've got quite a bit to go through. I'll try to go slow, but if you feel like you're getting lost, please speak up, okay?"

Blake rolled his eyes. I took that as assent to continue.

"I understand you are one of the players on the Rancho Linda High School soccer team."

The kid huffed. "I'm *the* player on the team."

"I see. All four years?"

"I transferred in last year, so no, dumbass. But I could have been."

I pulled my glasses off and made a show of looking at a blank page in my hand. "Oh, right. You were a student at Saint Frederik's. Why did you transfer to Rancho Linda?"

"I wanted to be close to my family, obviously."

"Obviously," I smiled. "Do you still play for the travel team that is based out of Saint Frederik's?"

"No."

"Ah," I nodded sagely. "You're on a travel team down here, then."

"No."

"Why not?" I frowned. "I hear you're thinking of going to Major League Soccer after graduation. I thought travel team work was required."

"I don't need it," he smiled back at me. Only then did I notice one of his incisors had apparently disappeared since the last time I'd seen him. "Rancho Linda is enough."

"I'm surprised you didn't do the college scholarship route."

"Not my deal, man. Not my deal."

"Well, to each their own," I said. "Except that you still seem to spend a lot of time up at Saint Frederik's." I ticked off the items on my fingers as I continued. "You're not a student there, and you don't play for any team based in Palm Springs. What's the attraction for going?"

"Girlfriend," he said quickly before flashing that smile at me. "Something you probably don't understand."

"On the contrary, I do," I smiled. "I actually had a girlfriend when I was in high school."

Blake scowled. "Fucking *Christ*. You're one of those bi swingers?"

"No," I said as I put down one piece of paper and then picked up a red file folder. I kept the label away from the camera, for Blake didn't need to know it held Alejandro's *Top Ten Tips for Professional Dress*. "I'm gay."

That seemed to befuddle Blake. "But you dated a girl?" he finally asked.

"I did."

Blake gaped for a minute. "How... does that work?"

"I'm sure you don't need pointers from me on how to get laid by a woman," I replied. "Or do you? Because my advice might be a little out of date, given how long it has been."

"*Shit* no — I don't need your advice."

I reached for and grabbed the small plastic bag that held the ring we'd recovered from the mansion; it, along with several other items had been pulled from the evidence locker and driven to me so I could use them during the interview. "Maybe you do," I said, holding the bag up. "Do you recognize this ring?"

Blake looked away. "No."

I shrugged. "The DNA we swabbed from it tells a different tale; our lab techs matched it to a website that sells the promise of 'curing' people's bad habits." I put the ring down and pulled out the bag holding the pornographic novel, which I held up to the camera. "It doesn't seem to have helped, in your case."

I caught the faint hint of embarrassment on the cheeks of the teenager. "That's not mine."

"This was in your truck," I reminded him. "If it's not yours, whose is it?"

"Teammate," he answered. "I give him a ride to practice."

There was no way to prevent the sly smile on my face. "Then the two of you must have gotten up to some interesting extracurriculars," I said. "This book was *literally* covered in your semen; was your *teammate* using a condom, then?"

That flush grew a darker shade of red. "Fuck you."

"You're not really my type," I replied easily as I put the book down. "So you're anti-porn, but have a novel full of it; you're anti-gay, but got your rocks off with another guy. Am I missing anything so far?"

"That's not what happened."

"Then correct me. Otherwise, I'm going to have to draw my own conclusions, and from where I'm sitting, they are rather intriguing."

I didn't think it was possible for Blake's face to get any more inflamed, but damn if it didn't get a shade darker. "I stole it from my mom's desk. I was looking for cash and found it under the checkbook and wanted to know why she was hiding it."

"Looks like you figured that out pretty quickly," I said, unsure I needed that particular new dimension on the principal's private life.

"Yeah."

"So no girlfriend, then? Or boyfriend, for that matter?"

"No."

I shook my head. "Then why were you going back and forth to Palm Springs?"

"None of your goddamn business."

"Look," I began, pulling my glasses off again and holding them like I was an exasperated senator at a congressional hearing, "you *were* there." I tapped at the stack of blank paper that was visible on camera. "The GPS data we have places you at the school on multiple occasions; I also have you at the Marriott on the night you tried to, well, do whatever it was you were trying to do."

"It wasn't me."

"So you loaned your truck to someone, then?"

"Yes."

"And your phone?"

"What about it?"

"You loaned them your phone, too?" I asked patiently.

Blake looked confused. "Why would I do that?"

"Great question," I smiled. "I certainly wouldn't — not even to my fiancé," I lied, for Alex would always be welcome to borrow *anything* of mine.

"Exactly."

"I bet your phone has never left your side," I continued.

"Not until you took it the night you ran me off the road."

I nodded again. "I can understand that, no question." I tried to look a bit confused then. "Except — if you loaned your truck to someone, and *they* were the ones that drove it to Palm Springs, why was your *phone* also there?" I waited a beat. "At the same *time*, on nearly the exact same coordinates."

"I must have left the phone in the truck."

"Ah." I frowned again. "For a phone that never leaves your side, though, you certainly seem to have forgotten it a quite a bit over this past week."

"It happens."

"Uh huh. Were you at the Halloween party on Monday?"

Blake looked like he was suffering from whiplash. "What?"

"The party you were at on Monday," I said, carefully adjusting my characterization. "Were you volunteering?"

"No."

I smiled. "I think that's the first truthful thing you've said so far." I flipped the blank pages. "Had you planned all along to kidnap Daniel

Kewley that night? Or were you intending to simply bully him into silence about the items you'd stolen from the soccer team?"

Blake blinked almost like an outdated computer processor that was having trouble keeping up with the commands being fed into it. "I didn't steal anything," he finally answered. "It was a misunderstanding."

"Oh? In what way?" I asked, noting that he'd not exactly refuted he'd had plans for Daniel one way or the other.

"I pulled a muscle last week while working out and needed to wrap it; the team had plenty, and I borrowed some."

"That sounds a little bit like stealing."

"The taxpayers of Rancho Linda paid for those supplies," Blake said smugly, clearly reciting something he'd heard elsewhere. "I'm a taxpayer, so I'm entitled to whatever was there."

"There are two things wrong with that," I sighed. "First, your *mother* is technically the taxpayer in question, and second, she's no more entitled to *take* those supplies as a taxpayer than the laser printer sitting on her desk at the school. It would still be theft and it would *still* be prosecuted as such."

That look something was slowly occurring to Blake appeared on his face, but he continued to press his point. "Whatever. It wasn't like the team would miss a few rolls of tape."

"Or a cooler?"

"Or a cooler. They had five of them, for shit's sake."

"Were you planning a party, then?"

"What?"

I shrugged. "The cooler you, uh, borrowed was large enough to fit a tailgate's worth of beer."

"I'm not old enough to drink."

"What were you using the cooler for, then?"

"Storage."

I nodded. "I suppose you could call it that," I said. "Did you accost Daniel at the party?"

"I don't know what that word means."

I sighed; so much for modern education. "Did you try to 'convince' Daniel not to speak to your mother?"

"I wanted to talk to him, yeah. I knew he'd be there."

Here we go, I thought. "And he refused?"

"Yeah," Blake nodded. "The shithead actually said I should go with him."

"That seems reasonable," I replied. "Then you could explain the situation."

"There was nothing *to* explain. Not to my mother, and certainly not to a stinking immigrant."

"You had some trouble with his group, didn't you? Over at the *Alternative Way*?"

"The fuckwads got those lesbian wackos to boot us."

"Why?"

Blake kind of shrugged. "They couldn't stand having *real* Americans in their presence? Bunch of pink commies that lot."

I was somewhat in awe at the rather large set of aspersions he was casting over a group that had, maybe, fifteen members in total. "Are you telling me that none of those kids were true citizens?"

"I'd be willing to bet half of them crossed the border, yeah."

I nodded. "Which is why they were so interested in helping *others* who had crossed?"

"Exactly," he nodded. "I read about it online — it's a pipeline, and it has to be stopped."

Because everything you see on the internet is truth, I thought. "And your group was dedicated to stopping it, then?"

"Yes." He looked at me for a moment. "You wanna know why we were meeting at that fucking bookstore in the first place?"

"That's easy," I smiled. "You were spying on KOTO."

He stared at me blankly.

"Kids On Their Own," I patiently added. "You wanted to watch their movements."

"Exactly. That's how we knew they were affiliating with the scum that crosses in the dead of night."

"Was that something you brought up with Daniel on Halloween?"

"Maybe."

"And the discussion grew heated?"

"If you mean did we start yelling at each other, yeah, we did."

"Who threw the first punch?"

"I did," Blake said proudly. "Knocked that spindly nerd's mask right off and floored him."

"But he got back up, didn't he?"

"Surprised the hell out of me. And then he ran — right back into that crappy hay maze they'd made." Blake smiled. "Dumbass didn't realize there was no way out."

"Except he did," I said. "You found him trying to open the door into the servant's corridor."

"He had his phone out and was dialing someone," Blake said. "I needed him to get his story straight before that happened."

"And that's when you hit him with the chloroform?"

"Yes," Blake nodded. "I needed to talk to him."

"Where did you get that from?"

Blake shrugged. "Some store on the web."

I nodded. "So, like any good television cop show, you came up behind him and pressed the rag to his face? And expected him to pass out on the spot?"

"Yeah."

"Which he didn't," I observed. "Chloroform takes time to work."

"The seller didn't mention that."

I'm sure they weren't planning on having it used to commit murder, I thought. "He fought back?"

"Got in a good punch or two," Blake replied, "but I hit him back, hard."

"And he went down?"

"Yeah."

"And hit his head on the hay bale beneath the electric chair?"

"Yeah."

"And stopped struggling?"

"Not at first," Blake said, his eyes going distant. "His arms and legs flapped for a bit, so I tied him up. By the time I was done, though, he'd stopped moving completely."

"You realize he was dead, right?" I asked quietly.

Blake shrugged.

"So it was an accident, then?"

"Yeah."

I nodded. "Well, that makes sense now that you've explained it. I'm not sure why you didn't come forward sooner, we could have short circuited this whole mess."

Blake frowned. "I thought I would be in trouble."

"Oh you are," I smiled grimly.

"But... you just agreed it was an accident?"

"No," I pointed out, "*you* said it was an accident. I say it was premeditated murder."

"Pre-*what*?"

"Blake, you've told me that you had a rag soaked in chloroform ready when Daniel didn't back down. You can't tell me you weren't planning on using it."

"I had it just in case he was an idiot."

"I see. And that's why you had the cooler in the back of your truck?"

"How did you know about that?"

"And why you'd driven up to Palm Springs to figure out where to dispose of the body?"

"I... well, wait—"

"You even parked your truck on the rear driveway at the mansion," I continued. "I think you'd intended on taking Daniel down the elevator and then out through the kitchen to avoid suspicion, but once you knew about the servant's corridor, you changed your mind — especially since dragging a dead body is far more obvious than waving a gun at someone and forcing them to walk out under their own power."

Blake just stared at me.

"You packed another human being into a cooler," I said, "then drove up to the school you'd been asked to leave and then out into the desert to dig a hole — something that is far more difficult to do in an *actual* desert and not a studio soundstage."

"I—"

"So, much like the cooler and the athletic tape, you *borrowed* a backhoe and dug the hole. Maybe you were running short on time, maybe you were afraid someone was going to find you out there, but for whatever reason you had to hurry the process along — enough that you, literally, ran out of gas." I paused. "That must have been a long walk back to your truck."

There comes a moment in every interrogation with a prime suspect when they realize they are down to a very binary choice: continue to deny everything and hope a reasonably good lawyer will clean up the mess they are in, or figuratively fall on their sword and plead for leniency. I had an instinct as to which way Blake was going to go and wasn't surprised when he met my expectations.

"I want my lawyer."

"Then we will get them," I replied.

Blake's face creased with confusion. "Aren't you going to offer me a deal? That's usually what happens when a suspect asks for their lawyer."

"I told you earlier that you believed too much in what you watched," I said. "Though, actually in this case you are right; some of my more wily suspects have used just such a tactic to try and elicit favorable terms from the prosecutor."

The teen actually smiled. "So you are going to offer me a deal."

"No, Blake, I'm not going to offer you a deal."

He looked startled. "Why?"

"Because I have enough evidence to bury you at trial and am quite happy to do so," I explained. "Every now and then, examples need to be set so the broader society knows that the sickening actions you took are not acceptable. You just happen to be that lucky person this week."

"You *fucking* cocksucker!" he yelled as he pulled at his handcuffs. "When I get out of here, I'm going to rip you to shreds!"

"Unlikely," I said. "Since by my count you'll be well into your eighties when they even *think* about granting you parole."

"Fucker!"

"Oh, and one more thing — Daniel Kewley was an American."

"No *fucking* way is that true! He had an accent and was black!"

"Maybe you shouldn't judge quite so quickly," I said softly as I reached to terminate the connection. "Hopefully *your* jury will be far more deliberative."

TWENTY-FOUR
AFTERMATH

Between the forensics, the GPS data and the damning interview, Blake Dolittle's lawyer saw the writing on the wall and managed to convince the teenager and his mother to plead out. I always assumed Janice Dolittle had hoped that preventing her kid from being convicted in a public trial was a pragmatic move designed to save her career; the school board saw things very differently, though, and by the start of Thanksgiving week, the principal had tendered her resignation at their request. Part of me felt badly that the fallout from Blake's actions had landed her on the unemployment line; blaming her for actions he admitted to taking without her knowledge felt a bit misogynistic, especially given the lack of female representation on the board. Then again, it probably hadn't helped that the *Orange County Register* had run a three-issue special report from Vivan Grandchester on the kidnapping, focusing on some of the more salacious evidence we had recovered. Discovering their highly decorated school administrator had a secret predilection for bad porn had probably doomed her career more than having a murderer for a son, given the conservative nature of Rancho Linda.

For my part, I had dutifully adhered to the terms of the medical leave I'd been ordered to take, which had boiled down to a few frustrated weeks cooped up in the condo with nothing more to do than stream bad television from Netflix or read the newspapers I had delivered daily. The latter had been my only connection to what was going on beyond the walls of my home, for Alejandro had cleverly locked away my MacBook to prevent me from sneaking onto the departmental network to catch up on what I was certain was a massive backlog forming in my absence. *Locked away* wasn't entirely accurate, actually, since my treasured laptop was simply sitting on the top shelf of the master closet, hiding behind a stack of sweatpants; after it had "disappeared" I'd done a thorough top-to-bottom crime scene search of the condo to determine its disposition. While I chafed at the imposition, I knew Alex was only doing what he thought would speed along my recovery; as I stood beside him in our kitchen preparing our Thanksgiving dinner, I had to admit he'd been right as always. For the first time in *years* I felt fully relaxed; my last appointment with the neurologist that Monday had confirmed no lingering effects from the concussion, something I credited squarely to the loving care I'd been fortunate to receive.

Unable to resist the urge to express how happy I was that Alejandro was in my life, I moved behind him and nibbled at his neck; he started to laugh, and was thoroughly unable to defend himself as he stirred the stuffing concoction he was making on the cooktop. "Someone is feeling frisky."

"It's your fault," I reminded him. "I've been stuck here at home with nothing to do save for fantasizing about my fiancé."

"I see," he said. "Hand me that bowl of apples, would you?"

I sorted through the amazing amount of food that was sitting on every countertop we had and located a small plastic dish holding sliced apples. "What are these for?" I asked as I handed them to Alex.

"They sweeten the stuffing a little," he replied. "And those sliced apricots over there — thank you — add a bit of tang."

Taking the two now empty dishes from Alex, I felt an eyebrow arch.

"Where did you get this recipe? And I can't believe you talked me into making a full-blown Thanksgiving meal."

"One of the counselors I work with at CSI is originally from New England. This is her family recipe, handed down generation to generation."

I put a hand on my hip, arched an eyebrow and tried to look skeptical. If I'd not been wearing a Ladybug-themed apron, it might have worked. "You said that about your enchiladas, my love. Those turned out to be from a Tyler Florence recipe."

Alejandro turned slightly, and was wearing the smile that always melted my heart. "All I can say is that she claims it didn't come off the back of a bag of breadcrumbs."

"Huh." I sniffed at the air and the pleasant aroma coming from the turkey currently baking in our stove. Alex had found a smallish one at Bristol Farms that I still felt was capable of feeding the entire floor of our building. "We should have invited Rosie over at the very least."

We'd seen very little of our favorite millionaire while I'd been on medical leave; partly that was due to my not leaving the condo for any reason, but I was privately worried I'd done some damage to our friendship the evening we'd hosted her for dinner. I'd not intended to be as harsh as I'd been at the time; I knew in hindsight I'd been working on too little sleep and too much caffeine, but that did nothing to assuage my guilt over rebuffing her offer of assistance.

I barely caught Alex's quick glance at the clock on the stove. "I'm sure she had plans."

That eyebrow of mine arched higher. "She lives alone, Alex. And we're the closest thing to family she's got."

"And there's a full slate of NFL games on today, too," he laughed. "She'll be in her element. Besides," he added as he turned and pulled me to him, "we've never had our own holiday celebration."

I started to argue and then realized he was right. "Son of a gun."

"After everything we've been through this year, I figured we could use a nice, quiet day together."

"With enough turkey to feed the entire swim team," I deadpanned.

"It'll freeze, silly," he smiled as he returned to the stove. "If there's anything left after I make the pot pie on Sunday."

"Oh wow," I sighed. "I've not had a turkey pot pie since I was in Windeport. Charlie had the most amazing pie crust."

"Well, I hope mine measures up," he chuckled. "Ours will be store bought."

"I'm sure it will."

We lapsed into a comfortable silence at that point; I'd wanted to help but had been chased out of the kitchen each time I'd made the offer. My fiancé seemed to be in his element, so I simply retreated to one of the bar stools on the other side of the counter and watched the magnificent male specimen who was my soulmate as he continued his preparations. Given how comfortable the moment was, I wasn't entirely sure if I should broach the topic that continued to be top of mind for me; deciding there was no time like the present, I cleared my throat and plunged ahead.

"Alex, about our wedding..."

"The one in January, *no?*" he smiled at me. "I wouldn't miss it."

"I should hope not." I paused. "Look, I just wanted you to know that I had a hard time keeping it a secret from you." I toyed with the saltshaker that looked like a Disneyland trash can. "In fact, I think I'm constitutionally incapable of keeping anything from you."

Alex looked at me with a soft expression. "You're not feeling guilty over what happened, are you?"

"Yeah, I am," I replied. "We should have done it together from the start."

"*Mi amor*," he laughed. "Whether you know it or not, we did."

Feeling like I was missing something, I frowned. "I'm not following you."

"Sean and Suzanne," he said patiently.

The penny finally dropped and I rolled my eyes. "It figures we would each pick one half of the only other duo that is just as incapable of keeping secrets from each other."

"Exactly," Alex said. "I talked to Suzanne after discovering what happened. The two of them were gently steering us toward making the same choices; they even reached out to the agents we'd been speaking with to ensure the right weekend was booked, regardless of which one of us managed to do it first." He smiled. "We got the hotel and weekend we wanted; as for the spot, I think we couldn't have gone wrong with either."

"I suppose not," I said. "You're really not upset?"

"Not in the least," he replied before tapping the end of the spoon he was holding to his chin. "Well, maybe with Suzanne. She's the one that spilled the beans to Sean."

"If she hadn't, though…"

"Exactly," he replied. "So, now all we have to do is decide on the final guest list."

"Would it be bad thing if it were just you and me?"

"No, but I think your best friend would be a little annoyed. Not to mention your mother."

"And yours," I nodded. "Okay, so how about this: Sean, Suzanne, Mama, your mom and Rosie."

"As long as Mickey and Minnie are also there, sounds perfect."

"I hope they can all make it."

Alex stirred something. "I think they will."

"Yeah," I said after a moment, "I think they will, too."

Alex leaned down and inspected the turkey through the oven's window. "*Caramba*. The pop-up thermometer says our bird is ready; why don't you uncork that red I bought and set our table?"

"Am I allowed to drink, now?" I teased as I pulled down two wine-glasses and then retrieved the wine opener from a drawer.

"Technically, yes," he reminded me, feigning obliviousness. "But after the rather orgasmic experience you had with your first cup of *real* coffee this week, I'm having second thoughts."

I smiled. "I don't do abstinence well."

"That I know," he laughed.

Seeing as though our *table* was pretty much just the breakfast bar, it didn't take long to get two place settings arranged; Alex had found a cute Disney-themed Thanksgiving tablecloth that he had carefully folded in order to have it fit. Getting into the spirit of things, I fluffed up the matching napkins much the way I'd seen our housekeeper do when Mama hosted a major gathering; stepping back to admire the tableau I'd created, I nearly stumbled over Chat as he appeared from wherever he'd been snoozing. I knelt to the carpet and scratched him under the chin; Chat rewarded me with a rumble of purrs before his nose twinged. I wasn't surprised when he dashed away from me and rounded the edge of the counter; a moment later, I heard the startled chuckle from Alex.

"I wondered when you were going to show up," he laughed as I stood. The turkey was sitting on the counter beside the oven, and Alex deftly sliced a small piece off before bending over. "*No mas*, Chat. Now go and lie down."

"Like he's really going to listen," I sighed.

"He minds me," Alex said matter of factly as he began dishing up.

"I don't think—" I started before I watched Chat come back around the corner and then head straight for his favorite pillow. My eyes widened more when I watched him curl up facing the kitchen. "Holy shit."

"It's all in how you speak to him, *mi amor*," he said as he placed two extremely full plates of food in front of me and then came around the corner to take his seat.

"Clearly," I laughed. "Happy Thanksgiving," I said as I held out my wineglass to him.

The gentle *tink* when his glass met mine felt perfect. "Same to you, my love."

"This smells divine—" I started but was interrupted when my phone went off. Pulling it from my shorts, I frowned when I saw it was the generic number for someone calling the condo from the front door. I looked at Alex. "Are you expecting someone?"

"Yes," he smiled as he stood from the barstool.

"Who—?" I began to ask before it finally dawned on me. Tapping answer, I smiled at Alex. "Rosie, you're late. We've already opened the wine."

The Lauren Bacall laugh that filled my ear warmed my heart at the same time. "Not to worry. I think there are still two bottles left from my last visit. May I come up? Halftime is almost over, and I don't want to miss a play."

As Alex pulled another plate out and began to add food from our miniature buffet to it, I had the most wonderful sense that the world was suddenly — or at least for the moment — in perfect shape. "I'll have the television on when you get here."

ACKNOWLEDGMENTS

An interesting post crossed my social media feeds just before I began work on this book — it was a question from one writer to the rest of the community asking if holidays played a key role in any of our works. In the process of deciding how to answer, I realized that nearly *all* my novels — both in this series and the *Sean Colbeth Investigates* companion — a holiday of some sort anchors the events of the story. I'm not certain I did this with any overt intention other than providing a generalized touchstone to the calendar so readers could form their own ideas about the time of year the events being depicted are taking place. *Blindsided*, appropriately, started this trend, featuring Halloween and that fateful costume party where Sean meets someone who will ultimately become his significant other; like *Masks*, I picked the October holiday more to evoke that strange transition period between Fall and Winter — and, maybe, with the hope to channel some of the spookiness that comes along with it. *Masks* leans into that creepiness a bit more, though in all honesty, I had a truly hard time turning Rosie's home into a weird version of the Haunted Mansion. Hopefully she will forgive me.

This particular novel dipped a toe a bit further into some compelling sociopolitical issues currently being experienced here in the States. I make no apologies for doing this; using fiction as a way to comment on our collective choices as a society is a time-honored tradition that I, sadly, have not done nearly as much as I should. Vasily's views are, obviously, an extension of my own; I know from reader feedback that some of the areas I've touched upon over the years are, frankly, uncomfortable topics, but I persist in putting them front and center in the hope that in my own, small way, I can effect change. I'm not a big voice in this area — at least, not yet — but every little bit helps.

Finally, a shout out to my lovely wife, **Paula**. Each time I feel like I'm writing my way into a corner that cannot be exited, she finds a gentle way to remind me of my creativity and its ability to take me anywhere I choose to go. Having someone like that in your corner is a blessing I am thankful for each and every day.

—C

December 31, 2023

About the Author

Born and raised in Maine, Chris has spent nearly three decades as an IT nerd, writing just about everything other than a novel in the process. That changed in early 2019 when he was advised to find a way to wind down from his day job; sifting through his options, he recalled a childhood ambition to become a writer and quickly found himself weaving an entirely new world from the comfort of his laptop. *Masks* is his eighth book of the *Vasily Korsokovach Investigates* series.

Despite his love for the Northeast, the author escaped the cold for Arizona, where he currently resides with his beautiful wife and a Staffordshire Terrier rescue who insists on being walked as frequently as possible.

For all of the latest information, including hints about upcoming books and an exclusive reader newsletter, please visit the author's website at https://chrisjansmann.com

a amazon.com/author/chrisjansmann

BB bookbub.com/authors/christopher-h-jansmann

g goodreads.com/chrisjansmann

m mastodon.coffee/@chrisjansmann

www.ingramcontent.com/pod-product-compliance
Lightning Source LLC
Chambersburg PA
CBHW052027240626
47153CB00006B/1981